An Ordinary Exodus

*For my mother, in memoriam,
this echo of her own story*

An
Ordinary
Exodus

ROGER BICHELBERGER

Translated by Toby Garfitt

A LION BOOK

Oxford · Batavia · Sydney

Text copyright © 1983 Éditions Albin Michel SA
This edition copyright © 1991 Lion Publishing

Published by
Lion Publishing plc
Sandy Lane West, Oxford, England
ISBN 0 7459 2483 2
Lion Publishing Corporation
1705 Hubbard Avenue, Batavia, Illinois 60510, USA
ISBN 0 7459 2483 2
Albatross Books Pty Ltd
PO Box 320, Sutherland, NSW 2232, Australia
ISBN 0 7324 0613 7

First edition published in 1983 by
Éditions Albin Michel SA, 22 rue Huyghens, 75014 Paris
entitled *Un Exode ordinaire*
First English edition 1991
Paperback edition 1992

British Library Cataloguing in Publication Data
  Bichelberger, Roger
  An Ordinary Exodus
  I. Title
  843[F]
  ISBN 0-7459-2101-9

Library of Congress Cataloging-in-Publication Data
  Bichelberger, Roger
  [Exode ordinaire. English]
  An ordinary exodus / Roger Bichelberger; translated by Toby Garfitt.
  ISBN 0-7459-2101-9
  PQ2662.I28E95 1991
  843'.914–dc20 91-12817 CIP

Printed and bound in Great Britain by
Cox & Wyman Ltd, Reading, Berkshire

*Then should I learn to go, not knowing whither or why,
without a backward look.*

JEAN-CLAUDE RENARD
La Lumière du silence (Seuil)

Translator's Note

The region of Lorraine, on the borders of France and Germany, changed hands four times between 1870 and 1945. Its sense of identity owes much to the Germanic dialect spoken there.

The use of dialect is central to this novel. It has been rendered in approximate phonetic transcription, with translations provided. Proper names, however, have been retained in their original form, designed for a French readership. Thus Millache'Babe should be read as 'Millash'Bab', i.e. Grandfather Müller, Wag-Nache'Péda as 'Wagnash'Péda', i.e. Peter Wagner, and Bêa-Yasse'Kette as 'Bêayas'Kett', i.e. Kate Berger.

Part One

THE DEPARTURE

1

She had been waiting for over an hour now, sitting on the stone in front of the house.

The little square of Lasting-en-Lorraine was swarming with people, and the other women had their hands full trying to control all the children who were rushing about enjoying themselves. For her, sitting there in the summer sunshine, the place might as well have been deserted. From time to time she was aware of the trickle of the fountain, singing for her alone. The sound seemed to come from a long way away, from deep in the well of her memory, as it had sung for her in the moonlight, the song of their hearts: *I love you, Angela, I love you, I love you.* And all the stars of heaven had joined in the chorus with Benoît, big Benoît of Siébert's Mill: *I love you, Angela,* while the fountain had tirelessly murmured words of love, so cool and fresh after the burning kisses. *I love you, Angela, I love you.*

'All ready, Angela?'

'Yes, all ready.'

'You're not going on your own, are you?'

'Not likely! I'm taking Manuel. I couldn't leave him behind.'

'Where is he?'

'Trying to catch the goat in the meadows. He's finding it hard to say goodbye to the animals.'

'Poor lad! But he'll just have to: there's no two ways about it.'

Yes, he'd have to. Manuel had known that when the evacuation order came last night. Of course he'd have to. They couldn't take the goat, or the pig, or the rabbits, or the pigeons. They'd simply have to abandon them, letting them go free, to face all the dangers that freedom would bring. How on earth would they cope? Manuel had lain awake worrying about that all the time that Angela was packing and tying up their bundles.

'Think of the pig! It'll never manage without us.'

'Oh yes it will, Manuel. It'll grub up enough food to stay alive.'

'I know what. First thing tomorrow I'll take it down into the Sûredal, by the Sime. It can wallow in the stream, and drink from it too. And there'll be carrots and cabbages in the allotments.'

'But what will people . . . ?'

'There won't be any people, Angela: we're all going.'

'So we are, Manuel: you're quite right.'

She had stroked her poor simple little brother's blond curls, and he had looked at her with an impish smile in his big blue eyes.

'The goat, Angela, what about the goat?'

'Take her down to the Sûredal too.'

'But she can't stand the pig!'

'Well, tether her a bit further on, then.'

'Tether her? But I'm not going to tether them, I'm going . . .'

' . . . to turn them loose: of course you are, Manuel, how silly of me!'

He had laughed his childish laugh, a laugh that unsettled you if you stopped to think about it, and she had noticed that he suddenly fixed his gaze uneasily on her bulge that was beginning to show.

'Goats will always manage somehow, Manuel.'

'Yes, that's true. I know, I'll take her down to the Hume instead. She'll find everything she needs there: water, allotments, and orchards too.'

'Don't forget the rabbits, will you?'

'I won't. I think I'll let them go in the Pré aux Pucelles, behind the house. At least everybody's taking their dogs with them...'

'Would you have liked a dog, Manuel?'

'Maybe, I don't know.' Then, after a silence: 'What's going to happen to all the dogs once we get going?'

'What's going to happen to all of us, Manuel?'

He had looked at her again with his big blue eyes, so serious sometimes, and she had stifled the real question that was burning her tongue: What's going to happen to me without Benoît?

The square was getting noisier by the minute, with everybody bustling about. Midday had been fixed as the departure time, and it was nearly that now.

Manuel had forgotten to let the pigeons out. She would remind him in a minute, as soon as he got back from the Hume.

There were three bundles on the doorstep: a big one and a little one for her, and a medium-sized one for Manuel. The push-chair was there too, but Le Voisin had already made it quite clear that there wouldn't be room for it on his cart. When it was time to go, she would put it back inside, before finally locking the door.

Last night, after discussing with Manuel what to do with the animals, she had put away what little crockery they had into the wall-cupboard, and then he had helped her push the heavy linen-press in front in an attempt to hide it. They had few illusions, though. Then they had bolted the doors and lain down together on the bare mattresses to wait for day to come.

What would become of them?

How would Benoît know where she was?

Would they ever hear from him?

Manuel dozed off just as day was breaking. She had lain there watching him sleep, with her hands folded on her stomach. She was in her fourth month now. How much had Manuel guessed? He was bound to realize: he knew all about animals and their litters. Why didn't he say anything? She was afraid of broaching the

11

subject with him, afraid of his boyish laugh, afraid of his big dreamy eyes that seemed to be somehow not of this world: she was always worried that they wouldn't understand what happened here. Yet he was such a nice lad. Tears had come to her eyes as she looked at him again. Why did this handsome young man of eighteen have to be an idiot?

It wasn't obvious when he was born, or even when he was little. In the wardrobe, now yellowed with age, there were photographs of him as a normal fair-haired toddler, and there were still some of his locks inside the wooden darning-egg. He had taken a long time to learn to talk, and even longer to start forming sentences. It was then that his mother had died, suddenly, without warning, and Manuel discovered her sitting on the garden steps, looking for all the world as though she were asleep. He called her, then tried shaking her, before eventually going off to look for help. For months afterwards he said nothing at all.

After that, their father neglected them, leaving an aunt to look after Manuel and Angela, who was just two years older. The father only came to see them occasionally. Manuel related best to rabbits: he really loved them, and Angela used to find him talking to them. Before the end of his first year at school, everyone in the village knew that Manuel was an idiot: he never managed to count further than twenty. His father despaired of him. But Manuel did at least start speaking again. Not much, but more or less correctly. And he was handsome to look at. The good folk of the village used to stop and exclaim at him as he was playing in front of the house: 'Goodness, what a pretty child! Isn't he adorable?' Manuel would stare at them and then carry on playing.

When their father had his accident, crushed to death by a runaway cart, Angela had just left school and they were living at home again: at fourteen she was a grown woman and capable of running the household. Despite their aunt's protests they decided to stay put and live their own life, on their own. All they needed was a bit of help now and then.

'Ready already, Angela?'

'I've been waiting for ages, Mother Rak'Onna.'

She had been waiting for over an hour now, sitting on the stone in front of the house. The sun was climbing in the sky. Still no sign of Manuel...

Sometimes he had been late home from school, and Angela would worry. Where could he have got to? Had he been fighting with the big boys again? At thirteen he had still been with the juniors because of his difficulties in keeping up, and he sometimes got bullied for it. He could fight pretty fiercely, and would come back all covered in blood. She used to undress him just as their mother would have done, put on the water to heat up and wash him. He would be crying his eyes out as she tried to comfort him, and even when she had tucked him up in bed he would still be sobbing. It was as if he were weeping for all the injustice in the world.

As long as he gets back in time...

When he left school at fourteen, she had got him an apprenticeship with the carpenter. He was good at sweeping up. He managed to saw planks, too, but he was clumsy, and the others laughed at him. One day they shut him in a coffin and left him there for what seemed like an eternity. When they unscrewed the lid, Manuel fled into the cellar. That was where Angela had found him when she came to look for him at nightfall, scared stiff that something awful had happened to him. It took him a week to stop shaking. He couldn't go to work, and it was a dreadful time for Angela. When he went back they left him alone for a while, until the evening when...

Angela could still see him standing on the doorstep, his mouth open in a silent scream, and his eyeballs bulging out of his head. She let him in, and he collapsed on the stone floor like a wounded animal. He stayed there for a long time, sobbing, before he could get a word out. What had they done to him? What had they said? But he couldn't explain. He used to tell his sister everything, but this was different: he just couldn't bring himself to. She ran straight to the carpenter, who of course couldn't find anything out until the next day. When he came to reassure her ... But what reassurance could he give after what they had done to him? They had stripped him naked and tied him down on the work-bench, they had shown him photographs of women, they had tried to 'make a man of him' ... Manuel never got over it. From being as natural as a little child, he developed an obsessive sense of modesty, as if to hide his shame. She didn't dare to talk to him about the facts of life. She simply removed him from his apprenticeship and kept him at home, where he helped her to look after their garden, their allotments and their animals, the goat, the pig and the rabbits. They lived frugally, but it was a good life. The sun rose every morning.

The church clock had just struck half past, bringing Angela out of her reverie. She got up and went into the house. As she was shutting the back door, she spotted Manuel slipping out of the garden with the last of the rabbits in a basket.

'Manuel! Manuel!'

He turned and gesticulated.

'Hurry up, Manuel, we're about to leave!'

But he had already disappeared towards the Pré aux Pucelles.

Angela came back through the deserted house. In the kitchen, she cast a last glance at her stove, now cold and likely to remain so for a long time to come. In the bedroom, the bed and the wardrobe looked lost, abandoned. It was as if the heart of the house had suddenly stopped beating. Angela escaped into the sun-scorched square, heaved a sigh of relief at finding her three bundles and the push-chair intact, stood for a moment looking at them, and then sank down again on the warm stone, indifferent to the noise and bustle around her.

As long as he gets back in time!

Le Voisin was harnessing up. He would be taking three carts, heavily laden, and pulled by three pairs of heifers. He couldn't make room for the push-chair. When the baby arrived, out there in the other world they were heading for, there would be no push-chair for it.

'I'm expecting your child, Benoît.'

That was how she had begun her letter, the one to which she had had no reply. Had Benoît even received it? 'I'm expecting your child, Benoît, and I'm four months gone already.' There couldn't be any mistake: the child had been conceived during that single night, back in the spring, well before Benoît went off to the war.

I love you, Angela, sang the fountain in the hubbub of midday. *I love you, Angela.*

They had succumbed to the blandishments of the sweet spring air, with its tender, intoxicating scents; they had succumbed to the wine of the first kiss, the magic of the first caress, the heady softness of bare skin. *I love you, Angela, I love you.* It was Benoît's voice that she could hear in the murmur of the fountain, in the stirrings of the new life deep inside her. *I love you.* But she wouldn't yield a second time, they could wait until their wedding night, they could wait, and she knew that Benoît was with her on that, except on those moonlit nights when the whole of nature was panting with love beneath the starry sky. *Angela, I love you.* Where was her Benoît at this moment? Where would her letter find him? Would it ever find him?

'Angela! Bring your things, we're loading up.'

It was Le Voisin shouting.

She got up, put her arms round the largest of the three bundles, tried to pick it up, and ended up by dragging it over to the cart. The man heaved it up on top. She went back and collected the other two, one in each hand. Le Voisin stowed them in a corner.

'That all?'

'There's the push-chair.'

'I've already told you we can't be lumbered with a push-chair. Look, why don't you come and make yourself comfortable in the corner over here?'

She could feel him looking at her.

'What about Manuel?'

'He can follow on foot. He's strong enough.'

She went back to the house, took hold of the push-chair, hesitated, and then abandoned it on the *gasse* (front yard), in the sun. Behind her, the noise of wagons manoeuvring to get into some kind of line, hooves scraping, men swearing—those young or old enough not to have been called up—women shouting, children squealing . . . Still no Manuel. As long as . . . She couldn't hear the fountain any more, only the noise of the key as she turned it for the last time in the lock of the heavy front door. On her cheeks she could feel the tears burning. She made no attempt to wipe them away, but she kept her back turned to the square and the scorching sun.

'Angela!'

Le Voisin was calling her again.

'Coming!'

Manuel still wasn't back.

The wagons now stretched right down the village street in a long line. She couldn't see the front or the back from where she was. The animals and the men were getting impatient.

'Let's get going!'

'Hang on! Manuel isn't back yet!'

'Where's he gone?'

'Down to the meadow, with the rabbits.'

'Go and fetch him, Victor.'

Le Voisin's boy let out an oath, and ran off.

The whole convoy was waiting in the baking hot sun, with the women enthroned on the carts, keeping a protective eye on their brood like so many mother hens, and surrounded by a sad, motley collection of objects which gave the wagons a monstrous and somewhat anachronistic appearance.

'Blimey! Trust him to want to be different from everyone else!'

Angela hung her head and said nothing. When Manuel turned up she wouldn't say anything about the pigeons either.

They had forgotten to let them out, so they were still shut up in the loft. No point: they couldn't wait any longer. There he was now, with Victor behind him. There was a broad smile splashed across his face, the smile of a happy child. At the very moment that the column started moving, he leaped over to the *gasse*, grabbed the push-chair and hung it on the back of the cart in triumph. Le Voisin hadn't noticed. Angela looked at him and smiled. He turned his big blue eyes on her, his sky-blue eyes, and she sensed that, paradoxically, he was happy beyond measure, as if he was off on a big adventure. But she suddenly remembered the pigeons cooing, first frenzied, then famished, and finally exhausted. She imagined their ghastly death, saw their fragile, feathered bodies littering the floor. She lowered her head to hid her tears.

They had now passed the last shuttered houses. In the deserted village of Lasting-en-Lorraine, all that remained alive were the animals—free to wander, free to die—and the clear trickle of the fountain. *Angela, I love you, Angela*. It would have been good to stay there in the square, alone, sitting on the warm stone, in the full summer sun. When she looked up, she could see Manuel striding along beside the cart. The noise of the wheels on the road was deafening.

But from the way his lips were moving, she could tell that he was singing at the top of his voice.

2

It was getting hotter all the time and, with the heat, exhaustion began to set in. The animals were steaming, the men sweated and swore, while the women dozed, slumped on top of the laden carts. Flanking the convoy were the older children, now dragging their feet, their early enthusiasm gone. Manuel's fair curls were plastered to his forehead, and his mouth hung open. He had stopped singing, and was gazing at Angela. She appeared to be drowsing, but then he saw that her eyes were open.

They could have been so happy together...

It wasn't the evacuation that was the real calamity, it was the war itself, setting men against each other and inciting them to kill. It was the war that had separated her and Benoît so that they didn't even know where to start looking for each other. The French forces were said to be quite close. But where was Benoît? And how would he go about finding her?

They could have been so happy together.

When she told him she was carrying his child, he would have taken her in his arms and rocked her gently in a long, warm embrace. They would have gone to see the mayor and the priest together. The wedding would have been fixed for before Christmas, that was definite, maybe even before Advent. Benoît would have come over to the house each evening from the mill, and they would have got things ready together: the upstairs room would have suited them nicely, with enough room for the double bed and the baby's cradle. After he left, she would have gone on knitting baby clothes until late into the night. They would have explained to Manuel all about their love and the baby that was on its way. He would have understood, and would have accepted Benoît into the family like a big brother. It would have been a simple wedding. Christmas would have been spent together round the tree, by the crib, in the 'bonne chambre'. Outside, the wind, the snow and the cold; inside, it would have been as snug and warm as a nest.

The child would have been born in February, a little boy or a little girl, and Manuel would have been thrilled to bits, and Benoît would have held it in his arms, clumsy but full of tenderness. With the new spring the child would have grown, the three of them would have made light work of digging and tending their garden and allotments, then the summer would have come, and the autumn and winter, and it would have been time to kill the pig despite Manuel's pleas: he had to be persuaded afresh each year. The carcass would have been split open and hung head-down from the ladder in front of the house all day. The bladder would have been dried for Benoît to make a lantern for the child: dear bright eyes, dancing like stars in the candle flame!

They could have been so happy together.

Manuel had joined Le Voisin by the heifers which were pulling their cart. They seemed to be locked in discussion like two grown men. Young Victor had run off some time ago, and now he was creeping back for fear of getting spanked.

Rédache'Momme's cart had got stuck in the ditch. They needed help to get it out.

Manuel was off already. What a to-do! Women got down to hold the animals, while men went off to lend a hand. There was the sound of raised voices, then finally a shout of triumph. Back came the men, rubbing their hands and talking loudly. Manuel was close behind. When he got back to Angela he said: 'This is fun, isn't it, Angela?' His face was wreathed in smiles, and she smiled back but said nothing.

'*Hue! Hotomohuohari!*'

The animals moved off again. Order was restored. The heat had dropped a little. The children were beginning to complain of thirst.

They could have been so happy together.

Manuel, striding along behind the cart, had got all his energy back. He checked that the push-chair was securely fastened, and started singing again. Then he changed to whistling, as if he were off to the annual 'Kirb de la Saint-Martin'. And why not? For him this exodus was as good as a festival.

Seeing him so cheerful, Angela felt her heart ache. If only he could understand...

In the wagons, the women dozed off one by one as the convoy wound slowly on between the meadows and into the gathering darkness. The men's voices were hushed now, the beasts were weary and even the children had calmed down: they were playing quietly, undeterred by the jolting of the carts on the uneven roads. Only Manuel, striding along tirelessly, was still singing, as though galvanized by the hope of a new life ahead.

What would become of them, though? They didn't even know where they were going—not that it made much difference to her. What did it matter where they went, here, there or anywhere else, if Benoît couldn't be there too... What skies would the child she was carrying, Benoît's child, be born under? Almost instinctively she lifted her eyes, and after a moment fixed them on the western horizon, where the sunset was fading into night. That's where they were heading, towards the sunset.

Suddenly a voice called 'Halt!' and the whole convoy came to a stop.

There was a lot of bustle around all the wagons. Manuel had

disappeared. When he returned with news, he seemed even more cheerful than before.

They were going to camp just here, in the fields on the right, in the open air.

'What, out in the open?'

'No shelter?'

'But there aren't even any trees!'

Yes, yes, that's right: Manuel nodded at the disbelieving faces round him.

'But what about aeroplanes?'

'And what if it rains?'

Manuel was relieved when Le Voisin confirmed what he had been telling everyone. There wouldn't be time to get to the first proper stopping-place tonight, so they might as well camp here, feed the animals and have something to eat themselves, and then get some sleep. They'd be moving off again at crack of dawn.

They might as well make the best of it, so with a few grumbles everyone clambered down and the wagons lurched across the fields to the appointed spot. Then the men got going trying to create some semblance of order, as if they had been waiting for this moment to throw off their lethargy and take charge again.

'Hue! Ho! Ha! Oh! Oha!'

The twilight echoed with the sound of voices mingling, tangling, as the carts started getting entangled, and the animals too. Backwards and forwards, shoving, bumping, provoking muttered oaths and noisy confrontations, each lasting no longer than the space of a swallow's cry—and above the convoy the swifts and swallows were indeed darting and swooping, slashing the melancholy sky with startled wings.

Little by little, as though under the orders of some invisible centurion, the wagons of the exodus were organized into a hollow square. The women and children, along with all the baggage, would be safe in the middle. The cows were unyoked and turned loose to browse nearby. Families were reunited. There were plenty of women on their own, though, those whose menfolk had been called up, and some of them formed a group in one corner of the camp.

In the space in the middle the children were playing, and Angela could see Manuel joining in, laughing as he used to when he was thirteen.

The life of the camp was getting organized. Some of the mothers went off armed with all sorts of receptacles and installed themselves underneath the cows after first patting their rumps and flanks. Milking was the first priority. By the time they got back, weighed down by the results of their efforts, the older women had changed the babies, while the men had collected flat stones, made hearths and got fires going. Now milk could be warmed for the babies' bedtime feeds.

Two of the big girls were standing stock-still, watching in fascination as Rosa unconcernedly gave the breast to her little one. A short distance away, some of the boys were sniggering: they had been spying on old Madamilla squatting down behind a bush. Victor was one of them.

When at last the babies were fast asleep, well wrapped up in a corner of the cart, their families could get on with the business of unpacking the food and eating. They ate in haste, in virtual silence, and without bothering to sit down. If the boys were too rowdy, or if the girls suddenly squealed like frightened birds, they were scolded and made to be quiet.

Manuel was with Angela, apart from the rest of the crowd.

When she had got down from the cart, she hadn't dared to join the other families, and she had stayed outside the square, watching everyone else busily rushing about.

When La Voisine brought her a bowl of warm milk she thanked her with a smile and drank it down slowly in little sips, thinking of Benoît's child in her womb. Then she leaned against the cart and gazed at the horizon, beyond the placid grazing animals, where the darkening sky merged with the earth. When Manuel arrived, she untied the small bundle and gave him the picnic she had made for the journey. He bit into it with gusto, abruptly silent, yet still radiant, happy as she couldn't remember having seen him before.

Night fell suddenly.

The refugee camp sank gradually into silence. Furtive silhouettes disappeared into the darkness and returned a few moments later. The women climbed back into the wagons, while the men and older boys slept on the ground, wrapped in blankets.

From time to time a dog barked, and others responded from the far side of the camp.

Angela, snug in her blanket between the bundles, lay with her eyes wide open, looking up at the sky. She wasn't worried about Manuel: he was safely asleep under the back of the cart, near the push-chair. She looked at all the stars twinkling, so far and yet so near that they were reflected in the tears which had started to well up. She was overcome with emotion at the sight of the many-splendoured firmament, at the vast tenderness of the heavens. Her lips parted to utter a prayer, but in the silence of the night only two words came, two words which she repeated over and over again: 'Our Father . . .'

If she had sat up, before her eyelids finally closed, she might have seen a figure vanish into the night. Would she have recognized her brother Manuel, who was not asleep as she had so fondly imagined?

The whole camp was asleep, or so any passing angel might have thought, unless he looked very closely, in which case he would have found plenty of eyes open in the dark, eyes full of anxiety and even terror.

Old Bêa-Yasse'Kette was weeping silently over her loneliness, which was magnified by the night. What would become of her?

Who would spare a thought for an elderly spinster in her seventies, with no family left? She couldn't even speak a word of French, which was all that would be understood where they were going. What would become of her?

'*O god o god o god! Honn'ish donn mousse so ald vêrre oun' dass noch êalêve! Vêrr'ish doch nid'ââ bessa dood vee ounsa Iéla!*' (O God, O God, O God! Why does this have to happen to me at my age? I'd have been better off dead like my Iéla!)

But there was no one listening. No one at all. She was listening, though, listening to the dogs howling in the night.

Millache'Babe was sitting up against his skimpy bundle. He looked asleep, with his bald, bony head nodding backwards and forwards, and his gnarled hands clasping his knees. He had come in his daughter's wagon. She had her hands full coping with her brood, and he didn't mind being on his own a lot: if he died where they were going, at least he'd have someone to bury him. Though it would be a shame not to be laid next to his Léna, in the same plot, nourishing the same geraniums. They'd meet again in heaven... but that wasn't the same, whatever people might say. No one had ever come back from there.

Millache'Babe certainly saw a figure slip away into the night, but then any number had been off to the bushes and come back again...

It was probably only the children who were really sleeping soundly.

Their mothers woke from time to time with a start, and some of them let out an involuntary cry, which caused the night birds to hoot in response.

The men had seriously considered setting a watch, but there weren't enough of them. Still, there was nothing to be afraid of out here in the country, and the dogs would do the job just as well. So the men snored, but the dogs kept barking and waking them up. They peered into the night, then lay down again on the ground.

'Dass'do honn'ish noch misse mêd'êalêve!' (Why did I have to live to see this?)

Old Bêa-Yasse'Kette was still moaning, and Fata Ioss and La Vieille could hear her from the next wagon. They snuggled up to each other for comfort. La Vieille was saying her rosary: Fata Ioss felt it when he tried to take her hand. That set him off thinking of the big rosary hanging above his bed at home, fifteen decades of boxwood beads, as big as green walnuts. He used to get through the lot when he came back drunk at dawn: all fifteen, on his knees by the side of the bed, to atone for his misconduct. Never had he allowed himself to get into bed without saying the rosary right the way through, and his drunkenness had never caused him any serious accident. He'd lost count of the number of times he had been picked up in the gutter, where he had crawled to escape being crushed by wheels and hooves. Stars? He'd seen billions of them, whirling round in a demonic dance: the sky tonight was practically empty in comparison, and what few stars there were were tamely staying put. If only their Iossep hadn't thrown himself into the Meuse! He'd have been a soldier today, though, so La Vieille would still have been sad. Such a fine lad, and as abstemious as a camel! What an end: all for a pair of pretty eyes, and not all that pretty either, he'd be bound.

What was that noise in the sky?

Bêa-Yasse'Kette had heard it too, and had lapsed into an anxious silence.

Millache'Babe couldn't hear anything. He was a bit deaf, after living with so many noisy children in the house. His head nodded backwards and forwards.

La Vieille muttered her prayers under her breath, while Fata Ioss listened attentively. The noise was getting louder. It seemed to be coming from all sides at once.

Aeroplanes! Aeroplanes ploughing noisily through the night sky.

The whole camp was alert now, but nobody moved. Had they

remembered to rake out all the fires?

The dogs howled in chorus, tugging at their chains.

Angela woke with a start. She stared up at the sky, straining her eyes to see, and just managed to make out the band of false stars dividing the real ones into two unequal groups. Instinctively, she covered her stomach with her hands as if to protect Benoît's child.

Would the aeroplanes never go away?

When they did, it took a long time for silence to return to the camp. For many of the evacuees, sleep had fled for good. There was still a long wait ahead of them.

'*Gegrüsset seist Du, Maria...*' (Hail, Mary...)

Bêa-Yasse'Kette had started on the rosary too, now. In German. You spoke to God in German, *ênn hochdêïd'sh*, not in patois, *ênn platt*. The village priest always preached in German for the benefit of the older members of the congregation. The restoration of Lorraine to France in 1919 had made no difference in that respect.

Millache'Babe had dozed off again.

Lying on his side, Fata Ioss was feeling in La Vieille's bundle. He pulled out a bottle, opened it carefully so as not to make any noise, and drank. Nothing like schnapps to put you back on top.

Somewhere a cock crowed, heralding the dawn.

The night air was cooler now, and Angela shivered under her blanket.

The cock crowed again, and then another. The stars were beginning to fade.

A frightened mooing came from a long, long way away across the meadow, or so it seemed. Could one of their cows have wandered so far off during the night?

Le Voisin emerged from under the cart grumbling, and Angela saw him stagger off towards the bushes.

The sky was imperceptibly getting lighter.

When Le Voisin returned, he busied himself round the make-shift hearth. He was the first to get a fire going. The crackle of kindling and the leaping flames were the signal for the life of the camp to revive.

Millache'Babe performed his morning ablutions in the wet grass and then trotted off in his turn to the bushes.

Angela hadn't moved. She lay on her side, watching the camp coming to life: fires being lit, women going off with buckets. Soon she could hear the cows lowing as they were milked. Good smells of coffee and hot milk started wafting across: there would be more than just dry bread to look forward to for breakfast!

There were children crying: they had been smacked for going too near the fire.

Suddenly, Angela realized that she couldn't see Manuel anywhere. She roused herself and struggled out of the wagon. There was nobody underneath. She went over to the fire.

'Morning, Angela. Sleep all right?'

La Voisine handed her a bowl of milk and pointed to the bread. Angela thanked her.

'Where's Manuel?' asked Victor.

Angela shook her had. La Voisine read the anxiety in her eyes, and said: 'Oh, he'll have gone off to the bushes! Or else he's just wandering about in the camp somewhere. You know he thinks the evacuation is fun.'

Angela smiled her thanks. Since they set out, La Voisine had been taking good care of her. As for her husband, he must have noticed the push-chair by now, but he hadn't said anything.

Where could Manuel have got to? It wasn't like him to go wandering off like that. Angela concealed her anxiety as best she could. She couldn't summon up the courage to go round all the wagons looking for him.

Time to pack up, and round up the animals.

'One of Wag-Nache'Péda's cows is missing!'

The news spread round the camp. Was he sure? Had he looked properly?

Still no Manuel.

After a thorough search, Wag-Nache'Péda's cow was still missing. The poor man was beside himself.

Everyone else was ready to go. Some of the wagons started moving over back to the road, and the convoy gradually reassembled.

Angela's worry reached a peak when Le Voisin's cart moved off across the field and she caught sight of the push-chair bouncing about on the back.

'What about Manuel?'

She went up to La Voisine and spoke to her in a low voice. La Voisine threw up her hands, and then joined her husband for a lengthy confabulation. He didn't get angry: he merely looked hard at Angela and then sent Victor off to search along the convoy.

When Victor came back empty-handed, Angela nearly collapsed. No one had seen Manuel, and now they all knew that he had gone missing. People started calling his name: men, women and children everywhere were shouting 'Manuel! Manuel!'

Angela was sobbing in the wagon. La Voisine tried to comfort her.

There was no sign of Manuel or of Wag-Nache'Péda's cow either. He must have gone off with it. That was the rumour that started going round. La Voisine, watching over Angela, swatted it away like a fly.

In the end they decided they would just have to get going. They couldn't wait for Manuel for ever, and in any case nobody knew where to start looking. When the convoy finally moved off, Angela tried to jump down: she'd wait for her brother at the campsite, he'd be bound to be back soon. Le Voisin had to help his wife restrain her by force.

At that moment there was a hubbub of voices up front, and Le

Voisin went off to see what was happening. Round the first bend they had found Wag-Nache'Péda's cow lying motionless in a dip in the ground. Everyone watched its owner as he rushed over to it, whip in hand. When he reached it, he threw his hands up in the air, then bent down and seemed to be shaking someone. He straightened up again, shouted something that no one quite caught, and eventually resorted to gestures. He was evidently asking for help. Two or three men went off to join him, including Le Voisin. When they got there, they too bent down. Suddenly Le Voisin stood up, holding in his arms the limp body of Manuel. It was clearly quite an effort to carry him.

La Voisine had stayed with Angela. She touched her shoulder. 'They've found Manuel.'

Immediately Angela sprang up, jumped out of the wagon, and made to run off into the field, but she was prevented. The men were nearly back, in any case, closely followed by Wag-Nache'Péda leading his cow, which had got up with no difficulty once Manuel had been removed.

'Manuel! Manuel!'

The lad's head was hanging like a dead weight as Le Voisin laid him in the cart. But at least he was alive: there was a muffled heartbeat. He was alive, but he wouldn't wake up, wouldn't come to.

Angela ran her fingers through her brother's blond curls and stroked his forehead. He was huddled against the cow when they found him, and the cow hadn't been able to move.

What on earth could have happened?

The decision was made to set off at once, without delay, so as to arrive as soon as possible and find a doctor, or at least the midwife who had gone on ahead.

Angela clambered up into the wagon next to her brother.

She couldn't take her eyes off him. He gave the impression of being sunk in a deep sleep from which he might never awaken.

A pale sun climbed above the horizon. Men's voices filled the morning air. In the wagons, the old women who felt the cold pulled the blankets closer round them. Children were frisking about. The animals were rested and pulling well. Despite the uncertainties of the exodus, and the unknown complaint that had afflicted Manuel the simpleton, the refugee convoy was in good spirits, almost in festive mood.

Angela, alone, was unaware of it. She cradled her brother's head on her knees, trying to spare him the worst of the jolting. He was breathing peacefully, and were it not for his dew-soaked clothes he might have been simply taking a nap. Bending over and putting her lips close to his ear, she tried gently calling his name: 'Manuel! Manuel!' But it was no good.

The sun had risen above the early morning mists and was gently warming the older women. The convoy was keeping up a good pace. Victor trotted along behind the wagon in Manuel's place, keeping an eye on the push-chair, while his mother kept hers, discreetly, on the two orphans, Angela and Manuel. They felt almost like her own children now.

'Hue! Hue!'

The dogs were chasing each other wildly all over the fields, then suddenly lying down flat in the grass when their owners called them.

The sun continued to climb in the sky. The morning was wearing on. Rumour had it that they would be there by noon.

Where was 'there'?

Angela leaned forward anxiously. Manuel had just stirred in his sleep for the first time. She couldn't help whispering his name once more and stroking his face. As if in a dream, she saw him open his eyes.

'Manuel! Oh, Manuel!'

He recognized her and smiled.

'Oh, I've been so frightened, Manuel!'

But he had already gone back to sleep. A great sense of peace descended on Angela, like an older sister putting a hand on her shoulder and calming her fears. She looked up, and La Voisine was surprised to see her smile. For the first time she noticed the fields, still wet with dew, the dogs rushing around madly, the sunshine, and she became aware of the men's voices urging on their beasts in the morning air.

'*Hue! Hotomohuohari!*'

She put her hand on Manuel's chest and felt his heart beating. All of a sudden she was so happy that she caught herself humming a tune. A little later, when the first thrill had worn off slightly, Angela returned to the question of where Manuel could have been in the night. And what was he doing with Wag-Nache'Péda's cow? He must have run a long way to be so utterly worn out.

'How's it going, Angela?' Le Voisin asked anxiously.

'All right now. He opened his eyes and smiled at me, but then he went back to sleep.'

'And is he still asleep?'

Angela nodded, and Le Voisin returned to his team.

When she next glanced down, Manuel was looking at her.

'I went ... to let out ... the pigeons. We ... we forgot them.'

'You what?!'

Angela couldn't believe her ears.

'I ran, I ran all night.'

'And did you manage? The house was all locked up.'

'I used Le Voisin's long ladder ... I've never run so far in all my life! I'm so tired!'

She smiled down at him and murmured: 'You silly old thing!'

But he didn't hear, he had gone back to sleep again.

Angela lifted her eyes heavenwards, and when she closed them again, dazzled by the brightness, she could see what looked like a flock of white pigeons taking off and rising into the sky above them.

3

Bermering.

Soon the name was on everybody's lips. Hardly anyone knew the place. Most of them had never left Lasting except to go to the market in Forbach or Sarreguemines; beyond that . . . Bermering.

A tiny village nestling in a little valley. The convoy slowed down and seemed to hesitate as the leaders caught sight of the first red-roofed houses in the midday sun.

Manuel was still asleep with his head on Angela's lap.

The village was dominated by a small, squat church perched on a knoll. The streets seemed quite deserted. The noise of the cartwheels on the road made it impossible to distinguish any other sounds.

Until now they had been deliberately avoiding human habitations. Those were their orders. Their exodus had taken them along side-roads and tracks. They had dropped out. It was almost as though they had never left Lasting-en-Lorraine, as though the long, straggling village on the main road, originally three separate farms which had become joined, had simply gone for a walk, snaking its way through the late summer countryside.

But now they were at Bermering.

Word went round that soldiers had been spotted in the main street, up by the church.

When Bêa-Yasse'Kette heard that, she exclaimed: *'Ish vill doch*

33

nid ênn'de greesh!' (But I don't want to be in the war!)

La Vieille, Fata Ioss' wife, crossed herself, while old Mill-ache'Babe's head nodded backwards and forwards.

The dogs were apprehensive and kept running under the wagons, narrowly avoiding being crushed by the wheels. The men swore at them. Someone claimed that she could hear all the dogs in Bermering barking together, quite distinctly.

Manuel slept on.

Was it the dogs that had brought the soldiers out? It wasn't just soldiers, though: they could make out some older folk too, who must be some of the local inhabitants. Angela wasn't looking. The bumpy ride, far from disrupting her happy reverie, was positively encouraging it. She was basking in the joy of having found her brother again, and for the moment she had even forgotten that Benoît wasn't there. Meanwhile the people of Bermering were watching the exodus in wary silence.

The leading wagons had arrived at the main road and were entering the village. It was true that the dogs were barking, but from inside the barns where they were chained up. Before long the convoy reached the church on the knoll and came to a halt. Hidden eyes were watching them from behind every curtain.

The sudden cessation of movement woke Manuel up. He sat up, rubbing his eyes. Was he dreaming? When he realized that the soldiers in the street were real, he let out an exclamation of surprise and jumped down.

'Manuel!'

Angela's quiet call went unheeded. He had already joined the group of refugees gathered round the villagers and the soldiers. Manuel had never seen soldiers before, and he gazed at them in wonder. Despite an encouraging smile from La Voisine, Angela couldn't help watching him anxiously in case he did anything silly.

One of the men had taken a piece of paper out of his pocket.

Others volunteered to show the refugees to their temporary quarters. The soldiers kept out of it: refugees were a civilian problem. The first wagon had already moved off down a narrow street by the church. The others moved up. All the women and children had by now disembarked, curious to know what was happening. The dogs which had come with them were hiding underneath the wagons with their tails between their legs. It might be the end of the summer, but the sun was beating down strongly.

Angela had only a vague idea of what was going on. She was in a dream as she walked beside the slow-moving cart. She found herself with Mother Rak'Onna, old Bêa-Yasse'Kette, Madamilla, La Vieille, Fata Ioss and Manuel, following an elderly man who was taking them just outside the village to a little two-storey house with a round orchard. Le Voisin had already put his cows out to grass there: his family was in a barn nearby, which was just as well, as Millache'Babe and his whole tribe were there too. Angela's group had a big ground-floor room with seven bundles of straw that would serve as mattresses. The upstairs had been requisitioned for the soldiers, and the sound of their heavy boots was audible through the ceiling. Would they have to set a guard tonight?

'*Do shdêav'ish fon ongshd!*' (I'll be scared to death!') wailed Bêa-Yasse'Kette.

Le Voisin was busy unloading the cart. Angela rescued her three bundles, and Manuel untied the push-chair and leaned it against the wall of the house. Mother Rak'Onna, bent double with rheumatism, was bravely starting to unpack the cooking utensils.

'Better start thinking about dinner. *Esse oun' dringge hêld lêib oun' séel sezomme* (food and drink keep life and soul together)! Fata Ioss, why don't you get on and make us a fire?'

Without a word, Fata Ioss beckoned to Manuel, who followed him outside, his eyes sparkling. Madamilla and La Vieille were getting their bundles sorted out. Angela had stowed hers in a corner, and now she was waiting with her hands folded on her stomach.

Fata Ioss and Manuel set to work collecting enough flat stones to build three hearths side by side: that should be enough. The old man noticed a bundle of sticks, and told Manuel to fetch it. Soon the flames were crackling, and out shuffled Mother Rak'Onna with a small milk churn.

'Go and fetch me some water, would you, Manuel?'

No beating about the bush with her. Manuel found a tap round the other side of the house, and made several journeys. There would be plenty of soup for everyone.

Bêa-Yasse'Kette had started unpacking her *saucisson*. La Vieille had some potatoes which she was peeling carefully: they could be fried. Madamilla offered some eggs. Thick soup, fried potatoes, and fried eggs too: not a bad dinner at all!

'Oun' minna vwashd?' (What about my sausage?) demanded Bêa-Yasse'Kette.

'We'll have that tonight. We've still got this evening's meal to think about, and tomorrow, and the next day.'

'It's Sunday tomorrow,' said Bêa-Yasse'Kette. 'A foreign church and a foreign God! I ask you!'

'God is the same everywhere,' Fata Ioss put in. 'When I was in Russia, I worshipped God there, and it was the same God, behind all those icons.'

'Vass ish donn dass?' (Whatever are they?)

Bêa-Yasse'Kette had never heard of icons before.

'Sort of little pictures of Our Lord and his Mother.'

'Dass hô'mir ââ!' (Oh, we've got those, too!)

How on earth did you explain to someone like Bêa-Yasse'Kette what an icon was?

'Soup, lovely soup! Come and get it!' called Rak'Onna.

'Where are we going to sit?' asked Madamilla.

Manuel had his eye on a wheelbarrow. He went and brought it over to the cooking area, turned it upside-down, and sat on it. The older folk could perch on packing-cases: there were several lying around.

'Better keep one for Angela. She needs one, in her condition...'

Manuel looked at his sister's stomach. How did it get like that?

Bêa-Yasse'Kette started saying grace in patois.

Manuel was thinking. 'She was found to be with child of the Holy Ghost.' Angela didn't know any men, except him, and he hadn't anything to do with it. 'With child of the Holy Ghost.'

'Pass me your plate, Manuel. What are you dreaming about?'

'The Holy Ghost.'

Everybody burst out laughing, and Manuel joined in. The mood was almost festive.

When Fata Ioss asked him what he had been up to in the night, and Manuel said, 'The pigeons! The pigeons!', the laughter redoubled.

'Don't tell me you saw the Holy Ghost in the form of a dove!'

Even Bêa-Yasse'Kette was splitting her sides. Angela alone didn't join in the general merriment, but sat drinking her soup in silence.

Two soldiers tossed them a friendly greeting on their way past. Bêa-Yasse'Kette hastily crossed herself.

Towards the end of the meal, one of the local inhabitants came bringing a bottle of red wine, and with it two pieces of news which hit them like a bombshell.

'Hitler has invaded Poland. And France has declared war on Nazi Germany.'

When the man left, there was a great silence, broken only by Bêa-Yasse'Kette's gloomy prophecy:

'*Do si'ma all' falôa!*' (Then we've all had it!)

Nobody felt like replying.

Fata Ioss got up, saying that he was off to talk to the other men. Manuel followed him. The five women did the washing-up. Angela refused to take La Vieille's advice and lie down.

Throughout the afternoon, the refugee camp hummed with rumour and counter-rumour. La Voisine dropped in to tell Angela that she was welcome to milk the cows morning and evening: she needed plenty of milk. Anyway, the exodus had united them all in one big family now.

Bêa-Yasse'Kette nodded in agreement: La Voisine was quite right, they must all help each other.

When Manuel came back with Fata Ioss, dusk was beginning to fall. They had been right round the village but there was nothing new to report. Everyone was more or less fixed up for the night. They were all worried about what they had left behind in Lasting, but at least they could feel safe behind the Maginot Line. The Führer wouldn't get past that in a hurry.

They had a quick bite of supper—Bêa-Yasse'Kette's famous sausage—and got ready for bed. They put out the bundles of straw, which took up all the floor-space. Overhead they could hear the soldiers' footsteps. Madamilla was getting worried.

'What are we supposed to do about relieving ourselves with all those soldiers about?' she complained.

They would just have to use the orchard. Madamilla decided to wait until it was dark.

They turned in.

Manuel, still tired from his escapade of the previous night, was asleep in no time. Angela lay awake, staring into the darkness. La Vieille was saying her rosary. Bêa-Yasse'Kette, despite all her anxieties, was snoring peacefully next to Rak'Onna.

Madamilla was hanging on until it was completely dark.

All of a sudden she burst out: 'I need to go! Who's coming with me?'

Silence.

They weren't all asleep, were they? Surely not!

'I need to go...!'

Still no reply.

'Angela! Angela!'

The poor girl must have been so tired she just couldn't stay awake any longer.

'Bêa-Yasse'Kette! Kette! Kette!'

But the old woman was sleeping the sleep of the just.

Manuel was breathing deeply. After last night's exertions, he must be out for the count.

'Fata Ioss! Fata Ioss!'

Madamilla resigned herself to asking a man.

'I need to go, I'm bursting! Ioss! Fata Ioss!'

'Wassamatter? Fire?'

'...need to go!'

'Well go on then!'

'I'm scared. You come with me!'

Fata Ioss turned over towards La Vieille. She seemed to be asleep. He got up quietly.

'Come on then.'

Madamilla heaved a sigh of relief, and the straw rustled under their feet.

Once outside, Ioss stood guard by the door, while Madamilla disappeared into the night. When she came back, she didn't notice his impish grin as he stood aside to let her in. He never would have imagined that one day he might have to escort Madamilla in such circumstances!

Fata Ioss found it hard to get back to sleep. He managed to lay his hand on the bottle of schnapps without waking La Vieille and had a good swig. He dreamed of Russian churches full of icons, and in the early hours he saw the shining face of Christ as represented...

Madamilla was up first.

Bêa-Yasse'Kette complained loudly at being roused from her

beauty sleep. What did Madamilla think she was doing, disturbing her at such a ridiculous hour? That woke La Vieille and Angela, who promptly burst into tears, diverting their attention on to her.

'What's the matter, Angela? Something wrong?'

Why cry if there was nothing wrong? Angela didn't reply.

La Vieille took her hand and held it, but didn't try to say anything. Meanwhile Fata Ioss and Manuel were oblivious to all this, and only woke up when the room filled with the smell of coffee and hot milk.

Angela had stopped crying.

It was Sunday morning, the first Sunday of the exodus, and the angelus rang out from Bermering church.

The long procession of refugees from Lasting-en-Lorraine wound up the village street towards the church. Yes, Hitler had invaded Poland. They were all looking rather solemn and awkward in their best clothes. Yes, France had declared war on Germany. The inhabitants of Bermering joined them, climbing the steep flight of steps to the church door: if they didn't hurry there might not be any seats left this morning!

La Vieille had stayed behind with Angela, who was feeling quite poorly. Was it because of all the jolting along country lanes? But she was only in her fourth month.

'Are you sure about the dates?'

'Quite sure. There can't be any mistake.'

'I was never as definite as that with mine.'

'But I'm not married. And it only happened once...'

Angela started crying again.

'Poor thing!' And La Vieille stroked her hair gently.

Manuel had set off for Mass with the others. Inside the church, much smaller than the one back home in Lasting, they had the same kind of chandeliers hanging from the roof. It wasn't that different. The prayers were still in Latin, even if the sermon was in French. It was standing room only, almost up to the altar. The coming of war had awakened people's religious feelings. Manuel was right in the front row, observing, listening, not missing a thing.

'*Accipite et manducate ex hoc omnes ...*'

He recognized those words, and he knew what they meant.

Angela was lying down on her straw mattress. La Vieille had managed to find the midwife. It was nothing serious: plenty of rest and she'd be fine. When the midwife had gone, Angela closed her eyes and La Vieille heard her murmuring 'Benoît'.

Where was her Benoît now?

When the others got back from church, nothing had been done about dinner, much to the surprise of Madamilla and Bêa-Yasse'Kette. Fata Ioss had stayed behind with the men. Manuel too, probably. That was the custom, and customs were what held a people together.

The women pooled their provisions. If all went well, there would be enough for two more days. After that... After that? Who knows, perhaps they would be able to get fresh supplies from somewhere. They would have to wait and see. Sufficient unto the day ... was the food thereof!

Bêa-Yasse'Kette was not so easily reassured. She liked to be prepared, and once she knew that they would soon run out ...

'Maybe the soldiers ...'

Soldiers were supposed to eat lots of tinned food. They could hear the ones upstairs coming and going on their mysterious errands.

When Fata Ioss at last got back, it was after midday.

Manuel was not with him. Angela had dozed off, and there was no question of telling her. La Vieille tore a strip off her husband.

'But I'm not his guardian, dammit!'

In the end they sat down to eat without Manuel. Just as La

Vieille was waking Angela up, he came into view across the orchard, carrying something in his arms. When he got closer, they could see that it was a rabbit.

Bêa-Yasse'Kette, Madamilla, Rak'Onna, Fata Ioss and La Vieille all stared at him. It occurred to Angela, who by now was installed on her packing-case, that they were expecting her to do the questioning.

'Where did you get that rabbit, Manuel?'

The lad looked at his sister, and a smile lit up his face.

'Over there.' A big sweep of his arm in the general direction of the fields. 'It was running about in the grass.'

Fata Ioss bit his tongue.

'Are you sure you didn't steal it, Manuel?'

The simpleton shook his head energetically.

'Because if you did, we must find the owner and ...'

More shaking of the head.

'But ...'

'It's mine. I found it.'

Fata Ioss decided it was time to intervene.

'Let him keep it, Angela.'

Manuel nodded vigorously.

'But where are we going to put it?'

'In a packing-case, of course!'

Rak'Onna had such a practical mind! She grabbed one of the packing-cases, put a handful of straw in it and placed it in front of Manuel, who was thrilled.

'Now, come on, food!'

It was a beautiful white female rabbit with red eyes.

Manuel gave it a bit of dry bread to nibble. Angela's mind was working hard. Had his love of rabbits driven him to stealing?

Manuel spent the whole of the rest of this first Sunday of the exodus with the rabbit. He let it run about and graze in the orchard, finding it the juiciest clumps of grass. Fata Ioss had gone back to join the men, while the women went for a walk round the village. Angela stayed behind on her own, resting on her straw mattress.

Up above, the soldiers were laughing and singing. One of them was playing the accordion. There were sounds of bottles clinking, and the ceaseless tramp of feet on the wooden stairs.

'Hello.'

Angela sat up.

A young soldier was standing in the doorway, with his cap awry. He smiled. His eyes were fastened on the girl's body.

'They haven't gone and left you all on your own, have they?'

'They haven't gone far,' Angela stammered, 'and anyway, Manuel's just outside in the orchard.' Her heart was racing, and she began to tremble.

'Can I come in?'

'All right. Sit down over there.'

How old could he be? Twenty-five? He had thick black hair, and his dark eyes were watching her intently.

'Been here long?' Angela asked.

'Not really. But it's pretty boring in this hole.'

'Where are you from?'

'Neuillé, north of Tours.'

'That's a long way.'

'Yes.'

'Married?'

'Yes. Two children, and the wife's expecting again, same as you.' He smiled.

Angela was scared, although what he had just said should have reassured her.

'You won't be staying here long, you know. Tomorrow or the next day they'll send you on to Lidrezing, and then they'll ship you off.'

'Ship us off?'

'By train. They won't let you stay near the Front, you'd be in the way.'

Angela said nothing. She was thinking that they probably wouldn't be able to take the cows with them on the train, and then they wouldn't have any milk. Where was she going to get milk from when the baby arrived?

The soldier got up. He looked a bit embarrassed.

'How about . . .'

He was right close to Angela now, she could smell the wine on his breath, feel his hot hand on her shoulder.

'Leave me alone!'

He laughed and tried to force her down on to the straw. Upstairs, the accordion was still playing.

'Manuel!' Angela screamed, pushing the soldier away. He gawped at her.

'Come on now, don't play hard to get, there's nothing to worry about.'

Manuel appeared in the doorway, with a look of grim determination on his face. He lunged forward and managed to topple the drunken soldier. He raised his fist menacingly.

'Stop, Manuel.'

He obeyed his sister, and slowly got up. The soldier muttered an oath through his clenched teeth. He hauled himself to his feet with difficulty and staggered back to the door glaring at them with hate-filled eyes.

'Slut!' he yelled, then ran off through the orchard.

Angela collapsed into Manuel's arms, sobbing. He murmured words that she couldn't understand. When she looked him in the face, she saw that he had gone as white as a sheet.

'Calm down, Manuel, calm down. He didn't harm me.'

When La Vieille and Rak'Onna got back, they found Angela and Manuel sitting on the doorstep, in tears, with the stiff body of the white rabbit by them. Manuel had found it in the orchard.

They realized straight away what had happened: it was the soldier's way of getting his revenge. But they weren't telling anyone. Manuel had promised to keep his mouth shut about the drunkard's visit, even if he didn't fully understand why. Bêa-Yasse'Kette and Madamilla were quite upset: they could have kept the rabbit in reserve in case their provisions ran out. Manuel wasn't listening.

Tonight, with Fata Ioss, he was going to dig a hole in the orchard and lay the rabbit in it.

At the burial, he cried like a little child. On top of the freshly-turned earth he set a large white stone.

Next day the order came to leave Bermering.

They repacked their bundles and carried them to the cart.

Manuel attached the push-chair to the back. Slowly the convoy reformed in the village street. La Voisine was glad to be with Angela again. Manuel, once more, was excited to be leaving: departures were joyful occasions for him.

Bêa-Yasse'Kette grumbled: *'Ma vaare doch so good sezomme!'* (But we were all getting on so well together!)

Fata Ioss and La Vieille tried to reassure her that they weren't going to be split up.

The dogs were frisking round the convoy, playing with the local dogs. How would they make sure they took the right ones with them?

The men swore.

The sky was overcast and, just as the exodus of refugees from Lasting-en-Lorraine got under way, rain began to fall, a peculiarly fine, penetrating sort of rain.

Manuel followed behind Le Voisin's wagon on foot, whistling. First thing this morning, he had been and checked that the white stone was still standing firm where he had put it, on the grave of the rabbit with the red eyes.

Angela was glad to be leaving Bermering. She was smiling.

45

She had not seen the soldier again. Her thoughts turned to the young woman in Touraine who was carrying his child and thinking of him.

4

This time they stayed on the main roads. A little while after leaving Bermering they turned left.

It was still raining.

Rédache'Momme was leading the exodus now. Next came Wag-Nache'Péda, no doubt praying that the cart he was following wouldn't fall into the ditch again. He looked relieved to have found his runaway cow. 'I don't suppose he'll be able to take it on the train, though,' Angela thought as she caught sight of him out of the corner of her eye, while huddling under her raincoat.

Manuel refused to protect himself from the rain. He marched along behind, bare-headed, keeping an eye on the push-chair.

The road wound gently up and down through a beautiful late-summer landscape which needed only the magic touch of a sunbeam to turn it into a fairyland.

They had just been through the village of Zarbeling, but Millache'Babe wouldn't have seen anything of it. His bald head, glistening in the rain, nodded backwards and forwards, forwards and backwards. Someone should have found him a hat. His eyes were tight shut, despite the bumpy ride and the whining of a dog: he must be thinking of his Léna whose mortal remains he had left behind in the safe, motherly keeping of their native soil, and of how he was unlikely ever to be laid to rest beside her now.

Manuel was watching him.

All of a sudden he dashed over to Angela, startling her, and grabbed a blanket from her bundle. Then he rushed off again to put it over Millache'Babe. The old man looked up at him with a seraphic expression on his face. Their two smiles together would have unlocked the darkest heart, bringing hope of a new dawn, a new birth. When Manuel returned to his post behind Le Voisin's wagon, Millache'Babe found that he couldn't take his eyes off him.

The fine rain continued to fall.

They could have been so happy together, Angela thought to herself when she noticed that Manuel was back. Her eyes filled with tears, which mingled on her cheeks with the raindrops. La Voisine observed her anxiously, and decided she needed to talk.

'Do you know where we're going next, Angela?'

'No.'

'Lidrezing. There's supposed to be food waiting for us there, so at least we'll be able to eat.'

'Until they ship us off.'

'Ship us off?'

'Yes, by train.'

'Whoever told you that?'

'The s... Well, that's what they were saying at Bermering, anyhow.'

'But they can't put us in a train! What would we do with the animals if we had to go in a train?'

'I don't know.'

'Victor! Call your dad for me, would you?'

Angela wished she hadn't said anything.

'He says he can't come just now. We're nearly there!'

At that moment they turned a corner, and a round church tower with a little steeple came into view between the overhanging branches of the fruit trees.

Lidrezing.

Manuel danced for joy round the wagon. Young Victor copied

him, though whether innocently or to make fun of him was anyone's guess, and La Voisine and Angela couldn't help laughing at the sight. The rain had stopped, and the sun was peeping out from between two thick dark clouds like a sign from heaven. The convoy wound itself round the little church and came to a halt by the fountain.

For some unknown reason the business of finding temporary quarters for the refugees took longer that it had at Bermering. They waited impatiently. Angela was getting worried. She had seen Manuel go into the little church, but she hadn't seen him come out. She looked at the building: it was tiny, with the nave and choir clearly older than the rest. What could be keeping Manuel?

Something had drawn him into the church. Something that took away the childish pleasure he had felt at arriving in Lidrezing and seeing the sun shining again. Something inside him, a deep peace and joy, but also a call. He had gone up the two rounded steps and pushed open the heavy door.

When he got inside he stopped, struck by the convex wall in the far left-hand corner: that must be the round tower, standing guard at the entrance to the sanctuary. He didn't notice the plain nave or even the little Gothic choir. His eyes were drawn irresistibly towards the gilded baroque altar on which a tiny light was shining.

Manuel was dazzled by it.

The noise of the exodus, temporarily forgotten, came surging back and filled his head, intensified by the silence of the empty church. In the gleam of the sanctuary lamp he could see the rainbow smile of old Millache'Babe as he sat in the freezing rain. He ran the length of the nave, oblivious to the clatter of his boots, through the gap in the communion rail, and up the few steps to the altar, where he stopped, open-mouthed, in front of the tiny, fragile, flickering light.

But Millache'Babe's friendly smile had disappeared.

Disconcerted, Manuel ran his hands over the altar. His fingers slowly tightened on the white cloth, crumpling it, crushing it, and finally pulling it on to the floor.

Underneath, Manuel was amazed to discover the stone tablet with five crosses carved on it. He felt them carefully, one after another, intrigued. He didn't know that they marked the location of the reliquary. But one thing he did know: in the tabernacle above the altar lived Jesus. Without meaning to, in his clumsy haste he pulled off the veil. His fingers tried feverishly to open the little door. His whole body was trembling.

'Come out! Come out! Come out!'

His voice swelled, mingling with the noise of the refugees outside.

'Come out!'

He didn't know why he was so desperate, why he was shouting. But if Jesus really did come out, to be with them ... Welling up inside him, Manuel could feel the same great, gentle, joyful peace and assurance that he had known at his first communion, a day whose memory he treasured like a foretaste of paradise. If the Lord Jesus Christ ... Suddenly the door swung open in his hand, and Manuel tumbled backwards down the steps and collapsed in a frightened heap at the foot of the ravaged altar. The blood pounding furiously in his head shut out all other sounds. His ears were buzzing, but then he thought he could hear a voice calling him. He turned round, but the church behind him was quite empty.

When he got to his feet again, his hands were no longer shaking. Imitating the priest at Bermering the previous day, he knelt down before going back up the steps to the altar. From the open tabernacle he took the ciborium, removed the white veil, lifted the lid, and stood there in ecstasy, contemplating the white wafers with which it was filled.

'Jesus!' he murmured.

His fingers had begun to tremble again. He picked up one of the wafers and put it in his mouth. Then another, and another. Manuel the simpleton consumed the bread of the Eucharist, slowly, conscientiously, until the sacred vessel was empty. A great joy filled his being. With his right hand he felt inside the tabernacle and took out the lunette in which the host would be exposed in the monstrance. O glory!

He turned the object over and over in his fingers until it came open. Then he took out the host, broke it, and ate it as well.

He stood for a long time gazing at the tabernacle and the ciborium, both now empty. Then he lifted his eyes to the crucifix above the altar and said: 'Thank you.'

Manuel was about to leave when he noticed a door to one side. He pushed it, and found himself in the sacristy. He went to the cupboards and opened them one by one, discovering chalices, patens, more ciboria, and monstrances, like beautiful suns. He took them out and held them up before his eyes, peering through the little window on to the other face of the world. He was intrigued by the censers with their long chains, smelling of prayers, and by all the different sizes of candles. Then he opened the big drawers holding the vestments. What a feast for the eyes! He held up white albs, tried on an amice, tied a girdle round his waist, examined stoles, chasubles, dalmatics of all colours: white, red, purple, pink, green, black ... Finally he discovered a huge golden cope which he threw over his shoulders, prancing about for sheer joy.

An enormous missal bound in red leather caught his attention. He opened it and deciphered a few words whose sense eluded him: *Introit, oremus, suscipe* ... He abandoned the missal, took off the great cope, and left the sacristy, walking on air.

As he came back down the nave he heard the noise of the wagons moving off. In the general confusion, no one noticed him emerge.

No one except Angela, that is. She had been watching the church door anxiously, from the presbytery across the road where they were to be quartered. Manuel looked up, saw her, and came rushing over to join her.

'What have you been doing in the church, Manuel?'

He eyed his sister, and said with a smile: 'Finding, eating, looking!'

'You...'

But at that moment Madamilla appeared on the doorstep.

'The house is full of food! Chocolate, sugar, coffee, you name it! Come and see, everybody! We're not going to starve here, anyway!'

Manuel seemed to have forgotten Angela's anxiety. He went over to join Madamilla as she stepped inside, beaming all over her old face, and joking: 'This must be the Lord's own house!'

'No it isn't,' came the voice of Bêa-Yasse'Kette from inside, 'it's the priest's!'

It was all the same to them: what mattered was that two of the rooms in the presbytery were stuffed full of provisions. One of them was piled high with loaves of bread. At the sight of them, the refugees felt as if they hadn't seen bread for decades. And besides bread, there was sugar, both lumps and loose, bars of chocolate (it was beginning to feel like the end of term!), and coffee beans which the women scooped up with both hands to enjoy watching all that abundance trickle through their fingers. The house rang with shouts of excitement, until eventually the mayor of the village arrived to supervise the distribution.

Then the refugees from Lasting-en-Lorraine formed themselves into a long line and filed past the mayor. Ably assisted by Fata Ioss, Manuel, Madamilla and even Bêa-Yasse'Kette, he doled out a ration of bread, sugar and coffee to the head of each family, and chocolate for the children. What a feast! The queue stretched out into the street, and it was not until quite late in the day, when the last people were collecting their rations, that the scandal burst like a bombshell. The inhabitants of Lidrezing were furious: their church had been profaned, the altar-cloth torn off, the sacristy pillaged, and horror of horrors, the ultimate sacrilege, the tabernacle had been forced open and the consecrated host removed!

At the thought that they might even be suspected of such a thing, the good refugees threw up their hands in protest: the mayor must come to the defence of their honour immediately. No sooner said than done: the mayor handed over the distribution of the remaining manna to Fata Ioss and moved to calm the crisis. The commotion caused by the arrival of the refugees had evidently been used as a cover for the perpetration of this heinous crime which they all deplored...

Manuel had gone as white as a sheet. He stood there, mechanically handing over one bar of chocolate to each person as they filed past him.

Angela's heart was pounding. Whatever could have got into her brother to make him do that? She only hoped no one noticed his hands shaking. He was so naïve, so innocent.

By the time the mayor got back, they had finished. He claimed that he had managed to convince the villagers that their guests were innocent. He had assured them that they were all good Christians: the parish priest of Bermering could vouch for the fact that he had seen them all at Mass on Sunday. But where could the so-and-so who had done it have got to? Just let him get his hands on him...

Manuel disappeared up the stairs at top speed: through a couple of doors, up more stairs and into the attic, where he sank to his knees right under the roof tiles and burst into tears. He went on crying for a long time, oblivious to the sound of rising discontent outside in the village, and to the lowing of the cows which had been turned loose in the fields prior to milking.

He hadn't done anything wrong. 'This is my body, take and

eat.' All he had done was obey. But who would believe him? He really hadn't done anything wrong.

His whole body was racked with sobs, and he didn't hear Angela anxiously calling his name out in the square. Fata Ioss needed him to help build fires. But how could he have heard? 'This is my body.' He had taken that at face value. 'Take and eat.' That's what he had done. Where was the crime in that?

'Manuel!'

He ran downstairs and fell into his sister's arms just as she came back inside.

'Where were you this time?'

'Up there.'

'Manuel, you mustn't tell them anything. Not a word. Promise...'

A stubborn look came over his face. He didn't understand.

'Don't tell them anything.'

'I didn't do anything wrong. Take and eat.'

Angela looked at him in perplexity.

'I didn't do anything wrong.'

'All right,' she stammered, 'you didn't do anything wrong, but they wouldn't understand. Just don't tell them anything.'

Her stomach was knotted with fear, and Manuel suddenly noticed that her whole body was shaking.

'All right, I won't say anything, Angela, I promise.'

That took an effort, but he couldn't bear to see her crying or feel her body shaking like that.

'Fata Ioss wants you.'

He went off straight away. As he came out of the door, Fata Ioss greeted him angrily: 'Where have you been hiding, then? Off you go and fetch me those big flat stones over there. You're stronger than I am.'

They were beginning to settle in. Women went off with pails to milk the cows. The angelus rang out from the round church tower. Joy would return round the fires this evening, despite the awkward feelings caused by the unfortunate incident earlier.

The following morning the women did a big wash. The sun had returned, and it was a fine September day among the orchards. The piles of washing were hauled over to the *lavoir* opposite the church, and the women knelt side by side at the bottom of the steps, along the water's edge.

It was a good opportunity to exchange gossip.

Manuel helped Angela to carry her bundle of dirty clothes.

He came right down to the *lavoir* with her, waited until she was safely installed between La Voisine and Rédache'Momme, and then went off to the fountain nearby where the children were sailing pieces of wood. It was a handsome piece of work for a village fountain, with a pair of metal troughs—now filled with boats—placed either side of a vertical column from which the water gushed. On top of the column stood a stone figure of a female saint, leaning on a sword. Manuel stood staring at it in some surprise before turning round to look at the church.

He thought he could hear the same voice calling him as the day before, but this time he didn't dare run over to the door and up to the altar to take and eat. Deep down inside, however, he was convinced that he could hear it. It was almost as loud as the voices of the women at the *lavoir* and the slapping of wet garments on stone.

He turned reluctantly back, remembering the scandal and his promise to Angela. He knew that he hadn't done anything wrong, but he forced himself to keep his eyes on the fountain.

'Hey, Manuel! have you seen my fleet?'

It was Victor, Le Voisin's boy. Yes, Manuel had seen it. He waved and smiled, but he didn't want to play just now.

A hubbub broke out suddenly on the other side of the square. A group of men had got hold of some poor blighter and were pushing him along in front of them. The local policeman, the *garde champêtre*, was holding him firmly by the collar with one hand, while with the other he was brandishing something in the air above their heads like a trophy, something that gleamed in the sun ... It was the golden ciborium!

Manuel felt as though he had been stabbed to the heart.

The women over at the *lavoir* had heard the noise over their chattering and thumping. They straightened up and stood watching. Most stayed put, but one or two climbed the steps up to the road.

The motley band, led by the *garde champêtre* and the vagrant, had by now reached the square.

'This fine fellow was making off across the fields towards Zarbeling when I caught 'im,' the *garde* announced to all and sundry, 'an' what do I find in 'is bag? This!'—and he pointed to the vessel. A murmur of disapproval ran through the group of assembled women.

'So he's the one as desecrated our church! What have you done with the consecrated wafers, eh, you cretin?'

The man was jostled and shaken like a sack of bran.

'It wasn't me! I didn't do it! Honest!'

'Liar! Just listen to him!'

One of them stepped forward and slapped him across the mouth.

Manuel wiped his lips on the back of his hand as if he had received the blow himself. He could feel Angela's anguished gaze boring into the back of his head. But he was incapable of calculation, and his mind was a blank. Suddenly, and quite simply, he went up to the *garde champêtre* and said: 'He didn't steal the wafers. Don't hit him.'

'What the hell are you talking about, funny boy?'

'He didn't eat the wafers, I did. I ate them. Take and eat. That's what he said.'

Angela had left the *lavoir* and was on her way across the

square, her hands still dripping wet and her apron stretched tight over her stomach.

'What's 'e trying to tell us now?' grumbled the *garde champêtre*. 'Look, the other bloke pinched this, didn't 'e?'

'Don't hurt him; he's my brother; he's innocent,' Angela stammered, standing humbly in front of him. 'He's a bit simple, that's all.'

They all stared at her. She could feel their eyes on her body.

'You're one of the refugees, aren't you?'

She nodded.

'So it was them as did it, after all,' said a voice from the crowd.

'It was me. I ate them. Don't hit him.'

The *garde champêtre* was thoroughly baffled, but he wasn't going to let go of his culprit. 'Look, 'e stole the whatsit, didn't 'e?'

There was a sound of rapid footsteps approaching, and everyone turned their heads. It was the *curé*. Since turning over his presbytery to the refugees he had been staying with a family at the far end of the village, and he had only just been alerted. The crowd parted to let him through. He was a white-haired old man, with staring eyes, and he wore a patched cassock that was green with age.

'Now what's all this about?'

"Ow about this, then?' The *garde champêtre* thrust the ciborium under the *curé's* nose, then pushed his wretched prisoner roughly forward. 'In 'is bag, it was!' Then he nodded towards Manuel. 'But this other feller, 'e says 'e ate the 'oly bread all on 'is own.'

'Don't harm him, he's simple, he's my brother,' said Angela.

The old priest looked at her and smiled reassuringly.

'Come with me, you two,' he said, taking Manuel's arm with one hand, and the vagrant's with the other. 'Let's go and sort this out together.' And he took them off towards the church.

After a moment, the other men in the crowd followed. At the

church door, the priest turned round and said: 'Not you: you wait outside.' They grumbled a bit, but stayed put.

Angela stood motionless a few yards away.

The *curé* took the two men right up into the choir. Manuel was glad to be back in the church. He looked at the tabernacle above the altar.

'Now, you sit down here, and you here.' The priest drew up two chairs, and the malefactors sat down, one on his right and the other on his left. He turned to Manuel.

'What's your name?'

'Manuel.'

'How old are you, Manuel?'

'Eighteen.'

'So you ate the consecrated wafers?'

Manuel smiled and nodded.

'You opened the tabernacle, threw the altar-cloth on the floor, got out the ciborium and the lunette, and ate the lot, is that right?'

'Take and eat, this is my body,' said Manuel in an undertone, with a smile on his lips.

The priest was taken aback. He looked at him and then asked: 'Why did you do it?'

Manuel hesitated. 'He said, Take and eat. That's what he said, and that's what I did.' He hadn't taken his eyes off the altar all the time they had been there, and the mysterious smile still hovered on his lips. The old priest smiled in his turn.

'You love Jesus, don't you?'

Manuel's reply was unhesitating: silent, but quite unmistakable.

'And what about my sacristy? Why did you make such a mess?'

Manuel evidently didn't understand the question. The priest pointed to the door of the sacristy. Ah! 'Beautiful!' Manuel said. 'It's beautiful!'

It took a while to sink in, but then the *curé* sighed and said: 'Yes, you're quite right, it is beautiful. But no one else notices.'

He turned to the vagrant and asked: 'Now, what about you? How did you manage to pinch the ciborium?'

The man gave him a shifty look and muttered: 'Well, I come in, see, an' everything was all topsy-turvy, so I thinks to myself, they're getting out, they've done a bunk with the communion bread an' all, so I might as well 'elp myself to what's left. There's a war on, y'know, an' it might come in useful.'

The *curé* smiled. He pulled an ancient purse from the pocket of his cassock, took the man's hand and poured the contents into his palm. The vagrant couldn't believe his eyes. 'Well, thanking you, yer honour, thank you kindly,' he mumbled.

'Off you go, now, and don't do it again.'

The man didn't need to be told twice. He backed away towards the door.

'Wait there,' the *curé* told Manuel, and he went after him. The *garde champêtre's* jaw dropped. The man took the opportunity to make a dash for it, and disappeared into the orchard. Someone picked up a stone and threw it after him. These Christians were hot on justice: they knew little of the difference between the love of God and the justice of men.

The *curé* went back into the church and shut the door. Angela was still standing there, flanked now by La Voisine and Madamilla, with tears coursing down her cheeks.

Manuel had not moved from his chair in the choir. As he gazed at the tabernacle he began to murmur: 'Come! Come out!' He didn't hear the priest come back. He only became aware of his presence when he heard him asking in a voice trembling with emotion: 'Would you like to receive?' He looked up and nodded. After a brief moment's hesitation, the priest went to the altar, opened the tabernacle, and then knelt down in a prolonged prayer of adoration. He had no need to ask forgiveness for what he was about to do from a God who knew the cost when he took the risk of the Incarnation, but it was unusual all the same. When he got up again, Manuel was standing beside him.

He took out the ciborium, opened it and held out one of the wafers which he had put in it only that morning. Manuel opened his mouth, but at the same time he took another wafer with his hand and put that in too. The priest was momentarily nonplussed, but he didn't stop him. Manuel then proceeded to eat all the wafers, one after another. 'Thank you, thank you,' he exclaimed, and went back to his chair.

The old man pulled a little book out of one of the deep pockets of his cassock, and holding it in his hand he came over to where Manuel was sitting. He sat down beside him, opened the book and said: 'Listen to the Word of God, my son.' Then he read: 'Jesus went out again beside the sea; and all the crowd gathered about him, and he taught them. And as he passed on, he saw Levi the son of Alphaeus... and he said to him, "Follow me." And he rose and followed him.'

Manuel echoed: 'Follow me.' Then he got up.

The priest got up too, and said: 'Tomorrow morning I'll come and find you, and you can receive Jesus again.' Manuel, thrilled, smiled and nodded. 'Come along now.'

They left the church together, their faces radiant, and passed through the middle of the crowd gathered outside, leaving them baffled. When he came to Angela, the *curé* said: 'Here is your brother, my daughter. He's a fine lad. Treasure him and take good care of him. Tell me, where are you staying?'

'There,' said Angela, pointing to the presbytery.

'Ah yes, well, that's a house I know! I'll come and see you both tomorrow. Off you go now.' When he turned round, he found the *garde champêtre* and his men right behind him.

'Just leave them alone, can't you?' he growled, to the astonishment of his parishioners. 'There are plenty of other things to think about, now that our forces have gone on the attack.'

'What? What's that?'

'Haven't you heard? A major offensive was launched this morning.'

The *curé* moved off, besieged by the men. Manuel and his sacrilege were forgotten in the excitement. Angela took her brother off to the presbytery.

'Manuel, you promised...' But he looked so happy that she didn't have the heart to say any more.

La Voisine and Madamilla had collected her bundle of washing for her: good old Bêa-Yasse'Kette had done it all.

In front of the house, Fata Ioss and La Vieille were busy round the fire: somebody had to think about eating! Manuel grinned broadly at them as he went past, and even Fata Ioss couldn't repress a chuckle. There was definitely something about that lad! Try as you might, you couldn't really get cross with him.

The women of Lidrezing could, though.

5

As soon as they spotted Manuel crossing the square after the meal, knots of women started forming. Even before he had reached the fountain the murmurings had begun behind his back: 'That's him, he ate the host, cannibal, God-eater, canni...' He wheeled round and confronted them, and they stopped immediately. Manuel smiled at them, then turned back and washed his face and hands in the clear jet of water, taking his time.

The sun was shining.

'There he is, cannibal...' The chant started again, as the women were joined by a group of boys with piercing voices.

Manuel straightened up, and at that moment a stone hit him on the shoulder.

'Justin, who told you to...?' There was the sound of two loud smacks.

His face still dripping with water, Manuel looked at them, and smiled. When he moved towards the crowd it parted like water under a ship's bows.

'Take and eat.'

The women looked at each other, not sure what to make of this.

'Follow me,' he added.

Young Justin sniggered through his tears. Manuel made his way between them and back to the presbytery. Behind him a shrill voice called out: 'He got his sister pregnant, he did, the cannibal, he sleeps with his sister...'

At that, the tears welled up, flowing unchecked and mingling with the water on his cheeks. He could see Angela's big tummy, and in his mind he could hear the apprentices sniggering. Of course it wasn't him that got Angela pregnant, but who on earth could it have been?

In front of the house he passed Fata Ioss, but didn't respond to the old man's expression of concern at seeing him crying. Madamilla shook her head. Angela saw him coming in and followed him all the way up to the attic before he would so much as look at her, despite her anxious pleading. When they were alone, with the door shut behind them, he turned to face his sister. Sadly, he let his eyes travel down to her stomach where the bulge was showing quite distinctly.

'Who got you pregnant, Angela? I know it wasn't me.'

Angela was taken aback, both by such unaccustomed language and by the mere suggestion...

'What have they been saying?'

'That I sleep with you.'

'But that's a foul lie!'

'Who did get you pregnant, Angela?'

Now it was her turn to start crying, and Manuel took her in his arms, cradling her head against his shoulder, but still doggedly repeating: 'Who was it?'

At last she spoke. She spoke as if Manuel was quite normal and could understand. She told him of the spring night by the softly-murmuring fountain. *I love you, Angela.* She told him of the breeze caressing the silky darkness. *Angela, I love you.* She told him of the sound of Benoît's voice and of the sound of their love springing from the very depths of the earth. She told him of their single night together, of their subsequent meetings, and of her dreams of their future. They could have been so happy together.

She told him of the war and their enforced separation, bringing with it such terrible uncertainty. Where was Benoît now? Somewhere in the Ardennes?

All this she told him and her voice comforted Manuel. He hugged his sister's fragile body, and at the same time he was embracing the baby she was carrying, Benoît's child, the child of happiness.

'When's the baby going to be born?'

'In February, probably, next year.'

Manuel looked surprised but said nothing. He smiled back at Angela and accompanied her downstairs. Fata Ioss called him and took him off to help Le Voisin mend his cart.

The following morning Manuel got up at crack of dawn. As soon as he was washed and dressed he sat down on the doorstep to wait.

The sun was not even up yet. Behind the round tower of the church a band of mist lay along the horizon, making the house of God stand out sharply against the white background. Manuel gazed intently at the porch, as if he could make the door open simply by looking at it. Somewhere a cock crowed hoarsely, and others replied from the outskirts of the village. In front of him, in the orchard still partly wreathed in mist, the cows were placidly chewing the cud. It was not yet milking time. One of them, seeing Manuel sitting motionless on the step, lowed softly, and its greeting was like a caress in the freshness of the dawn. Manuel contemplated the clouds of incense escaping from its nostrils into the September air, and shivered.

How long did he sit waiting? Angela came into his thoughts, and with his eyes closed he imagined her sleeping with her hands folded over her stomach, as she always did these days. He smiled, and his lips moved as he murmured the name, 'Benoît'. It was Benoît who got her pregnant. Not Manuel.

At that moment the *curé* appeared in the square, draped in his tattered cape. Manuel jumped up, rushed over to the old man and stopped in front of him, panting.

'It was Benoît who got Angela pregnant!'

The priest was baffled to begin with, but then he remembered and smiled. He still didn't quite understand, though. 'Now, why are you telling me that?'

'It wasn't Manuel, it was Benoît.'

'Why, did they say it was Manuel?'

'Yes, the women did.' Manuel's arm swept round in a big, clumsy gesture as he pointed to the area round the fountain.

The priest shook his head in distress, but his smile soon returned, and he took Manuel off towards the church. 'Come along, we're expected.'

Manuel followed him across the square through the lingering traces of mist. When they reached the porch the *curé* fumbled in his pockets, pulled out a big key, and gave it to his companion. Manuel took it, examined it happily, inserted it into the lock and gave two turns, then pushed open the heavy door and penetrated into the silent church.

At the far end of the nave a single light was burning, the sanctuary lamp whose steady glow fascinated him.

The priest closed the door quietly and knelt on the bare stone floor in a long, silent prayer of adoration. Manuel copied him, without taking his eyes off the tabernacle.

When the old man rose from his knees, his wrinkled face had taken on a look of remarkable youthfulness. He gave Manuel a playful nudge and pointed to the bell-rope.

'Let's go and ring the angelus, the two of us together.'

They both took hold of the rope and pulled on it with all their might. At last the single bell high up in the tower began to swing, and the rope jerked up, nearly sweeping them off the ground. They came back to earth, looking for all the world like two excited little boys. The angelus pealed out in the muffled expectancy of the dawn, and Manuel imagined it piercing the mist and wafting over the village and over the fields, awakening men and beasts and celebrating the miracle of a new day.

At a sign from the *curé* they started to slow down the wild dance of the rope and of the bell up above until it stopped. No one but the old man knew how little time remained before that bell was to be condemned to a long silence. They crossed the nave, pausing to genuflect before the gilded altar, before going into the sacristy. Manuel felt a mixture of happiness and anxiety at the memory of the riot of colours the first day. The priest took a taper, lit it and handed it to him.

'Take this and light the candles on the altar.'

Manuel was jubilant. When he got to the altar he hesitated. Which candles should he light? The two little ones at the end, or the six big ones in the middle, flanking the tabernacle? Eventually he decided to do all of them, to have as much light as possible. When he returned to the sacristy holding the smoking taper at arm's length, he gasped with surprise. The old *curé* had removed his threadbare cape and thrown it over a chair, and he was in the process of putting on the priestly vestments one by one, undergoing a metamorphosis before Manuel's fascinated gaze.

A white alb, whose girdle he was tying, covered his clothes completely and made him look like an apparition, like Moses and Elijah on the Mount of Transfiguration. The purple stole crossed on his breast marked him indelibly with the sign of the Master. The maniple hung from his forearm. By the time he finally turned round, the purple chasuble had completed his transformation, and now he looked like every other priest that Manuel had ever seen officiating at the altar. Seeing him rooted to the spot, the old man interrupted his silent prayers for a moment, smiled, and beckoned. Manuel stepped forward.

'We're going to pray for peace, the peace that the Lord alone can give.' Then, with a twinkle in his eye, he added: 'We'll make you as beautiful as an angel, my lad.'

Out of the cupboard he took another alb and put it on Manuel, who let himself be dressed like a child. Then he strode out of the sacristy and into the choir, with the simpleton at his heels. Manuel failed to notice the scattering of older women kneeling in the body of the church; they couldn't believe their eyes.

'*Introibo ad altare Dei.*'

'*Ad Deum qui laetificat juventutem meam.*'

Never had they heard their old *curé* say the service with a voice so full of youth and enthusiasm. Kneeling just behind him, the 'God-eater' appeared to be in ecstasy. At the sight of him, the good ladies fell into the sin of distraction.

'*Confiteor Deo omnipotenti...*'

A conscientious smiting of the breast did not prevent them peering over their spectacles at the young simpleton who had come with the refugees.

'*Et plebs tua laetabitur in te.*'

The voice of the celebrant boomed out from the sanctuary:

'*Da pacem, Domine...* Give peace, O Lord, to all them that put their trust in thee.'

Then came the ringing *Kyrie eleison*, followed by the prayers. May God grant that peace which the world cannot give. The reading in Latin from the second book of Maccabees passed over the heads of the pious ladies in the congregation, but when it came to '*exaudiat orationes vestras*' they fingered the worn black beads of their rosaries with fierce concentration, while still not taking their eyes off the motionless, radiant 'God-eater' for a second. The Gradual, the Alleluia and the *Munda cor* left them unmoved. At the *dominus vobiscum* before the Gospel they scrambled to their feet. '*In illo tempore...*' But what had got into the *curé* today? Turning towards them, he started proclaiming the Gospel in French! 'Jesus came and stood among them and said to them, "Peace be with you." ' Unable to believe their ears, they looked at one another in disarray.

As for Manuel, he kept his eyes fixed on the priest, drinking in every word. He even forgot to kneel down again after the Gospel, or to fetch the elements at the Offertory. The women were indignant, but the old priest was at peace as he celebrated, indeed he had never known such peace in his heart as on this morning in wartime. *'Laudate Dominum quia benignus est'*: yes, the Lord was indeed good to have given him such consolation today, something that would stay with him throughout the remaining years of his life. *'Suscipe, Sancte Pater'*: never had his offering been so richly thankful as on this day of apocalypse. *'In spiritu humilitatis'*: joy mingled with the humility of his heart as he washed his sinner's hands.

Manuel's eyes did not wander for an instant. Of course he had seen Mass being celebrated before, but only from a distance, in the congregation at Lasting-en-Lorraine. Last Sunday, at Bermering, it was different: and this morning, again, he was seeing things in quite a new way. Kneeling on the stone floor, rooted to the spot, he gazed and gazed.

The priest started singing the *Sanctus* in his old, cracked voice, throwing the good ladies into sudden confusion: was this a Low Mass or a high one? They looked at each other, but by the time the *Benedictus* came their quavering voices joined in with that of the celebrant. Then he moved into the Prayer of Consecration, giving to the words of Christ at the Last Supper an emphasis that they had never heard from him before. *'Hoc est enim corpus meum... Hic est enim calix sanguinis mei... in mei memoriam facietis.'* He even went as far as to translate the Latin words, saying out loud: 'Take, eat. This is my body.' The elevation lasted an eternity, and during it the women of Lidrezing watched the uplifted, motionless face of Manuel the simpleton.

They thought they could catch the sound of his voice blending with that of the *curé* in the *Pater noster*. When they came forward for Communion, their bowed heads did not prevent them seeing him get up and follow the old man to the rail with a mute plea in his eyes. After making their Communion they hurried back to their places in case anything happened while their backs were turned.

But nothing happened. All there was to see was the *curé* at the altar, giving Communion to his strange server. Did they discern a movement of his arm? And did their ears deceive them, or did they catch a whispered 'Thank you', picked up and amplified by the building and transmitted down the nave towards them? But by that time they were in the middle of their prayers, and Manuel was once more kneeling on the stone floor of the choir, as still as a statue.

'Pacem relinquo vobis; pacem meam do vobis,' the old priest recited, before giving the blessing to the congregation and then reading the closing Gospel verses in an undertone. Manuel did not follow him when he retired into the sacristy, but remained kneeling on the flagstones, with his face uplifted.

At the back of the church, the women finished mumbling through the rosary, genuflected awkwardly and hobbled out. Angela, concerned at Manuel's long absence, spotted them standing gossiping in front of the porch: what were they finding to talk about?

Inside, the old man and the lad were left alone, one now wearing a cassock and standing in his stall, the other still robed in white and kneeling on the ground. The voice of the priest suddenly filled the silence:

Blessed are the poor in spirit, for theirs is the kingdom of heaven.

Blessed are those who mourn, for they shall be comforted.

Blessed are the meek, for they shall inherit the earth.

Blessed are those who hunger and thirst for righteousness, for they shall be satisfied.

Blessed are the merciful, for they shall obtain mercy.

Blessed are the pure in heart, for they shall see God.

Blessed are the peacemakers, for they shall be called sons of God.

Blessed are those who are persecuted for righteousness' sake, for theirs is the kingdom of heaven.

Blessed are you when men revile you and persecute you and utter all kinds of evil against you falsely on my account. Rejoice and be glad, for your reward is great in heaven.

When he had finished, Manuel looked up at him and murmured: 'Blessed are the poor ... Blessed are the meek ...' Then he got to his feet and went over to the priest, who opened his arms and embraced him at length, before giving him a blessing, there in the choir of his own church.

Back in the sacristy, Manuel took off the alb. When he turned round, the priest was hovering just behind him, with a smile on his face.

'Never forget, Manuel,' he said.

The lad looked at him with a puzzled expression.

'Say after me: Come, follow me.'

'Come, follow me,' Manuel repeated.

'Take, eat. This is my body.'

'Take, eat. This is my body.'

'Blessed are the poor, the meek, the merciful.'

'Blessed are the poor, the meek, the merciful,' said the simpleton.

And the old man added: 'Abide in my love.'

'Abide in my love,' Manuel stammered.

'Never forget, Manuel.'

He shook his head, impressed by the priest's solemn air. His lips were half open, but no words came out. The *curé* looked at him and smiled. 'You won't forget, I know you won't,' he said, suddenly forceful. 'It's time to say goodbye now, my lad. I don't suppose we'll meet again.' After a long silence, broken only by the heavy breathing of the simpleton, he added: 'I have to go soon, before midday. You'll be leaving early tomorrow morning, with all your folk.'

'Leave?' Manuel could hardly get the word out.

'Yes, my lad. You have to. All the refugees must go. You'll all be put on a train tomorrow, at Hampont. You're going to France.'

Manuel shook his head vigorously.

'Yes, you must,' the old man repeated. 'You must. The war ...'

'Peace,' said Manuel loudly, startling him.

'Peace will come when men, free men, curb their murderous madness enough to allow God to restore it to us. God is the prisoner of men, Manuel.' The simpleton didn't understand. 'God can do nothing against the freedom of men, my child. All that God has to set against the guns and bombs of men is the weakness of his immense love. That is why he needs us.' His voice had dropped to a whisper. 'The power of God lies in sons of men like you, my child. Your love is stronger than death. What is foolishness in the eyes of men ...'

'Foolishness,' echoed Manuel.

' ... is wisdom in the eyes of God.'

'Wisdom,' said Manuel.

There was another long silence in which they could hear a dog barking in the square.

'Goodbye, Emmanuel,' said the priest.

'Goodbye, goodbye, goodbye!'

The old man hugged the child once more and pushed him gently but firmly out of the sacristy with the words: 'Whatever happens, don't forget.' They knelt together before the altar, then came down the nave and opened the door on to the square outside which was flooded with sunlight. 'Come on,' muttered the *curé*, as if to himself.

Manuel stepped forward. He had seen Angela waiting on the doorstep of the presbytery, wide-eyed with anxiety. The sight of the priest emerging behind her brother helped to reassure her. The *curé* gave Manuel a slap on the back and sent him off towards the house. He ran across the road to Angela without a backward glance. When they had both disappeared inside, the *curé* walked slowly over after them, as if going home. In the little front garden, he stopped by Fata Ioss who was crouching down by the fire.

'Morning, Father.' Fata Ioss heaved himself up and took his hat off.

The priest gave a conspiratorial grin, fumbled in his pockets, and eventually pulled out a small, battered volume. 'Would you be so good as to give that to Manuel for me?'

Fata Ioss took the book, hesitated, and then said: 'But he can't read.'

'You can teach him.' And before Fata Ioss could think of a reply, the *curé* had turned and disappeared round the corner.

Fata Ioss was just about to go inside and look for Manuel when the mayor arrived. 'Morning, Fata Ioss. You are to tell everyone here to start getting packed up. Only things you can carry, mind you. You'll be taken to catch the train before the night is out.'

'What about the animals?'

'You'll have to leave them behind, I'm afraid: cows, dogs, the lot. Sorry: orders is orders.'

6

Ioss stood on the doorstep, reeling. In the orchard across the road
the cows were grazing peacefully. Who would milk them in the
morning? The old man was moved to pity by the thought of the
poor creatures being abandoned. He could intuitively hear their
plaintive lowing, and then the lowing turning into subdued protests that were not even aware of being protests. He could see
himself being pursued from station to station by the gentle but
persistent reproach of these trusting animals, always audible
through the rumbling and bucketing of the train. It was like a
startlingly clear memory of the future, it was intolerable. Fata Ioss
couldn't bear even to think what might happen to the dogs. As if to
escape from it all, he turned to go inside.

As he did so, his eyes fell on the title of the little book which
the *curé* had left for Manuel: *The New Testament*.

'Manuel!' he shouted once he was in the hallway, 'Manuel!
Manuel!'

But Manuel had disappeared up to the attic, and it was Angela
who answered. Her anxiety had returned, and she peeped timidly
round the door.

'What is it, Fata Ioss? What do you need Manuel for?'

'Isn't he here?'

'No. I think he's gone up to the attic.'

'Angela, my girl, we're off in the morning, by train. We'll have to leave the cows and the dogs behind. The mayor has just told me.'

'What were you calling Manuel for?'

'The *curé* gave me this for him.'

With a smile of relief, Angela thanked him and took the book. Fata Ioss was a bit put out at her lack of response to his momentous news, and he stood there watching her as she climbed the stairs heavily. Then he pushed open the door of the downstairs room where the other women were expecting him: La Vieille, Bêa-Yasse'Kette and Madamilla. They gave him the opportunity to enjoy his role as bearer of bad tidings, and Bêa-Yasse'Kette's lamentations more than made up for Angela's self-centredness.

'Dass'do ivalêve ma nid'! Dass'do ivalêve ma nid'!' (That's the end! We'll never survive that!)

La Vieille was the first to pull herself together and dry her tears. 'We'd better make the most of today, then,' she declared. 'Milk the cows frequently and drink plenty: that'll give us strength for the journey.'

Madamilla's bonnet nodded in agreement, and she picked up her churn and went out, followed by La Vieille and Bêa-Yasse'Kette who was convinced that the end of the world was at hand.

Outside, the square was already alive with people.

As for Fata Ioss, he went straight to his wife's bundle, rummaged about until he found the bottle of schnapps, and had a long drink to steady his nerves.

Meanwhile Angela had at last reached the attic. When she opened the door, she was surprised not to see her brother straight away. But then she found him, sitting in his favourite place tucked away in a corner under the skylight, singing softly to himself. He looked up at her, and Angela was struck by the light which appeared to be radiating from his face despite the semi-darkness.

'We've got to move on,' she said, not fully understanding the note of apprehension in her own voice.

'Yes, Angela, tomorrow morning.'

'How did you know?' Angela was astonished to see tears shining like pearls in her brother's eyes. 'We're going to have to leave everything behind, the wagons, the cows, the dogs, everything.'

A shadow passed over his features. 'The goat, the pig, the rabbits, the pigeons,' he said.

'Yes,' she nodded. Once again the thought came to her that the freedom which they would give the animals tomorrow was the freedom to die.

All of a sudden Manuel said: 'Follow me.'

'What's that?' asked Angela in surprise.

'Come, follow me.' The sun was shining again through the tears in the simpleton's eyes. Angela didn't understand. 'Take, eat. This is my body.'

'Manuel, promise...' She was scared. 'Promise me you won't ever go and do it again!'

Still smiling, Manuel went on: 'Blessed are the poor, the meek, the merciful... Blessed.' Then: 'Abide in my love. Love, Angela, just love.'

She reeled. *I love you, Angela,* murmured the voice from deep down in her heart, *Angela, I love you.*

'Benoît!' she sighed.

'Abide in my love,' Manuel repeated. 'Just love.'

Now she could no longer hold back the tears. Not wanting to alarm her brother, she thrust the *curé*'s book at him and fled to the shelter of the stairs.

Manuel recognized the book at once. He ran his fingers over the cover, stroking it, then put it to his lips. What a treasure! He turned to ask her how she had come by it, and it was only then that he noticed that she had gone. He got slowly to his feet and followed her down.

At the front door he met Fata Ioss looking distinctly unsteady. The old man accosted him and asked: 'Well, did she give you the book, then?'

'Oh, yes,' said Manuel.

'D'you know what the *curé* said? He told me to teach you to read it!'

'Oh, yes!' said Manuel again, pulling himself away with a laugh.

'Bloody hell!' muttered the old man as he staggered out. Outside, the women were sitting on the steps with their full churns beside them. Angela was standing, drinking. 'It's good for the baby,' Madamilla assured her.

'*Dass ââme kênnd!*' (Poor child!) said Bêa-Yasse'Kette, shaking her head. La Vieille gave her a meaningful nudge.

Fata Ioss stopped in his tracks, surprised to see Angela's eyes full of tears. He had often felt maudlin after drinking in the past, and now his eyes started misting over too. 'Bloody hell!' he muttered again as he set off down the street.

Soon he bumped into Le Voisin, La Voisine, Rédache'Momme and Wag-Nache'Péda.

'What are we going to do with our wagons and our animals?' They were all distraught, and young Victor was in tears. Manuel came over and tried in vain to comfort him. 'What about my dog, Piano? What's going to happen to him?'

'And the pig, too, and the goat,' said Manuel. 'What about them?'

'Idiot,' said Victor crossly. 'They're not the same as a dog.'

Manuel didn't react to the insult. 'And the rabbits,' he added under his breath.

'I know,' Victor piped up, 'I'll kill him, that's what I'll do. I'll kill him.'

'No, don't do that!' Manuel begged.

'Yes I will. I'll kill him.' And Victor ran off towards the fountain.

Le Voisin had decided to ask a local farmer to look after his wagons for him.

'What about the cows?' his wife asked anxiously.

'Maybe we can persuade them to take care of them too.'

And off they went across the square with heavy hearts.

Fata Ioss had gone into the church. The women were already there to say their prayers. He knelt down, smelling strongly of drink, and started doing the rosary, fifteen full decades, counting the *Aves* on his fingers.

'He's been drinking again,' said La Vieille as soon as she saw him come in.

'Let him be,' replied Madamilla. 'Let him drink if he wants to. It helps take his mind off things.'

'*So a élênnd*!' (What a misery!) wailed Bêa-Yasse'Kette.

Suddenly a dog started howling from the other side of the orchard. Manuel heard it too and dashed off. 'Manuel!' shouted Angela anxiously. No good. He was already out of earshot. The dog was still howling, but less loudly. By the time Manuel reached the far end of the orchard, scattering the cows as he went, it was all over. Victor was standing with the stick still in his hand, crying, and in front of him on the ground lay Piano, dead. The boy had tied him to a tree by his lead and clubbed him to death.

'You shouldn't have done it,' said Manuel.

'I've killed Piano,' Victor blubbered.

The dog's teeth were bared, his tongue was hanging out, and blood was trickling from his mouth.

'Poor Piano!' said Manuel.

'At least he didn't have to die of hunger and a broken heart,' said Victor, between sobs.

Manuel stroked the dog's coat, feeling the body, still warm, from which the life had now gone.

'We'll bury him, shall we, Manuel?'

'Just like the rabbit,' Manuel mused.

'I said dogs were different, didn't I?' snapped Victor.

'But they're not really,' said Manuel, 'not when they're put in a hole and covered with earth.'

'All right, have it your own way.' Victor was drained now, and it was all he could do to stretch out his hand and touch the creature he had just killed.

'He was looking at me all the time, Manuel, and howling. I'll never be able to forget that, never.'

Manuel said nothing, but went on stroking the dead animal.

Victor noticed in amazement that the tears were streaming down his cheeks. 'I'll go and get a pickaxe,' he said, and rushed off.

Piano was well and truly dead. Manuel tried hard to detect even a flutter of life, but it was no good. The corpse was already starting to grow cold. When Victor came back with the pickaxe, Manuel showed him the best place to dig the grave. He had found a beautiful white stone to put on it. Victor started digging first, and Manuel took over when he got tired.

'That's deep enough, isn't it?' said Victor at last. Manuel carried on digging without a word. When he eventually stopped, Victor whispered: 'I can't bear to touch him, Manuel.' So the simpleton picked up the bloody carcass and placed it gently in the hole. Victor was crying again.

'Throw some earth in, Victor.'

Victor picked up a handful of loose earth and threw it on top of Piano, lying lifeless at the bottom of the hole.

'Poor Piano!' he sobbed. Manuel took the pickaxe and used it to shovel the earth back in until the dog was covered and the hole was filled. Then he put the stone on top. It stood up proud in the midst of the orchards and fields.

'When the war's over,' said Victor through his tears, 'I'll come back and visit your grave, Piano.'

Manuel grasped him by the arm and took him off towards the village. The midday angelus was ringing. High in the pale blue sky the sun was shining, surrounded by little white clouds. They walked a long way in silence. Then Manuel asked: 'What's your father going to say?'

Victor swallowed a last sob. 'Don't tell him. Lots of dogs have gone missing these last few days. Piano could easily . . . You won't say anything, will you, Manuel?'

Manuel shook his head. ''Bye, then,' said Victor, striding off with the pickaxe over his shoulder.

''Bye!'

When Manuel got back to the house it was well after midday. He found old Madamilla bustling about on her own round the fire.

'Ah, there you are, young man,' she said when she saw him. 'They've all gone crazy! You can't not eat, even if you are going to be packed off by train.'

The soup she was stirring smelled good, and Manuel was hungry.

'Go and call them, there's a good boy. Some warm soup is just what they need to bring them down to earth.'

Manuel went inside. He found La Vieille and Bêa-Yasse'Kette busy with their bundles; Angela was lying down at the far end of the room with her hands folded on her stomach and her eyes closed. When he came nearer, he could hear her murmuring Benoît's name. There had been no news from the Front. As if to break the spell, he shouted at the top of his voice: 'Food! Come and get it! Madamilla's special soup!'

'*Ish honn' kê houn'ga!*' (I'm not hungry!) moaned Bêa-Yasse'Kette.

La Vieille was more positive. 'Come on, we've got to eat. Especially you, Angela, in your condition. Come along, now.'

'*Ish moon' nix!*' (I don't want anything!) Bêa-Yasse'Kette

continued.

'You too,' said La Vieille, grabbing Bêa-Yasse'Kette's arm and hauling her off.

Manuel held out his hand to Angela. 'Come,' he said simply. She got up and went out with him.

La Vieille had already disappeared. She had gone off to the church to look for her husband. She found him slumped on a chair, fast asleep, with the tear drops still clinging to the ends of his moustache. 'You ought to be ashamed of yourself!' she grumbled as she shook him. He looked up with sad, staring eyes, and followed her in silence when she beckoned. He even forgot to genuflect.

By the time they got back, the others had started eating. 'Well, we shouldn't come to much harm now,' quipped Madamilla, 'not after all those prayers Fata Ioss has been saying for us!'

The old man didn't respond. The praying had sobered him up—unless it was the nap he had just had—and he applied himself to drinking his soup while it was hot. Nobody else said anything, either, so there they all were, more solemn than ever, eating in absolute silence. The arrival of Le Voisin came as a relief.

'I've come to tell you to be ready to leave at half past three tomorrow morning.'

'*So free!*' (As early as that!) exclaimed Bêa-Yasse'Kette in horror.

'They're sending military trucks to pick us up.

'What about the animals?' asked Madamilla.

'They'll stay here, where there's pasture,' said Le Voisin. 'Some of them will go to local farmers. The rest will probably be slaughtered for meat for the army.' No one said anything. 'After all,' he added, 'quite a few of them are in a pretty sorry state. I can't tell you how many cows' legs my wife has had to bind up. Their poor feet are bleeding after all the distance we've covered.'

Bêa-Yasse'Kette, who had a soft spot for the animals, nodded her agreement.

'As far as I can gather,' he went on, 'the train or trains will be leaving Hampont station at four o'clock sharp, so we'd better not be late when they come to collect us.'

'We'll be ready,' said Fata Ioss, breaking his silence.

The women nodded. As soon as Le Voisin had gone, everyone started talking at once. The women washed up the pots and pans, for the last time, according to them: tonight it would be a cold meal, and they could drink milk.

Manuel had gone to fetch water from the fountain. Justin, the boy who had thrown the stone at him the other day, was there. He got a shock when he turned round and saw Manuel behind him, and terror showed in his face. Manuel's cheeks flushed, but he heard a voice repeating the *curé*'s words: 'Abide in my love.' He smiled at Justin and said: 'We're off tomorrow, you know.' The boy hesitated, unsure of his intentions. 'You heard, didn't you? We're all off tomorrow.' Justin gave a faint smile, but said nothing. He only regained his composure once Manuel had gone off carrying a pail of water in each hand. He returned to his game.

Manuel had just remembered the push-chair. How on earth would they manage to take that with them in the morning?

As soon as the washing-up was done, the women set themselves to tearing up handkerchiefs and making little bags in which to put as much coffee, sugar and as many other provisions as possible. Fata Ioss had gone to help Le Voisin put the wagons away: there was always the hope that they could collect them again when the war was over.

Manuel went off to look for a large cardboard box which he remembered having seen in the attic. He brought it downstairs and squatted in front of the house. With the patience of a saint he unscrewed the wheels of the push-chair one by one and stowed them at the bottom of the box. Then he took the frame to pieces as far as he could, and at last succeeded in fitting it all in. He wrapped the box in a blanket and tied it up securely. By the time he came back inside carrying his parcel, the women had nearly finished repacking the bundles.

'Whatever's that, Manuel?' asked Angela, eyeing it dubiously. Manuel gave a mysterious smile. When she repeated her question, he leaned forward and whispered in her ear: 'Push-chair for the baby.' She was touched, and thanked him.

Bêa-Yasse'Kette, who had been watching all this, hadn't grasped what it was about. *'Vonn'a noua nid' nomal de dêivl on'geshdeld had', dêa do!'* (The rascal hasn't gone and put his foot in it again, has he?) Angela's face should have been enough to reassure her though. Madamilla told her off.

The evening angelus rang out from the round tower of Lidrezing church. Someone must have been standing in for the *curé*. On hearing it, the women went out for the last time with their bowls, buckets and churns to milk the cows in the orchard. They lingered beneath the plum trees, and patted Bella and Bless, poor creatures, on the flank. When they returned, for the last time, everybody had a cold supper outside, without bothering to light a fire.

Conversation did not flow. It was as though they were all in mourning for their village, due to die a second death before dawn. The first death had taken place that hot afternoon a few days before when the exodus had begun, and they had set off leaving their houses, their pigs, their goats and their chickens behind. But at least, as they made their way along lanes and tracks, it was as if the whole of Lasting-en-Lorraine was coming with them on their lurching wagons. Now that those wagons and the remaining animals were being abandoned, what would remain of their village once they were in the train? A few wretched bundles, and the inhabitants themselves, dispersed to the four corners of an unknown desert...

Bêa-Yasse'Kette was very upset at the thought of it, and was weeping bitterly.

For the last time, as soon as the light faded, they settled down on the straw and tried to sleep, but the silence was heavy and full of foreboding. It was no good. Even Manuel lay awake, excited by the prospect of a new departure. After a while the *Aves* of La Vieille established a rhythm which at least offered an alternative to the periodic lamentation of Bêa-Yasse'Kette, amid the crackling of the straw and the gurgling of Fata Ioss' bottle of schnapps: his wife, for once, had no objections.

Angela was crying silently, with her hands folded on her stomach. They could have been so happy together. Tonight, no voice whispered *I love you, Angela*: the very memory of Benoît seemed to have flown far, far away, to the distant Ardennes. Where would the train take them? They could have been so happy together. How would Benoît manage to trace his sweetheart? How would he find out where to write to with his news? The church clock marked the long hours of the night. They could have been so happy together.

On the stroke of one, Bêa-Yasse'Kette, who must have drifted off, woke with a start and roused everyone else: '*Sishdzid! Ma mousse oufshdéénn!*' (It's time! Come on, up we get!)

Fata Ioss turned on the light and consulted his watch. Bêa-Yasse'Kette didn't catch what he grunted as he turned the light off again. An hour later, when he put it on again to wake everybody up, she was fast asleep, snoring happily.

They were all ready and waiting on the doorstep well before time.

When the distant roar of the trucks reached them through the darkness, the whole exodus of Lasting-en-Lorraine was out in the streets of Lidrezing. The dogs barked excitedly. There were lights everywhere. The sight of the first headlamps in the distance drew a lament from Bêa-Yasse'Kette: '*Yéd'sd gééd de vêld ouna!*' (It's the end of the world!) But nobody heard.

The ground shook and a convoy of trucks invaded the square. A dog, trying to cross the road at the last moment, was hit by one of them and killed on the spot. A little girl cried in the night. Young soldiers leaped out of the trucks, leaving the engines running. 'In you get!' The younger refugees climbed in first. For them this new departure was fun. Angela could see the joy on Manuel's face: he made no attempt to hide it.

'Come on granny, your turn!' Bêa-Yasse'Kette was outraged, but she accepted the help of the two cheeky soldiers and scaled the vehicle, eyes bulging, in the glare of the headlamps. Next it was the turn of La Vieille and Madamilla. The soldiers were in a cheery mood. One of them had spotted Angela. 'Come on, then, gorgeous!' She stepped forward, and they helped her to clamber up into the truck. She did not react when the younger one's hand brushed her breasts. Manuel jumped up behind her, closely followed by Fata Ioss and all of Le Voisin's family. Rédache'-Momme and the midwife came last.

The dogs frolicked round the trucks, and some even tried to jump in, especially when the vehicles started moving. The story went that they ran behind, leaping and falling back, panting, only to disappear in the dazzling lights of the truck following. Some said that they could hear them howling even over the noise of the engines. But soon there was nothing more than a few isolated barks piercing the night.

In the trucks the women counted their bundles to make sure that none had been left behind. Manuel was keeping his eye on two, one of them being the box containing the dismantled push-chair: he was guarding that with his life. In his jacket pocket was the book the old *curé* had given him.

After a journey of about half an hour through the darkness, the trucks turned to the left and pulled up with a screeching of brakes in front of a dimly-lit building. Hampont Station. It was still pitch dark. In the distance a few points of light indicated the location of a village. The baggage was passed to the younger passengers, who had already jumped out, and to the soldiers who were helping the older ones to clamber down. The same young soldier hovered near Angela and tried it on again. When he saw her eyes filled with tears, he gave her a knowing wink and whispered: 'Well, it's wartime, isn't it?' Angela didn't even notice.

Manuel carried their bundles one after the other and piled them with all the rest by the imposing stone entrance. Babies who had not been properly fed yet were crying. Old women disappeared to the right, towards the toilets. Victor and some of the other children had gone off to explore the station. It stood alone in the middle of the fields, outside the village of Hampont. They were fascinated by the waiting-room with its huge windows, and by the goods train standing in the station, perhaps waiting for them.

Manuel stayed close by Angela. She had stopped crying now. A handful of other women were with her too, full of sympathy.

It was time to board the train—yes, in the cattle trucks. They all retrieved their belongings and dragged them along the platform amid shouting. Somehow or other their group all ended up in the same wagon, piled on top of each other, and surrounded by their stuff: Le Voisin, La Voisine, Victor, Rédache'Momme, Wag-Nache'Péda, Madamilla, Bêa-Yasse'Kette, La Vieille and Fata Ioss, Manuel and Angela, the whole of Millache'Babe's tribe, and the midwife. The children were squealing because they couldn't see in the dark.

Gradually the platform cleared, leaving only a few soldiers.

At last, just before the train started moving, the heavy doors were shut with a clang. It was as if the very doors of life were being shut on a convoy of condemned prisoners.

Part Two

THE EXODUS

1

When the train moved off, a long line of trucks pulled by a wheezing locomotive, the noise it made was drowned by a chorus of sobs, shrieks and desperate prayers. It was still pitch dark outside, and dark too in most hearts, with a few notable exceptions: children who hadn't been on a train before, and Manuel. In his heart there shone a secret sun, brighter than the one that would shortly rise out of the autumn mists to illuminate the desert called France which they would be crossing. The memory of his last meeting with the old priest the previous morning was still strong, and it was to that that Manuel's gaze was directed.

All the excitement didn't stop the children crying. They were as scared of the unknown as the grown-ups, and Millache'Babe's daughter and even the old man himself had to keep soothing and scolding in turns, in an attempt to quieten them down.

'Soon, when it's light, you'll be able to see . . .' What would they be able to see, shut up in their cattle truck? But the promise did the trick, for the time being at least.

Another distraction was provided by a disturbance at the other end of the wagon, centred on Bêa-Yasse'Kette who was suffering a sudden attack of colic.

'*Ish konn's nimmé hébbe!*' (I can't hold on any longer!) Madamilla tried to calm her down, but to no avail. They couldn't stop the train: there was no communication cord or any other means of alerting the driver. In any case, was it fair to stop the whole convoy every time anyone...?

Wag-Nache'Péda had a good idea. He gallantly offered his hat to old Bêa-Yasse'Kette, who accepted it. Tears turned to suppressed laughter, and off she went behind the piles of baggage, glad that it was not yet light. The hilarity of the younger members of the party was infectious and soon spread to everyone.

'*Péda, dina houd'!*' (Peter, your hat!)

That was Bêa-Yasse'Kette's voice.

'You're not expecting me to put it on again now, are you?' replied Wag-Nache'Péda, slapping his thighs.

'*Vass soll'ish donn demêt ounfongge?*' (What shall I do with it, then?)

Everybody laughed.

Wag-Nache'Péda good-naturedly relieved her of the offending object, managed to slide one of the doors open a few inches, letting in some much-needed air along with the pale light of dawn, and hurled it on to the bank beside the track. It rolled down to the bottom.

'*Mêa'si, Péda.*' (Thank you, Peter.)

Bêa-Yasse'Kette was all right now, and the whole truck was at peace with the world once more. A new day was dawning.

This experience reawakened the women's sense of organization. Even La Vieille put away her rosary and began looking through one of the bundles.

Madamilla, with her practical common sense, was the first to discover a hole in the floorboards near one corner. The area was screened off by a pile of baggage and promoted to the rank of official latrine. The various families staked out their territory in the remaining space. The midwife stayed with Angela, who was complaining of intermittent cramps. La Voisine lent a hand too, when she wasn't staring open-mouthed at Manuel who kept murmuring: 'Blessed are the poor...'

It was daytime at last, and the pale grey light that crept into the cattle truck set tongues wagging.

The motion of the train reminded Fata Ioss of Riga and his Russian exile on the Dvina in 1917. He started talking about the icons...

'*Dass hash'de shoun gesââd!*' (You've already said that!) interrupted Bêa-Yasse'Kette mercilessly.

That stopped him in his tracks.

Now it was Madamilla's turn to recall an exodus, that of her ancestors from Kleinblittersdorf in the Saarland in 1786.

'Now they were a tough lot...'

Following the partition of Poland in the 1770's, the rapid modernization of the country made it sound like an earthly paradise. Many of the inhabitants of Kleinblittersdorf decided to emigrate, including Madamilla's ancestor, one Iob. He sold all his possessions for a pittance: his house, with its barn and other outbuildings, fetched only three hundred francs. And off he went.

'Go, sell all that you have, and come, follow me,' said Manuel.

Nobody heard except Angela.

Madamilla carried on with her story.

'Iob set off for Poland with one of his neighbours. They eventually crossed the frontier near Lvov, and found several estates that were going cheaply. There was only one that really appealed to them, but when they tried to buy it they discovered that it had just been sold. Other disappointments followed, and they began to regret having left their native land so lightly. Their passports had already been confiscated, and they had to redeem them at considerable expense. Some of their compatriots who were unable to do so were rumoured to have been deported to Hungary. They decided to go back home. Never had they sunk so low. The old nag that pulled their wagon collapsed and died outside St Ingbert in December 1786. They were reduced to hauling the wagon themselves, and that was how they arrived home, so the story goes, on the evening of the feast of Saint Nicholas.'

'*Di hêdde yo kinne de'hêmm blee've!*' (They should've stayed at home!)

No one paid any attention to Bêa-Yasse'Kette's caustic comment. Somebody was anxious to know whether Iob and his friend ever managed to recover their possessions.

'Not likely!' said Madamilla. 'My ancestor turned distiller. He went round collecting all the rotten pears that nobody wanted, distilled them, sold the resulting liquor, and fed a family of seven children on the proceeds.'

Bêa-Yasse'Kette opened her mouth to say something, but at that very moment the train braked sharply.

'*Vass ish donn yéd'sd looss?*' (Whatever's happening?) she gasped.

Wag-Nache'Péda soon had the door open. It looked as though they were stopping in the open country. Ribbons of mist were still floating on the meadows, caught here and there on bushes. There was no village in sight.

Once the convoy had come to a complete halt, rumours started flying up and down the track: first of all that it was a comfort-station, and then that the Red Cross were waiting just round the corner to distribute food-parcels.

To begin with, no one dared to leave the train. What if it went off without you? Wag-Nache'Péda was the first to jump down on to the embankment and set off towards the bushes, followed by Le Voisin and Victor, with Madamilla not far behind. It was a chilly morning, and the weak September sun had not yet dried out the grass, even though someone claimed it was after eight o'clock.

Fata Ioss leaned against the door of the cattle truck and smiled at the sight of the entire exodus from Lasting-en-Lorraine scattered across the fields. Even La Vieille had just trotted off towards the bushes to join Rédache'Momme, the midwife and Angela. As for Manuel, he was on his way back to the train, with his trousers wringing wet from the knee down.

'Time I taught you to read from the *curé*'s book,' said Fata Ioss.

'Yes! Yes!' agreed Manuel, jumping up into the truck.

The old man did not relish the prospect of giving a reading lesson, but he had promised.

'Let's see your book, then.'

Manuel dug it out of his pocket and handed it to Fata Ioss, who opened it at random.

'Right, then, have a go at reading that. Blessed ...'

'Blessed are the merciful ...'

'Very good, my lad. You missed out a few words, but never mind. Keep going!'

'Blessed are the pure in heart ...'

'Who can still claim to be pure in heart these days?' murmured the old man to himself.

'Me,' said Manuel. 'And you.'

Fata Ioss looked at him in astonishment.

At that moment the others returned from the bushes and swarmed into the truck.

'We'll carry on some other time, Manuel.'

Fata Ioss gave him back the book, and Manuel put it in his pocket. The old man eyed the simpleton briefly, with new respect.

'All aboard!' called a voice. 'Close the doors, please!' It sounded so absurdly normal that everybody laughed. Then, almost before they realized that the train had started, it stopped again, the doors were flung open to let in the sunshine, and there in front of them were the Red Cross lorries ready to distribute the manna that had fallen from heaven in the middle of the fields: loaves of fresh bread as big as your thigh, bars of chocolate, milk and water.

The exodus burst into shouts of joy. The Red Cross people set to work with a will. The whole convoy was jubilant.

When the train moved off again, the doors of the cattle trucks closed slowly on scenes of families seated in a circle, eating and talking, with the little ones, their faces smeared with chocolate, tumbling about in the middle.

The only complaints came from Bêa-Yasse'Kette, whose colic had returned. It must have been the milk, of which she had drunk large quantities the day before.

Only when what was left of the chocolate had been wrapped up and put away with the remaining loaves in the corner by the bundles did boredom take over again. The day was warming up, and the atmosphere in the trucks was growing heavy.

Madamilla suggested telling stories.

Wag-Nache'Péda had a better idea.

He took from his pocket a page torn from a newspaper which he had found in the attic of the house where he was billeted in Lidrezing. It was the story of events that had happened long ago in the neighbourhood, by the lake known as the Etang de Lindre, over towards Tarquimpol.

'I'll read it to you if you like,' he offered.

'*Favass donn nid?*' (Why not?) said Bêa-Yasse'Kette, sounding interested.

Only Victor pulled a face: he had never had much time for reading, even when done by someone else.

'Is it a love story?' asked Madamilla.

'Yes, sort of. A sad one, though.'

'*Di honn'ish gêa!*' (My favourite kind!) simpered Bêa-Yasse'Kette.

Her dreams had doubtless always been of impossible love.

La Voisine was observing Angela, but she seemed to be asleep. Manuel said nothing.

'Come on, then. Let's hear your story,' said Fata Ioss.

Wag-Nache'Péda coughed to clear his throat, held up the sheet of newspaper in front of his nose—there was little enough light to see by—and began:

'Be quiet!...'

'*Ma honn'doch gââ nix gesââd!*' (But nobody said anything!) wailed Bêa-Yasse'Kette.

'Shush!' hissed Fata Ioss. 'That's how the story begins.'

'*Das honn'ish yo nid gevissd?*' (Well, how was I to know?)

Wag-Nache'Péda looked at her, shrugged his shoulders, and started again:

' "Be quiet!" The giant's voice covered the hysterical cries from the big ship and the sounds like the squealing of a pack of hounds gone mad which rose in sinister fashion from the shore where the ragged men lived. A dark silence fell over the calm waters of the lake and, now that the oars themselves were still, the only sounds left beneath the lowering sky were the cry of a moorhen and the shivering of the leaves in the wild wind. They were close enough to the shore now for no one to drown before reaching the land of the curse.'

Wag-Nache'Péda was no better at reading aloud than a schoolboy, but everyone in the truck, even Victor, was listening with rapt attention.

'At a signal from the giant, the warders came, seized the first member of the terrified band, and threw him overboard in the direction of the island.'

'*O Iérum Maria!*' croaked Bêa-Yasse'Kette.

Wag-Nache'Péda looked at her and then continued:

'He was a young man, powerfully built, and he managed to swim and then wade half-naked to the shore, where he was immediately surrounded. He shook off his attackers and fled to the woods, with a few men still on his heels. Meanwhile the warders had already seized a young woman and dragged her screaming to the side, where she fell into the water like a stone.'

Bêa-Yasse'Kette heaved a deep sigh.

'They had to push her towards the shore with a long pole... So, one after another, the whole boatload of a dozen mad prisoners, men and women, were thrown into the lake and left to the mercy of the inhabitants of the island. By the time it was all over, the woods on the island were echoing with cries, wailing and sinister laughter.

'What an inspiration it had been when the Lord of Lindre decided to round up all the problem cases periodically and exile them to the middle of the lake! It was good riddance! The few unfortunates who had dared to try to escape had been publicly flogged as an example and sent back. After each trip the warders regaled the villagers with horror-stories: newborn babies left lying on the beach like a litter of puppies, or unburied corpses at the mercy of the wild beasts and the elements.'

'Ugh!' The reaction of horror and disgust was universal, and for the moment the discomfort of the bumpy cattle truck and the muggy weather was forgotten.

'The good folk of the village,' Wag-Nache'Péda went on, 'were too frightened to say anything. Anyone who expressed pity for the plight of the exiles would immediately have been pronounced mad themselves and sent off to join them on the sinister island from which no one ever returned.

'One day the chaplain was rash enough to rebuke his master. He soon discovered what it cost to stand up to the Lord of Lindre, even in the name of the Holy Gospel! He was handed over to his master's henchmen. Subjected to hard labour, beatings and other humiliations, he lost his reason and joined the next exodus to the island.'

'I'm not sure I've understood it all,' put in Madamilla, 'but that old Lord of Lindre seems to have been pretty much of a monster.'

'Quite right,' said Fata Ioss. 'Carry on, Péda.'

Ioss evidently didn't appreciate interruptions.

The hesitant voice of Wag-Nache'Péda resumed reading:

'The fate of Alexandre the serf, who rebelled against the brutality of the bullies, came as no surprise: one fine evening he, too, disappeared in the direction of the island. His son Hanno swore to set him free but, after roaming the countryside all night, he came across Lioba and her flock of sheep on the threshold of the new day.

'How long did he stay listening to her, before continuing on his way? She spoke the language of the wind in the tall trees, and the words that came from her mouth were as smooth as the pebbles from the stream behind the bushes. Her voice was like the murmur of the leaves whispering freedom, her sighs were those of the night, and her lament was the long complaint of the tree tortured by the storm. In her black eyes rolled the dark clouds of low autumn skies, speaking, like the flight of migrating birds, of departures and long journeys. Her lips sang of dreams and happiness: dreams of happiness and the happiness of dreams... How could Hanno not forget for a while the ruffianly henchmen of the Lord of Lindre?'

Angela, too, had forgotten: forgotten everything except the fountain murmuring words of love in the night, *I love you, Angela*, and the soft, strong voice of Benoît, welling up from the depths of her memory, murmuring *Angela, I love you*. She was crying gently—they could have been so happy together—and never even noticed that the train had stopped again in the middle of the countryside. Manuel took her hand and sat holding it, quite still, without a word.

Wag-Nache'Péda stopped reading and opened the door.

Another train came past in the opposite direction, full of young soldiers bound for the Front.

'*Di ââme bouve!*' exclaimed Bêa-Yasse'Kette. '*Canône foudda!*' (Poor lads! Cannon-fodder!)

When they had settled down again and the refugee convoy had resumed its bumpy journey, they automatically fell silent to allow Wag-Nache'Péda to carry on reading.

Angela's cheeks were still wet with tears.

'By the time Hanno reached the castle, his father had already been taken away. The young man was arrested, beaten almost to death as an insolent peasant, treated as mad, and sent off to the island. When he got there he ran off into the woods: it was only to stumble over his father's corpse.'

'Oh!!!' A long moan rose from the corner where Bêa-Yasse'Kette had taken refuge.

'But it was the sight of that corpse that gave him the strength to face his pursuers and overpower them one by one. The poor madmen were won over by this display of force and treated him with the admiration and respect due from slaves to their master. He led them back to the shore as the first light of dawn reached the tree-tops, and they helped him to round up all the scattered inhabitants of the island of fools in the course of the rest of that day. Hanno spoke to them, and was somehow able to touch their poor distracted hearts and minds: all the time that he spoke he was thinking of Lioba the shepherdess, and his language was that of Eden before the Fall. He and they resolved to organize the life of the island.

'He chose a spot near the spring and sheltered from the wind to build a small village. After seeing to the burial of the dead, he got the able-bodied men to clear the ground, and he then traced out the plan of the hamlet himself. In the middle he left a large space for people to meet, and for games and festivals. The next days and weeks were spent erecting huts made of branches all round the central square. When the work was finished and the huts were ready to be occupied, there were terrible problems, because the men each had several wives and the women had several husbands, while the children were in the care of a few older women who were unwilling to relinquish them. Compromises had to be worked out.'

Compromise was the order of the day in the wagon too. Those who couldn't wait to know what happened next were faced with seeing Wag-Nache'Péda fold up his sheet of newspaper and stow it away in his pocket. The convoy had once again stopped in the open countryside, and once again the doors opened to reveal Red Cross lorries with provisions. It was after midday. Goodness, how the time had flown!

This time, everyone got out and went off into the fields for a picnic. Gossip got round quickly, and soon the whole convoy was splitting its sides over the episode of Wag-Nache'Péda's hat. Only Bêa-Yasse'Kette, offended, retreated into a sullen silence. The wretched inhabitants of the island of fools were quite forgotten ...

Only Angela, eating on her own in silence, was still pondering the impossible love of Lioba and Hanno. They could have been so happy together! She scarcely noticed Manuel playing football with Victor and some of the other children a little further away. What if Benoît, like Hanno, were never to come back?

Wag-Nache'Péda redeemed himself in Bêa-Yasse'Kette's sight by bringing her back something for her colic from the Red Cross dispensary. Once the convoy had resumed its journey across unknown France in the heat of the afternoon, she was the first to demand the rest of the story. He didn't need to be asked twice.

'One day, at dawn, a man in tattered clothes was discovered wandering back and forth across the village square singing the *Alleluia* and *Kyrie*.'

Manuel pricked up his ears.

'Hanno thought he recognized the former chaplain to the Lord of Lindre, and he asked him to say Mass for them. A huge cross was set up, and an enormous block of pink sandstone rolled in front of it as an altar. Then the ex-chaplain was summoned to come and celebrate.

'As if suddenly recovered from his madness and overcome instead with terror, the man tore himself away, screaming that he was unworthy, and disappeared mysteriously into the woods. They started to search for him, but while they were combing the island he reappeared as mysteriously as he had gone. They were overjoyed to see him but took a while to understand what he was trying to tell them.

'They were still clamouring for him to recite the *Confiteor*, the *Gloria*, the *Credo*, the *Sanctus* and the *Agnus Dei*, but he was trying to tell them that a boat was approaching the shore with men dressed in black habits on board, priests for certain, who would be much better...

'But they were no longer listening. They were running as fast as their legs would carry them, down to the shore, full of excitement and apprehension at the same time. When Hanno got there he could make out the boat clearly and, at the prow, five silhouettes standing with their faces turned towards the island. At a signal from him, his companions fell back to the edge of the wood, and they all watched as a mysterious cargo of chests was unloaded into the water. Before the boat turned to go back, the thunderous voice of the giant reached them: "Never forget, gentlemen, that his lordship has only allowed you to settle on the island of fools on the express condition that you never return. If any of you were to attempt to..."

'But the monks were no longer paying attention.'

In the overheated wagon the attention of the refugees, too, was beginning to wander. Wag-Nache'Péda could not help having a monotonous reading voice. As he looked round at his audience he was on the point of putting the newspaper back in his pocket, but he caught Manuel's fervent gaze, and he also detected encouragement in the eyes of Fata Ioss. So, taking a deep breath which seemed to last an eternity, he continued:

'They had fallen to their knees, and with their faces to the ground they kissed the earth of their new land. Then with one voice they started to chant: "*Suscipe me...*" Hanno could only catch the odd word. "*... venite... jubilemus...*" When at length they got up, Hanno stepped forward.

'"Who are you? What do you want?" he asked.

'"We are monks," replied the one who seemed to be the leader, "seekers after God. We live according to the rule of our father Benedict. I am Luitwin..."'

'Then he introduced his brothers.

'"I am Hanno," said the young man. "What do you want?"'

'"As we were passing through the country, we learned of the existence of this unfortunate colony, and we understood that it was there that we were being sent. We asked for permission to come and live with you here. It was granted, and here we are, at your service."'

'*Di braafe leed!*' (What good folk!) The voice of Bêa-Yasse'Kette came from the far end of the wagon, where the others thought she was fast asleep.

Wag-Nache'Péda looked at her before continuing.

'When Hanno grasped the hand which the monk held out to him the poor mad men and women besieged them with cries of jubilation. The chests were hoisted on to strong shoulders, and Hanno led the monks off to the new village where they sang the *Magnificat* at the altar beneath the cross. The mad chaplain and Brother Luitwin, who was an ordained priest, conducted marriages and baptisms, and the people sang hymns and chants so lustily that the sound carried across the waters of the lake and reached the ears of the villagers there, and even the Lord of Lindre heard it. No one ever discovered what he thought, but when a few weeks later a fresh consignment of exiles was thrown into the water, the monks trembled. The new arrivals were dying of the plague.'

'Oh! How horrible!' Madamilla's cry awoke the whole wagon. Bêa-Yasse'Kette joined in, and La Vieille, who had been asleep, asked what was the matter.

'*De péshd!*' (The plague!) said Bêa-Yasse'Kette.

No one except Angela heard Manuel asking: 'What is *Magnificat?*'

Wag-Nache'Péda, rather proud of the effect he had produced, continued to read in a loud voice.

'Brother Luitwin none the less welcomed them, as did the other monks, among whom Hanno was now numbered. The mad men and women followed their example, and life carried on, with the work of cutting stone and ploughing made easier by the tools which the monks had brought in their chests. But alas, it was not for long. The disease spread with frightening speed, sparing no one. The whole island was soon filled with cries and groans, dominated from time to time by the fervent strains of a hymn. In the evening, those on the mainland could hear the choir of madmen singing the *Salve Regina* at the foot of the great cross.'

'What is the *Salve Regina?*' asked Manuel.

'Then came the autumn, and the weather changed. Rain set in, and strong winds buffeted and twisted those trees which had been spared by the lightning. The Lord of Lindre sent his warders to see what was happening. They ventured quite close, and brought back tales of love and mutual help among the wretched inhabitants of the island in the midst of their dreadful suffering. Sometimes, at night, snatches of Latin chants could still be heard above the storm: "... *mater misericordiae* ..."'

'The story goes that a terrible tornado swept across the lake one December night, and that in the morning, when the grey light began to disperse the bands of mist which hung in the air like mourning veils, it could be seen that three quarters of the island had been engulfed. It was later confirmed that there were no survivors.'

'Oh!' The whole wagon was aghast.

'Only the great cross,' Wag-Nache'Péda went on, 'remained standing like a sign of defiance. It is said in the region that on stormy nights one can still hear a distant choir of infinitely pure voices, like angels, tirelessly singing: "*O clemens, o pia, o dulcis virgo Maria.*" The last note dies away only with the end of the morning angelus.'

After Wag-Nache'Péda had stopped reading, there was a long silence, broken only by the rhythmical noise of the wheels beneath them. The sound of the newspaper being carefully folded and put away seemed inordinately loud. Then, suddenly, Fata Ioss began to sing: '*Salve, Regina.*'

After a moment's hesitation, everybody joined in the hymn to the Virgin. They all knew it well for having faithfully attended Vespers on a Sunday. Manuel, too, recognized the tune and smiled, glad to have discovered what *Salve Regina* was. Even Angela, normally tight-lipped, was singing now.

In the trucks in front and behind, the other refugees thought they could make out snatches of liturgical chant, but they weren't sure. The steam engine gave a few last hiccups before coming to a halt, and suddenly the final notes of the chant rang out much more clearly than the rest.

Once more the train had stopped out in the country. The sun was low down over the western horizon. They had been travelling west for nearly a whole day now. The sliding doors were opened and the refugees poured out on to the embankment, all except those with Wag-Nache'Péda, who remained frozen in a kind of sacred horror and took some time to realize that they had stopped. Fata Ioss eventually appeared at the door of their truck, rubbing his eyes.

Once more everybody disappeared into the bushes, before coming together again round the Red Cross lorries for food and medicines.

Angela and Manuel remained in the wagon, alone.

Angela was still pondering the impossible love of Lioba and Hanno. She could hear the language of the wind in the tall trees and the murmur of the leaves whispering freedom; she could see the dark clouds of low autumn skies speaking of departures and long journeys; she could imagine the dreams of happiness and the happiness of dreams ... They could have been so happy together. And what if Benoît never came home from the war, just as Hanno had never returned from his island, in spite of his promises to Lioba? What would happen to her, with Benoît's child?

Manuel could still see the huge cross standing like a sign of defiance. He could hear the chants of the madmen and the monks, the raging of the storm and the floods which engulfed both land and people. Had the monks then come only to adore the cross and perish, when they had hoped to save a whole community of hapless people? Why did that cross have to come between them and their good intentions? Had they crossed the desert of their lives only to end up at the foot of a gallows-tree?

Neither Manuel nor Angela heard the others return, bringing with them provisions for the two of them. Wag-Nache'Péda would never even know that his story of the island of fools was intended principally for the brother and sister, who would guard it in their hearts like a precious seed.

Madamilla was all in a flap about the news she had heard, and as soon as they were on their way again she poured it all out.

Some of the young people in the other wagons had come through villages that had already been evacuated and taken over by the army, and they claimed to have seen soldiers pillaging houses and raiding wardrobes, killing animals that they found abandoned, and looting whatever took their fancy.

'*O Iérum Maria!*' exclaimed Bêa-Yasse'Kette indignantly. In one village, having drunk too much, they had performed a sinister masquerade. One of the soldiers had found a wedding dress and put it on, and they had all paraded through the streets, pretending that they were marrying War, or Death. They had even compounded their sacrilege by going into the church.

So that was what was happening to what they had left behind them. They had no illusions now. And as for the future ...

Some said that they had heard that children would be separated from their parents. And, as far as they knew, they were heading for the sea...

'Fââre di ouns nid ênn's méa?' (Aren't they sending us into the sea?)

Bêa-Yasse'Kette was panicking at the thought that the whole refugee convoy might be sent straight into the sea, before they knew what was happening, still shut up in their cattle trucks. She was terrified of drowning, as she kept trying to tell old Mill-ache'Babe, but he just sat there, his bald head nodding backwards and forwards, forwards and backwards: so it was true, he would never be buried beside his Léna.

Darkness gradually filled the wagon as night fell outside. There was darkness in many hearts, even the bravest. Silence soon reigned, punctuated by deep sighs. Bêa-Yasse'Kette had sworn to escape the next time they stopped, and she was listening for any sign of the engine slowing down.

When Wag-Nache'Péda, who had pulled the heavy door open a few inches on to the night, suddenly announced that they had just passed through Angoulême, that he had seen the name Angoulême on the station with his own eyes, there was consternation.

'Angoulême, where's Angoulême?'

'Somewhere in the Charentes.'

'And where's that?'

'By the sea.'

Bêa-Yasse'Kette let out a scream and had to be forcibly restrained from throwing herself out of the moving train. Young Victor was obviously enjoying the tussle.

When at last, on the stroke of nine o'clock, the train slowed down and stopped and the doors were opened, the sea that first greeted their eyes was a sea of people: nurses and volunteers who had come to welcome the people of the exodus.

Hiding away at the far end of the wagon, Bêa-Yasse'Kette observed them with deep suspicion.

2

The refugees from Lasting-en-Lorraine had arrived at Châtelaillon. There were crowds of people milling about on the platform under the harsh electric lights. Priority was given to young children and their mothers, pregnant women and the elderly.

Standing at the door of his wagon, Fata Ioss watched Rosa dashing after her baby which was being carried off in the arms of a nurse. The poor girl had dropped her bundles and was running for dear life, like a madwoman. Was she, too, afraid that her child would be taken away from her? Ioss shook his head.

Behind him, Bêa-Yasse'Kette was muttering: *'Ish géén nid dorouss! Nimols!'* (I'm not coming out! Never!)

It was only to keep her company and to try to persuade her to come out that Fata Ioss had stayed in the wagon. All the others were waiting on the platform: Le Voisin and his family (Victor had been watching Rosa running, no doubt remembering the milk-white breast which she gave to her child in the meadow), Millache'Babe with all his tribe, Rédache'Momme and Madamilla, Wag-Nache'Péda, La Vieille, Manuel and Angela.

Angela was looking distraught in all the crush. Manuel, on the other hand, was quite cheerful. The bustle and confusion amused him, and he kept picking up his bundle and the box with the push-chair in it, as if eager to go off and explore the town.

Bêa-Yasse'Kette was still obstinately refusing to get out.

'Mish green'se nid dorouss!' (They'll never get me out!)

But when Fata Ioss eventually grew tired of cajoling her and jumped down on to the platform, she wailed: *'Fata Ioss, faloss mish nid!'* (Fata Ioss, don't leave me!) and rushed to the door of the wagon carrying her things. She was helped down.

'O Iérum Maria!'

Poor old Bêa-Yasse'Kette was rolling her eyes in alarm like a mother hen who had lost her chicks. Fortunately no one attempted to separate her from the rest of the group when the time came to leave the station. She held on tightly to her precious bundles as long as she possibly could, only letting kind hands relieve her of them when she could carry them no longer.

After negotiating unfamiliar streets in the pitch dark, they boarded buses bound for an unknown destination. Manuel and Victor were all excited. Angela, worn out, dozed in her seat. The old women said prayers. Fata Ioss tried to see where they were going, but the windows were steamed up and he couldn't make anything out.

When they eventually arrived in the foyer of the Grand Hotel, which had been converted into a dormitory, they found Rosa already there, feeding her baby in the corner. Victor went straight over and camped a few yards away, unable to take his eyes off her generous breast. Manuel smiled tenderly at the sight, but it reawakened his concern for Angela, who was finding it hard to keep up with him. Before too long she would have a little one to feed as well. Benoît's child... It would have to have a name, but what would it be?

'Angela,' he asked, turning round, 'what are you going to call your baby?'

Angela was taken aback by the question. 'I... I don't know.'

Manuel didn't understand. He stared at his sister in amazement and opened his mouth...

'You two over there, come on, there's room this way,' called a voice from the back of the foyer. They hastily obeyed.

Angela was asking herself what on earth she would call Benoît's child.

Soon the foyer of the hotel was buzzing like a beehive as the refugees settled down for the night.

Bêa-Yasse'Kette had been put with the older widows, Madamilla and Rédache'Momme, and she was not pleased. She could be heard complaining loudly to the voluntary workers in her harsh Lorraine dialect, but they couldn't understand a word she was saying, and in any case they were too busy to do anything about it. Madamilla tried in vain to calm her down.

Gradually the place quietened down as everybody got sorted out somehow or other. They moved next door for a quick supper. The local people had done them proud.

Not surprisingly, the refugees found it hard to sleep on their first night in a strange place. Bêa-Yasse'Kette dreamed aloud about the sea and screamed fit to wake the dead: she had had a real fright. As soon as it was light, Rosa's baby woke up and started crying, and she had a hard job keeping it quiet. Manuel heard nothing of all that. He slept like a child, and Angela had to shake him awake in the morning.

After breakfast the refugees were distributed round the town. Bêa-Yasse'Kette had her back to the wall again, declaring: '*Ish géén nid alêên fouwad!*' (I'm not going on my own!) What would become of her in this foreign place where she couldn't speak the language?

Millache'Babe and his tribe had already gone off to the centre of the town where they had been allocated an empty house. The old man brought up the rear, with his bald head nodding backwards and forwards, forwards and backwards. Whatever would poor old Léna have said if she could see him now?

Rosa, too, had gone with her baby, and Victor was very much

afraid that he had had his last chance to feast his eyes on her milk-white breast. He was certainly heading for quite a different part of the town with the rest of his family.

'We'll try to meet up, Angela. I'll come round,' shouted La Voisine from the steps of the Grand Hotel.

'What about us, then?' grumbled Madamilla. Bêa-Yasse'Kette, for once, said nothing.

Next it was Wag-Nache'Péda's turn to leave, with the midwife, La Vieille and Fata Ioss.

At last they came for Madamilla, Bêa-Yasse'Kette, Angela and Manuel. The two older women were to be lodged together. Angela and her brother set off through the streets of Châtelaillon with a strapping young fellow who carried her two bundles. Manuel wouldn't relinquish the box with the push-chair in. They stopped at the entrance to a narrow street which their guide said came out on the beach. He pointed with his chin to the Villa Suiram. 'That's where you'll be,' he said.

A woman came out of the house. 'Two people for you, madame,' he announced.

She smiled at them, clearly noticing Angela's condition. Did she take them for husband and wife? 'Come on in,' she said.

She opened a gate leading to a small courtyard at the side of the villa and pointed to an annexe beyond. 'That's where you'll be staying. I'm sure you'll be all right there.'

She led the way into the building. The young guide put the two bundles down at the door and took his leave. Angela and Manuel went in. First there was a short passageway with a well in it. Manuel, intrigued, put his hands on the wide stone rim and leaned over. The passageway led into a sparsely-equipped kitchen. Then they came to the two bedrooms.

'There's more than enough room for a young couple,' said the lady.

Manuel looked at Angela.

'Manuel is my brother, madame. Benoît is in the army, away at the Front.'

'Oh, I'm so sorry. I hadn't realized. Well, in that case ...'

They re-emerged into the courtyard to be shown the lavatory. Then the lady said: 'If there's anything you need, just come over and knock at my door,' and off she went to the Villa Suiram, casting a slightly surprised glance over her shoulder at Manuel.

Angela picked up one of the bundles by the door and took her brother inside, fighting back the tears which welled up at the thought of this strange house where Benoît's child was going to be born. They could have been so happy together.

Manuel inspected the rooms one by one, opening the wardrobes, feeling the beds, taking in every detail. He was particularly interested in the well, and he couldn't rest until he had hauled up a bucket of water, using the squeaky pulley, and taken it over to the kitchen sink.

There was plenty of time to unpack their bundles and spread out all their worldly possessions. Angela wouldn't have to cook today, as lunch was being laid on again for them at the Grand Hotel. Together, meticulously, they put their things away in the wardrobes. Then Manuel undid the cardboard box and started putting the push-chair together, piece by piece. Angela had a job getting him to stop when it came to midday. He was thrilled that he had managed to bring it safely all the way.

There was a noisy reunion at the hotel. Everyone had a story to tell about their new quarters and about what had been happening in their particular household, and even Bêa-Yasse'Kette was happy.

'*Di honn'ouns amol good êmb'fong!*' (They've really done us proud!) And she tucked in hungrily.

Washing up together was fun. Those with no one at the Front almost forgot that there was a war on. Some of them had been down to the sea already.

Then it was time to explore. Madamilla and Bêa-Yasse'Kette took a whole party off to see their delightful two-roomed apartment with its own courtyard. On the way, they looked in on La Vieille and Fata Ioss, discovered Le Voisin's family installed at the end of a cul-de-sac, and bumped into Millache'Babe in the square, his head nodding as always.

'Whatever are you up to, Obba?'

'I'm just going round to Léna's grave.'

Had the upheaval of the exodus turned his brain? They took him back to the tiny house where his whole tribe was quartered. 'It's the second time he's gone off like that,' complained his daughter.

Bêa-Yasse'Kette shook her head knowingly: if they only looked after him a bit better... Meanwhile the old man had recognized Manuel and smiled broadly at him. Manuel waved back happily, watched by Madamilla.

Since Lidrezing he had been rather lost sight of in the exodus of the refugees from Lasting-en-Lorraine, but Madamilla knew that people tended to keep a wary eye on him. What would he do next to bring discredit on them? Nobody dared say much for fear of upsetting Angela, but she knew how deep feelings ran in some quarters against poor simple Manuel. Some even thought he ought to have been locked up after the scandal in the church at Lidrezing. Madamilla promised herself to keep her eyes and ears open and forestall any malicious moves.

Here they were at the Villa Suiram, home of Manuel and Angela.

'More like the Villa Douckdish (Duck-your-head)!' said Wag-Nache'Péda, who had just joined them, and everybody laughed.

Manuel got straight back to work, and while the others exclaimed over the well—hardly any of the houses in Lasting-en-Lorraine still had them, they had been supplied with running water for such a long time—he finished putting together the push-chair for Benoît's child, the child that Angela was carrying.

'Come along, Manuel, we're going down to the sea!' said Angela.

Manuel stood up, with the others round him. 'What's the sea, Angela?' he asked.

They all burst out laughing, and Manuel stared at them in astonishment. Had they managed to see the sea in Lasting-en-Lorraine, or what?

Arm in arm, the refugees marched off towards the sea at the bottom of the street. They emerged by the Hôtel de la Plage, crossed the boulevard, and halted when they got to the sea wall, their breath taken away by the sheer immensity of the ocean stretching away in front of them.

There it was, alive, creeping sinuously towards them in a manner that gave Bêa-Yasse'Kette the willies. Manuel stood silently, taking it all in. The white-crested waves chased each other, caught up, overlapped and devoured each other with a dull murmur, finally expiring in a whispering, lacy froth at their feet.

Manuel was still silent.

There was the sea, green and blue and grey and mauve, with a few objects bobbing about like corks on the surface: one or two swimmers near the beach and, much further away, on the horizon, tiny boats whose sails traced a mysterious message between heaven and earth.

Manuel gazed and gazed, open-mouthed.

There was the sea, a moving monster, and you couldn't tell whether it was coming or going. It was like the beast of the Apocalypse, its multiple body glinting with scales of silver and iron, an elastic mass of constantly changing form, never still enough to be grasped and fixed by a landsman's memory, accustomed to stable landscapes and rolling hills.

There was the sea, and there was Manuel, still silent.

When, despite Bêa-Yasse'Kette's cries of ill omen, the first of the refugees from Lasting-en-Lorraine ventured down the stone steps which nestled against the sea-wall, Manuel was quick to follow, with Angela close behind him, unhappy about letting him go on his own. When they got down on to the beach and stood by the edge of the vast ocean, they stopped, as at the frontier of a new and unknown country.

Then Manuel crouched down and wrote with his finger in the sand, tracing mysterious symbols. Only Angela, who was watching him attentively, saw what he was doing.

Above them, in the sky, a solitary seagull screamed.

Manuel went on writing in the sand.

A wave, bigger than the others, came and licked the feet of the people of the exodus with its thousand tongues of foam. They drew back in alarm.

Now they noticed Manuel and started staring at him, but nobody said anything.

When the playful ocean finally washed over his mysterious symbols, inking them in with salt water, the simpleton pulled himself upright and hurried off up the stone steps with a tense expression on his face.

The others followed, chattering away about the need to reconnoitre the local shops and buy in food before evening.

Angela was anxious about Manuel, whom she had seen disappearing up the street.

The older women were complaining about being split up: they had all been good companions in misfortune. Madamilla pointed out that there was no reason why they shouldn't get together every day. Bêa-Yasse'Kette said it wasn't the same. Well, of course not. Eventually they all went their separate ways and Angela went back, alone, to the Villa Suiram. Wherever could Manuel have been going off to in such a hurry?

On the way she met Fata Ioss and La Vieille, arm in arm, who were off to see the sea for themselves. No, they hadn't seen

Manuel, but they reckoned that he must have been going back to the house: after all, he didn't know anywhere else yet.

The sea... La Vieille was all excited when she spoke about it. She had heard that Al'mongs'Péda's little Denise, who was only just twelve months old and hadn't learned to walk yet, had taken one look at the sea, jumped up and run towards it as if by a miracle, and that she had had to be chased and caught before she reached the edge of the water. How about that!

Fata Ioss smiled indulgently and reassured Angela again that Manuel couldn't have gone far, before taking his wife's arm and continuing on his way. The town hadn't seen that kind of holiday-maker before!

When she got home, there was no sign of Manuel. It only took a few moments for her to check the three rooms and the passage-way, and she even looked down the well before coming out into the courtyard again: no Manuel anywhere, and he evidently hadn't been back at all or he would never have left the push-chair outside.

Standing in the doorway of the strange house, Angela sobbed softly to herself.

Meanwhile Manuel was investigating the new church of Châtelaillon-Plage.

It was when he saw the ink of the sea flowing into the lines that he had drawn in the sand that he heard it. It was like an irresistible voice telling him to get up and run and seek until he found. The voice was not in the deep roaring of the waves, it was not in the screaming of the gulls overhead, it was in the silence of the meeting of sea and sand, in the silence of his heart which was open to hear the call.

Rise, said the voice, and Manuel arose.

Run, said the voice, and Manuel ran.

He ran up the steps to the top of the sea-wall, he ran across the boulevard and up the street to the Villa Suiram. But the voice said no.

Seek, said the voice, and Manuel sought.

He ran like a madman through the streets of the town, seeking, and the people turned to look at him racing past.

He ran and sought, sought and ran, for a long time.

At last, there he was in front of the church, and he knew that he had found what he was looking for. He had the assurance of joy in his heart.

He took several deep breaths and pushed the heavy door. It was as if he was coming home.

Slowly his gaze swept round the vast building. There was no longer any hurry. It was his house, and he happily started to walk round it.

The first thing that caught his attention was the way the nave was filled with heavy pews. Moving round to the left, he saw at the far end of the side-aisle a statue of Our Lady of Lourdes, just like the one in the grotto at Lasting-en-Lorraine. But he was in no hurry to get to it. He was enjoying looking round.

The statues, particularly, intrigued him. Here, on the wall, was a little figure of a young girl standing, draped in a great white mantle, with a long veil on her head. She was smiling. What was her name? Manuel had the impression that he might have seen her before somewhere, in a previous existence, back in Lasting-en-Lorraine, but he was not certain.

Then he saw a beautiful image of the Blessed Virgin against a pillar. He was sure he had seen that one before. He looked at all the bouquets of flowers laid at her feet by the people of Châtelaillon.

He glanced up at Our Lady of Lourdes as he went past, and crossed in front of the choir with a delicious burning sensation in his breast. But he kept going, as if saving the best until last.

In the other aisle he paused in front of a statue representing an angel in white showing a kneeling child the cross of the Lord Jesus. That reminded him of a little picture that he had had over his bed when he was a child, of a guardian angel leading a child by the hand, showing him the safest way.

Manuel sensed that he was on that safest way, and that all he had to do was allow himself to be led.

Next to the angel there was a very young priest, wearing a long black robe and a white surplice. His eyes were lifted heavenwards.

Further on, against the second pillar on the right, Manuel discovered a bearded man, dressed in a coarse brown habit, with a white cord round his waist. He was holding a child in his left arm, like the babe in the manger, but a bit bigger.

Now he was at the back of the church again. He glanced briefly up at the white stone vaulting and then yielded to the feverish impulse which swept him up the nave towards the choir. He could feel the burning, right there in his chest.

When he reached the altar rail he stopped and knelt down. But he soon got up again: he wasn't close enough yet. *He* was there, he knew it, *He* was there, and Manuel threw himself down at the foot of the steps to the left of the altar and stayed huddled there. Nothing else mattered.

He had been sorely tempted to go right up to the tabernacle and try... But he hadn't dared. Remembering Lidrezing, he hadn't dared, for Angela's sake. So there he stayed, not moving a limb.

Sometimes he shut his eyes and breathed deeply as if he were peacefully asleep; sometimes his breathing got faster and he looked up at the altar, letting his eyes linger on the fine lace cloth, the tabernacle up high, the six huge candlesticks flanking the golden cross, and the great wooden cross which soared majestically above everything, topping even the windows of the choir. When his gaze returned to the door of the tabernacle he stiffened, made a great effort, and forced himself to shut his eyes and breathe more slowly. There he stayed, not moving a limb, overwhelmed by an unimaginable happiness.

That was how Angela and Fata Ioss found him as they explored the church which at first had seemed empty.

Angela, utterly distraught, had waited at the door of her house until Fata Ioss and La Vieille came back from the sea. She was almost certain that they would look in on her on their way past, in view of her anxiety, and she was not mistaken.

'He's not in the house, Fata Ioss!'

'Why don't you two go and look for him in the town while I stay and look after the house?' offered La Vieille, taking pity on her.

So off they went, the old man and the girl together, with not much idea of where to look, one of them handicapped by age and the other by the child she was carrying.

Fata Ioss was the first to think of the church: 'What if he's done the same as at Lidrezing...?'

'Oh no, don't tempt fate, Fata Ioss!'

They asked where to find the church. As soon as they opened the door, Angela looked towards the altar. Even when she got as far as the communion rail, nothing seemed to have been touched: the altar with its cloth was intact, as was the veil over the tabernacle. Relieved, she murmured: 'He isn't here.'

But Fata Ioss nudged her, and pointing with his chin towards the left-hand side of the choir he whispered: 'Yes he is, over there.'

Manuel didn't hear them. It was only when Angela called to him softly that he gave a start and looked at them, wide-eyed. Then, very slowly, and as if with regret, he got up and joined them.

'What are you doing here?' he asked.

'Looking for you, of course, what else?' grunted Fata Ioss. 'Your poor sister has been beside herself.'

Manuel gave Angela a smile. 'You shouldn't have. I must...'

Fata Ioss hesitated, then said: 'The next time you come here, sit in the front pew, or else kneel down, but there, where we can see you,' and he pointed to the pew in question.

Manuel looked sullen. He didn't understand.

'Up there I'm closer,' he muttered.

'Look, Manuel, Fata Ioss is right,' said Angela. 'If someone came into the church while you were up there in the choir, they wouldn't understand, and they'd think you were up to no good.'

But Manuel couldn't see what they were getting at. He'd controlled himself, hadn't he, and not gone right up to the tabernacle?

'They'd suspect you of trying to steal something, like at Lidrezing, remember?'

Fata Ioss was getting nowhere.

'Come on, Manuel,' said Angela. 'Time to go home now.'

She genuflected and turned to go back down the nave, followed by Fata Ioss. Manuel hesitated. He looked at all the statues populating the church and had the impression that all these men and women of stone understood him far better than his own sister and Fata Ioss. He felt a twinge of envy that they should be able to dwell in the house of the Lord all the days of their life, but not him. Yes, he would get on well with them.

When at last he descended the nave, he stopped again at the first pillar on his right, and spent a long time gazing up at the white body of the crucified Christ hanging there, high up under the roof. The others waited for him at the door. Then they walked back through the streets of Châtelaillon-Plage in silence. Angela was brooding about the future, and even Fata Ioss was troubled.

Back at the Villa Suiram, La Vieille was looking out for them on the doorstep. She didn't ask any questions, but stood aside to let them in and said: 'I've taken advantage of your absence to get the shopping for you, Angela. I've put it all away in the cupboard.'

Angela thanked her.

Out in the courtyard, as they were leaving, Fata Ioss said to

Manuel: 'I'll call in tomorrow to do some reading with you, from the *curé*'s book.'

The sound of the sea came to their ears from the far end of the street. Somewhere away in the town the evening angelus rang out.

3

The refugees from Lasting-en-Lorraine gradually settled into their new life in Châtelaillon-Plage.

Coming as they did from the interior, the September sunshine seemed quite different to them here on the coast. They couldn't get over the vastness of the blue sky and the equally blue ocean. Their exile introduced them for the first time to horizons that were not clearly marked, not even finite. They could see the sky without lifting their heads as they were used to doing in their own land of hills and valleys. Lifting one's head takes an effort, an act of will: here it was more a question of responding to a friendly invitation.

Exile was like being on holiday.

Not that the exodus wasn't marked by poverty. But they were lodged only a stone's throw from the beach, with unrestricted sea views, unlimited stay, and change of scenery guaranteed.

To begin with it was the change of scenery, in its broadest sense, that they noticed most, every single day. Like simply being in strange houses which somehow had to be tamed and made familiar.

Millache'Babe kept getting mixed up. Either he would go into the wrong bedroom at night, or else he would end up in the street instead of in bed, and the children would have to be sent after the venerable ancestor of the tribe to fetch him back.

Rumour had it that old Mother Rak'Onna mistook her wardrobe for the door and was eventually discovered huddled inside in a state of shock. It was true that she was old and bent, unable to lift up her eyes and see straight ahead.

The older women found the streets of the little town too much for them to cope with. Between the shops and their lodgings they succumbed to the malicious labyrinth and wandered up and down, lost, under the astonished gaze of the greengrocer who saw them coming past for the umpteenth time.

Even the shops were different. The products they stocked were unfamiliar, as were the eating habits and of course the language of the local people: the oldest among the exiles couldn't speak French at all, although most of them could just about understand it.

That led, naturally, to misunderstandings. One day Bêa-Yasse'Kette, who now insisted on doing her shopping herself, asked for *kêêz* (cheese) and got a case, a crate, instead, fetched by the shopkeeper in desperation.

On another occasion she met with blank incomprehension when she asked for *aya*. She tried drawing an egg-shape on the counter and even pointing to the white colour of the scales, but to no avail. In the end, beside herself, Bêa-Yasse'Kette squatted down and clucked like a hen laying an egg—and at last they understood! Half a dozen, that's right, she nodded, holding up the five fingers of her right hand and her left thumb, and gave a grin of satisfaction.

Things were different at church, too. They used Latin for talking to God, of course, that was only right and proper, but the hymns and canticles were in French and sounded foreign.

The first Sunday left a deep impression on the refugees.

As the clock finished striking they surged into the street and went off to Mass, looking dignified in whatever they had managed to salvage of their smart clothes. The local people were amazed at how devout they appeared to be. Certainly the new church of Châtelaillon-Plage had never been as full as it was that Sunday and the weeks that followed.

They naturally sat together in the pews, which had the effect of creating zones of loudness (for the bits in Gregorian chant) and silence (for the other hymns and canticles, sung only by the handful of locals).

The correct pronunciation of Latin caused a bit of rivalry. While the locals sang *Et com spiritu tuom*, the visitors were responding *Et coum spiritou tou-oum*. Both sides looked at each other out of the corners of their eyes, across the aisle.

And what about knowing when to stand, when to sit and when to kneel? They all belonged to the same Roman Catholic Church, but clearly they had different ways of doing things. That caused a bit of confusion, so that even the priest up at the altar noticed. But that was nothing to what was to come, and anyway the refugees soon gave in and bent the knee with the rest.

Communion time came. The visitors waited to see what the regular congregation would do. All except Manuel, that is. As soon as they got to the *Domine, non sum dignus*, and before Angela could restrain him, he strode up the aisle, his eyes alight with the fire from his heart. Fata Ioss saw what was happening and tried to reach him, but he was too late: others had got up and were shuffling forward, and he was trapped.

Manuel had reached the front of the nave, and now he was standing before the priest, not far from the altar, waiting. The server, a young choirboy, sniggered. Manuel opened his mouth. 'Pssst!' the priest whispered: 'Kneel down!'

Manuel complied, and some of the old ladies of the town knelt down beside him.

He opened his mouth wide. '*Corpus Domini nostri Jesu Christi ...*' As he shut his mouth, his fingers closed over the wafers in the ciborium.

'Oh!' exclaimed the priest. 'You can't...'

'Sacrilege!' bleated one of the old ladies.

Manuel got to his feet and slowly put the wafers one by one into his mouth. The priest managed to rescue the last one from his fingers. He couldn't understand that great love may imply profanation—what ordinary people consider profanation—and that such profanation may be the sign of great love. All he could see was the scandal of the sacrilege, along with the rest of his flock who were now recoiling in horror from Manuel as if he were an emissary of Lucifer himself.

'Father, please, Father!' It was Fata Ioss who had at last managed to get through, and who had a good idea of what must have happened even if he didn't see. 'He's the village idiot, he doesn't mean any harm.'

'Ah!' The *curé* sounded relieved. 'All right, then, but you ought to watch him more carefully. *Corpus Domini nostri...*'

With Fata Ioss close behind him, Manuel returned to his seat, with his eyes half-closed, and looking extraordinarily calm and happy amid the scandalized whispers of the congregation.

He sat down and shut his eyes completely. Angela heard him murmuring: 'Come, follow me...Blessed...Blessed...Blessed... Thank you.' She couldn't bring herself to get up and go forward to the communion rail. She wished she could hide under the pews for shame. Then she remembered what the old *curé* of Lidrezing had said: 'Watch over him like a treasure,' and those words gradually restored her calm during the rest of the service. Before long the *Ite missa est* released a wave of parishioners down the aisle. They all stared at Manuel as they went past, but he didn't notice.

Outside in the square, Madamilla was trying to reassure the others. They were afraid Manuel would discredit them in the eyes of their hosts.

'He ought to be locked up!'

Madamilla gave the speaker a withering look.

'Now look here, he's a lovely lad, I'm not hearing anything against him!' She was getting angry.

When they came out of the church, Angela, La Vieille, Fata Ioss and Manuel were oblivious to everything. As they went up the street to the Villa Suiram, Ioss was trying in vain to make Manuel see reason.

'Look, each wafer is the Body of Christ. You don't need more than one.'

Manuel wasn't having any of it. He laughed and shook his head, pretending not to know what he was talking about.

'If you go on grabbing wafers like that, the *curé* won't let you take communion any more.'

That was different. Manuel stopped, first puzzled and then furious, as furious as he had been happy a moment earlier, but seething in silence, with his head down.

'Come along, Manuel,' said Ioss.

He followed them sulkily. What were they trying to do to him?

'At Lidrezing...' he began.

'We're not at Lidrezing any more, Manuel, and people won't understand like the *curé* who gave you the Gospels.'

At that Manuel perked up. Ioss was relieved.

'Will you come and read with me this afternoon?'

'All right.'

The lad seemed to have forgotten what had just happened, which the old man found disconcerting. It was as if each moment was fresh, a new start in life.

'Don't forget!'

'I won't.'

No, he wouldn't forget, any more than he had forgotten on previous afternoons. Fata Ioss had come each day with La Vieille and sat down next to Manuel on the little bench in the courtyard, with the Gospels open on his lap. He had quickly realized that the simpleton couldn't actually read, but that he had a wonderful memory for everything to do with the book. So, day after day, Fata Ioss had read to him, amazed at what he was rediscovering on every page.

That afternoon, however, Angela's landlady had been. She had had wind of the incident at church in the morning.

'You never told me he might ...'

'It's all right, madame, he isn't dangerous, quite the opposite.'

'If you'd said, I ...'

Angela knew very well what she meant: she wouldn't have taken them in the first place. That hurt her.

Fortunately Manuel was outside on the bench.

When she passed him on the way out, the lady looked at him, hesitated, looked again, summoned up her courage, and then stepped forward and patted his blond curls with a little laugh, relieved at her own daring.

Manuel looked up at her with his sky-blue eyes and gave her a dazzling smile. Reassured, she returned to the villa, adding as she noticed the empty push-chair: 'I'll bring you over some cushions and some lace.'

'Thank you, madame,' said Angela.

But when Fata Ioss and La Vieille arrived they found her in tears in her tiny kitchen. They could have been so happy together. So while Fata Ioss joined Manuel on the bench outside, La Vieille tried to console her and cheer her up. Why not come down to the beach? All the others would be there, and the men could come on later.

The beach was quite crowded when they got there, and none of the people of the exodus were missing. Even Bêa-Yasse'Kette had turned up with her folding stool, and was sitting apprehensively watching the waves eat up the sand. The beach, more than anything, was foreign to these folk from the interior. As at church, they seemed strangely out of place.

For a start they were the largest group there. Then they had dug themselves in at the very edge of the sand, as far as possible from the dangerous, shifting domain of the unpredictable sea. Their camp was divided into smaller, compact units which stayed tightly together the better to resist the enemy. And they were all rigged out in their country clothes—today their Sunday best—staring at the few bathers who dared to tease the sea as if they came from another planet, and visibly shocked by this exhibition of half-naked bodies.

La Vieille and Angela joined Bêa-Yasse'Kette and Madamilla.

Angela was glad to be back with the women of the exodus. When they saw her, Rédache'Momme and Rak'Onna came trotting over. They had all half-adopted her, and the baby to be born would be spoilt for grandmothers.

La Vieille told them about the landlady's visit.

'Well,' someone said, 'you can understand it...'

'Let's hope she knows what's what now,' put in Madamilla, 'and won't come sticking her nose in any more.'

Someone else suggested that Manuel needed to understand the situation too, to which Madamilla replied: 'I reckon he understands a lot more than the rest of us put together. We just don't understand him, that's all!'

That was one in the eye for her opponents.

There was Manuel now, coming down the stone steps off the sea-wall in front of Fata Ioss. He was beaming all over his face. Huffing and puffing, Fata Ioss came over to where the women were sitting.

'Angela,' he asked, 'look, can Manuel read or not?'

Angela was taken aback by the question.

'You know very well he can read,' said Bêa-Yasse'Kette. 'He read all right in the train!'

'Yes, but...'

'Yes but what?'

'Oh, be quiet! You wouldn't understand!'

That upset old Bêa-Yasse'Kette, who turned her back on Fata Ioss. He looked at Angela and waited for an answer.

'Well, he used to be able to make out a few syllables here and there, the odd word, nothing more. But it may have changed for all I know.'

'In that case let me tell you that your brother can now read perfectly well. Slowly and still rather hesitantly, mind you, but he can read. He's just been showing me...'

And Fata Ioss recounted what had been happening.

Meanwhile Manuel had gone down towards the sea. He gazed at it, breathed in deeply, and started laughing. It was for himself that he was laughing, there was no one there to see him. His heart was bursting with joy. 'Be of good cheer, it is I, be not afraid.' Those words which he had just been reading with Fata Ioss came back to him as he stood at the edge of the ocean. It reminded him of the Sea of Galilee. He could hear Peter saying to Jesus: 'Lord, if it is you, bid me come to you on the water.' Manuel didn't need to ask if it was the Lord. He knew. Hadn't he just been walking on the water like the apostle? And he hadn't sunk beneath the waves of the text which usually made him feel he was drowning. He had experienced a sense of liberation, and as his eyes studied the Gospel text the letters had suddenly started coming together to form syllables, the syllables words, and the words sentences, sentences which rolled over each other like waves, and he, Manuel, had ridden on them as though borne up by the gaze of the One towards whom he was walking.

The joy in him was so strong that he suddenly turned away from the sea and crouched down to write with his finger in the sand. He wrote and wrote, until he saw the women coming towards him with Fata Ioss in their midst. Even Bêa-Yasse'Kette was trotting along behind with her folding stool under her arm, burning with curiosity. Then with a great sweep of his hand he effaced the secret message, his own secret, which he had written, glanced impishly at his frustrated visitors, and ran off laughing.

At the other end of the beach he noticed Victor, who had just arrived and was getting undressed. Victor waved to him. He was the first of the refugees to dare to put on a bathing-costume.

'*Dass ish yo noch a lauss'boub'!*' (He's still a youngster!) commented Bêa-Yasse'Kette.

Would she be so tolerant of those who were no longer so young?

After waving to Manuel, Victor soon joined the group of boys and girls who were playing further down the beach.

Manuel sat down on the sand and watched them playing until evening, ignoring all invitations to join them, and even ignoring Angela behind him who eventually gave up and went off home without him. Far beyond the figures running about at the water's edge, Manuel's eyes were fixed on the horizon, on the band of light which proclaimed the marriage of the visible and the invisible.

In the coming days and weeks, Manuel and Victor would often come down to the beach. September was generous with fine sunny days, and it would be hard to go back to school when the refugee nuns arrived, to settle to dictations and arithmetic, when the gulls and the waves still called them.

Victor played truant on more than one occasion, and his parents received official complaints during the months of September and October, more like months of Sundays to Victor.

Victor was discovering life, while Sister Irma, blinkered by her stiff nun's cap, was trying to control it.

Life can't be controlled.

It was the life of the moving sea, immense, alive, into which Victor threw himself with all the eagerness of a young animal rediscovering the fields after months spent cooped up during the winter. When he was in the sea, he felt as though he was in the arms of life itself, a weird and wonderful womb which held him and rocked him and carried him, and he was never frightened. It only took him a few days to learn to swim, and soon he could move about like a water-baby, a child of the sea, a child of life.

It was the life of the thousands of shellfish that he found

clinging to the rocks or hiding under stones, asking to be hunted. Everything that moved, that was alive, was there for the taking.

How could Sister Irma understand what life meant to Victor?

She kept her class of little savages seated in rows, two to a desk, and governed them by the bell and the stick. Prayers before school, stand up, sit down, fold your arms, now religion and morals, now reading.

Reading sometimes managed to open a window on to life, but Sister Irma took good care to close it at the slightest sign of a gust of fresh air.

Recitation.

The poems of the sea and of life had no place in her pattern of recitation of dead texts, killed by formal lessons and raps over the knuckles.

Mental arithmetic.

How could anyone be expected to get the right answer when their mental powers were all directed towards working out how to get away at break-time?

Problems. If a tap drips into a tank ... If one train leaves La Rochelle at 8.47 for ... and another train arrives at ...

Life had arrived and was waiting at the beach.

Victor was waiting for life, waiting for the ten o'clock bell announcing freedom, when he could rush off down the path behind the lavatories to the sea.

Down on the beach, Marie was waiting.

A little further over, Manuel would often be sitting on a rock. As Victor was changing he would wave to him, but stay put.

Victor and Marie ran down to the sea, frolicked in the edge of the waves, laughed, splashed each other, went in deeper.

Standing in the living waves, alone beneath the sky, alone in the whole world, apart from the seagulls and Manuel, over there, who wasn't looking at them anyway, they were inventing life amid the turbulent silence of the sea.

They had met on the beach and fallen in love. She was fifteen, he was fourteen. Every day she waited for him, and every day he ran to join her at the edge of the water.

Victor's fingers traced her features: her thick hair, the small forehead, the eyelids, closed over the hazel eyes, the high cheeks, the fine nose, the full lips, the chin which he drew towards him, bringing her intoxicated face close to his so that he could tame it as he was learning to tame life, avidly.

They sat down in the waves, and the water came up to their shoulders.

He slipped Marie's bathing-costume down so that the sea caressed her youthful breasts. They were both drunk with life.

Over there, Manuel was just a dot on the beach. He was gazing at the light on the horizon, dazzled by it. For Marie and Victor, he was like the guardian of their freedom, the guarantee of their innocence.

Marie was on her knees, discovering Victor's body.

Victor was discovering Marie, love, life.

If Manuel looked, he would no longer be able to see their heads, but he was not looking.

Lying down in the edge of the water, the two children were one with the waves.

Manuel was in the light.

It had suddenly fallen from heaven, flooding his whole being with its brightness, giving a totally new quality of illumination, as pure as love, to the sand of the beach, the silver of the waves, the blue of the sea and sky, and the horizon, which now seemed so close that you could touch it with your hand.

Then the horizon and the waves and the beach faded from view, leaving nothing but the light, in which he felt taken up and transported to another world. Joy flooded him, and he waited, oblivious to the passage of time.

When the light at last began to fade, the joy remained, and it was while he was still intoxicated with that unspeakable joy that Manuel saw Victor and Marie walking towards him, hand in hand.

They went past without saying a word, shining with water, sun and contentment, and Victor looked at Manuel as a man looks at a child.

That night his father, informed by Sister Irma that his son had missed school again, unbuckled his belt, and when Victor next appeared on the beach two days later his backside was still smarting. Marie had waited patiently for him all the previous day, alone by the edge of the water, with Manuel nearby.

There would be many other occasions when she would wait and sometimes weep. Then Manuel would get up, come over to her and put his hand on her shoulder, without a word, until the tears ceased flowing. The firmness of that hand was like an assurance of forgiveness and absolution to Marie.

Not that the refugees forgave her, on the contrary. To them she was nothing better than a loose girl who had led Victor astray. And if they only knew...

His mother, La Voisine, was the recipient of much commiseration. As for Le Voisin, he was in a permanent fury.

Victor was kept at home, and only let out under strict supervision.

Until the day, at the end of October, when he gave strict Sister Irma the slip one last time.

He found Marie waiting for him on the beach, under the watchful eye of Manuel.

A cold breeze like a shroud was blowing off the sea, and the tide was right out.

They smiled at Manuel as they walked past, hand in hand.

Much later, when Manuel returned from his house of light, he was surprised not to have noticed them coming back. Yet the tide was in now, right at his feet.

He went back home, a little anxious, but only a little.

That evening, Le Voisin came round. Victor wasn't back. Had he seen him?

Manuel said nothing, which exasperated Le Voisin still further.

The next morning, Manuel went down to the beach first thing, before anyone else. As the tide turned, he found the two naked children's bodies in the water. He carried them out and laid them side by side, hand in hand, on the sand. Le Voisin came running, too late, and broke down at the sight.

The refugees of the exodus were broken by the disaster too. Victor was the first of their number to have died on foreign soil. A child too. Le Voisin's child. One of theirs. The one who looked at Rosa's breasts while she was feeding her baby, the one who had gone to find Manuel originally, the one who... Victor was dead.

Dies irae, dies illa.

The church of Châtelaillon-Plage was packed for his and Marie's funeral. The two coffins lay side by side before the altar, just as the two young bodies had on the beach.

Love, death.

Love, life, thought Manuel, as he sat in the front pew. Victor had found death and love and life. With Marie.

The tolling of the bell was like rain falling on the square, on the town, on the beach, with the last few sad droplets taken by the waves and carried far away into the unknown.

The sky, too, was raining, for the first time since their arrival.

It was raining in their hearts, except in Manuel's, where a different sun was shining.

When the simpleton walked through the streets with a smile on his lips, there were always those who took offence. It was no different now. Manuel didn't notice. He went off towards the beach, down the stone steps, and over the sand, in the rain. When he reached the flat rock he sat down and watched the grey horizon where the grey sky met the grey sea. Only the gulls were there to keep him company this time.

That night, when the bell started tolling again, people looked at each other in consternation.

Manuel was back at home with Angela. He gave her a questioning look, but she didn't know what it was all about.

Then La Vieille and Fata Ioss arrived.

'Millache'Babe died this evening, suddenly, without any warning.'

Manuel shivered. He could see Millache'Babe's open smile, and his bald head nodding backwards and forwards, forwards and backwards.

'He spent the whole afternoon sitting in the doorway, despite the rain. They couldn't shift him.'

In the morning he had been to the burial service.

'Then, not long ago, he suddenly got up and went inside. Apparently he said to his daughter: "*Dêa do greesh nimmd sobal' kê ênd'mé! Ish konn'nid lênggâ vââde!*" (This war shows no sign of ending. I can't wait any longer!) And then he sat down in his armchair—the new one given to him by the folk here. A quarter of an hour later his daughter realized that he was dead.'

So old Millache'Babe couldn't wait to go home to his Léna, back in their own land, beneath the geraniums, he couldn't wait for this interminable war to end, so he died, there and then, simply turning his back on the war. As though young Victor's death had suddenly given him the idea. As though he had just realized that his Léna might be waiting for him somewhere other than in the heavy soil of Lorraine.

Having buried Victor in the morning, the people of the exodus now had the body of Millache'Babe, their oldest member, to see to. More than one of them thought of their own dead lying in the cemetery in Lasting-en-Lorraine, abandoned, with no one to look after their graves or to bring them flowers this coming All Souls' Day.

4

Yet no one forgot the war.

How could they?

For a whole month, they had to take their gas masks with them everywhere. The children cried when they were put on, which was hardly surprising, since they made them look like aliens from another world.

Which they were, in a sense. Here they were living in a foreign land, anyway.

No, no one forgot the war.

The Charente region was still foreign soil, even if they had already planted two seeds for eternity in the form of Victor and Millache'Babe; and even if they had found a warm welcome... for the most part...

It hadn't been easy. Old Bêa-Yasse'Kette had been called a '*Boche*' almost from the start.

'They called my boy a "*Boche*" too!'

'And my grandad!'

It hadn't been easy to swallow.

Of course there was the weekly sermon in dialect on Radio Bordeaux on Sunday mornings, but then, who had a wireless to listen to it? And if they did, all the more reason for people to call them '*Boches*'. Anyway, Alsatian wasn't that easy to understand: they came from Lorraine, not Alsace.

They couldn't get away from the fact that they were refugees, in receipt of a daily allowance. Of course it was a help to have that ten francs a day, but it was just as humiliating as having your young people deported to work in the industrial towns.

'They tried to take Manuel!'

'*So ebbes! So ebbes!*' (Well, I never!), gasped Bêa-Yasse'Kette in outraged surprise.

It had taken all of Angela's determination and Fata Ioss' firmness to get permission for Manuel to stay.

And then he got called lazy and work-shy, labels that are always hung round the necks of young people who find it hard to get a job.

Not that Manuel minded.

'He must be getting even more simple.'

He was getting more and more happy, that was all. How could you explain that?

Those with their man or their boy at the Front weren't happy. How could they be? In the first place they only got half the daily allowance, and then they received hardly any letters. Mail took three weeks to get to the Front and the reply took another three weeks, so that was six whole weeks without news.

And the news wasn't always good when it did come. It was a funny, phoney kind of war they were having back there in Lorraine. In the villages behind the Front the soldiers appeared to be on holiday, and they were living it up at the expense of the refugees whose property they were squandering. They were living it up, that's what. That's how it had started, and that's how it was carrying on.

Whenever would it all finish?

And what were they to make of the newspapers, which said the opposite of what they gathered from letters and from the first soldiers to come to the town on leave?

Those soldiers made Angela's heart beat faster. If only Benoît could be among them one day! Since leaving Lasting-en-Lorraine she had been entirely without news. Had her letters even reached him? Did he know...?

No, they couldn't forget the war.

They could have been so happy together.

Those who returned on leave were fathers with young children or husbands whose wives were pregnant.

Angela was in her sixth month. But still no one knew who the father of her child was, no one except Manuel and the *curé* of Lidrezing whom he had told. But he was a long way away. None of the women round her, La Vieille, La Voisine, Rédache'Momme, Madamilla, Bêa-Yasse'Kette, none of them knew whose child she was carrying.

How could they tell old Siébert from Siébert's Mill that he was going to be a grandfather? He must know where his son was, over there in the Ardennes somewhere.

Old Siébert knew everything.

He was the one who had kept Fata Ioss, Wag-Nache'Péda and the others up to date with how things were developing, week by week.

'Canada has joined the war...'

That was shortly after their arrival in Châtelaillon.

'The Russians have invaded Poland.'

Fata Ioss knew all about the Russians.

'I saw how they operated in the last war, the Great War.'

'This one seems set to be an even greater war, Fata Ioss.'

'Think so?' Fata Ioss was sceptical. 'Anyhow, I know what the Russians are like.'

'They've circulated a pamphlet in Paris calling for "Peace Now!"'

'Good for them,' said La Vieille. 'That's what we all want.'

'Not Hitler.'

'Oh, him...'

He was their *bête noire*.

'In Paris, they've dissolved the Communist Party.'

La Vieille disliked the Communists, but she kept her mouth shut. Two days later, old Siébert announced: 'The Germans and the Russians have divided up Poland between them.'

'Poor old Poles!'

In the streets, all the talk was of the defence of Warsaw. People brandished newspapers and shouted: 'Warsaw will never fall!'

Warsaw fell.

The Germans entered Warsaw on the twenty-ninth of September.

'It'll be Paris next,' said Fata Ioss. 'If they can enter Warsaw, they can enter Paris.' That scandalized everyone.

'Now come on, Fata Ioss...'

'If the Poles couldn't stop them...'

'Ah, but they didn't have the Maginot Line.'

Some time later, they heard that the French divisions which had advanced into the Saarland had now withdrawn voluntarily.

Some of the soldiers on leave said that French troops had been punished for firing at the enemy.

'What's the point of being a soldier then?'

They couldn't understand that.

No, there was no chance of forgetting the war.

'Apparently Maurice Thorez has deserted.'

'Who's he?'

'Anyway, if he's deserted...'

'Deserters...!'

Then the rumour came that Hitler had proposed a peace conference. They found that hard to believe. They also found it hard to believe that the government should have had the Communist deputies arrested.

'But if Thorez has deserted...'

'But they are deputies like any others.'

'Anyone who goes over to the enemy...'

There was talk of Public Enemy Number One.

What a funny, phoney war.

After the burial of Victor and Millache'Babe, there was news of a bomb in Munich after one of Hitler's speeches.

'They'll get rid of him in the end, the Germans will.'

As if they were relieved to think they wouldn't have to do it themselves.

But the assassination attempt failed, and winter came.

The war would never end.

Apparently it was a really harsh winter back home.

It would be a white Christmas in Lasting-en-Lorraine, and they wouldn't be there to see it. They wouldn't see the white forest of fir trees down by the Hume, or the bare beeches on the Gréderich, or the spooky black shadows of the Athisberg. Who would take the animals their fodder up in the clearings? Who would look after the young hinds? Would the edge of the Sime freeze over? Who would put out the birdseed, or hang bacon-fat and rind from the beam for the tits? How would the village get through the winter with all those foreigners, whether French or Germans, who understood nothing of its secret life and treated it like a trollop?

'Bloody war!' grumbled Fata Ioss, to his own surprise.

The next day, they heard that the Russians had attacked Finland...

France, Germany, Canada, Russia, Poland, Finland...

'It's a world war!' exclaimed La Vieille, not knowing how right she was.

How could they prepare for Christmas in circumstances like that? Peace on earth, good will towards men: not much chance of that...

The four Sundays in Advent came and went, all equally bleak.

Often, in the evenings, Manuel would look at Angela.

She was sitting by the table, knitting. The little charcoal stove didn't give out much heat. From time to time Angela furtively wiped away a tear. In her room at night, Manuel knew that she wept: he had often heard her. When she felt him looking at her, she started talking without lifting her head, asking him how his day had been.

Despite the winter weather, he still often went down to the sea. He would go to the edge of the sea-wall and lean over, watching the waves battering the stones and the flight of steps and throwing the spray as far as the road, soaking him in the process with fine spindrift which the wind then carried far, far away. When he passed his tongue over his lips he could taste the salt as he had at his baptism so long ago, and that gave him the sensation of experiencing a new birth, as though each time he was being more fully born into a mysterious life, unknown yet much more real than anything he had known before.

When he felt that sensation welling up in him, overwhelming him, he would set off along the sea-wall until he reached the sand, and then he would go for a long walk along the beach, sometimes as far as Les Boucholeurs, where he was intrigued by the fishermen's cottages. He would often stop and look at the low, grey sky, pressing down on the sea which might be iron-grey or green beneath its crests of foam. He searched in vain for the horizon, dissolved in all the greyness. Where had the light of those blue September days gone?

Sometimes, during those long halts, Manuel would think of Victor and Marie, and then he would close his eyes and see them coming out of the sea towards him, hand in hand. But he couldn't make out their faces: the mist had erased them, and they were no more than grey patches on the moving, menacing ocean. As soon as he moved towards the edge of the sea they disappeared, reclaimed by the waves, and Manuel stopped, wondering.

He no longer went to sit on the flat rock. He still went to the spot, however, when the sea uncovered it, and stroked the stone with his hand like a pet. He used to talk to it, too, asking when the light would come again.

He thought of Fata Ioss, busy for several days now on a Christmas crib. Straw was easy enough to find, and he had made a stable with a roof supported by four branches and a manger full of hay. From shapeless bits of wood he had carved an ox, an ass and Joseph. Now he was doing the Virgin Mary, and then there would be just time to do the Christ-child. He couldn't spare the time to come round in the afternoons, and it was too cold to sit on the bench outside, so Manuel went to him now, setting off across the road as soon as La Vieille came to join Angela, with the book which the *curé* of Lidrezing had given him tucked under his arm. He found Ioss in the kitchen surrounded by wood-shavings, and stood watching him work until the old man commanded: 'Read!'

Then he opened the book at the page that was marked, always the same one, and began painstakingly: 'And she gave birth to her first-born son and wrapped him in swaddling clothes, and laid him in a manger... Unto you is born this day a Saviour, who is Christ the Lord.' Fata Ioss listened attentively, his penknife suspended in the air, as if he were expecting to receive precise instructions from what Manuel was reading. When he resumed his work there was a look of calm concentration on his face, and Manuel watched him with boundless contentment.

He experienced the same contentment in the evenings in front of the fire whenever he looked at Angela. He was always taken by surprise by her regular question, and he looked startled, unable to tell his disappointed sister what gave him such secret happiness.

'I went down to the sea...'

'Do be careful, Manuel, and don't go too close. Remember what happened to Victor. With all these storms about...'

'Then I went to see Fata Ioss...'

'Well, that's all right, at least I don't have to worry about that!'

No, she wasn't going to worry, especially not this Christmas Eve of 1939 when the two of them were waiting to go over to Fata Ioss and La Vieille's house for the traditional vigil. That afternoon the old man had finished carving the baby Jesus and he had promised Manuel that he could be the one to place it in the manger. The simpleton was getting very excited, Angela could tell, as she finished getting herself ready. She was both happier and sadder this evening, feeling lighter and heavier at the same time, more alert and yet slower, as if the waiting was urging her forward and yet at the same time dragging on her. They smiled at each other and then started in surprise as they heard someone knocking crisply on the shutter of the front window. Whoever could be coming to see them at this time of night? Had Fata Ioss come to collect them after all?

After a moment of hesitation, they both headed for the door together. Angela slowly pulled back the bolt and opened it a crack. At first neither of them recognized the huge dark figure on the doorstep with the soldier's cap and the heavy greatcoat and leggings. Then Angela burst out:

'Benoît!'

Did she recognize him, or was she afraid it was someone bringing bad news? But who would think of telling her? No one knew...

Benoît, for he it was, stooped to come in. Then he took Angela in his arms, watched by Manuel who didn't understand straight away. His face had gone numb with the shock, but naturally the lovers didn't notice. Angela was sobbing on Benoît's shoulder, saying his name over and over again. Benoît held her close, murmuring words of love like those of the trickling fountain back at Lasting-en-Lorraine in the moonlight. They were so happy together that they forgot all about the simpleton, standing staring at them, open-mouthed. Angela's sobs made his face twitch, and his hands kept half reaching out as if they wanted to rush to the rescue of his sister, caught in the arms of the man who had made her pregnant. It was her eyes that stopped him, eyes filled with tears yet shining like the sun after a storm, or like a summer morning after a night of rain. They were so happy together.

'You know your letter...' stammered Benoît.

'My letter,' echoed Angela.

'The one you wrote before leaving...'

'Yes...'

'Well, I only got it ten days ago...'

Gently, he pushed her away and stood back with his two hands on her shoulders to look at her body, heavy with the child, their child, which she was carrying. He smiled with contentment, and the smile Angela gave him in return was like a reflection in the water of a fountain. Their smiles restored Manuel's calm, too, smoothing away the stiffness from his face, awakening the mysterious complicity of another smile.

'The moment I read it, I dashed off to the captain, and... here I am!'

They fell into each other's arms again, and suddenly their happiness bubbled up inside Manuel and came out in a burst of wild laughter. Benoît looked at him in astonishment.

'What's come over him?'

Angela stood back to look at him, only to see Manuel rush off into the night.

'Manuel! Manuel!'

She stood on the doorstep and called out into the starlit night of the Nativity, 1939: 'Manuel, Manuel! Where are you off to?'

Her brother's voice came back to her as a distant echo: '...Fata Ioss!'

'It's all right, he's just going to Fata Ioss' as planned.'

'Well, let him go, then.'

Benoît's hand was warm on Angela's shoulder, and she could

145

feel the warmth going all through her body, making her quiver.

'Come back inside, you'll catch your death.'

Benoît drew her to him and gently closed the door. Angela didn't try to stop him.

Manuel was running through the night, and it was Christmas.

The sky above was full of stars. He stopped for a moment on the sea-front to draw breath. Suddenly motionless, he lifted his head, looking for all the world as though he was drinking in the starlight. When he lowered his eyes again he saw the dark waves twinkling like another firmament, and he shivered.

When he started off again, he realized abruptly that he had forgotten his book, his Gospels. He turned and came slowly back to the house. Somewhere in the night, in spite of the war, people were singing Christmas carols. They were happy.

He tiptoed across the courtyard. As he opened the door quietly he could hear Benoît's loud voice and Angela's happy laugh. At last. There was his book, in the hall, on the edge of the well. He put out his hand to take it, and through the kitchen door he saw Angela on Benoît's knees. He had taken off his coat, his cap and his leggings, and his shirt was undone. Angela was letting him caress her.

They could have been so happy together.

Manuel felt left out. He stood gaping at his sister's happiness, then turned and tiptoed away, careful not to make the slightest noise. When he got out into the street he didn't run: he walked slowly through the labyrinth of streets to Fata Ioss' house.

The old man was looking out for them. When he saw Manuel he greeted him with: 'Ah, there you are!' and wrapped the blanket tighter round his shoulders. Then he asked: 'Have you come on your own?'

Manuel said nothing, but went on into the room where all the others had gathered for the vigil: La Vieille, Madamilla and Bêa-Yasse'Kette.

'Have you come on your own?' they all chorused. 'Has Angela...?'

'She's back at the house. With Benoît.'

'Benoît...?' The women looked at each other.

'Would that be Benoît from Siébert's Mill?' asked Fata Ioss.

'That's him,' said Manuel. 'Benoît who got Angela pregnant.'

The women looked at each other again.

'Well, now, isn't that nice for her that he's been able to get here
for Christmas?' said Fata Ioss.

'They are happy together,' murmured Manuel.

'Well, well, well! They'd best be left to themselves tonight.
Come along, it's getting late. We nearly couldn't wait for you any
longer.'

And Fata Ioss took Manuel off to the corner where the crib
was. La Vieille quickly lit the candles and turned off the lights.

Manuel was dazzled. Joy flooded through him, wonderful,
intoxicating joy, and everything else was forgotten.

In Fata Ioss' stable, the ox and the ass were waiting for the
child Emmanuel along with Mary and Joseph. One was standing
up, the other lying down, looking at the empty manger, ready to
warm the baby with the breath from their nostrils. Leaning on his
staff, Joseph had one eye on the door and the other on Mary. She
was kneeling by him, her head on one side, attentive with every
fibre of her being to the life inside her, the life which was to
become the way and the truth as well for many, this very night.

Fata Ioss gently took the book from Manuel's hands.

'Here you are,' he said, and he placed in his open palm the tiny
baby for Manuel to lay in the manger. Nothing else seemed to
exist in that moment.

'And Joseph also went up from Galilee, from the city of
Nazareth, to Judea, to the city of David, which is called Bethle-
hem, because he was of the house and lineage of David, to be
enrolled with Mary, his betrothed, who was with child.'

The deep voice of Fata Ioss filled the little room.

'And while they were there, the time came for her to be delivered. And she gave birth to her first-born son and wrapped him in swaddling-clothes, and laid him in a manger, because there was no room for them in the inn.'

Manuel leaned forward and placed the baby in the manger.

'And in that region there were shepherds out in the fields, keeping watch over their flock by night. And an angel of the Lord appeared to them, and the glory of the Lord shone round about them, and they were filled with fear.'

Manuel had fallen to his knees before the crib, with the women round him, and was listening to Fata Ioss' words as if in a dream.

'...good news of great joy which will come to all the people... a Saviour who is Christ the Lord...lying in a manger...'

Light shone around the simpleton, and he allowed himself to be embraced and comforted by it as he had seen Angela being embraced by Benoît. Joy filled him and radiated from him, as if he had become a little child again.

> *Glory to God in the highest,*
> *and on earth peace among men with whom he is pleased.*

The quavering voice of La Vieille launched into the *Gloria in excelsis Deo*, and the other women and Fata Ioss joined in. Then, for the sake of Bêa-Yasse'Kette, Madamilla struck up *Ihr Kinderlein kommet*, and with the old familiar tune came back memories of childhood Christmases long ago and far away, right over the other side of France, where today men were fighting each other. The women's eyes misted over, and even Fata Ioss' voice had a catch in it. Then, all on his own, Manuel sang the *Gloria* a second time. When he had finished, Fata Ioss said: 'Come along, it's time we were off to Midnight Mass.'

The women stood up and got ready to go.

When Manuel at last rose to his feet, the old man blew out the candles, wrapped himself in a heavy overcoat and led the little band out into the street.

Outside, the night was cold.

'Bi ouns' dehêmm' lêid' beshdimmd' shnée' (There's bound to be snow back home), said Bêa-Yasse'Kette.

No one answered. They were hurrying towards the new church of Châtelaillon-Plage, and Fata Ioss was doing his best to keep Manuel close to him. He sensed that he might have to look sharp tonight.

Dominus dixit ad me.

A scratch choir sang the introit.

When it came to the sermon, the priest spoke of the soldiers at the Front and invited the congregation to pray for peace. Some of the women got their handkerchiefs out.

At communion, Fata Ioss went up to the rail with Manuel the simpleton, and as soon as the priest had placed the wafer on his tongue, he steered him gently away. Manuel co-operated, *in splendoribus sanctorum.* Fata Ioss was mightily relieved.

After the service, in agreement with La Vieille, Fata Ioss wanted to take him home with them, but he was surprised when Manuel refused.

'No, I want to go home.'

'But Angela isn't on her own, she's with Benoît, so you don't have to worry about her.'

'I want to go home.'

Even Madamilla couldn't persuade him.

He went off in the direction of the Villa Suiram, but as soon as he was out of sight he doubled back towards the sea, with the *curé* of Lidrezing's book stuffed safely in his pocket.

He didn't stop running until he got down the steps and right to the edge of the water. There, under the formidable but gentle gaze of the starry heavens, he dropped to his knees on the cold, wet sand, exhausted. He stared wild-eyed at the rolling waves, and then all of a sudden he burst into tears, softly at first, but soon more and more violently until he was sobbing his heart out. How could he know what was happening inside him? It was because he was happy that he was crying, because of the tiny baby in his hand and then lying naked in the manger, because of the white communion bread on his tongue, because of ... But because of Benoît, back at the house, and Angela in Benoît's arms and on his knees, he was unhappy, and that made him cry too. Manuel was inconsolable, and the tears rolled off his cheeks into the water, mingling their salt with the salt of the ocean.

He didn't feel the gentle hand on his shoulder. He didn't hear the voice asking: 'What's the matter? Whatever's the matter?'

He had to be shaken before he would respond, before he would look up at the face leaning over him.

'What's the matter?'

He didn't recognize the young woman who was speaking to him, and he wondered who on earth she could be to be wandering about on the beach at night.

'What's the matter, darling?'

'Who ... who are you?'

The young woman drew her coat closer round her body and smiled at him from under her mantilla. 'Oh, I'm just the whore. Who else would be out at this time of night, on Christmas Eve too?'

She squatted down on the sand next to the simpleton and wiped a tear from his cheek with her finger.

Manuel didn't know what a whore was, and he didn't bother to ask. He couldn't control his tears, with that soft, soft hand stroking his cheek. They started flowing again.

'There, there!'

She sat down and took his head in her hands, resting it first against her shoulder and then on her knees as Manuel abandoned himself to her. He was lying flat out now, staring up into the sky and crying, with unfamiliar fingers drying his tears and his soul comforted by this woman who had come to him out of the night. The only noise was that of the waves licking the sand at their feet.

'What's your name?' asked the whore.

'Manuel.'

When he looked up into her face, he thought he detected tears in her eyes too.

'What about you? What's your name?'

'They call me Gina, but my real name is Elisabeth.' After a long silence, she added: 'My parents used to call me Lisbeth, when I was little.'

Manuel smiled at her through his tears.

'We'll catch cold, sitting here like this,' she said suddenly. 'Come with me.'

Manuel didn't hesitate for a second. He jumped up and followed Lisbeth along the beach and up the steps. When they reached the road he took the hand which she held out to him, and together they walked through a maze of narrow streets which were quite unfamiliar to him.

'It's cold enough,' whispered Lisbeth with a shiver, and she hurried them along.

When they stopped in front of a tiny cottage she turned to him and said: 'I don't suppose you've got any money, but never mind. Christmas Eve, and all that . . .'

Manuel had never had any money of his own, and he couldn't think why she had mentioned it. He simply echoed: 'Christmas Eve . . .' and followed her inside. She took him into a small bedroom warmed by a stove in one corner.

'That's a bit better!' she said, taking off her coat and putting some wood on the stove. Then she turned to Manuel. 'Come on then, don't just stand there! Oh, but look at you, you're all wet!'

Manuel smiled.

Lisbeth had by now removed her mantilla and he could admire her long black hair.

She took off his jacket. 'Sit down on the bed over there.' Next she undid his shoes and pulled off his socks. 'You'll soon warm up, you just wait.'

Manuel thought of Angela who used to undress him like that when he was younger. He felt at home and, anyway, Angela was with Benoît...

She took off his shirt and vest. When she undid his trousers Manuel was quite innocent. There he was finally, sitting in front of her, naked, like a little child.

'Who's a handsome fellow then?'

Lisbeth rubbed him all over with a warm towel.

'Now, you just lie down and wait.'

She pulled back the sheets and Manuel snuggled into bed and closed his eyes. When he opened them again, he saw the whore who was finishing getting undressed. He looked at her small breasts. He knew quite well what Angela was like, but his sister never walked about in front of him like that.

'You're my Christmas present,' murmured Lisbeth, sitting down on the edge of the bed.

Manuel looked at her as if what she had just said had brought him out of his dream.

'Christmas,' he said. Then he suddenly jumped up.

'What's got into you?'

He rummaged through his clothes until he found his jacket, pulled a book out of the pocket, and went back to Lisbeth.

'What's that?'

Sitting on the bed, blissfully unaware of his state, he opened the book.

'Listen,' he said. And he began to read: 'Joseph went up from Galilee, from the city of Nazareth...'

Lisbeth listened, open-mouthed: she couldn't believe it. Never since she had started...

'... she gave birth to her first-born son and wrapped him in swaddling-clothes, and laid him in a manger...'

Manuel read through the whole Gospel passage that Fata Ioss had read earlier before the crib. 'It's odd,' thought the whore to herself, 'he reads much too badly to be a *curé* and yet...'

When he had finished, Manuel gave her a look of triumph. 'It's Christmas,' he said, and he put the book down on the chair.

Lisbeth snuggled up to him without a word and took the blond lad in her arms. Manuel smiled and let her rock him, with his cheek resting against her soft breast. She was completely at a loss for words.

When she eventually plucked up courage to start stroking him, she was amazed to find that he had gone to sleep against her, and he had a seraphic smile on his face. She laid him down next to her, passed her fingers through his unruly blond curls, planted a kiss on his forehead, and carefully covered him up. She couldn't stop looking at him.

At last she turned the light out, but as she lay there in the darkness next to him, waiting for sleep to come, she could still hear the echo of the words Manuel had just been reading: '... on earth peace among men with whom he is pleased.' It was as though the voice came from the depths of her childhood. As she drifted off to sleep she could hear the voices of the children of her native village singing: *'Il est né le divin enfant...'* Did she dream that she was crying, or was she really crying? Did she dream that she was happy?

When Manuel woke early in the morning, he sat up in bed and was astonished to see the face of the whore still wet with tears. He shivered in the chilly air as he stood by the bed where Lisbeth slept. He got dressed without making any noise and tiptoed out of the room, holding his shoes in his hand. Once he was outside he wasn't sure which way to go. In the silence of the dawn he caught the sound of the sea, and he walked towards it through the maze of streets until he came to the sea-wall. The ocean was calm and grey as far as the eye could see. The simpleton looked at it, shivered, then crossed the road and went up towards the Villa Suiram. Somewhere in the town, a peal of bells rang out.

5

Angela didn't hear him come in.

She had stayed up with Benoît until the early hours, happy beyond words; never in all her wildest dreams could she have hoped for such a Christmas Eve. When he had finally left, only a few minutes earlier, amid mutual promises to meet again first thing, she wished she could have grabbed him and held him tight and taken him off to the bedroom and never been separated from him for a single instant... But with her arms still stretched out, seeking him, in the darkness of the courtyard, she had let him go, with a heavy heart and eyes dim with tears. The tears didn't stop until she went to sleep, at last, quite untroubled on Manuel's score: La Vieille and Fata Ioss must have realized what the situation was and kept him there for the night. When he came back in the morning he could simply collect the key from its hiding place as usual. Angela's sleep was deep and dreamless, black as a bottomless well, as if the angels of the night were afraid to come near her in case their watchfulness should be caught out by one of those eloquent fantasies which humans sometimes see in their dreams.

She didn't hear Manuel come in.

Shivering with the cold, he took the key from the recess in the wall, turned it as quietly as possible in the lock and opened the door, careful to avoid making any noise that might disturb his sister. When he was in the passageway he took the New Testament out of his jacket pocket and put it back on the edge of the well. The kitchen was dark and deserted. Benoît must have gone home, unless he was with...

Manuel stopped, stupefied at the thought.

On tiptoe he went to the door of Angela's room, put his hand on the latch and opened it a crack: his sister was fast asleep, and she was alone. Relieved, Manuel smiled, pulled the door to, hesitated, then came out into the corridor and went to his own room. He was cold. That was why he wanted to go back to bed. Huddled under the blankets, he suddenly found himself thinking of the whore and her soft, warm body. The thought warmed his own body up and made his heart beat faster. He tried to work out where her little cottage was, but his mind got lost in the maze of tiny streets, and soon, drowsy from the warmth, he fell asleep.

Both of them were awoken by Benoît hammering on the front door. Manuel leapt out of bed, but stopped at the door of his room to give Angela time to get there first. He could hear her slippers on the stone flags of the passageway, then the noise of the bolt being drawn, a creak as the door was opened, and then silence. He knew that Angela was in the arms of big Benoît of Siébert's Mill, and he leaned forward and listened before turning away slowly back to his bed. After a while he tore off his pyjamas and got dressed as fast as he could, angrily. When he got to the kitchen, Benoît was already sitting at the table. Angela was making the coffee.

'Morning, Manuel,' smiled his sister. 'How did it go at Fata Ioss' last night?'

'All right.'

'And the Midnight Mass?' enquired Benoît, trying to show interest.

'All right.'

Angela hadn't seen Manuel putting on his jacket, and when

she turned round at Benoît's question she asked: 'Where are you off to?'

'To see Fata Ioss. He said...'

But Manuel no longer knew what Fata Ioss had said, if indeed he had said anything. He gripped the latch tightly.

'You could at least have had your coffee first!'

Manuel shook his head, smiled, and went out.

Once in the street he started by going towards Fata Ioss' house, but he could hear the noise of the sea, growing louder and louder in his head. So he changed direction and came to the grey ocean, whose moving surface constantly betrayed the presence of a mysterious life deep down. Then, turning his back on it, he looked at the town as if trying to find his way. Suddenly he dashed off like a madman through the narrow streets, sometimes retracing his steps, then rushing off again, until finally he stopped in front of a small cottage and beat on the door with his fists.

'All right, I'm coming!'

He carried on knocking in spite of the sleepy voice which he could hear muttering, 'All right, all right, I'm coming!'

When the door at last opened, Manuel stepped inside, took the whore in his arms and hugged her tight.

'Let go, can't you! You're stifling me!'

Manuel laughed.

'You gave me a real fright, you did,' said the whore. 'First of all you went off and left the door unlocked, and now here you come banging on the door like a madman. What's got into you?'

Manuel went into the living-room, followed by Lisbeth. He sat down at the table and waited.

'What are you waiting for?'

'Coffee.'

'Well, I never!'

Lisbeth, in amazement, pulled her dressing-gown tighter round her shoulders, got the fire going, and put the water on to heat up. While she was laying the table, Manuel sat watching her. Intrigued by her visitor, she said nothing. She cut the bread, buttered it, and finally poured out the coffee and milk.

'All right? Happy now?'

Manuel smiled and nodded as he took a bite of bread and butter.

'What made you disappear earlier on, then?'

Manuel smiled at her and went on eating.

'Don't say much, do you?'

Lisbeth, in her turn, went on eating in silence. When they had finished, she got up to clear the table. Suddenly, Manuel pulled her to him, opened her dressing-gown, undid the buttons of her nightdress, and nestled his curly head against her warm bosom.

'You funny old thing!'

Lisbeth couldn't get over it. She didn't try to stop him, and when she felt his hand on her breast she said: 'Do you want it?'

'Oh, yes!' said Manuel.

'Go and get into bed, then, and I'll be right with you.'

In a flash Manuel was naked and snuggling under the blankets. He lay there watching Lisbeth getting undressed. When she joined him he hugged her so tightly that she had difficulty in shaking herself free.

'Let me breathe!'

Manuel laughed.

Faced with this little boy with a man's body, Lisbeth went from surprise to surprise, and finally, like Manuel himself, from marvel to marvel. It was as if what she was doing and saying were for the very first time. Everything was different from usual, and before the blond lad's look of childlike innocence Lisbeth rediscovered a sense of modesty. He was so clumsy that she felt as shy as a bride on her wedding night.

'Is that nice?'

'I love you.'

He said it as if it were really true.

'You're my Christmas present.'

Lisbeth sensed that everything Manuel said or did was true.

'I love you just like Angela ...'

'Who's Angela?'

'... just like Angela loves Benoît.'

He was careful not to say: like Benoît loves Angela.

'Who's Angela?'

'My sister.'

'And Benoît?'

'He's the one who got her pregnant.'

'What a funny thing to say!'

Lisbeth didn't know what to think.

'Manuel's getting the whore pregnant.'

She gaped. She wanted to shout out that for him she wasn't the whore, she wasn't acting like a whore, she ... And she burst into tears like a little girl beneath the astonished gaze of Manuel.

At first he just watched her, uncomprehending, but then he took her in his arms and cradled her like a child. She cried and cried, as she hadn't cried for months, as she used to cry when she was little. She had suddenly discovered that deep down she was still that little girl, however sordid her life had become. Manuel continued to cradle her, murmuring over and over again words which Lisbeth only started to catch when she was calm again: 'Blessed are those who mourn, for they shall be comforted.'

'What's that you're saying?'

'Blessed are those who mourn, for they shall be comforted.'

'Manuel ...'

'Blessed are the pure in heart, for they shall see God.'

Lisbeth opened her eyes wide. 'Why do you say that? You know very well ...' But she didn't dare finish and say that he knew very well that she was not pure, she was a whore.

'Blessed are the pure in heart,' repeated Manuel, and then:

'You are the light of the world.'

The grey light of Christmas morning penetrated into the small room through the openings in the shutters which were still closed. Lisbeth's head lay on Manuel's shoulder, and he wiped away her tears with his fingers as she cried silently. They remained motionless for a long while. When she eventually stopped crying he kissed her eyes and repeated: 'You are the light of the world.'

Lisbeth didn't quite know what to do. She sat down and said: 'I'll get us something to eat.'

By the time they sat down at the table the midday angelus had long stopped ringing in the December air. The shutters which Lisbeth had opened revealed a day that was already declining. Between their two plates she had lit a little red candle, the only one in the house. The flame danced in Manuel's eyes and kindled in them a joy which Lisbeth drank in avidly, as if she couldn't get enough of it. Can one ever get enough joy? Or enough of a childhood that seemed to be lost for ever and that is suddenly rediscovered? Or enough love? The whore was like a little girl seeing a lighted Christmas tree and a crib for the first time, lost in wonder. She scarcely bothered to eat herself, she was so happy gazing at Manuel's simple face opposite her: not that she knew that he was simple, rather she found him genuine and pure like the finest gold.

'How about a walk, Lisbeth?' Manuel's voice brought her out of her dream.

'A walk? Where to?'

'With me. Come on!'

'Just give me time to get dressed.'

They both got dressed as quickly as they could, laughing like children, happier than they had probably ever been on Christmas Day.

Manuel took Lisbeth's hand and they ran through the streets. Where was he taking her? Heedless of the approaching sunset, indifferent to those who might pass them or see them from behind their closed curtains, Manuel led her on, deaf to Lisbeth's questionings, straining towards his secret goal.

His goal was the great new church of Châtelaillon-Plage.

When they arrived in front of the doors, Lisbeth shrank back. It was years since she had set foot inside a church...But Manuel led her on irresistibly. Fortunately, the door swung open as he pushed it. Inside it was already dark in the corners and behind the pillars. There was only one light, the tiny, intense glow of the sanctuary lamp at the far end.

Manuel first of all headed towards that with Lisbeth, but when they got to the crossing he noticed the crib in the shadows of the transept. He let go of her hand and poked round until he found a box of matches behind the angel. He struck one and patiently, like a verger, he lit all the candles, so that they illuminated the stable and the mother and child, between the ox and the ass. He looked round at Lisbeth, smiled and pointed almost timidly at the tiny figure lying in the straw. Then he knelt down in silence.

Lisbeth stood behind him staring at the crib. Soon the tears started trickling down her cheeks, but she didn't notice, any more than she noticed that Manuel had disappeared. How long did she remain motionless, dazzled by the twinkling stars of the candles seen through her tears? Where were her thoughts?

She was brought back to earth by the sound of the main door creaking on its hinges. She shot to a pew and knelt down like any devout churchgoer, rediscovering a pious but misleading habit which she thought was dead and buried in her. She could hear heavy footfalls coming up the nave behind her, and at the same time her eyes recovered from the glare of the candles and grew sufficiently accustomed to the dark for her to make out the figure of Manuel slumped at the foot of the altar steps.

Someone had put a hand on her shoulder. She looked up.

'It's time to go home, madame. I'm shutting the church now.'

It was the *curé*, looking enormous in his black cassock and cape. Manuel didn't appear to have noticed him.

Lisbeth got up. What should she do? The priest was still standing next to her in the aisle. She gave him a distraught glance.

'Is he at the Front?' he asked.

Her only response was to stretch out her hand and point to the figure up in the choir, by the steps.

'Who is it?' said the *curé*, dropping his voice to a whisper.

'Manuel.'

'Manuel?' And after a moment: 'The simpleton who came with the refugees?'

Lisbeth looked at him in astonishment.

The *curé* hesitated, then said: 'Go and tell him it's time to go home.'

After a moment, she obeyed.

She walked slowly, as if reconsidering before each step whether she dared go on. She went through the gate in the communion rail, and on up the steps to the sanctuary. As she advanced her heart raced in her breast, galloping like a runaway horse, and her stomach tied itself in knots as though she was about to encounter the unknown. And yet it was Manuel who was there in front of her, she could see him against the light, as it were, with the red glow of the sanctuary lamp giving him a halo, an aura of mystery. There he was, motionless, with his head bowed and his arms hanging loose, with hands open. When she came up close, only a few feet away from the tabernacle, she sensed that he was somehow absent. She hardly dared lean forward and touch his shoulder with her hand.

'Manuel!' She could hardly force her lips open. 'Manuel! Manuel!'

He raised his head, but it was not her he was looking at. He was gazing longingly at the tabernacle, and Lisbeth, in amazement, heard him murmuring: 'Come! Come out!'

Wasn't that precisely what she was supposed to be saying to him?

'Yes, come out, Manuel,' she echoed. 'The *curé* is going to shut the church.'

As if waking out of a wonderful dream, Manuel at last became aware of her and looked startled. Then he smiled and said: 'All right, I'm coming.' Almost immediately he added, as he got up: 'It's a lovely crib, isn't it?'

'Yes,' murmured Lisbeth, 'but come now.'

She took his hand, and they went down past the *curé* still standing in the front pew. Manuel didn't notice him, but the whore gave him a discreet nod, which he returned.

After he had watched them go, the priest remained alone in his dark church. Was he meditating on those things which have been revealed to the simple but hidden from the wise and understanding? Was he worried by Manuel's way of praying? Was he frightened by the wildness of his faith and love, which escaped from reason, habit and rules?

Out in the street Manuel went off hand in hand with Lisbeth, a Lisbeth who felt all small and who didn't dare to ask any questions. She thought of her ecstasy just now, before the arrival of the *curé*, and was filled with a nostalgic yearning for love and tenderness. Night had fallen, and through the closed shutters of the houses she could sense something of the warm, happy family life inside, or what she took to be such. In her own little cottage she could see her mother busying herself round the hearth in her long skirts, and her father sitting smoking his pipe beside the fire, as he did every evening. Was it before or after the death of Alexandre, her elder brother, who had gone off to sea as a cabin-boy and never come back, struck down by a fever on the other side of the world? It must have been after, because that was when her father started going downhill, dying slowly like a candle burning down. Her mother followed him before the year was out, and Lisbeth remained alone, looked after by old Aunt Agathe, a cantankerous spinster whose insufferable yoke she had fled by following the first young fellow she met to the bright lights of the big city. After that...

After that, Lisbeth had died and Gina was born. She tried to survive in the city, but she was at the mercy of her pimp, and there was little let-up. Until she had been given a break this Christmas, as a present, because she worked hard and she was a good sort, really. But she'd better be back the day after Christmas without fail: she'd be needed for the end of the holiday period when they should be doing a roaring trade.

'I have to go tomorrow, Manuel.'

'Go. Where to?' Manuel was quite taken aback, and he looked at Lisbeth as though he had never seen her before. 'Where are you going?'

'Paris.'

'Paris? Whatever for?'

Lisbeth tried to explain, but the words wouldn't come.

'Come along, let's get back.'

She took his hand again and they ran through the streets. Manuel enjoyed that, and seemed to have forgotten his question. When they got to the little cottage, they stirred the fire into life and lit the candles.

'Don't go,' said Manuel.

'But I must, Manuel, I really must.'

'Benoît has to go too. Angela said so.'

'There you are, then, you see.'

Manuel didn't see. He was heartbroken, and he started crying, with his head on Lisbeth's big white pillow.

'Don't cry...' Lisbeth sat by him, wiping away the tears as they rolled down his cheeks, until he went off to sleep. Then she got up, collected her few belongings and put them in her case, before tidying up the kitchen. When would she be able to come back again?

She had difficulty lying him down with all his clothes on and leaving enough room for her to lie next to him. She lay there looking at him, full of emotion, until she too drifted off into a light sleep. She woke up as soon as Manuel stirred. Whatever time could it be?

She watched as her strange lover got up, put on his jacket and tiptoed out of the room, as he had done the previous night. She lay absolutely still until she heard him going off down the street. Surely it was better for her to disappear while he was out? She got up, made the bed, had a quick wash, got dressed, tidied up, picked up her suitcase and left, double-locking the door. She left a note for Manuel, if he ever came back. The sun was rising, and her train, earlier than the one she had been intending to catch, left in half an hour.

Manuel had gone off to the sea. He stood for a long time looking at it before making his way, with his hands in his pockets, to the Villa Suiram. He was surprised to see lights on. Hadn't Angela gone to bed yet? He approached the house stealthily and looked in through a crack in the shutter.

Benoît was standing in the middle of the room under the light, rigged out in his leggings, his greatcoat and his cap. His suitcase was by the door. He was holding Angela in his arms. She was crying, and he was trying in vain to comfort her. Manuel couldn't hear what he was saying, but he gathered that Benoît was off for good, back to the war. Manuel immediately felt ashamed of the feeling that rose up from the depths of his being, an odious feeling of joy that made him blush. He suddenly remembered what the whore had said to him: 'I must go, Manuel.' Benoît was going, Lisbeth was going. A light dawned in his head: if Benoît was just on the point of leaving, then Lisbeth ... And he wasn't there to hold her in his arms and comfort her as Benoît was doing for Angela!

No sooner had the thought come to him than he turned and rushed off towards the sea, not caring how much noise he made. In the half-light, Manuel ran as fast as his legs would carry him, waking the sleepy streets as he went, until he stopped in front of the little cottage. The door was locked and the shutters closed, and all that was waiting for him was a small piece of white paper. He went up to the door and deciphered it: MUST GO. 'BYE MY CHRISTMAS PRESENT. GOD BLESS. L. Manuel didn't understand. He tore the paper off the door and read it again. Then he leaned his forehead against the doorpost and burst into tears. He didn't hear the shutters opening behind him, didn't see the heads being shaken or the knowing looks. Simply, like a child who has been unfairly punished, he cried his eyes out, oblivious to all but his own grief.

It was not until long after Benoît had left that Angela started wondering where Manuel was. She looked all round the house, then decided he must be with Fata Ioss and La Vieille. When he was not there either, they all went off together, first to Madamilla's house, then to the church, but it was deserted. Eventually they got to the sea-wall, where the cold wind whipping off the ocean caught their throats, and there they saw him, far away across the sand, sitting on his rock, motionless, and deaf to their shouts. They ran to him, even La Vieille and Madamilla, braving the icy water which was already lapping round Manuel's ankles.

'What on earth are you doing there, Manuel?'

The simpleton made no response to Fata Ioss' question, as if he hadn't heard it. The old man grabbed his shoulder and shook him: 'Manuel! Manuel!'

Manuel looked up at them all as if he had never seen them before in his life.

'Manuel!' Angela suddenly burst into tears, and that was what did it. He got up, took her in his arms and comforted her.

'Wherever have you been, Manuel?' sobbed Angela.

'With the whore,' he replied.

Madamilla and La Vieille, taken aback, exchanged glances. They all went off up the beach towards the sea-wall, taking Manuel with them.

When they had climbed up to the road, Fata Ioss explained to the women that that was what he had heard sailors call the sea. Angela and Manuel walked on in front, holding hands like children.

6

The days followed each other like the olive-wood beads on Madamilla's rosary. For the refugees from Lasting-en-Lorraine it was the
routine of exile, aggravated by the monotony of a war which
seemed to be making no progress but which they knew to be
ravaging their homes. Fata Ioss had put his Christmas crib away
in a box, and he could sometimes be seen with La Vieille, walking
up to the cemetery and standing by the graves of Millache'Babe
and Victor, the old man and the child of the exodus, its first victims
on a road whose destination was uncertain. They might meet Bêa-
Yasse'Kette, grumbling about the cold, a damp cold which got right
inside you, wherever you were.

'*Bi ouns dehêmm . . .*' (Back home, now . . .)

That was what she always said. Then they might go round
together by the Villa Suiram, where Angela was spending more
and more time in the house. She still lay awake at night sobbing,
or so Manuel said. In the daytime, old Siébert of Siébert's Mill
came to see her with increasing regularity: he had quite taken to
her since his son had spilled the beans. He sat down by the stove,
just as he presumably did in his own house, and he didn't stop
talking until it was time for him to get up and go. He had worked
everything out in his head, had their future as a family all planned
out, and he told them about it at great length, for hours at a
stretch. Manuel was astonished to see it all laid out in front of

his eyes like that. Sometimes he had doubts about what the old man was saying, because after all who knows what tomorrow may bring? But he said nothing and went on listening. Old Siébert seemed so happy to be able to talk away to someone.

One Sunday, after Mass, the *curé* beckoned to Fata Ioss to join him in the sacristy. He told him that he had found Manuel in the church on Christmas evening, in the company of a woman whom he did not recognize. Fata Ioss said that he didn't know any more than the *curé* did, but that he would keep his eyes open, and he thanked him for the information.

'It would be such a pity, wouldn't it,' added the *curé*, 'if such a pious, pure lad...'

'Yes, yes, of course,' said Fata Ioss, rolling his hat between his fingers. Manuel's words about 'with the whore' were drumming inside his head, but he said nothing and took his leave.

La Vieille, Madamilla and Bêa-Yasse'Kette were waiting for him outside to find out what the *curé* had had to say. Fata Ioss was surprised to notice that his hat was shaking in his hand, and he hastily put it on.

'He said... that he had found Manuel praying on his own in the church again at night.'

'*Ma konne doch nid ôônbênne!*' (But we can hardly keep him tied up!) said Bêa-Yasse'Kette.

'Anyway, why shouldn't he go and pray in the church like anyone else?' demanded Madamilla.

They were astonished to hear Fata Ioss muttering: '... You just don't find women like that in church...'

Had he realized that he had said that aloud? At any rate, he gave his arm to La Vieille as if nothing had happened, and they went off up the street, with Madamilla and Bêa-Yasse'Kette following.

That afternoon he went round to the Villa Suiram, and was furious when he found that old Siébert of Siébert's Mill was already there. He'd be sleeping there next!

'Ioss! Hello there! Just the man I wanted to see.'

'Why? What's up?'

'Don't you ever read the papers? Haven't you heard...?'

No, Fata Ioss hadn't heard that the French troops massed on the Belgian frontier had broken ranks in the middle of January, that the soldiers were demanding wireless sets, musical instruments, sleeping bags, books, that it was 20 degrees below at the front and 25 below in Alsace—25 below!—and that they had held open-air masses at midnight under the snow-laden fir trees.

'Didn't you know there was a war on, Ioss?'

But Fata Ioss was wondering why on earth the *curé* had waited so long, more than six weeks, to tell him about that woman Manuel had been with in the church.

'D'you know what?' shouted old Siébert, brandishing a letter in his bony hand. 'Some of our lads managed to get as far as Forbach! Benoît has written and told me all about it. One of his friends was there.'

Manuel, who was sitting in the corner next to Angela, grinned.

'Just you listen to this! "Very early in the morning, about four o'clock, three platoons of chasseurs set off for Forbach. The town had been evacuated. One platoon under Lieutenant Agnely and Lieutenant Darnand advanced to the edge of the town, covered by the other two. They occupied two buildings by the main road, with instructions to observe what was going on. Guess what they saw! Germans, sentries, soldiers reading the newspaper, a gang of forty men on fatigue duty laying booby-traps, officers (including a Kommandant) coming to inspect them... All sorts of things. It was all going fine and they were waiting until it was dark to get back, but then a couple of looters entered one of the houses. Sergeant Polverelli dealt with them, but the Germans down below heard the shots. I don't know why he had to shoot them. There must have been some other way, surely? Anyhow, along come the SS, and our lads had to run for it, through gardens and over walls and fences, which held them up badly. It took them more than five hours to get back, and they lost a lot of men. Lieutenant Agnely was killed, and Sergeant Baroni with a couple of men managed to get his body back. They buried him with some of the others at Morsbach. General Laure was there, and he pinned the Legion of Honour on Agnely's corpse. Major Gérodias was there too, and so was Father Bruckberger, who gave absolution to the men who had gone to get the body. So that's what's been happening in our sector, and I thought I'd write and tell you about it straight away." '

Old Siébert stopped reading and looked across at Fata Ioss as if to say: 'Well! How about that, then?' Fata Ioss couldn't stop rubbing his painful knees with the palms of his hands and muttering: 'Well I never! Well I never!'

Angela was crying quietly to herself. When old Siébert noticed, he asked in surprise: 'What's the matter with you, then?'

'Benoît might have been with them!' she sobbed.

'But they're heroes, think of that, my girl!'

'But he might have been killed!'

The old man was momentarily nonplussed. Manuel spoke up: 'Why did they have to kill people? You shouldn't kill people. You should love them.'

'Because it's war, that's why!' Benoît's father couldn't take any more. He stood up and said to Fata Ioss: 'Come on, Ioss, let's take a turn outside.'

Once they were on the doorstep he grumbled: 'You can't talk to her about anything like that. As for the lad . . .' and he tapped his forehead with his finger.

'But he's right, you know,' protested Fata Ioss.

Old Siébert turned and stared at him in blank incomprehension.

'He is, he's quite right.'

From behind the curtain Manuel watched them as they walked off down the street. Now why had Fata Ioss come round today? They'd have to wait to find out. He turned to Angela and said: 'I'm just going out for a bit.'

She was still sitting down, wiping away the last of her tears. She was looking enormous.

'Don't stay out too long, Manuel.'

'No, I won't.'

And off he went, down to the sea, with his hands in his pockets, holding the whore's note in his fingers. When he got to the end of the street, in full view of the ocean which had completely covered the flat rock, he took the piece of paper out, unfolded it and read it for the umpteenth time. 'God bless.'

Manuel stood and looked at the maze of narrow streets, but this time he didn't plunge into it as he sometimes did, ending up looking stupidly at the empty cottage, but set off instead towards the town centre. Soon he was pushing open the door of the church and, when he had checked that it was deserted, he went and crouched down right underneath the tabernacle again.

Angela was waiting for him, hunched up on the chair by the window. She was in pain and unable even to drag herself to the villa and ask for help. When she saw him coming up the road she opened the window and gesticulated until he started running.

'Quickly, Manuel, go to La Vieille and tell her to come with the midwife. Hurry!'

Manuel got the message. The baby was coming. He ran like the wind to Fata Ioss' house and hammered on the door like a madman until he came to open up.

'What's up, my lad?' grumbled Fata Ioss over his shoulder as he went back inside. 'Fire or something?'

'Yes ... I mean no ...' Manuel was out of breath. 'It's the baby. Angela and Benoît's. It's coming.'

'Oh, is that it? You had me frightened.' The old man turned

and called: 'Mother! Mother! Quick, you're needed round at Angela's. The baby's coming.'

La Vieille appeared, all flustered, pulling a shawl round her shoulders.

'Ioss, you go off and get the midwife, and Manuel, you run round to Madamilla's. We may need her.'

'You're not going to try . . . ?' said Fata Ioss doubtfully.

'Why not?' she retorted. 'Go along with you! There's no reason why I shouldn't!' And off she sped down the street without even bothering to lock the house.

Manuel had already gone. Ioss turned the key in the lock before setting off in his turn.

When La Vieille arrived at the little house next to the Villa Suiram, she found Angela slumped on the chair by the window.

'How are you feeling, my dear?'

'Bad, bad . . .'

'Come along, let's try to get you on to the bed.'

It was as much as La Vieille could do to lift Angela off the chair and help her to the bedroom.

'The midwife's on her way.'

But Madamilla arrived first, despite being old and bent, preceded by Manuel who hadn't had the patience to stay with her.

'Where's the baby?'

'Patience, my lad, it doesn't happen as fast as that. Why don't you stay in the kitchen, you'll be all right there.'

But Manuel was already by Angela's bedside. He laid his cool hand on her clammy forehead and looked at her as if he was seeing her for the first time. Angela tried to smile at him. Then she gasped: 'Go and see if Fata Ioss is on his way.'

'All right.'

Fata Ioss and the midwife were just at the end of the street.

'Hurry up!' shouted Manuel.

When the midwife was safely installed, Ioss took Manuel by

the arm: 'Come on, my lad, we'll go off for a bit of a walk, down to the sea.' Manuel seemed reluctant, so he added: 'Come along, this is women's work, and we'd best leave them to it.'

Side by side they set off towards the sea-wall. Fata Ioss couldn't think how to begin. He'd never have another opportunity like it, though.

'Manuel... At Christmas, you weren't at home. Oh, I quite understand,' he hastened to add. 'You weren't with us either. We've often wondered, Angela and Mother and I... Angela didn't dare ask you straight out, you see, after the... I'm sure you understand. Anyway, my lad, where were you that night?'

For a long time Manuel said nothing, and Fata Ioss didn't know whether to try again. After several minutes' silence, he added: 'The *curé* told me he'd seen you in church the next day with a woman.'

Manuel still said nothing.

'Where were you?'

'I've already told you, with the whore.'

It was quite true, he had already told him.

'Manuel, I don't quite understand. What whore?'

'Lisbeth.'

'And you were in church with her?'

'Yes.'

'All on your own?'

'Yes. I was her Christmas present.'

'Manuel...'

Fata Ioss didn't know what to say. Was Manuel even aware what a whore was? As if recalling a wonderful memory, Manuel's face suddenly lit up and he murmured: 'Blessed are the pure in heart, for they shall see God.'

The old man was stupefied. What on earth was all that about? 'You didn't...?' But no, he couldn't probe any further. God alone... 'Come along,' he said gruffly as if talking to himself, 'it's

175

time we were getting back. Perhaps the baby . . .'

As soon as Fata Ioss mentioned the baby, Manuel wanted to run.

'Hang on! Wait for me! I'm not as young as you, remember.'

Behind them they could hear the sound of the sea. When they finally got back to the Villa Suiram after a silent walk which seemed interminable to Manuel, they could hear women's voices in the kitchen. Manuel stood anxiously on the doorstep, not daring to go inside. Fata Ioss gave him a push, and at the same moment there came a cry from the back room, a loud one, and then another, more fragile and hesitant.

'Angela!' shouted Manuel, and he shot inside despite Fata Ioss who tried to restrain him. As he got to the door of the bedroom the midwife came out carrying a red baby in her arms.

'Angela!'

'Let her rest, young man,' said the midwife in a tone that brooked no argument. 'She needs it.'

Manuel reluctantly complied.

'Come and have a look at your little nephew instead.'

'The baby . . .'

'Yes, come and see the baby,' agreed Madamilla as she brought the basin full of warm water.

The midwife looked at Fata Ioss standing idle on the doorstep. 'Go and put some wood on the fire, Fata Ioss, and shut the door, do,' she said. 'In weather like this . . .'

La Vieille went off to shut the door while Fata Ioss came in without a word and started dealing with the stove.

Manuel was standing next to the midwife who at last folded back the blanket to reveal the baby.

' . . . Baby . . . Baby . . .' He was thrilled. 'He's gorgeous!'

Madamilla thought it looked rather crumpled.

The midwife took the baby and held it in the basin with her left hand while washing it delicately with the other.

La Vieille had disappeared into Angela's room.

Madamilla was ready with some wraps.

'Swaddling clothes, like baby Jesus,' said Manuel.

'Yes, just like baby Jesus,' said the midwife, 'except that this one was born a little later.'

La Vieille came back into the kitchen, plucked Manuel's sleeve and took him off to the bedroom.

'What's he going to be called, then?' asked Fata Ioss.

Manuel, coming back unseen into the room, replied: 'His name is Sébastien Benoît Emmanuel.'

'Sébastien?'

'Yes: Sébastien Benoît Emmanuel.'

'Sébastien's a lovely name!' said the midwife as she wrapped the baby up.

'Lovely,' echoed Manuel, and then: 'Sébastien is lovely.'

'Let's take him to his mummy. Come on!'

Although she was still feeling tired and weak, Angela gave a big smile as she took the child. The midwife went off to the kitchen and left the three of them alone together. For the first time.

'Our Father,' said Manuel.

'Our Father,' repeated Angela in a whisper.

'Thank you,' said Manuel.

'Thank you.'

Out in the kitchen the women were making arrangements: La Vieille would stay that night, Madamilla would take over in the morning, and the midwife would come too.

'What about Manuel?' someone asked.

'His place is here,' replied Fata Ioss. 'Anyway, you'd never get him to budge. I'll go and tell old Siébert.'

'All right,' said La Vieille, 'but for goodness' sake don't let him come here before tomorrow. We musn't tire Angela.'

We musn't tire Angela. It was that thought that would prevail in Manuel's mind and make him go to bed that night as soon as

Angela dozed off and little Sébastien was soundly asleep.

'He's lovely.'

'Yes, he is, isn't he? But it's time we all went to bed.' La Vieille could hardly stand up straight, she was so tired.

'Good night, Manuel.'

'Good night, good night, Mother.' It moved her deeply that Manuel should call her Mother, like Fata Ioss. 'Good night, my boy.'

But she was still busy in the kitchen when Manuel was already snoring. She peeped round Angela's door once more just to check that all was well, that mother and baby didn't need anything. Then she went out and stood on the doorstep for a while before finally lying down for a few hours of sleep in a strange bed.

... A strange bed. As she lay in the darkness trying to get to sleep, La Vieille smiled at that thought. Did she ever sleep in a bed that was not strange these days? No doubt tonight it was the unaccustomed absence of Fata Ioss beside her that made her particularly aware of the strangeness; no doubt the presence of her husband was what helped to preserve a sense of familiar, domestic life. Fata Ioss. Was he feeling equally bereft tonight? La Vieille was suddenly frightened. Perhaps he would start drinking again tonight, after managing to stay sober ever since Lidrezing. Oughtn't she to ...? No, she must stay here, with Angela. Well, it was in God's hands. She tossed and turned on her mattress and, just as sleep came, she heard the voice of Sébastien from the bedroom, still hesitant but imperious as a summons. She got up quietly without complaining.

Next morning she was woken from her sleep by Madamilla.

'I went round to see Bêa-Yasse'Kette,' she said as she took off her coat. 'She'd never have forgiven me if I hadn't told her the news. And she's keen to take her turn. She'll be here this afternoon.'

Angela had had a quiet night. Manuel was still asleep, and the two women were sitting on their own in the kitchen making coffee when Bêa-Yasse'Kette burst in in an agitated state.

'I thought you weren't...'

'*Do droumm géds nimmé!*' (Never mind that!) she interrupted. 'Fata Ioss...'

'What is it?' exclaimed La Vieille, jumping up from her chair. 'Oh, I do hope nothing's happened to him! Oh dear, oh dear!'

'*So shlimm ish's ââ vila nid!*' (It's not as bad as all that!)

All that had happened was that old Bêa-Yasse'Kette had found him dead drunk by the church porch when she went to fetch bread.

'Oh dear, oh dear!' sighed La Vieille. 'That's all it needed. I wondered last night if that might happen.'

Bêa-Yasse'Kette had tried to get him home, but it was no good. He wouldn't hear of it. What he wanted was to go into the church, but luckily the door was still locked. So she had run here, knowing she would find La Vieille, and...

'What's up?'

Manuel was standing in the doorway, his blond hair all tousled. They hadn't heard him coming.

'*Gââ nix!*' (Oh, nothing!) said Bêa-Yasse'Kette. She wasn't going to reveal Fata Ioss' unfortunate lapse to the lad!

'What's the matter? Is Angela...?'

'Angela's still asleep,' said Madamilla, 'and so is Sébastien.'

Manuel smiled at the name.

'Manuel...'

'Yes, Mother?'

La Vieille hesitated, then plucked up courage and said: 'Fata Ioss is by the door of the church. He's been drinking. You're the only person...'

'All right, Mother, I'll go.' Manuel passed his fingers though his hair and put on his jacket.

'Take him back home if you can. I'll go straight there.'

Manuel shot off, leaving Bêa-Yasse'Kette speechless, and disappeared round the corner, passing old Siébert without even noticing him.

'I'm off,' said La Vieille, barely responding to the old man's greeting as she came out of the door.

Manuel reached the church to find Fata Ioss negotiating with the *curé*.

'But monsieur Josse...'

'No! No! No! No b..buts! I'm g..going to take the B..Blessed Sac..Sacrament in p..procession d..down to the sea!'

'Monsieur Josse, monsieur Josse! You've been drinking!'

The priest was outraged. Then he saw Manuel the simpleton coming towards him like an apparition. That was all he needed, the old drunkard and now the God-eater!

'Fata Ioss, come!' said Manuel, putting his hand on the old man's arm.

'That's right, my lad, you take him away.'

'In the church!'

'Oh, no you don't!'

But Manuel was already past him, with Fata Ioss clinging to his arm. The *curé* followed them anxiously up the nave, not knowing what to do, and casting imploring glances at the statues of saints as he went past.

'Look here, just stop a minute!'

Manuel and the old drunkard had gone into the choir and up the steps of the high altar, where they at last stopped, closely pursued by the *curé*.

'You sit down over there, Fata Ioss, next to him.'

Ioss staggered over and collapsed on the steps.

The *curé* gave a worried look back down the nave to the open door, hoping that none of his parishioners would choose that moment to come in.

Manuel stood motionless, gazing at the closed tabernacle with eyes full of love, desire and expectancy. Had he forgotten Fata Ioss and the *curé*? His face was radiant, as if a light had shone on it from heaven, and the priest had the impression that he too was bathed in that light, and the old man as well.

'Manuel...' He didn't hear the *curé* whispering his name. He didn't hear anything. All he was aware of was the light. Could he still see the tabernacle or the walls of the choir? The priest looked with a kind of awe at his eyes, filled with a huge, wild joy. He bent towards Fata Ioss. 'Can you... Can you see?'

Fata Ioss lifted his head, as though he had suddenly sobered up, and looked first at Manuel, then at the *curé*, then at Manuel again, noticing his absent air, as if he was somehow no longer with them, but had been caught up and taken elsewhere.

'Manuel!' He couldn't hold back what sounded like a cry for help. 'Manuel!'

A shudder ran through Manuel. The *curé* was certain, he saw it quite distinctly, just as he saw the light dim as at the onset of dusk.

'Manuel!' The third time Fata Ioss called his name, Manuel at last heard and lifted his hand and placed it slowly on the old man's bowed head.

The *curé* couldn't believe his eyes or his ears when he heard Manuel say quietly but perfectly audibly: 'Your sin is forgiven, Fata Ioss, for you loved much.' Then, after a long silence: 'Go, and do not sin again.'

'I won't, never again,' murmured Fata Ioss, quite overcome.

'But look here...' The *curé* could get no further. Manuel turned and looked at him, and in that look he could see the incredible joy with which his heart was overflowing. Strange and wonderful thoughts passed through the *curé*'s head as he accompanied the two men back down the nave.

'Goodbye, Father. And sorry.'

'Not at all, monsieur Josse, not at all. Goodbye . . . Goodbye, my lad.'

He went back and sat down in one of the pews of his deserted church and started thinking. It was not easy. By what authority had the simpleton forgiven the drunkard's sin? Could it be true, as he had once read while he was in seminary, that the power to forgive sins could be given to an unordained . . . *saint?* He hesitated to use the word. Surely their village idiot couldn't be a saint, could he? He was just a fool . . . A fool? Was the greatness of man not precisely in his folly? That folly which might be the Spirit present in the heart of man? Perhaps Manuel's simpleness allowed that folly freer rein in him . . . His simplicity, his childishness. Perhaps his heart was like a blank sheet on which God could write directly, in letters of fire. But in that case . . .

The *curé*'s hand unconsciously but firmly rubbed his chin, his cheeks, his forehead, as though trying to remould his anxious features.

Meanwhile Manuel had take Fata Ioss home, with the old man managing to walk almost straight. La Vieille couldn't believe her eyes when she saw them. The most surprising thing of all was the smile they both had on their lips, a smile of complicity. And when she thought of just how much schnapps her husband had consumed—look at the bottle!—her astonishment knew no bounds.

'Ioss!'

'He won't do it again, Mother, he's promised,' said Manuel with such compassion in his eyes that she was moved to tears. Then he went in, leaving the old couple to follow together.

'Mother . . .' stammered Fata Ioss. That was as far as he could get.

'Bring me your schnapps, Fata Ioss, all of it.'

Ioss looked at his wife doubtfully but then obeyed Manuel's strange command. The few bottles that he had managed to salvage from the shipwreck of the exodus were lined up on the table. Manuel took the first one, most of which Fata Ioss had drunk the previous night, and put it to his lips.

'Manuel!' shouted La Vieille and Fata Ioss in unison.

'What?'

'It's poison, or it is for you, anyhow!'

'There you are, you see, Fata Ioss.' And he calmly poured the contents of the bottle down the sink under the old man's incredulous gaze. He did the same with the second bottle, and the third. When he came to the last one, Fata Ioss stepped forward.

'What about your rheumatics, Mother?' he asked plaintively.

Mother said nothing. Manuel proceeded to open the last bottle and pour it away. The gurgling of the precious liquid seemed to dance drunkenly in Fata Ioss' ears, but he managed to keep smiling. A heady smell, like that of a distillery, filled the room.

'Time I was off,' said Manuel at last. 'Angela and the baby will be awake by now.' And off he went down the corridor before La Vieille or Fata Ioss could say a word.

He ran to the house and his feet scarcely touched the ground. When he got to the kitchen he found Madamilla bustling about and old Siébert sitting in a corner with the child on his knees. Angela smiled at him through the open bedroom door.

They were going to be so happy together!

7

Sébastien was christened the following Sunday. The *curé* kept his eyes fixed on Manuel throughout the ceremony, but in vain. The face of the young godfather displayed nothing unusual: it was simply radiant with joy. Old Siébert of Siébert's Mill was none too pleased that Manuel should have been asked to be godfather. He had had one of his cousins in mind, but Angela would have none of it.

She had written to Benoît the day after the birth to tell him the happy news. All week she had been hoping against hope that he would be given special leave to attend the baptism, but she was disappointed.

At the celebration meal, for which La Vieille, Fata Ioss, Madamilla and Bêa-Yasse'Kette joined Angela, Manuel and the baby, grandfather Siébert dominated proceedings, talking endlessly about the war. 'Did you hear how well our soldiers were treated at Christmas? Quarter of a pound of ham apiece, a cigar, an orange, and a bottle of champagne between four! France knows how to look after her sons!'

Bêa-Yasse'Kette nodded in agreement, but really in the hope of making him shut up or at least change the subject. She even tried saying: *'De klêêne va so brââf ênn de kiaish!'* (Wasn't the baby good in the church!) But it was no good. The old man didn't even hear.

'Morale is high on our side, so the *Boches* had better keep their heads down!'

Fata Ioss ate in silence. From time to time he glanced at Manuel and smiled. La Vieille helped Angela back to bed, while Madamilla changed Sébastien and wrapped him up again. Only three men were left round the table, and old Siébert was on about the Communists. He was still talking about them when he left the house with Fata Ioss, late in the afternoon.

Benoît came home on forty-eight hours' leave the next Sunday. Angela wept for joy. They gazed at their little son together, and Benoît talked about the future. Manuel commented to himself that Benoît's plans were very different from his father's. Later, Manuel looked after the baby for a bit so that Angela and Benoît could have some time on their own.

He cradled little Sébastien in his arms and rocked him, and it was his own dream that he was cradling at the same time. He couldn't help thinking of Lisbeth the whore, of her soft, warm body, of her sad heart, of her loneliness. The tears rolled silently down his cheeks, and he made no effort to wipe them away. As he rocked the child, his eyes staring at the dusk falling in the little courtyard outside, it was the coming night that he was holding in his arms, and forgotten tenderness, and love.

When Angela came into the kitchen she was surprised to find his eyes full of tears. 'What's the matter, Manuel?' But he shook his head: no, nothing was the matter.

That night, he slipped out of the house unseen and ran down to the sea. The waves were lashing the sea-wall, and at one point he got drenched, but he hardly noticed. His salt tears mingled with the salt of the ocean. Then he turned and plunged into a maze of tiny streets until he reached a small, abandoned cottage. He leaned his head against the locked door and remained there for much of the night, weeping, and waiting for one who would not come. At first light he crept back into the house like a thief. When

Benoît left, Manuel had to be woken up to say goodbye to him.

'We're going to get married in the spring, Manuel, in May! Isn't that wonderful!' Angela's eyes were sparkling through her tears as she told her brother the exciting news. 'May! It's not long to wait: Sébastien will be just three months.'

She was so happy in the midst of her sadness that Manuel threw his arms round her neck and gave her a kiss. Then they both hurried to the bedroom to see the baby, who had just woken up.

In the days that followed, and the weeks that passed like days, the child occupied them fully, and their lives were regulated by the rhythm of his tiny life.

The women came less often, except for La Vieille who still accompanied Fata Ioss when he came to read with Manuel from the book. Ever since the scene in the church, when the simpleton had forgiven his sin, the old man had had a new respect for Manuel, and he sometimes looked at him as if he came from another world, as if he knew something that no one else did, as if his mere presence in the kitchen was somehow miraculous. Manuel didn't appear to notice, and he carried on living quite normally, overjoyed to have the baby there.

Every time old Siébert encountered Fata Ioss on one of his visits he brought up the subject of the war. He discussed the decision to ban the Communist deputies and then to bring them to trial. He talked and talked, oblivious to the signs of spring. Yet the buds were bursting in all the little gardens along the street, the air was sweet and getting warmer in the evenings, and the refugees were beginning to linger outside on the doorstep now that the days were starting to lengthen.

'Do you realize, Fata Ioss?'

Did he realize? Finland seemed so far away and, even when Denmark and Norway were invaded, what could he hope to do about it, when M. Reynaud and the Allied forces seemed powerless?

'Oh yes, I realize...'

'Do you think...?'

The moment old Siébert had his back turned, Fata Ioss started dreaming about spring in Lasting-en-Lorraine, spring which would be surprised this year to find the land abandoned and the gardens neglected.

Perhaps there had been no one to see the snowdrops in front of the grotto of Our Lady of Lourdes in the churchyard, great clumps of them, flowering and then passing over, unappreciated. Had anyone been to pick violets under the hedges in the Waldagasse, or gather bunches of primroses in the Pré aux Pucelles, or the short-lasting cowslips by the fountain at Ruchling? There would have been no one by the Hume early in the morning, feeling the buds bursting with sap, no one on the Gréderich, no one on the Athisberg, no one down in the valley of the Sime to dig the allotments on either side of the stream.

The lilac must be coming into flower now, draping its heavy bunches over the warm tiles of the shed in the courtyard. Were there still any stray cats left to sun themselves by the roadside? If so, would they see anything growing in the gardens, any peas, any beans, any lettuces? There was no one to sow, no one to look after the vegetables. And it would soon be the middle of May, and time for the cherry trees to burst forth in their splendid blossom, gracing the empty fields and hillsides, the abandoned village, and the soft spring night whose only inhabitant might be a lovesick nightingale.

Quite distressed, Fata Ioss bent his head and discreetly wiped away a tear with the back of his hand. Would this stupid war never end? When would they be able to go back home, dig and rake the soil—heavy up on the hillside and sandy down in the valleys—cut the young grass, breathe, and live again?

Easter was long past, early that year, just as spring was early, and it was already nearly Whitsun. Nothing seemed to be happening at the Front, whatever old Siébert might say. Benoît was quite clear on that score in his letters, most of which were devoted to plans for the wedding.

'Fata Ioss! I say, Ioss!'

Fata Ioss was on his way down to the sea that Friday lunchtime, and was surprised to hear his name being called.

'Wait for me, Ioss! I've got some news for you!' Old Siébert came puffing up behind him. 'Things are beginning to happen over there,' and he waved his hand in the general direction of the east. 'Apparently the *Boches* are on the move, and they've invaded Luxemburg, and last night they attacked Belgium.' He waved a sheaf of newspapers.

'Don't tell Angela. That's where Benoît is, up in the Ardennes.'

'It's just as well,' the old man carried on, paying no attention to Fata Ioss, 'it had to come some time. And fancy them attacking just where we expected! They're in for a hiding, I can tell you.'

'Don't tell Angela.'

'Why ever not? It's good news!'

'Look, Benoît, your son, is up there.'

'That's true.'

The two men walked on in silence for a few moments towards the sea. It was obvious that old Siébert was put out by the other's lack of enthusiasm.

'We'll get them,' he growled, and left Fata Ioss to carry on alone.

Next day Fata Ioss found him in the kitchen with Angela, surrounded by papers. It was a glorious day, Whit Saturday, and the streets were full of people doing their shopping for the holiday weekend.

'Ioss, it says here that the Dutch and the Belgians are resisting the German advance, so our boys will be all right.'

Over by the stove, Angela was clearly very upset. Fata Ioss was furious with the old man, but he managed to hide it.

'It says they're blazing away and that Stukas are falling like flies all round them! They're doing a grand job.' Ioss nodded but said nothing.

Old Siébert proceeded to tell them about a countess who had managed, with the help of her people, to capture the crew of a German plane that had come down on her estate.

Manuel listened solemnly, holding Sébastien in his arms. What thoughts were going through his mind?

In church next day, Fata Ioss saw him going up for communion with his face streaming with tears. He didn't dare ask him afterwards in the square, where old Siébert was brandishing the newspapers and holding forth about a German offensive in the Ardennes.

The refugees stood about in groups and talked and talked. The sky was clear and bright that Whitsunday afternoon, the twelfth of May, 1940, and Bêa-Yasse'Kette shouted across the square: *'Dehêmm bliye beshdimmd de ebbl'bêêm!'* (The apple trees'll be in blossom now, back home!) But nobody was listening.

Fata Ioss could see Manuel wandering from group to group, with the tears still coursing unchecked down his face. As he passed close to him, he thought he heard him murmuring Benoît's name, but he couldn't be sure. People were staring at him in amazement.

At lunchtime, Manuel was late back. He had been down to the sea, just long enough for his tears to dry up when faced with the hugeness of the salty ocean.

'Why are you so late, Manuel? Nothing's happened, has it?'

'Oh, no! Where's Sébastien?'

'Are you sure nothing's happened?'

'Of course I'm sure.'

But Angela could tell that her brother was being evasive.

'Come on, eat your soup: it's delicious! Were they talking about the war again in the square?'

Manuel nodded.

'What were they talking about?'

'They were talking about bombing raids on the northern Front...'

'Oh, no!'

'Come on, Angela, eat up. Your soup's getting cold.'

In the afternoon, La Vieille and Fata Ioss came to keep them company. Then Bêa-Yasse'Kette arrived, still talking of apple-blossom: *'Mouss dass so shéén sinn!'* (It must be so pretty!)

Manuel closed his eyes. On Monday, Tuesday, Wednesday, Thursday and Friday, every day of that fateful week, old Siébert of Siébert's Mill made his way to the annexe of the Villa Suiram with the newspapers under his arm. He believed he had encouraging news: 'In Belgium, our forces have successfully counterattacked!' he announced. 'The *Boches* are retreating, d'you hear that, retreating! And anyway, Belgium is a long way from home.'

Angela breathed a little more freely.

'The Front stretches 400 kilometres from the Moselle to the Zuiderzee,' he read out on his next visit. 'Wherever's the Zuiderzee, now?'

Nobody knew. Two days later he was rather less cocky. 'Repeated enemy attacks along the Front between Sedan and the Meuse.'

Angela winced.

'The Dutch have surrendered.'

Silence.

'How could they?' The old man was appalled.

On the sixteenth, the news came that the enemy had managed to cross the Meuse at several points.

'Let's hope our men remembered to blow up the bridges behind them!'

On the seventeenth, it was fighting everywhere. By the Saturday morning, old Siébert was beginning to make comparisons with the 1914–18 war, and he could be heard muttering: 'That's just like 1916! That's how it was in '18!' But they didn't quite know what to make of it.

On Sunday, after church, he spoke of the Marne. 'They'll never get across the Marne! Never! Never!'

Later on he would evoke Verdun, and the Somme. That must have been in the course of the following week. 'They'll never cross the Somme. Their heavy tanks won't get any further. And anyway, even if they did, our forces are lined up on the other side waiting for them. They'd give them a roasting!'

But he no longer sounded so confident, and he no longer came to the house so often to hold his grandson. He couldn't cope with the anguished look in Angela's eyes.

Was it the following Sunday that the first carload of refugees arrived in the square? Those from Lasting-en-Lorraine couldn't understand what was happening to begin with. Did that mean that they were no longer the only refugees? They pressed round the driver who gave them all the details. Gradually they began to register: it was the whole of France that was going to constitute the people of the exodus. It had already begun in the north and the east.

The man spoke of the air raids at dawn on the tenth of May: 'It couldn't have been worse if the sky had caved in, that's all I can say! It was raining bombs!'

He described the rush of air that told you a bomb was coming, the ear-shattering noise as it exploded, the soldiers running for cover.

'But you don't run for cover if you're a French soldier!'

'Come off it, grandad, you'd have done the same.'

Old Siébert of Siébert's Mill was livid. His Benoît never ran for cover. But no one took any notice of him: their ears were glued to what the driver was saying.

Everybody was getting out, apparently. Looting was commonplace. People saw spies everywhere. 'Disguised as nuns, think of that!' And he told them the story of the Sister of Charity whose ample head-dress concealed the ugly mug of a German officer. 'They dealt with him all right, I can tell you!'

Then he reverted to the dreadful bombings, telling them about the little spy plane which always looked so harmless but which prepared the way for the squadrons of Stukas.

'Well, why don't they get on and shoot it down, then?'

'Just go and see for yourself, grandad!'

He described how columns of refugees had been machine-gunned on the roads, ending up in a tangle in the ditch, with a woman ripped right open, still clutching her little daughter in her arms, and children wandering about lost, and animals everywhere, abandoned and terrified.

'*Genau vi bi ouns!*'

The man stared at Bêa-Yasse'Kette in disbelief. Had he, or had he not, just heard her speak German? Who was she? But when he mentioned the word spy, they all laughed at him. As for Bêa-Yasse'Kette herself, she rushed off to find La Vieille.

'*So ebbes! So ebbes!*' (Well I never! Well I never!) The driver watched her go. 'Are you sure...?'

"Course we are! She's one of the refugees from Lorraine.' By the time he restarted his limousine, he had sown consternation in the hearts of all the inhabitants of Châtelaillon-Plage, whether refugees or permanent residents.

'What if he was making it up?' old Siébert wondered aloud. But he wasn't making it up. That much was obvious over the next few days, as more cars arrived, full of refugees.

One of them stopped in the square, and someone asked for Benoît Siébert's father.

'There's his young wife too, of course, but it'd be better...' The man was taken to Fata Ioss.

'You Benoît Siébert's father?'

'No, but I know where to find him.'

Fata Ioss understood, and he sent La Vieille round to be with Angela before setting out himself.

The old man had seen them coming, and he was waiting for them on the doorstep.

'You Benoît Siébert's father?'

'Yes.'

'Right, well ... I've got a mate who was with Benoît, and when he heard I was coming down this way, he told me to tell you ... Benoît was killed by a bomb on Whitsunday.'

Fata Ioss immediately had a picture of Manuel's face bathed in tears. Old Siébert had turned away.

'It happened in the morning. Benoît had gone out to help a friend. That's when ...'

'At least he didn't die hiding.' Those were his father's first words.

'No, that's true, he didn't ...' The man took something out of his pocket. 'Look, here's his penknife. My mate said: "That's for his wife, or rather for his son, for Sébastien." That's it, that's what he said: I remembered the name.'

At the name Sébastien, old Siébert suddenly broke down. Fata Ioss and the messenger looked away. The man hesitated, before saying: 'I must be going. They're waiting for me in the square. We're going on further. Not that there's much point: we've had it. Sorry and all that, but ...'

The old man went inside and came back with a bottle of schnapps which he gave to the messenger. 'Thanks for coming,' he said. 'Thanks a lot. Goodbye.'

'Goodbye.' And off he went without a backward glance. After a while Fata Ioss said: 'Come on, we've got to go and tell her.'

The old man was clutching Benoît's penknife in his hand. 'I shan't even be able to visit his grave,' he muttered. Fata Ioss didn't reply. When they arrived at the little house next to the Villa

Suiram, Manuel was waiting for them outside. He had been on the lookout for them ever since La Vieille had come.

'Benoît's dead,' he said.

Old Siébert stared at him in amazement.

'Who on earth told you?'

'He died on Whitsunday, during Mass.'

'Does she know?'

'No, I haven't dared tell her.'

Angela came out. 'What's the matter?'

'It's Benoît...' stammered the old man, and the tears started to flow again, quietly.

'Benoît...' Angela repeated the name of her beloved, and everything swam in her head: the wedding, the war, death.

'He's dead,' said Manuel.

La Vieille was holding Sébastien in her arms. Angela let out a cry, a taut, tense cry. Then, as white as the shroud that would never cover Benoît's body, she turned away, tottered to her room and collapsed on to the bed as though dead herself. It seemed an eternity before the sobs came, convulsing her whole body and giving expression to the grief of her heart.

'I'll stay with her,' said Manuel.

Little Sébastien had begun to cry too. Old Siébert patted his cheek with his big horny hand as he murmured: 'Sébastien... Benoît... Sébastien...' and the tears trickled down his wrinkled face.

Fata Ioss was at a loss to know what to do. La Vieille hunted in the folds of her big apron for a handkerchief. In the bedroom Manuel had laid his hand on Angela's head. 'He's dead,' he said in a low voice, 'so he's alive.' Listening to him, his sister redoubled her sobs. 'He's alive. He who believes in me, though he die, yet shall he live.'

Out in the kitchen La Vieille gulped: 'They could have been so happy together.'

Fata Ioss said nothing. Old Siébert of Siébert's Mill turned his son's knife over and over in his fingers.

'Cry, Angela, cry,' said Manuel. 'He will wipe away every tear from your eyes.'

'Like Hanno, like Hanno, like Hanno...'

Manuel didn't understand to begin with, but then he remembered the story Wag-Nache'Péda had read them in the train.

'He'll never come back, never ever!' sobbed Angela.

'He'll never come back; he's here for ever and ever.'

'Manuel...'

'Yes, Angela, he's here for ever.'

'But I'll never see him again.'

'You... But he's here, he's here.'

Angela was just beginning to regain her composure when Bêa-Yasse'Kette started wailing loudly in the other room. The news had spread quickly round the refugee families from Lasting-en-Lorraine. That set Angela off again.

'If only we had the body to prepare for the burial!' wailed Bêa-Yasse'Kette. It would be some consolation to be able to dress him and give him a good send-off. But they had nothing, nothing at all, no body, no coffin, no flowers, nothing!

La Vieille nodded.

Madamilla came in haste and settled down to say her rosary with the big olive-wood beads. Bêa-Yasse'Kette was still moaning about there being no body to pray beside.

Madamilla prayed out loud, her eyes glued to the penknife in old Siébert's open hand.

'*Gegrüsset seist du Maria, voll der Gnade* ...' (Hail Mary, full of grace.) She was praying in German, as she always did back at home, for the repose of the soul of the young Frenchman.

'*Herr, gib ihm die ewige Ruh.*' (Lord, grant him eternal rest.) '*Und das ewige Licht erleuchte ihn.*' (And may your light shine upon him for ever.) If any new refugees happened to pass the window, whatever would they think? *'Herr, lass ihn ruhen in Frieden.'* (Lord, may he rest in peace.)

The lady from the Villa Suiram arrived and wanted to see Angela. She helped her up, embraced her, tried to console her: 'You're young! You'll be able to rebuild your life once the war is over.'

As if a life could be rebuilt! As if the past was not definitive, try as you might to change it. As if past, present and future were not all one. Why try to deceive people?

Manuel looked at her without saying a word. She would give the money to him before leaving.

At that point Angela collapsed and sank into a kind of stupor. Nothing could get her out of it, not even Manuel speaking to her.

When evening came, La Vieille decided to stay with her that night.

Old Siébert put the knife down on the waxed table cloth and left, looking older and more bent. Fata Ioss went home with him.

The next day the *curé* came. He suggested saying a Mass for the repose of Benoît's soul.

A few days later old Siébert received the official notification.

There were more and more refugees on the roads. The whole of France was fleeing towards the south. On the main road there were people escaping on bicycles and on foot, with tales portraying the Germans as barbarians who would cut off your children's hands, rape your daughters and slit your throat if you happened to be rich. The folk from Lasting-en-Lorraine shook their heads in disbelief. They knew the Germans quite well. All that couldn't possibly be true.

Then it was reported that they had crossed the Somme, that they were at the gates of Paris, that the government was somewhere in the Loire valley, that the Germans had entered Paris.

'It's all over, then,' said someone.

Old Siébert had nothing to say these days. He never even went out.

Angela had put the knife, a knife that she knew well, on the table in Benoît's place. Now that she was prepared to take a little food again, she would eat it staring at the knife and thinking of what Manuel had said. From time to time she would hear Sébastien crying and get up to go to him. That was the only sound that reached her.

It was reported that the Germans were on the Loire and were getting ready to advance southwards to Bordeaux.

It was reported that the government had arrived in Bordeaux. The wife of a minister had apparently summoned the chief of police to order him to find her dog among the nine hundred thousand refugees who were cluttering up the town.

It was reported that collections had been taken to feed the refugees.

It was reported that the Germans were being kind to the wretched civilians stranded on the roads. The folk from Lasting-en-Lorraine shook their heads again. They knew the Germans, and knew that they were no better nor worse than anyone else.

It was reported that Marshal Pétain had asked for an armistice.

The lady from the Villa Suiram had packed up and gone too.

That was the day when Bêa-Yasse'Kette burst into the kitchen complaining at the top of her voice: *'Di sinn gonns farick'd!'* (They've gone crazy!) One kilo of peaches for sixteen francs, and seven for a kilo of tomatoes! Three francs for just one liddle egg!'

She had learned a bit of French by now, and the rocketing prices scandalized her.

Angela stared at her without a word, as if she were living in another world. Manuel kept a watchful eye on his sister.

She hadn't even replied when the lady had invited her to move into the big house.

The Germans were advancing at prodigious speed. They would be here tomorrow. They were here.

Some people went to see the procession of Panzers through the streets, out of curiosity.

In the little annexe, Manuel held the child on his knee. Sébastien was crying. Angela was washing up, but her mind was elsewhere.

People said later that the man had thrown himself at the leading Panzer as they entered the town. The whole column had had to halt. He had hammered on the tank with his fists, yelling: 'You won't get past, you bloody *Boches! Stinckpreusse!*'

Some of the German soldiers seized him, but he struggled and shouted: 'Butchers! *Mörder! Mörder!*'

Then one of them hit him.

The caterpillar tracks began to roll again. The man suddenly stiffened, then collapsed in the arms of the German soldiers who were holding him. When they laid him out on the pavement, one of the bystanders recognized him. It was old Siébert of Siébert's Mill.

Part Three

THE DESERT

1

It was the news of old Siébert's death that brought Angela back to herself, as though she no longer had the right to be absent. The child had no father or grandfather, only her: and his godfather, Manuel, was simple.

She dressed herself in black from head to toe to go to her father-in-law's funeral, which was held as soon as the Germans released his body. The *curé* celebrated a Requiem Mass, including Benoît in his intention as well, so that it was like burying him at the same time as his father. The whole of Lasting-en-Lorraine was there, except of course the men who were still said to be 'at the Front', although no one actually knew what that meant these days. After the service, the coffin was interred alongside those of Millache'Babe and Victor.

When she got home, Angela devoted herself to looking after the household. There was nothing else to do. Next door, at the Villa Suiram, there was constant noise now that the Germans had taken up residence. Even that was nothing compared to what they had to put up with at night.

From the very first day the Germans had requisitioned all the smartest houses which had been abandoned by their owners, and they had set about enjoying themselves. There were loud voices and laughter, and the sounds of glasses clinking and plates breaking. *Man lebt wie Gott in Frankreich* (You can live like the gods in France), as the saying goes. They were even agreeably surprised to find folk from Lorraine who understood German. There had been the unfortunate incident of the old protester the first day, of course, but that had been quickly forgotten: there would always be the odd nutcase, and anyone could have a heart attack.

Old Bêa-Yasse'Kette, once she plucked up courage to go out again, had even been bold enough to go up to two young German soldiers in the street and ask them if they had come through Lasting. They had explained to the old woman that no, they had come through the North of France, but she had still insisted on telling them exactly where her house was, *enn'da Shnidda gass'* (Tailors' Street), and they had gone away laughing. She had found them nice but a bit cheeky: *'Lauss'bouve! Loudda lauss'bouve!'* (Rascals! Young rascals!) Fortunately they hadn't heard that.

There was a tacit agreement among the refugees from Lasting-en-Lorraine that they would reply if spoken to by a German but that they would not speak first. The invaders were very sensitive to that kind of treatment. Spurred on by her curiosity, Bêa-Yasse'Kette had broken the rules. She was left standing in the middle of the road, shaking her head: *'Lauss'bouve!'*

Everything had changed with the coming of the Germans. In the first place, a significant proportion of the inhabitants had fled. Several of the shops were shut, and that was inconvenient. But at least prices were starting to go down again, even if there were shortages of some things.

'S'ish doch bessa sôô!' (It's better that way!) Bêa-Yasse'Kette evidently meant the prices.

Manuel was listening to her story of her encounter with the two young soldiers. *'Lauss'bouve! Loudda lauss'bouve!'*. He smiled, but he didn't actually agree that they were *Lauss'bouve*. Not all of them, anyway.

The day after the Germans arrived, he had gone out shopping

as usual. When he saw a group of soldiers he went up to them, as he had done at Bermering. He was fascinated by their uniforms. When they shouted at him he just smiled.

They got cross, and seized him and took him to a building on the main square where their commanding officer had his headquarters. They mentioned the word spy, and Manuel shook his head, desperately. When they realized that he understood what they were saying it got worse: they hadn't, after all, forgotten the incident with the old man the previous day. Another of that dangerous lot from Lorraine! What really infuriated them was when they called him an idiot and he nodded: he knew he wasn't quite the same as everyone else, and some people did use that word to describe him. An idiot, that's right, that's what he was.

When Fata Ioss arrived, tipped off by someone, they had just started hitting Manuel. He had a terrible job convincing them that Manuel was all right, just a bit simple in the head. In the end the officer had to admit that an *Einfältiger* wasn't necessarily dangerous. But he'd better be watched a bit more carefully if he was going to keep out of trouble.

Manuel stayed indoors after that, and didn't even go to the Requiem Mass. Fear had somehow got inside him, making him hide behind the curtains all day long. Whenever he spied the soldiers from the Villa Suiram, he retreated to his room and stayed there, not coming out again until long afterwards. Sometimes he would get out his book and pore over it for hours at a time. Angela could hear him reading from the kitchen.

'... And he was in the desert till the day of his manifestation ... What's the desert, Angela?'

He had already asked her that, and Fata Ioss too.

'Lots and lots of sand, nothing but sand.'

'Like the beach?'

'I suppose so, but much bigger.'

'As big as the sea?'

'Maybe, I don't know. Nothing grows there and nobody lives there, nobody at all.' She remembered the oases, but didn't mention them. 'Sometimes people go into the desert to seek God.'

'Like John the Baptist?'

'I suppose so.'

'Are there Germans in the desert?'

Angela laughed.

'What about the beach, are there any on the beach?'

'I don't know.'

'Can I go and see?'

He was already pulling his jacket on. Angela watched him anxiously. But he couldn't be kept shut up like an animal all the time.

'All right, but don't stay out too long, and whatever you do, don't hang about in town.' He shook his head. No chance of that!

The beach, when he got to it, was almost deserted. Manuel smiled as he climbed down the stone steps from the sea-wall. Over there his favourite rock was waiting for him, by the vast ocean. He headed towards it, ignoring the people he passed on the way. In any case, men in swimming costumes all look the same: here there were no longer 'French' and 'Germans'.

He sat on his rock and looked down at the sand. The desert. His eyes were almost closed, and when he lifted his head all he could see was sand, sand, stretching away into the distance, even where the ocean had been a moment before. That God was to be found in the desert he could well understand: this was where he had already been visited by the light, after all. He suddenly caught himself murmuring: 'Come! Come!' but nothing came, no burning fire, nothing. The desert of the sea was empty this evening. No path of light crossed it.

Manuel the simpleton shivered and started remembering. His thoughts turned to the deserted village of Lasting-en-Lorraine, to the abandoned animals, to the pigeons he had set free. He remembered Lidrezing, bare fields, the long crossing of the desert of France, and then the desert of Judea where John lived and where Jesus withdrew to pray. It was as if a huge unknown country was opening up before him. He thought of old Siébert and his plans for the future, and of Benoît's plans. The future had escaped from the hands of both of them, father and son, and now it was a foreign land in which they were going to have to learn to live. Fear gripped Manuel, and he looked round him in terror.

He saw the four young men coming down the beach towards him. Soon they had surrounded him.

'*Was macht denn der da?*' (What's he doing there?)

'*Wer bist du denn?*' (Who are you, then?)

They were blond like him, blue-eyed too, just like him.

'*Ach, das ist ja der lothringer Idiot!*' (Oh, it's the village idiot from Lorraine!)

They roared with laughter and slapped their bare thighs.

'*Wie heisst du schon?*' (What's your name?)

'Manuel.'

His reply came in a murmur. Inside him a voice was trying to make itself heard, as fragile as the wind in the reeds, and threatened by the frightened thumping of his heart.

'*Manuel heisst du!*' (So you're called Manuel!)

'*Ach ja, Emmanuel, Gott mit uns!*' (I know, Emmanuel, God with us!)

And they roared again, laughing until they cried. But Manuel could hear the voice now: 'Love one another as I have loved you.'

'And what are your names?' he asked them in the dialect of Lasting-en-Lorraine.

They looked at each other and then answered:

'Dieter.'

'Karl-Peter.'

'Wolfgang.'

'Werner.'

Manuel got up and held out his hand. They took it and shook it one after the other.

'Have you been here long?'

'I don't know.'

'What are you doing on that rock?'

They had by now sat down on the sand at his feet.

'Looking at the sand and the sea.'

'Dreaming of Lorraine?'

'Yes.'

'You'll probably be able to go back soon. You'll become Germans again, now that the Führer has liberated you.'

Manuel listened in surprise. He didn't quite understand.

'Don't you want to go back to Lorraine?'

'Is Lorraine the desert too, now?'

The young Germans burst out laughing again. 'When you lot get back, it won't be!'

One of the others asked: 'Who do you live with, by the way?'

'With Angela, that's my sister, and Sébastien.'

'Is that her husband?'

'No, that's the baby. Benoît was killed by a bomb, in the Ardennes. He was a soldier.'

'Oh! I'm sorry.' They seemed to be genuinely sad.

'How old was he?'

'About the same as you.' Manuel looked at them, and that look spoke volumes.

'That's war, I suppose,' said one of the soldiers.

'War is bad,' said Manuel. 'It kills people who haven't done anything wrong. For nothing.'

The German soldiers looked at each other. One of them bent down and drew in the sand with his finger.

Manuel said: 'Love one another as I have loved you.'

Then he stood up, walked through the middle of them and went away. They watched him go.

He did not want to worry Angela, so he didn't tell her about his encounter with Dieter, Karl-Peter, Wolfgang and Werner.

The following day, Fata Ioss passed on some of the rumours that were going round: the Germans were leaving to go further south, the men were coming back from the Front, they themselves were going to be repatriated. Some of them didn't want to go home if it meant living with Germans; others retorted that the Germans were everywhere now anyway. Old Siébert, though, he'd never have gone.

'It seems to me,' said Fata Ioss, 'that we probably ought to.'

Angela wasn't sure. She was afraid of the Germans, more for Manuel than herself.

'Mother thinks we ought to go, too.'

Manuel said nothing.

A few days later they were all round at Fata Ioss' house in the evening, discussing what to do. Rédache'Momme was there, along with the whole of Millache'Babe's clan, Rak'Onna, Madamilla, Bêa-Yasse'Kette, Le Voisin and La Voisine who had hardly been out since Victor's death, the midwife, and even Sister Irma whom someone had gone to fetch from the school-house. There were many fewer Germans in town now, most of them having moved on southwards with the occupying forces. Manuel had stayed at home to look after Sébastien, so that Angela could go with La Vieille.

'We've got to make a decision, so you ought to be there.' In the end she had decided to go along.

'But make sure you don't open the door to anyone, Manuel!'

'No, I won't.'

Wag-Nache'Péda was the first to speak. 'We come from Lorraine, and our place is back there. A Frenchman from Lorraine is only truly French when he's at home in Lorraine.'

Silence greeted this opening.

'In any case,' he went on, 'that's where all our roots are ... Like many of the rest of you, my French nationality was reinstated in March 1920. And quite right too! My paternal grandfather was born French under Napoleon III, as his father was before him under Louis-Philippe. And *his* father was born under Napoleon Bonaparte in 1802, the same year as Victor Hugo. Before that there was still one more generation that was born French, that's my ancestor Henri, even if Joseph and Georges-Adam before him were citizens of the independent Duchy of Lorraine. We're as French as the rest of them, but our roots are back there in Lorraine. You can't transplant an old tree, mark my words!'

Then Sister Irma got up. Without batting an eyelid, she pulled a piece of paper out of her pocket and began: 'Of course we're French. I'm going to read to you the declaration made by the deputies for Lorraine and Alsace at Bordeaux on the first of March 1871, as France, defeated, prepared to sign the Treaty of Frankfurt which ceded us to the Reich.'

As soon as she opened her mouth there had been an almost instantaneous silence. Fata Ioss' kitchen felt like a classroom as she declaimed in her clear schoolmistress' voice:

'Having been given up, in defiance of all justice and by an odious abuse of force, to the domination of a foreign power, we have a last duty to fulfil. We repeat that a pact which disposes of us without our consent is null and void... As we leave this place, the sentiment which remains uppermost in our hearts is a sentiment... of unbreakable loyalty and attachment towards the land from which we are being so violently torn... Your brothers in Alsace and Lorraine, now separated from the remainder of the family, retain for France a lasting filial affection, and look forward to the day when the two households will once again be reunited.'

Sister Irma finished reading and looked round at the assembled company. She noticed that Fata Ioss was surreptitiously wiping a tear from the corner of his eye. Then she added: 'I might point out that in Berlin they knew very well that the German soldiers serving in Alsace-Lorraine were camping in enemy territory. That proves that we're French, if any proof were still needed.'

Someone sitting next to the cold stove put in: 'That's all very well, but it's not the point.'

'Oh yes, it is,' she interrupted, 'it's very much the point, in fact it's the first point we'll have to get straight. Soon they'll be trying to tell us that we were under the rule of the Holy Roman Empire for centuries. You may not get a chance to reply, but at least your heart will tell you that the Frankish Victory over the Alamans goes back to the fifth century and Clovis: that's when they introduced the Frankish dialect that we still speak. They built a royal villa near Sarreguemines right at the beginning of the Merovingian dynasty and, later on, after AD750, it was given to the abbot of Saint-Denis, counsellor to several French kings, who kept it quite a while... Anyway, Lorraine was Frankish, and hence French, along with many other parts of Gaul, long before it came under the Holy Roman Empire. That should be enough.'

When she had finished there was a pause, and then Fata Ioss got up to speak.

'Our land needs guardians to look after it. We must go back.'

The others listened in silence. Wag-Nache'Péda and some of the women nodded their agreement.

'We must go back,' he repeated. 'Back to our homes and our gardens, back to mow the Pré aux Pucelles, dredge the Sime at the bottom of the Hume Valley, and climb the Gréderich and the Athisberg. We must look after our land and our houses and preserve them for France. If we don't go back, they'll send Prussians, and then our land will have a Prussian soul. We must go back and preserve the soul, the French soul, of our village, Lasting-en-Lorraine. The rest will only be a matter of time, all we have to do is hang on.'

'The people of Lorraine are good at hanging on,' agreed Sister Irma.

By the time they broke up that evening, the decision had been taken to go back. But when, and how? On the faces of those who were hurrying home, the word haste seemed to be written. They repeated what had been said earlier: those who wanted to stay could stay, they wouldn't bear any grudges.

The first men to return from the Front arrived in Châtelaillon-Plage that night. It was the following evening before most people found out about it: their wives had been too scared to go round spreading the good news until then.

During the day, Manuel went down to the beach again, looking for Dieter, Wolfgang, Karl-Peter and Werner. He even wandered round the streets, but in vain. He would have liked to see them again.

There was another gathering, this time at the Comm'nickels' house. Their Maax was sitting by the fire in his slippers, smoking a pipe. He'd just come back, and he'd seen worse in his time.

'We were fighting up till ten days ago.'

'But Pétain signed the armistice on the twenty-fifth of June!'

'Well, we didn't know that, did we? And what bloody difference would it have made to us, anyway?'

Mother Comm'nickel eyed her son anxiously.

'We were waiting for them behind the Maginot Line. We were expecting them from the north, and they came at us from the south, from the French side. They caught us in a pincer movement.'

No one spoke.

'We fought like savages. For nothing. Damn all. One night we realized it was all up, when we saw our officers making a bonfire. Guess what they were burning? Bundles and bundles of banknotes!'

'Oh!'

'They were! So they wouldn't fall into the hands of the *Boches*. And we hadn't got two sous to rub together! Nothing to buy civilian clothes with, nothing to get us back home! Bloody fools!'

Silence.

'That's when we got out. There was nothing left to defend, so why stay there and look silly? We got as far as the first farm in uniform, and the people there agreed to hide us for twenty-four hours until the *Boches* had been past.'

'Didn't they search?'

'No, Fata Ioss, not likely! They just wanted to be through with it. The farm people gave us civilian clothes, we burned our uniforms, and off we went back to Lasting.'

'Didn't anyone stop you?'

'There wasn't anyone. All the villages were empty. And we avoided the Germans as much as we could. But remember, we can speak their language, and when we did bump into them there wasn't any trouble. They left us alone when they discovered we were from Lorraine.'

'*Oun' de hissa? Shdéénn'se noch?*' (And the houses? Are they still standing?) Bêa-Yasse'Kette couldn't keep quiet any longer.

'*Ya. Noch all'.*' They were all still intact.

'*God sai donk!*' (Thank God!)

That was a relief, at any rate.

'Well, the walls and the roofs are.'

They looked at each other, not understanding what he meant.

'Your house, for instance,' said Maax, looking at Bêa-Yasse'Kette, 'has all its shutters open, and the front door won't close properly.'

Bêa-Yasse'Kette opened her mouth in horror.

'I went in and had a look. There's hardly any furniture left. They'd smashed it all up and made a fire on the floor, in the middle of the *shdob* (living-room). The floorboards are all burnt.'

'*O Iérum Maria!*' Poor Bêa-Yasse'Kette had to be supported, or she would have collapsed completely.

'But who...?'

'The French, the Germans, who knows? We've all done it. That's what war's like.'

Bêa-Yasse'Kette stared at him, her mouth still hanging open. But he was on to another subject now.

'The *Boches* took masses of prisoners.'

'You were lucky to get away,' said someone.

'Oh, but you know, all the other ranks from Lorraine have been released anyway. They're doing that to butter us up, see?'

'What about the animals?' someone asked. 'Did you see any in the fields?'

'Not a sausage. They must have eaten them all.'

'Oh!'

'Well, what do you expect? That's war for you.' That's what their Maax kept saying.

'*Grouss'lish!*' (Horrible!) groaned Bêa-Yasse'Kette.

In the days that followed, other men came back. They had all been round through Lasting-en-Lorraine. Many of them, with not a franc to their name, had travelled by night, stowing away in cattle trucks.

When they were taken out in the streets of Châtelaillon-Plage, a few days after their arrival, they were like owls blinking in the sunlight. They had returned from the land of war, from the dark land of night where death was their constant companion. They found the bright summer of the Atlantic coast strange and surprising.

They found it strange to see women in bathing costumes sitting on the beach in the afternoon knitting, with their children playing round them.

They found it strange to be able to go for long swims, and they hid their feelings by splashing about and making plenty of noise.

They preferred the beach in the evening, when the sun sank

into the ocean, the sea withdrew to a great distance and everything was deserted.

One evening, Maax found Manuel on his rock.

'Hullo, what are you doing there?'

They had known each other since they were children.

'Nothing. Just waiting.'

'What for?'

'The light.'

Maax laughed. 'You'll have to wait a pretty long time. At least until tomorrow morning!'

Manuel shook his head.

'You mean you can see the light at night?'

Manuel nodded. Maax looked at him in astonishment.

'And I'm waiting for Dieter, Wolfgang, Karl-Peter and Werner, too, in case they come this way again.'

Maax opened his eyes wide in amazement. 'Germans? You don't mean you're waiting for Germans?'

'Yes.'

'You must be absolutely round the bend!'

Maax regretted it as soon as he had said it. But Manuel smiled and murmured: 'Love one another.'

Maax stared at him, opened his mouth as if to say something, shut it again, turned, and walked away with his hands in his pockets and his head down.

Everything had changed, even the village idiot! Let's get back home to Lorraine as quickly as possible! When he reached the Comm'nickels' house, he met Sister Irma coming up the street carrying a suitcase.

2

The return convoy was finally organized. There were no more cattle trucks, and everyone could take all their possessions with them. Not that that amounted to very much.

The fine summer of 1940 ended at the station for the refugees from Lasting-en-Lorraine. There they turned their backs on the sea and waited, surrounded by their bundles, with their hearts quickened by the mere thought of the Sime flowing through the valleys of the Sûredal and the Hume.

Like everyone else, Manuel was waiting. While it was still night he had been to bid farewell to the ocean and to the little cottage in the middle of the maze of narrow streets. He had sat on his rock for a long time hoping the light would come, but there had been nothing but a pale band on the horizon behind him, the signal for departure. He had leaned his forehead against the door of Lisbeth's house, and just before leaving he had written on it with his finger, in invisible letters, the words *God bless*. If she ever returned, she would surely be able to read them with the eyes of the heart which alone can see what is invisible. And now he was waiting, and propped against the pile of bundles was the push-chair which had travelled so far and had done such good service already.

Angela was holding the baby in her arms and crying, no doubt at the thought that a part of her life was dying, the house where she had known her only hours of happiness, the bedroom which meant love and life to her, the birthplace of little Sébastien for whom Lorraine would always be a foreign land. His native town was here on the other side of France. Angela was crying, and Manuel watched her without thinking of trying to console her. He knew now that tears do not spring only from suffering, and that one must respect the mystery of every individual being. Happiness too can be bathed in tears, and suffering may be the twin sister of joy. Manuel knew that, and perhaps La Vieille knew it too as she waited with Angela and placed her hand on her shoulder.

Fata Ioss said nothing. He had carefully packed up his Christmas crib with all the figures so lovingly carved, and he was clutching the parcel which contained them to his heart. Was he reflecting that it was best to hold on tight to your hope if you were lucky enough to have one in these uncertain days? What would tomorrow bring? When he closed his eyes, all he could see was night and fog, and he sometimes thought that old Siébert of Siébert's Mill must be glad to be enjoying eternal sleep, even if it was in foreign soil.

La Voisine and Le Voisin, next to Fata Ioss, looked broken. There was a child-sized space between them, and every so often they would glance pathetically sideways as if expecting to find their Victor restored to them.

There were no such sentiments in the noisy ranks of Mill-ache'Babe's clan. The old man, whose nodding head had been such a familiar sight in rain and shine, was well off where he was, even if he couldn't share the yellow clay of his Léna's grave. One day, perhaps, his body might be brought home, but there was no time to think of that now.

Wag-Nache'Péda had a goldfinch in a cage, which he was having a hard time trying to protect from all the children who were rushing up and down the platform. He cuffed one or two of them on the way past. The bird flapped its wings in fright. It had been captured as a fledgling in its nest in May, and so was a kind of symbol of France, now trapped as in a cage and deprived of her freedom. Wag-Nache'Péda had sworn to take it back to Lasting-en-Lorraine and keep it until the day this horrid war was over and the door of life stood wide open once more.

Bêa-Yasse'Kette, whose skirts concealed her innumerable bags and parcels, gazed at the bird with a tear in her eye.

Madamilla, Rak'Onna and Rédache'Momme were bustling about like clockwork toys wound up and set going by the exodus. It was hard to imagine them ever stopping, but deep inside them must have been the secret hope that when they at last got back to their own homes they would find peace and rest.

Rest was the last thing in Manuel's mind. He wasn't even thinking of the excitement of further adventures. Perhaps he was already aware that there are no returnings, only new beginnings, and that the 'return' to Lasting-en-Lorraine was not the second half of a straightforward journey, there and back, but a new phase of an exodus that would never end. If he wasn't aware of it, who else would be? Who else would suspect that the village awaiting them when they got out of the train was not the Lasting that they knew, but a strange place, the same but different?

Sister Irma, maybe, sensed it, as she stood, silent and motionless, at the end of the platform, with her little suitcase at her feet and her big black rosary in her hands.

Maax stared at her as he went past with Shong, another of those who had just returned from the Front. They had been making plenty of noise, but they were suddenly reduced to silence by the sight of the old nun's lips moving as she told her beads.

Just as the signal to board the train was finally given, the primary-school teacher from Grandbourg turned up with his daughters to say goodbye to Sister Irma. They lingered on the platform as the others piled into the carriages, finding the parting almost more than they could bear. He could have gone back too, but French culture meant something rather different to him, and indeed to his two daughters, who had already left Lorraine to pursue their studies. They had decided to stay put, preferring their intellectual homeland to the land of their birth. Not everyone understood the reasons for their choice, despite protestations to the contrary, but there was no ill-feeling.

When the train started moving, amid a sudden flurry of handkerchiefs, the old teacher was seen to wipe away a tear. How many eyes remained dry on that platform where those who had chosen to stay mingled with the local inhabitants who had befriended them and come to support them today? On the train, too, some of the passengers had to blow their noses hard once the town was out of sight, despite the joy of going home which tended to eclipse everything, even Sister Irma's warnings.

As they crossed France from west to east the whole country seemed to be full of German uniforms. Every time they passed through a station they gathered at the windows and stared in horrified disbelief. Whenever they stopped, the women tried to hold on to their menfolk and prevent them wandering off in case they never came back. Maax was very nearly left behind somewhere in central France.

Wag-Nache'Péda was fussing round his French goldfinch like a mother round her baby. At each stop he would go off along the platform or across the fields in search of fresh water, with the cage dangling from his hand. The bird was getting over its initial fear and would even sit on its perch sometimes. Everyone was feeling happier in the sunshine, and the children would play on the bank alongside the railway track.

It was after one such halt that Shong divulged what he had picked up some kilometres back: 'We're going to have to cross the frontier.'

'What's that?'

'What did he say?' The news spread like wildfire along the train.

'*Vou ville donn di mêd' ouns anouss?*' (Wherever are they taking us to?) exclaimed Bêa-Yasse'Kette, all worked up.

Some people claimed that they were going to be exiled to Prussia, to Pomerania, and replaced in Lorraine by Prussian colonists, *Siedler*.

That provoked a few tears among the women. Fata Ioss was sceptical. So was Sister Irma, only more so. She managed to restore a bit of calm by getting out at the next station and making enquiries, although those enquiries were to cost her dear later on.

'Jean was right,' she said, using the French form of Shong's name, 'there is a frontier to cross, but it's not the Prussian one. The Germans have established checkpoints all along the line of the old Franco-German frontier of 1870. That can only mean one thing, that they intend to annexe us again.'

Her companions stared at her.

'What are we to do, then?'

'We'd have been better off staying in Châtelaillon,' said someone.

'Oh no we wouldn't!' rejoined Sister Irma. 'If we had, then they certainly would have brought in *Siedler*. No, we must definitely go back. We're on our way, and there won't be any difficulty crossing this frontier; it's only a temporary one anyway.'

'If only we could be sure of that!'

'That's one thing we must be sure of!'

They looked at each other, saying nothing, and trying to be sure. But their original enthusiasm had gone.

Manuel had not contributed to the discussion. In fact he had said practically nothing since they had left, except the odd word in reply to his sister and a few sweet nothings to Sébastien whom he held occasionally. The rest of the time he sat quite still, with the *curé* of Lidrezing's book open on his knees. Sometimes he looked out of the dirty window at the countryside going past, and sometimes he rested his head against the back of the seat and closed his eyes, but mostly he read, slowly and painstakingly, chewing over each word.

'Well, well! So you can read now, can you?'

Maax couldn't sit still for more than a few minutes at a time. He had just come along, and he was amazed at what he saw.

'That's right,' said Fata Ioss, 'Manuel can read.'

'How on earth ... ?'

'He just taught himself, like a big boy.'

Manuel merely smiled.

Maax leaned over and looked at the book, then suddenly straightened up and went off down the train.

'Manuel!' said Fata Ioss. 'You'd better hide your book when we get to the frontier, because of the Germans.'

'Why should I?'

'Because it's in French. You never know ...'

And since no one knew exactly where the frontier was, they decided to hide it under the seat at every stop.

'I'd be surprised if they did search the train, though,' grumbled Fata Ioss.

Manuel was a bit upset, and Bêa-Yasse'Kette was getting at him: 'Why does he have to read all the time?'

Nobody bothered to reply.

When they stopped at Saint-Dizier, they realized straight away that something was going to happen: the station was crawling with German soldiers.

'*Kontrol!*'

The word was on everybody's lips.

First of all they were told not to get out. Then they were told to leave everything in the compartments and form into groups on the platform. Their identities were checked and their names ticked off on a long list by *Unteroffiziere*.

'*Schwester Irma, bitte vortreten!*' (Sister Irma, step forward, please.)

She stepped forward. The other women trembled.

The *Unteroffizier* looked at her. '*Hohlen Sie bitte ihr Gepäck.*' (Fetch your luggage.)

Without a word, Sister Irma climbed back into the carriage and reappeared with her little suitcase.

'*Kommen Sie bitte.*' (Come this way.)

One of the soldiers took her to join a group on the other side of the railway line which was growing in numbers. She seemed quite impassive, and she had wound her black rosary round her hands. When her eyes met Manuel's she smiled.

Then the Germans boarded the train. That was the most anxious moment for Manuel, but he breathed again when they came out empty-handed.

'*Einsteigen, bitte!*' (All aboard!)

'*Oun de Shvesh'da?*' (What about the Sister?) Bêa-Yasse'Kette called out.

'*Einsteigen!*'

And they got in.

As the train moved off, the group of *Zurückgewiesenen* (those who had been turned back), who were standing by the line, waved. Sister Irma remained motionless. Maax said later that he had seen two tears roll down her cheeks.

Manuel had retrieved his book from under the seat and clutched it to his heart under his jacket. Occasionally he still brought it out and opened it, but he couldn't read. For him as well as everyone else, hope only revived once the convoy finally reached Forbach, where buses were waiting to take them the last few kilometres to Lasting-en-Lorraine.

They somehow managed to pile into the buses, and the hubbub didn't die down until they had got to the top of the Brigandal and were about to go through Spicheren. They were expecting to see a few people about, but what they found was a desert, with some of the houses sacked and grass growing between the paving-stones and even on the doorsteps. Anxiety gripped them again, and the final two kilometres took an eternity.

'*Yéd'sd gééd' de vêld ouna!*' (The world's coming to an end!) wailed a lone voice amid the silence, and no one felt like laughing at Bêa-Yasse'Kette.

At the *Dodekritz* (war memorial cross) the bus slowed down as the first houses came into view. A sob was heard, and some of the women crossed themselves.

They could see at once that Lasting-en-Lorraine was a desert too, a dead place, without a living soul, not even an animal. Everywhere doors were open and shutters hanging loose. Oh, if only one single chicken could run squawking across the road to avoid the wheels of the bus! But there was nothing at all—all that remained alive was the water of the fountain. When Angela shut her eyes she could hear its murmuring trickle, and the sound broke her heart. They could have been so happy together.

When they pulled up, some German soldiers were there waiting for them. The returning exiles looked at each other, not saying a word. The Germans held out their hands for the luggage, laughing and joking, and in the end they handed them the cases and bundles. They could hardly leave them standing there not doing anything.

'*Guten Tag! Guten Tag!*'

'Hello. *Eea sinn ava leeb, minne hêrre!*' (Well, that's very kind of you!)

They smiled at old Bêa-Yasse'Kette, but when she added '*Mêa'si filmols mêa'si*' (Thank you very much), they didn't find the mixture of French and German so amusing.

'Heil Hitler!' It was an NCO who saluted and offered to help too, but they busied themselves with their own things and hurried off to find their houses, without even bothering to take leave of each other. They'd be seeing each other before long in any case, now that they were back home.

Back home? Manuel had never felt less at home than he did now, looking at the ransacked houses and not even recognizing them, staring at the deserted streets.

'Come along, Manuel,' called Angela. She was waiting for him with Sébastien in her arms, accompanied by a German carrying two bundles.

'Go on,' said Fata Ioss, who had stayed behind on purpose.

'*Was hat denn der Kerl?*' (What's the matter with the lad?) The NCO sounded irritated.

'Go on, Manuel,' Fata Ioss repeated. Then, turning to the German, he explained: 'He's a little simple, *einfältig*, and this homecoming is just too much for him.'

'*Ist er ihr Mann?*' (Is he her husband?)

'No, he's her brother.'

'*Und ihr Mann?*' (And what about her husband?)

'*Tod*' (Dead), replied Fata Ioss. 'Killed in the Ardennes.'

'*Ach so!*' The man looked rather shamefaced.

Holding the push-chair in one hand, Manuel had at last tagged along behind Angela. He was still clutching his book, hidden underneath his jacket, next to his heart.

'I'll be along soon, Manuel,' said Fata Ioss, but the simpleton didn't turn round once.

'*Schade für das Mädel, dass sie mit dem Dorftrottel leben muss!*' (Sad for the poor girl, having to live with the village idiot!)

'Oh, they get on very well, the two of them,' replied Fata Ioss.

But he didn't elaborate any further. Perhaps it was just as well that the NCO should think of Manuel as the village idiot: it was as good a way as any of guaranteeing him a little bit of freedom.

When Manuel and Angela got to their house, they found it open. A scene of utter chaos awaited them as they went inside, and they couldn't suppress a cry of surprise and shock. The little hallway where the soldier had left their bundles was untidy enough, but when they set foot in the *shdob* they found that the table-legs had been broken off and used for a fire in the middle of the room, badly damaging the wooden floor. The doors of the heavy linen-press were hanging open to reveal empty shelves, but at least it hadn't been moved. Rubbish was piled up in one corner of the room.

In the kitchen the cooking-stove had gone, but the table and two chairs were still there. The tap was dripping on to the dirty floor.

In the first of the upstairs rooms they were astounded to discover half a dozen mattresses piled on top of theirs, along with pillows and big red eiderdowns: the place had obviously been used as a kind of storehouse.

When Manuel saw what a shambles the room was in he recovered from his initial stupor and laughed out loud, making Angela smile in spite of herself. Little Sébastien wriggled in her arms.

The small room at the end was almost intact: there were still blankets on the bed and linen in the wardrobe. Angela would be able to sleep there tonight with the baby.

'Hello! Anyone at home?'

'Coming!' Angela shouted down the stairs, but Manuel was already on his way.

'I thought perhaps you could do with a hand.' It was Fata Ioss, standing in the hall with a little rabbit in his arms.

'Oh!' Manuel was in ecstasies over it. 'Where did you find it?'

'One of the Germans gave it to me as I was going home just now. I thought you'd...'

'Oh, thank you, thank you!' Manuel had taken the frightened animal and was cuddling it.

'You'd better go and put it in the hutch,' said Fata Ioss, glad to see the joy that had returned to Manuel's eyes.

The yard was in as much of a mess as the house, but at least nothing was actually broken.

'Anyone would think they'd had nothing better to do than move everything round,' grumbled the old man. Then he added: 'But here's the stove, at any rate. Give me a hand to bring it in and get it set up, and then you can have something to eat.' He rolled up his sleeves, and Manuel laughingly copied him.

In the wall-cupboard Angela had found all their crockery and cutlery intact.

Soon the fire was roaring in the stove and the water was singing for the baby's bottle.

'Come on, Manuel, let's get things sorted out upstairs.'

By the time Fata Ioss went off homewards, their house was beginning to feel lived in again. People had finished collecting their mattresses from the *gasse* outside. Others had been found out in the fields: whatever could they have been used for there?

Manuel had helped old Madamilla to get her belongings sorted out, and then he had carried on down the main street as if in response to a mysterious call. People were too busy in their homes, with darkness about to fall, to notice him going past, and only the German soldier on duty saw him slip into the church at dusk through the doors that were now permanently open.

As soon as Manuel walked down the nave, he felt a tide of well-being surge over him, something like a warmth invading each of his limbs and reaching right to their extremities, or cool water drunk straight from the fountain on a scorching summer's day, refreshing his body in the noonday heat. His whole being quivered. Despite the darkness which lurked in the corners like a wild beast seeking someone to devour, Manuel's eyes could see a great light which seemed to come from nowhere and everywhere. It shone inside him and around him and was as familiar and friendly as a happy memory, so much so that he opened his mouth and let out his joy in a cry that was as deep as a well and yet as calm as the reflection of a star in the water. He advanced with arms outstretched as though someone had come to greet him and take him by the hand. His feet hardly touched the ground. Filled with wonder, he looked at all the statues of the saints on either side of the church and greeted them one by one, like long-lost friends. They were all there to welcome him back: the curé d'Ars, smiling gently in his white surplice; Saint Antony of Padua, holding the child Jesus in his arms; Saint Louis de Gonzague; Saint John; John the Baptist clothed in skins; Joan of Arc with her banner; Saint Nicholas; little Saint Theresa of Lisieux with her eyes lifted heavenwards; Saint Joseph; and finally, wearing a queen's crown, Mary, the Holy Virgin, the Mother of God. Manuel went to each of them in turn but in front of Mary he stopped as if seeing her for the first time.

'Hail, Mary.'

The words had come spontaneously, and Manuel repeated them without attempting to continue any further with the prayer, although he knew it well enough.

'Hail, Mary.'

Mary, young girl who loved enough to accept that your God should become your son, who said yes without any strings attached, whose self-giving was total, Mary whose soul magnifies the Lord and whose spirit rejoices in God your Saviour, humble handmaid glorified, epitome of the miracles of the Holy God, guarantee of his love to all who love and of his terrible power to the proud and the mighty, gentle to the poor and hungry, Mary with hands full of sunshine, you had come to Manuel the simpleton, never to leave his path.

'Hail, Mary.'

And always to point him to God.

'Do whatever he tells you.'

Manuel bowed his head, and the smile continued to illuminate his face as he proceeded slowly up towards the choir. It was night outside, and in the church it was difficult to see between the dusty pews, but for Manuel the sun was shining and he climbed the steps to the sanctuary without stumbling. He walked with arms outstretched and his heart overflowing, and he stopped only when he came to the foot of the altar. There, a little to the right of the altar itself, he sank to the ground.

He could see perfectly well that the stone table had been stripped of its cloth, that the sacred vessels were empty and the candlesticks had been thrown down, and that the tabernacle itself had been violated, its open doors revealing nothing but an empty container. But he could identify that prodigious absence with the presence which so transported him and in which he joyfully lost himself. This edifice, though abandoned for months past, still signified the presence of Him whom his soul loved. How could he not be overwhelmed and satisfied?

There he lay, the village idiot, the only one wise enough to have found that love which no man has ever seen with his eyes or touched with his hands, but which he, the simpleton, had received for good. While the darkness deepened outside, Manuel was in the light and the light in him, beautiful as a flight of doves in the midday sun, as a garden of lilies at dawn, or as apple blossom on May morning. His heart leapt in his breast like a gazelle or a young hind upon the mountains.

... Angela was anxious again, and she ran to tell Fata Ioss.

'Hurry up and get dressed!' said La Vieille urgently. 'You never know what might have happened with all these Germans about.'

How could she know that Manuel was quite safe, but that he had lost all notion of time and was like a log consumed by the flames?

'Poor fellow! He must have been badly shaken...'

Fata Ioss lost no time. Accompanied by Angela, he headed up

the main street towards the church.

'Do you think...?'

The old man didn't reply.

He was gripped by a secret apprehension at having to face the unknown again. He walked on even faster, and Angela had to run to keep up with him.

When they got to the church, Fata Ioss was at first reluctant to use his torch, but it was pitch dark and they couldn't see a thing without it. The feeble cone of light swept the nave, passing quickly over the empty pews, and up to the communion rail. The old man knew that Manuel was up there, and his hand shook as he directed the torch to the altar steps. Angela let out a cry, not very loud although it seemed so in the silence, and then she put her hand over her mouth and stared at her brother as though seeing him for the very first time, with Fata Ioss equally motionless beside her.

With his head bowed, his mouth half open and his eyes closed, Manuel looked like a child innocently sleeping. His features were those of an adolescent, but they were marked by the firm resolution of an adult and the wisdom and serenity of an old man, which shone through them. When she eventually plucked up courage to approach him, with Fata Ioss close behind, she panicked at the sight of the tears on his cheeks.

'Manuel! Manuel!'

She had to touch his shoulder to get any response. His body shook. Fata Ioss' torch made a pool of light on the stone floor of the choir.

'Angela...' He smiled at his sister and pulled himself to his feet.

'Why did you do it? I've been so worried!'

'Why? Didn't you know that...' But he didn't finish the sentence.

'Come along,' said Fata Ioss, 'time to go home.' Then, more

combatively: 'Just look at the state they've left our church in!'

Outside, the street was deserted. Even the soldier on duty had disappeared.

Fata Ioss walked in front, holding his torch, but it had gone out.

3

The next morning, the French flag was flying from the top of the church steeple, just below the weathercock. In no time at all the news had spread from one end of the village to the other, and the men, laughing up their sleeves, were climbing up to their attics to lift a roof-tile and peep delightedly at the blue, white and red colours streaming out against a cloudless sky in the fresh September breeze. The older ones among them brushed away a tear with the back of their hand, and the women's cheeks were flushed. But no one ventured out except the children, and they interrupted their games in the streets to stop and look up, shading their eyes with their hands, before swarming round the group of German soldiers who were locked in discussion.

Manuel had slipped out of the back door without Angela noticing. In the narrow lane behind the house he met Maax, who seemed in a hurry.

'Where are you off to so fast?'

'Can't explain now, Manuel. Look, take this and keep it: it might be of some use to you, and you can wear it quite safely.'

Maax disappeared rapidly, leaving Manuel turning his friend's blue beret over and over in his hands. He didn't understand what Maax had said, but never mind, it was a nice beret and he put it on before making his way up to the main street. As he got there he heard some children talking about the flag on the church.

He hurried on until he could get a look, then lifted his eyes to the top of the steeple without paying any attention to the group of soldiers.

'*Was macht denn der Kerl da?*' (What's that lad doing there?)

The German NCO had noticed him at once. Two soldiers advanced towards Manuel, shouting at him, but he didn't understand.

'What's the matter? What's up?'

'*Heil Hitler!*' bellowed the NCO.

'Good morning.'

'*Mütze abnehmen!*' (Take your hat off!)

Manuel had completely forgotten he was wearing Maax's beret. The man glared at him.

'*Warst du gestern Abend in der Kirche?*' (Were you in the church last night?)

'Yes, of course,' Manuel replied.

The German was taken aback. '*Abführen!*' (Take him away!) he barked, but then suddenly changed his mind.

'*Stehenbleiben! Was warst du in der Kirche machen?*' (No, stop! What were you up to in the church?)

Manuel lowered his eyes.

'*Raus mit der Sprache!*' (Out with it!)

'I... He called me, and I came. Come, follow me.'

The NCO looked at his men. '*Hälst du mich zum Narren?*' (Do you take me for an idiot?)

'It was wonderful...' As Manuel murmured those few words, a hint of a mysterious smile hovered over his lips.

'*Du lügst!*' bawled the German. '*Du hast den Lumpen angebracht und du wirst ihn auch wieder runter holen!*' (You're lying! You put that rag up there, and you're going to get it down again!)

Manuel shook his head.

'*Das werden wir sehen!*' (We'll see!)

The NCO looked up as though estimating the height, and then gave orders. Soon two soldiers came running with a long ladder which they leaned against the base of the tower. They had ropes hitched round their shoulders. They seized Manuel and manhandled him into the church and up to the organ-loft. He barely had time to glimpse the crowned statue of the Mother of God and whisper: 'Hail, Mary.' There was a passageway behind the organ, and the door to the tower was open. One of the soldiers leaned out of the first window and tied the rope to the top of the long ladder, while the other said to Manuel: '*Du musst dich vorbereiten.*' (You'd better get ready.) He himself took off his military cap and jacket and rolled up his sleeves.

Manuel put Maax's beret down in a corner and imitated the German. Then he asked him: 'What's your name?'

The soldier was taken aback. '... Wilhelm,' he replied.

'*Und du?*'

'Manuel, I'm called Manuel.'

The soldier lowered his eyes and motioned to him to go in front of him up the narrow stairs, towards where the bells hung, far above them.

When they reached the second window, the first German threw the rope up to them and Wilhelm and Manuel hauled the ladder up through the window and made the rope fast round the stair-rail.

'And what's his name?' Manuel asked, pointing to Wilhelm's companion who was coming up after them.

'Dieter,' said Wilhelm.

'Blimey, you can't have done it all on your own last night!' said Dieter as he reached them, puffing and blowing.

'I didn't do anything' said Manuel.

'*Natürlich,*' snapped the German. 'Must have been the angels!'

'There are hooks outside, a bit further to the right,' said Manuel. 'That's what you hang the ladders on.'

Wilhelm couldn't help laughing. 'You might have said so before!'

'I never thought of it. We've been away such a long time.'

The two Germans looked at each other. After that they had a terrible job getting the ladder out through the window and hanging it on the hooks.

'Jetzt weiter!' (Up we go!)

When they reached the great bells with their huge open mouths, Manuel got all excited and wanted to ring them. 'Like at Lidrezing,' he said.

Dieter and Wilhelm looked at each other again.

At each landing, all they had to do now was to haul the ladder up by the rope and hang it on the next set of hooks. Soon the stairs gave way to steep wooden rungs which led up the beams support-ing the steeple. By the time they got to the top, the three men were streaming with perspiration. The two Germans had a job keeping the heavy ladder steady and they nearly dropped it once, but eventually they managed to stand it up and then lower it towards the slates. It fitted snugly on to the metal cramps and reached right up to the weathercock, resting against the horizontal bar from which the flag was fluttering.

'All yours now.' They looked at Manuel. 'Not feeling dizzy?'

Manuel was remembering the famous night when he had used Le Voisin's long ladder to climb up to the pigeon-loft and let the birds out. And on that occasion he was already exhausted from having run all the way back.

'Sure you're not feeling dizzy?'

'No, thanks, Wilhelm.'

'He's done it once already ...'

'No, I haven't. I didn't do it, Dieter, believe me.'

'But in that case ... you're innocent.'

From the street below came a long despairing cry: 'That's my brother! He's innocent!'

Manuel leapt to the parapet and looked over. Angela was pleading with the German NCO. La Vieille and Fata Ioss were with her. The little square was black with people.

'Yes, I am,' said Manuel, looking at Wilhelm and Dieter as they tied the rope round his waist.

'But why...'

Manuel didn't wait to hear. Already he had swung himself on to the ladder, and with his eyes steadfastly fixed on the sky above he was climbing slowly, keeping his body pressed flat against the slates and every muscle in his body tense.

Down below in the square, an equally tense silence reigned.

Suddenly the prayer came to his lips like someone gasping for breath: Mother of God, pray for me. Mother of God, pray for me. Mother of God, pray for me. Up he went without a backward glance down into the abyss. Mother of God, pray for me. When at last he reached the top of the steeple, his stiff fingers took ages to untie the flag which kept wrapping itself around him and blinding him.

Everybody in the square had their heads back, straining to see. Some were biting their nails. Bêa-Yasse'Kette, standing next to the German NCO, was praying out loud: '*Gegrüsset seist du Maria, voll der Gnade...*'

Up there, Manuel was still at it. The big flag hid him almost completely from view.

'*Heilige Maria, Mutter Gottes...*'

The soldier never even turned to look at the old woman praying at his side.

Angela was trembling in La Vieille's arms.

At last the final knot was undone. Manuel tried to roll the flag up but a gust of wind caught it and nearly blew it away. He was leaning dangerously.

'*Lass ihn runter fallen!*' (Drop it!) shouted the NCO.

Manuel appeared not to have heard. He was still struggling with the folds of the material, when he suddenly started trying to come down the ladder blind.

'Werf ihn doch runter!' (Throw it down, for goodness' sake!)

Wilhelm and Dieter were leaning out of the top window and twisting their necks trying to see him. At that moment Manuel missed a rung; his body jerked down at full stretch, and his right hand, the only one he was holding on with, let go. He was slipping, falling, as a confused noise came to him from below.

'Mother of God...'

He must have closed his eyes at the same time as Angela did. By some miracle he managed to catch hold of the second to last rung with both hands. He felt as though his arms were being pulled out of their sockets, and he wasn't immediately aware of the firm grip pinning his legs.

Wilhelm and Dieter were leaning right out into space. The great tricolour flag seemed enormous as it floated away from Manuel and down, down, slowly, towards the waiting crowd. The two Germans managed to haul him back and get him inside the tower. They helped him down to the first landing. Questions of nationality had vanished, and it was just three exhausted young men who fell into each other's arms and wept. The NCO couldn't believe his eyes when he found them. Angela was close behind, despite Fata Ioss' attempts to restrain her, and she now threw herself into her brother's arms. He held her in silence, drying her tears.

Dieter and Wilhelm had gone back up to fetch the ladder. The NCO retired to the organ-loft, leaving Angela and Manuel on their own. When he eventually came down with them, his men were waiting with the French flag rolled up, and behind them stood the villagers, silent and resentful. Manuel looked wide-eyed as he fingered the blue beret that Maax had given him.

'You'd better come to my office,' the German said.

'He's innocent! He's innocent!' Angela pleaded, clinging to his arm.

The NCO motioned to Fata Ioss. 'Take her away. I'll let the lad go in a minute, I promise you.'

'She's right, he's innocent,' said Fata Ioss.

The man made no reply. He took Manuel through the crowd to Sister Irma's house, where he had set up his office. He went in first and stood behind his desk. Manuel stood in front of it and waited. The two men looked at each other for a long time.

'So, you're innocent,' the German said at last.

Manuel smiled and nodded.

'But why...?'

'I've already told you.'

The man pulled himself up straight. 'Why on earth did you go up, then?'

Manuel hesitated before replying: 'Greater love has no man...'

The German's grey eyes lit up. 'John chapter fifteen, verse thirteen,' he said, and a shy smile spread over his face.

'You know it?' asked Manuel, slipping naturally into the familiar 'Du' form of address.

'You bet! I'm a Lutheran.'

'Christian?'

'Of course.' The man was laughing now.

'And you made me...'

The reproach stung him. 'We're in a war,' he said. 'I must do my duty.'

'War is bad,' said Manuel. 'Love one another as I have loved you.'

There was a silence. Then the German said: 'You're right. But I had to get that flag taken down, and it was probably better for you to...' He paused, then added: 'Can you forgive me?'

Manuel's reply was immediate: 'Of course I can. Until seventy times seven.'

The German looked at him. 'What can I do for you?'

Manuel smiled again. 'Nothing. But don't try to find out who put the flag up.'

'But...'

'You know perfectly well that I was the one who put it up last night and this morning you made me take it down. Everybody knows that.'

The NCO stiffened. 'Ah, yes, of course,' he mumbled.

Manuel was still standing in front of the desk, smiling and twisting Maax's beret in his fingers.

'They'd better not try it again,' the German added.

'They won't,' said Manuel.

'How do you know? Do you know who it was?'

'No, but they wouldn't want me to have to go up there again.'

'Would you really?'

'Of course I would. Who else?'

'Well, whoever put it up there, of course!'

'You don't think they'd let themselves get caught, do you?'

The German gave Manuel a puzzled stare.

'There's Wilhelm and Dieter, of course,' Manuel went on. 'They were fine as far as the top of the tower, but they wouldn't be any good out on the steeple. They'd fall off.'

The man found himself asking: 'Wouldn't you want them to fall off?'

'No, of course I wouldn't. Love one another...'

'Yes, all right, I know.'

'We're good friends, Wilhelm and Dieter and I, we love each other.'

Still standing rather stiffly in his uniform, the German held out his hand to Manuel. 'Müller's the name,' he said. 'If you need me, I'm always here.' After a moment he added in an undertone: 'Because I love you, too... now.'

As Manuel was opening the door, the other said loudly: '*Heil Hitler!* That's what you have to say, Manuel.'

'What does it mean?' Manuel turned and faced Müller, who looked rather disconcerted.

'Well, Hitler, you know, the Führer.' He pointed to the photograph hanging on the wall behind his improvised desk.

'Yes, I saw the picture,' said Manuel. 'What does *Führer* mean?'

'It means the guide, the one who shows the way, who leads his people.'

'I am the Way,' murmured Manuel, 'I am the Good Shepherd.'

'Don't confuse things,' said the German.

'It's the truth. There isn't any other truth. And what about *Heil Hitler*, what does that mean?'

'It has three possible meanings. First, hail Hitler, like saying *guten Tag*.'

'I understand.'

'Then it may be a wish for Hitler to be saved, in other words to win the victory.'

'And the third meaning?'

'Well, I suppose it could mean that Hitler alone brings salvation.'

'God is the only one who can do that, Müller.'

'Yes, but that's not the...'

'And that's why I wouldn't ever be able to say *Heil Hitler*, although I very much hope that God will save the man called Hitler.'

Before the NCO could recover, Manuel had left the room, quietly closing the door behind him.

Angela and Fata Ioss were waiting for him in the square. The simpleton put on Maax's beret, waved to Dieter and Wilhelm who were busy a little further on, and went to join his folk as if nothing had happened.

In the church tower, now deserted, there was no one to ring the bells for the angelus, although it was by now midday.

In the afternoon Maax slipped into Angela's house through the back door. He had come to thank Manuel on behalf of all of them, and particularly Shong, but he didn't find him. Angela had had enough difficulty getting Manuel to go upstairs and lie down—he was complaining of pains in his arms, chest and stomach—and now that he was dozing she wasn't prepared to let him be disturbed. She would tell him about Maax's visit when he came down.

But he didn't come down that evening. Angela put the baby to bed and then went off early herself after glancing into her brother's room. He seemed to be sleeping peacefully, and there was no reason to be worried. In the middle of the night, however, she was suddenly woken, first by groans coming from Manuel's room, and then by his voice which seemed to be calling. She hurriedly got out of bed.

'What's the matter, Manuel?'

He was tossing in his bed, with his eyes still shut. His blond curls were plastered to his forehead with perspiration. He suddenly threw off the blanket with both hands and his fingers reached out as if trying desperately to hold on to something. His whole body tensed, then stiffened, and from deep in his chest there rose a series of spasmodic, frenzied groans which never quite escaped from his closed mouth. When he fell back on the bed his lips parted and the same cry came twice, the same call for help: 'Mother of God ... Mother of God ...' To begin with Angela didn't understand what he was saying, and then she waited for something to follow, but nothing came. She wiped the sweat from Manuel's brow and placed her cool hand on his head in the hope of calming him down. But in vain: there was not the slightest remission, and dawn arrived without any noticeable improvement. Angela got dressed as quickly as she could and went to find La Vieille and Fata Ioss. When she returned there was still no sign of change in Manuel's condition.

Fata Ioss went off to fetch the midwife. She couldn't make head or tail of it. It was obvious that Manuel had a high fever, but all she could do was give him the only sedative she could lay her hands on and hope it would have some effect. When she left, promising to call back later on, Fata Ioss declared that he would stay by Manuel's bedside: Angela should get on with seeing to little Sébastien, who had finally been woken up by all the comings and goings.

Manuel didn't wake up at all that day; the fever showed no signs of falling, and if anyone tried to rearrange the bedclothes he cried out in pain. The next night passed without any improvement, and then another day. The midwife was at her wits' end. What was needed was a doctor, but their regular doctor, the old man from Grandbourg, hadn't returned from the exodus, and she didn't know anyone else who had.

They tried to force some soup down him. By now the whole of Lasting-en-Lorraine knew about Manuel's mysterious illness, and some of the women gathered each evening in the church, which had at last been cleaned and tidied, to pray the rosary, under the leadership of Bêa-Yasse'Kette, who would then go on round to the house. She and Madamilla tried to give some comfort and support to Angela, whom the old lady now referred to as *dass ââme kênnd* (the poor child).

In restoring her patois, the return to Lasting had given old Bêa-Yasse'Kette a new lease of life and she seemed to be everywhere at once, enjoying every moment. Even the Germans could understand her.

The Germans. They came round to Angela's house on the third evening and introduced themselves: Dieter and Wilhelm. She wasn't at all sure, but in the end she took them up to Manuel's room.

'*Was hat er denn?*' (What's wrong with him?)

Angela shrugged her shoulders. Wilhelm took Manuel's hand

in his and squeezed it gently. Dieter ran his fingers through the simpleton's damp hair.

The next morning a staff car drew up in front of the house, and Müller got out, accompanied by the *Amtsarzt* (official doctor) from Sarreguemines. Angela took them up to see her brother.

Müller must have told the *Arzt* about Manuel's experience and how he had slipped and nearly fallen. The German doctor felt all the patient's muscles, provoking groans of pain. Then he sent for the midwife and gave her enough drugs and needles to give Manuel two injections a day, morning and night. He would come back himself in a few days.

'*Docda, ish's shlimm?*' (Doctor, is it bad?)

Bêa-Yasse'Kette was waiting for him by the front door. He was reluctant to give an opinion.

'*Es kann lange zugehen.*' (It can last a long time.)

'*Ea hêêld ava doch?*' (But he'll pull through?)

'*Wahrscheinlich, ja.*' (Probably, yes.)

Whereupon Bêa-Yasse'Kette pronounced sententiously: '*Do mousse ma hald de roserkronn's viddash'd bêêde!*' (All that remains for us to do is to carry on saying the rosary!)

The two men looked at each other, saluted and got back into their car.

Shong, Maax's friend, arrived at that moment to ask after Manuel, and Bêa-Yasse'Kette told him that the Germans really weren't as bad as all that. '*Dass sinn mênnshe genau vi mia!*' (They're people just like us!) And when the young man replied that they were just trying to butter them up, she wouldn't hear of it. 'Ta! Ta! Ta! Ta! Ta! Ta! Ta!' Their welfare people had organized soup-kitchens in Sarreguemines, hadn't they?

That really made Shong see red, but she carried on regardless. Wasn't the *Winterhilfswerk* organization handing out clothes for the coming winter? And weren't their own menfolk finding work, one after another, at the *Organisation Todt*? There was plenty to do, repairing electricity lines and rebuilding bridges.

Shong couldn't take any more. He nearly knocked old Bêa-Yasse'Kette over as he pushed past her to go up the stairs. When he came to Manuel's room and found him lying apparently lifeless in his bed, he shrank away like a frightened animal. 'When's he going to get better, Angela?' he asked.

'I don't know. No one knows.'

'*Gêd'sh bessa bêêde!*' (You'd do better to pray!) came Bêa-Yasse'Kette's voice, and the young man fled to avoid any further persecution.

But he came back. A few days later, Manuel's condition seemed to improve slightly, although he was still very weak. When Manuel opened his eyes and looked at those around him as if awaking out of a long sleep, it was Shong who gave him the news. 'They' had started setting up commissions of expulsion to deal with undesirable elements in the population, particularly French-speakers, who would be given the choice between Poland and France...

'*Vass soll ma donn noo Pôôle mache géén?*' (Whatever would we go and do in Poland?)

And German settlers would come in to replace them.

'*O Iérum Maria!*'

Shong glared at Bêa-Yasse'Kette before continuing. In Sarreguemines they had changed all the street-names and were now starting on people's Christian names. 'So I'm to be no longer Jean or Shong, but Johann!' On the twelfth of September they had piled up all the French flags and French books they could get hold of and burned them publicly in the street. '"*Hinaus mit dem welschen Plunder!*" (Out with all that foreign trash!) they said.'

'*Ounsa bish'hof honn'se yo ââ ous'geveesd!*' (And they've expelled our bishop too!)

Despite the seriousness of the situation, the bathos of Bêa-Yasse'Kette's comment was so great that they couldn't help laughing. That sent her into a huff, and she shut up.

There was no problem about retrieving their carts and wagons from Lidrezing where they had left them, and Le Voisin went to collect his. Some people even came away with more than they were entitled to.

From now on it was forbidden to say *Bonjour*. The official greeting was *Heil Hitler*, but *G'môa'ye* and *G'nôô'vdd* were still just about tolerated. There was talk of rationing, with coupons for food and even for buying a pair of boots.

No, of course the Germans weren't as bad as all that!

Shong let out a mocking laugh, and Angela tried to shut him up so as not to tire Manuel. He seemed to have dozed off again in any case.

'We'll get them in the end!'

Fata Ioss hadn't missed a single day. Throughout September, during Manuel's mysterious illness, he had come regularly to keep Angela up to date with what was happening, now that Maax and Shong came less often. Manuel only listened with half an ear, as if he was in another world, and it was only when Fata Ioss read from the *curé* of Lidrezing's book that his eyes lit up and he seemed a bit more alive.

The Germans had appointed one Josef Bürckel as *Gauleiter der Westmark* (Governor of the Western Marches), an area which covered the Moselle, the Saarland and the Rhineland Palatinate. 'In other words, they're treating the Moselle as German territory just like the rest.'

Dieter and Wilhelm came regularly to see Manuel, and even Fata Ioss no longer regarded them primarily as Germans. The *Amtsarzt* and Müller had also been back, but Ioss escaped to the kitchen as soon as they arrived.

Wag-Nache'Péda had been made *Ortsbauerführer* (local farmers' leader). Someone had to be, and how could he refuse? There was no point in waiting until they sent a settler to do the job! That had nearly happened already for the *Ortsgruppenleiter* (district head), but luckily someone had come forward. Fata Ioss felt it was silly of the young people to blame those who took on such responsibilities.

The school had also reopened, with a new teacher who only spoke German. How on earth had they got hold of all those school books in German so quickly? *Lesebuch, Rechenbuch, Geschichte...* Reading, arithmetic, history books... Everything was there, filling the satchels of the children who were now known as *Volksdeutsche*, or German stock.

'Oh, if only Sister Irma was here! As if we were German stock. We're from Lorraine, and proud of it! Do you remember that history lesson she gave us that night at Châtelaillon? That was something!'

On the thirtieth of October, the part of Lorraine known as the Moselle was formally annexed by the Third Reich. German troops took over the police and other services: *Schutzpolizei, Sicherheitsdienst, Geheime Staatspolizei.*

That evening, as the shadows were already beginning to blur the outlines of things, the old man sat alone in Manuel's room and cried bitter tears, which coursed freely down his wrinkled cheeks. Fata Ioss had been to Russia in the time of the old Kaiser, but that was nothing like as bad as the present horror.

4

November never seemed to end. It lingered over the *gasses* which were deserted as soon as the light faded, a little earlier with every passing day. The nights were interminable, like the long, twisting main street of Lasting-en-Lorraine. The old men who couldn't sleep lay there counting the hours, while the women stared into the darkness and fingered the big black beads of their rosaries under the warm sheets. From time to time there came from the courtyard the noise of a rabbit—excited or frightened, who could tell?—scrabbling on the walls of its hutch with a sound like gunfire. There were still few cocks about, and the houses were slow to awake in the morning, despite the clatter of hobnailed boots in the street, under the pall of mist that hung over the village. People rose late, particularly the older folk, who sometimes at last found a few minutes of precious sleep in those in-between moments before the day really started, or lay awake trying to recover the tatters of dreams and sew them together as they stared up at the ceiling, low and grey and heavy with menace like the eastern sky.

Fata Ioss would lie there next to La Vieille, listening for the slightest noise, always on the alert. Occasionally he spoke aloud, and La Vieille was astonished to hear him talking about the Beast, but in rambling, disconnected sentences, like a simpleton. She let him babble on in the silence and safety of the bedroom, but sometimes she would take his hand and squeeze it gently in hers under the sheets.

'So long as nothing happens to them!'

'It's all right, we're here...'

That was always the signal for him to get up at last, put on his trousers, jacket and hat and tiptoe out of the room as if he didn't know that his wife was awake.

'All this fog...'

She could hear him going off down the street muttering as his old shoes slipped on the smooth stone of the gutters: 'Hope nothing's happened to them!'

Then La Vieille would get up in her turn, get dressed and hasten down to the kitchen where Fata Ioss had put the handful of straw and the kindling ready to light the stove. As she cleaned the grate she could hear herself murmuring: 'Hope nothing...' But she pulled herself up short: 'There's nothing that can happen.'

The baby was nearly nine months old now, and Angela was looking after him as well as she could. The problem was that Manuel couldn't bring himself to leave his bed. He lay there the whole day long, staring at the whiteness of the ceiling. He hardly spoke unless asked a direct question, and he scarcely ever smiled.

The flame sprang up, bright, warm, beautiful. La Vieille smiled at the fire as she often did at Manuel to try to make him smile in return. Then she trotted over to the sink and filled the kettle. When the water boiled she poured it on to the *Malzkaffee*. She had placed the two bowls on the table and cut the bread, the *Schwarzbrot* which she found so difficult to digest, and was just spreading it with *Harzschmeer* when Ioss came in. She looked at him inquiringly.

'All's well,' said the old man, 'in a manner of speaking, that is...'

La Vieille sighed. 'But they said he'd get better.'

As if he hadn't heard, Fata Ioss continued: 'Apparently

they've expelled more than two hundred priests.'

'Oh, no! Are you sure?'

'That's what everyone's saying.'

'They'd take God himself away if they could!'

Fata Ioss looked at her in silence for a moment and then added in a whisper: 'As long as we've still got Manuel...'

But he didn't finish the sentence, and he lowered his eyes before his wife's gaze as if he was afraid he had already said too much.

La Vieille dipped her black bread into her coffee and said nothing. Even if she didn't fully understand what her husband meant, she somehow sensed that what he had said was very significant and that there was nothing to add.

Outside the window it was a murky day, or rather the same murky day that returned with every new dawn, merely a little greyer and a little shorter with every passing week. Moving through time was like crossing the desert, with the constant risk of losing one's bearings. Then suddenly it was the sixth of December, and Saint Nicholas' Day was upon them like a mirage rising up out of the sand.

Dieter and Wilhelm came round to Angela's house for the evening, bringing some *Gebäck* which their parents had sent. La Vieille had brought some of her own too, but Manuel preferred to nibble the little cakes which the two Germans offered him with a smile of encouragement. At one point he asked them: 'Isn't the war over yet?'

"Fraid not, old chap.'

That was Wilhelm who replied, a Wilhelm who was taken aback all of a sudden to see two big tears rolling from the simpleton's wide blue eyes down on to the pillow, where they soaked in.

'But it'll be over one day, Manuel,' said Dieter.

'One day...'

Manuel didn't utter another word the whole evening. The lads from the other side of the Rhine played with little Sébastien for a while and then left.

When La Vieille and Fata Ioss went home later, they nearly got lost in the fog which was swirling everywhere. In fact, if La Vieille hadn't been talking non-stop about Christmas and about the crib and all the other things that help one to survive, shining at the end of the night like a star fallen from the sky, they might well have taken the wrong road and carried on walking, arm in arm, right into the dark kingdom of death. But there was Christmas to prepare for, and her words, murmured in the darkness, were like a light guiding them home and helping them to pick up the trail of everyday living once they got there.

The first snows had come before Ioss got out his Christmas crib and started re-doing all the little figures, one by one. La Vieille had known at once, before opening the shutters, before even getting out of bed, because there was no sound of boots in the street and even the noise of dogs barking out in the countryside was muffled. For once, Ioss had not gone straight out when he got up, but after lighting the fire and the candle he had sat, lost in contemplation, looking at the Joseph figure that he had carved the previous winter in Châtelaillon. When La Vieille came and asked him what he was doing, she didn't quite catch what he muttered: 'Better re-do it... not finished off properly... haven't got the look quite right.'

Later, when she was pouring the coffee, he added: 'It's like us, there's always more to do, more finishing touches.'

La Vieille said nothing.

Then, as the days went by, Fata Ioss spent long hours putting the 'finishing touches' to his characters. Joseph gave him a lot of trouble. It was odd that he should have to expend so much effort on him, when the Virgin and Child were so much less bother. He sat staring at him for ages, turning him this way and that, and then stopping and gazing at him as if he were looking at himself in a mirror. Was he trying to recognize himself in his handiwork? La Vieille had to keep prodding him: 'You'd better get a move on if you want to have it all ready for next week!' Then he would give a start and put Joseph the foster-father down, only to pick him up again the next minute and fall back into silent contemplation, while La Vieille shook her head.

All the same, come the morning of the twenty-fourth of December, he was able to go off to Angela's house with a box on his shoulder. He had decided to set up the crib in Manuel's room.

Christmas was a strange festival that year.

When La Vieille and Fata Ioss returned to Angela's house that evening, they found Müller, the German NCO, standing to attention by Manuel's bedside, straining to hear what he was whispering:

'This war must end... Love one another, Müller, remember: love one another.'

'Ich weiss, Manuel, aber...' (I know, Manuel, but...)

'No buts: it's vital.'

Manuel fell silent and Müller turned away, stiff in his uniform and as white as a sheet.

'Ich hab was mitgebracht... (I've brought something) for Manuel, for the baby, and for you.'

'Oh, you shouldn't have,' murmured Angela, 'really you shouldn't... Thank you, thank you very much.'

'Frohe Weihnachten!' (Happy Christmas!) That was Müller the NCO's parting greeting.

As soon as he had gone out of the front door, Shong and Maax came in through the back carrying a huge fir tree with the branches tied up. Fata Ioss looked at them, intrigued.

'Plenty of fine trees up in the forest, grandad. No point in leaving them to be flattened by our bombs when the time comes to send Fritz packing.'

They took the tree up to Manuel's room and set it up beside Fata Ioss' crib. Then they stuck little white candles all over it and lit them.

'Happy Christmas, Manuel.'

'Peace on earth, peace on earth,' said Manuel over and over again, not taking his eyes off the tree for a moment.

Sébastien tried to catch the bright candles with his little hands. His eyes were shining with happiness.

At that moment the two young Germans, Dieter and Wilhelm, turned up. Shong and Maax made to disappear.

'No, stay,' said Manuel, sitting up in bed. 'Please stay.'

The four young men looked at each other suspiciously.

Dieter had brought some more home-made *Gebäck*, and Wilhelm took his *Quetsch Kaste* (accordion) out of its case.

'*Frohe Weihnachten*, Manuel!'

'*Frieden auf Erde* (Peace on earth),' said Manuel. Then he turned to Angela and asked her to fetch more chairs so that everyone could sit down round the crib.

Ioss and La Vieille couldn't get over how excited he seemed. Wilhelm started up on his accordion and Sébastien clapped enthusiastically in La Vieille's arms. Soon everybody was sitting round the crib: Angela, La Vieille holding the baby, Fata Ioss, Shong and Maax, then Manuel in his bed, then Wilhelm and Dieter. Dieter launched into *Ihr Kinderlein kommet*, accompanied by Wilhelm and by the gently quavering voice of La Vieille. Then Fata Ioss started to sing *Il est né le divin enfant*, and even Maax ended up by joining in in his gruff voice. Finally Wilhelm struck up *Silent Night*, which the German-speakers knew as *Stille Nacht, heilige nacht* and the French-speakers as *Douce nuit, sainte nuit*. They each sang in their own language, and even Sébastien chirped along merrily. Manuel's face shone as if mysteriously illuminated from within and, looking at him, Fata Ioss was suddenly struck by how white his hair had gone. To begin with he thought he was dreaming, and he was just nudging La Vieille to see what she thought when the carol ended and Manuel said 'Fata Ioss, read us the Christmas gospel.'

Everybody watched as Fata Ioss got up and went to fetch the *curé* of Lidrezing's book from under Manuel's pillow. He opened it and, still standing, started to read the story of the Nativity. They all listened, even the two Germans, who seemed to be following well enough. When he got to the place where it says that Mary laid her newborn child in a manger, Fata Ioss stopped, put his hand into his jacket pocket, pulled it out and then opened it to reveal the Christ child. He held out his hand towards Manuel and looked at him. And the miracle happened.

Without a moment's hesitation, Manuel threw back the bed-clothes, heaved his legs out of bed and pulled his long nightshirt down over them. Angela let out a cry but Fata Ioss held her back with his free hand. The simpleton was standing by his bed now. When he tried to walk he was rather unsteady, but Maax and Wilhelm jumped up at the same time and supported him on either side as he shuffled towards Fata Ioss with outstretched hands. Barefoot, the white figure approached the crib, and the others all held their breath. Ioss placed the baby in his cupped hands, whereupon Wilhelm and Maax, still supporting him, knelt down with him. Then he leaned forward and laid the new-born child on the straw. Behind him, Fata Ioss began to read again in a voice trembling with emotion. When he had finished, the three young men got slowly to their feet. Manuel's face, though still shining, was bathed in tears. He was murmuring words that no one could understand as they took him back to bed and made him lie down.

'Now eat,' he said at last.

Angela had put the German *Gebäck* and the French cakes together on the same plate.

To disguise his emotion, Shong went to see to the little candles on the tree, some of which were leaning dangerously. Wilhelm played some squeaky notes on his *Quetsch Kaste* to amuse Sébastien, who was beginning to get tired.

Angela's plate of cakes went round. Dieter spoke of a letter from his mother, and of the present his little sister Ruth was getting: *'Ein Schaukelpferd, wie für einen Jungen!'* (A rocking-horse, just the same as for a boy!) Maax recalled the rocking-horse he had had as a child, which his mother still had at home in the loft over the shed.

'I'll bring it for Sébastien next year.'

Everybody laughed, even Manuel, whose face was still wet with tears.

... That evening, or rather that night, when they left long after everyone else and were on their way home, with La Vieille wrapped up in her coat to keep warm, Fata Ioss couldn't help thinking over what had happened earlier. His wife heard him muttering: 'The strangest thing about this evening was Manuel's hair: it was so white!' What he was thinking was that it looked like a halo round Manuel's childlike blue eyes. 'I'm sure I didn't dream it,' he added.

La Vieille looked at him and said nothing.

Next morning she was out early as soon as there was a glimmer of light, and as she went up the main street towards Angela's house there was no one else about. Angela had scarcely had time to get the stove going...

'Anything the matter?'

'No, my dear, I just needed to see Manuel, that's all.'

'But he's still asleep...'

'Just to see him. Can I go up?' And already she was halfway up the old wooden stairs. Angela followed her with her eyes.

When she got to the landing, La Vieille pushed the door gently open. She could smell the fresh scent of the fir tree. Manuel was lying on his back, asleep. She leaned over and had to clap her hand over her mouth to stifle a cry of stupefaction. Manuel's hair...

'Angela! Angela!'

'What is it? What's the matter?'

'Manuel's hair, it's gone all white.'

'Yes, I know.'

'Is that all you can say?'

'What do you expect me to say? He's my brother, but at the same time he's like a stranger living among us.'

La Vieille went out shaking her head. Out in the street she remembered what Fata Ioss had said. No, he hadn't dreamed it, Manuel's hair was as white as an old man's, while his face was still that of an adolescent, even of a child, with those pure, laughing eyes. However could it have happened?

How was it that La Vieille never noticed the snow falling that Christmas Day? When it was time to close the shutters, she went over to the window as usual, and Fata Ioss heard her exclaim: 'White! It's all white, I can't be dreaming...'

'No, you're not dreaming,' he said with a laugh. 'It's been snowing all day, nearly.'

'Snowing?'

'Yes, snowing! What's come over you?'

'Oh, nothing, nothing.'

All that whiteness which sent a pale, milky light into even the darkest corners at night also had the effect of burying the secret of Manuel's white hair. Nobody spoke of what had happened in the village, neither Fata Ioss, nor La Vieille, nor Angela, nor Wilhelm, Shong, Dieter, Maax, Müller, not even Bêa-Yasse'Kette who was speechless for quite a while when she first saw what had happened. What is the use of speaking about mysteries? Who can find the tracks of the unknown visitor when once the snow has covered them? Who could have traced the Lord's footsteps on the waters of the Sea of Galilee? Throughout the long dark January days, their thoughts often turned to Manuel's white hair as to a beacon, but they never spoke of it except at night, in their dreams... Time was passing like a dream in any case, and sometimes like a nightmare when the news was bad.

'They've abolished the religious orders and communities.'

It was in mid-February that Fata Ioss announced that to his wife one evening.

'What's that you say?'

'There aren't going to be any nuns any more.'

'Who says so?'

'Hitler.'

'Let him say. Nothing can stop Sister Irma being Sister Irma. Hitler can't do anything about that.'

'But they stopped Sister Irma coming back.'

'That's different.'

Later, when March was nearing its end and the rain had washed away the last of the snowdrifts, Ioss came back from the village shop and told her: 'In Sarreguemines and Forbach all the crucifixes have been removed from the hospital wards.'

'The brutes!' muttered La Vieille, crossing herself.

'And all the nuns who were teachers or nurses have been expelled.'

'Are you sure?'

'So they say.'

'Well, who's going to look after the sick, then?'

The old man shrugged his shoulders. 'Another thing they say is that we're being given a last chance to go and live in France.'

'They'd be only too glad if we went and left them free to come in and take over. Don't you think?'

'Yes, that's right. But some are going to take up the offer...'

'Not me, anyway,' said La Vieille decisively. 'I'm not going to give them the pleasure of driving a wedge between France and Lasting-en-Lorraine. This is France, here, where I am.' And she added, almost shouting: 'And here I stay!'

'Some people claim that those who choose to go are taken back to the frontier.'

'Which frontier?'

'You know very well which frontier, Mother.'

La Vieille looked at Fata Ioss, shaken to the core.

'They also say that some are deported.'

'Where to?'

'Germany.'

She looked away, and Fata Ioss caught her wiping away a tear.

'Maybe they're just rumours, you know.'

Rumours or not, it was towards the end of April, when the cherry trees were in blossom everywhere, that the news came of the institution of compulsory *Arbeitsdienst* (labour service). It went from house to house, like the plague, but was soon over-taken by another piece of news, so good that no one could believe it to begin with: 'Manuel is out walking with little Sébastien under the cherry trees.'

He hadn't been out of bed, far less out of the house, for months...

That morning, when Angela had brought up his coffee, she had found him standing in the middle of the room. He had opened the shutters, and he was gazing out at the orchards.

'Manuel!'

'Morning, Angela. I'm coming down for breakfast, you know.' Then, pointing to the cherry-blossom outside: 'Look, it's spring.'

'Yes, Manuel, it's spring.'

'I can't think where I've put my clothes, Angela. Can you help me to find them?'

Nearly six months had gone by since he had taken them off...

'Wait a moment, I'll just go and find them, but...'

But she bit her tongue, for fear of seeing the tall thin body of her brother, draped in his nightshirt like a priest in his Easter alb, collapse on her like a dream. She opened the wardrobe and took out his trousers and pullover. When she handed him his clothes, she was struck by the shock of white hair which stuck out all round his head like the glory surrounding the figure of Christ in some medieval paintings.

'We ought to have got Julien to come and cut your hair.'

'Why, is it too long?'

'It is a bit, yes.'

'Not to worry, Angela.'

Did he realize that it had gone all white? He hadn't looked at himself in a mirror for a long time.

When Angela went downstairs to lay the table, Manuel got himself dressed slowly. Although his legs were shaking, he felt a new strength circulating in his body, like sap rising in the spring.

'Where's Sébastien?'

'He's still asleep, Manuel.'

'I'll take him out for a walk through the cherry trees.'

'Oh, do you think . . . ?' But she didn't dare ask if he would be strong enough to carry the child, who was only just beginning to walk. She was so happy to see Manuel up and dressed that she wouldn't have stood in his way for the world, in case he had a relapse.

'He's not very good at walking yet, you know.'

'Never mind, I can carry him,' Manuel replied. 'When do you think he'll wake up?'

As if in response to Manuel's question, Sébastien started crying.

'I'll go and get him.'

When she came down again with the child in her arms, Angela found her brother standing in front of the mirror, somewhat startled at what he could see.

'Say hello to Manuel, Sébastien.'

Angela had to force herself to sound normal. Sébastien produced his version of a greeting, and Manuel held out his arms to him with a smile, saying: 'Angela, you never told me that I looked like the cherry-blossom.'

When he went out of the house a little later he had a job making Maax's beret sit properly on his head.

'You were right, I'd better go and see Julien. But he mustn't cut too much off...'

As he walked down the street, surprise and pleasure were written all over the faces of the people he met. 'Manuel, well I never! What... How are you? You better now, then?'

'Yes, I'm fine now, thanks. 'Bye!'

'Goodbye.'

And off he went, down the lane and across the Pré aux Pucelles to the Jardin des Cerisiers, the cherry orchard, now in its full spring glory.

'Morning, Manuel!'

'Morning.'

'Better now, then, are you?'

'Yes, as you can see.'

The orchard had never been so full of people. They pretended that it was little Sébastien they had come to see—as if they hadn't seen him only the day before in the grocer's with his mother!—and used that as an excuse to get close to Manuel and touch him.

When the news reached Fata Ioss he rushed off to the orchard like the rest. Yesterday he had left Manuel lying in bed, apathetic, and seemingly resigned to his strange illness for ever, and now they were saying that he was out with the child up beneath the cherry trees.

'I just can't believe it!'

'But that's what they're saying,' La Vieille countered. 'And I don't suppose they're all dreaming.'

Many of them thought they were, though, when they saw Manuel with his long white hair sticking out from under his beret.

'It must have been the shock,' said Madamilla to Bêa-Yasse'Kette. 'When he fell, he must have had a terrible fright, so...'

'Think so?' said Bêa-Yasse'-Kette doubtfully. 'He's better, that's the main thing.'

Ioss came past only a few feet away, without noticing them. 'Morning, Manuel.'

'Oh, good morning, Fata Ioss! Have you come up to admire the cherry-blossom too?'

'I heard you were up here.'

'Isn't the earth beautiful, Ioss? Look how Sébastien's eyes are shining!'

'Yes, it really is, it's beautiful.'

Manuel picked two primroses and gave them to the child who was standing in the new grass. The birds were singing in the trees.

'I've brought the book, Ioss.'

'Oh, you found it, did you?'

Manuel smiled. 'Would you read me a passage?'

The old man felt his heart swelling: Manuel was well and truly back. He opened the book and read: 'And very early on the first day of the week they went to the tomb when the sun had risen. And they were saying to one another, "Who will roll away the stone for us from the door of the tomb?" And looking up, they saw that the stone was rolled back—it was very large...'

From time to time Fata Ioss stopped and looked at Manuel, who was happily drinking in every word, and at the same time keeping an eye on the child playing in the grass. When the old man at last finished reading, Manuel took the open book from his hands and proclaimed in a loud, clear voice: 'And these signs will accompany those who believe: in my name they will cast out demons; they will speak in new tongues; they will pick up serpents, and if they drink any deadly thing, it will not hurt them; they will lay their hands on the sick, and they will recover.' He closed the book and slipped it into his pocket, and then went off to fetch Sébastien who had wandered a few yards away. He didn't hear Fata Ioss murmuring in amazement: 'His head and his hair were white as white wool, white as snow.'

The first petals drifted down from the cherry trees of Lasting-en-Lorraine and landed like snowflakes in the morning breeze.

5

In July, the Germans expelled another two hundred priests and turned them loose in the open countryside near Verdun. When the news reached Lasting-en-Lorraine, there was much silent head-shaking, conveying reproach, indignation and powerlessness. Just as they had been powerless to refuse their forced enrolment in the *deutsche Volksgemeinschaft* (Community of the German people) although none of them wanted to belong to it in the slightest.

'We're French, we are,' bellowed Maax, 'and we'll show them, too!'

'*O Iérum Maria!*' groaned Bêa-Yasse'Kette.

'If only Sister Irma could be here ...'

That was a sentiment frequently expressed in the village during the summer of 1941, and the autumn and winter that followed.

'In any case,' said Shong one day, 'the Germans have had it.'

'If only that were true!'

'But it is! Look, Hitler signed his death-warrant when he gave the order to invade Russia. If Napoleon himself couldn't succeed...'

'Well, that's what they say, I know...'

'If Sister Irma was here, she'd say the same thing, and she knows everything there is to know about Napoleon's Russian campaign!'

Maax didn't attempt to reply. He was well aware of the extent of Sister Irma's knowledge of the subject, from having had it dinned into him at school.

Instead, he watched Manuel get up and go off out into the fresh snow by himself, as though indifferent to what he had just heard. His beret still didn't cover his mass of white curls. Under the huge cape which enveloped him, Maax knew that he was clutching the *curé* of Lidrezing's book. Large snowflakes had begun to fall, covering his footprints. Maax remembered a poem by Victor Hugo which he had once learned at school, about the retreat from Moscow in 1812.

> *Il neigeait. On était vaincu par sa conquête.*
> *Pour la première fois, l'aigle baissait la tête ...*
>
> *(It was snowing. Vanquished by victory itself,*
> *For the first time, the eagle bowed its head.)*

Was it the snow that awakened old memories in Maax's head, or was it what Shong had just been saying? Could it be true that Hitler's eagle was at last to bow its head, like Napoleon's? If only that poem could turn out to be prophetic! If only the Germans could end up having to go back home again!

Maax was still gazing out of the window in the direction that Manuel had taken, as if he expected to see him come back any moment. He knew perfectly well that it would be a couple of hours before he returned, as always. He knew, because he had watched him often enough, in the blistering heat of summer, and then all through the autumn, with the dead leaves crunching beneath his feet. He knew, because he had followed him—and even Müller's Germans knew, even the latest arrivals who quickly discovered that the strange young man with the white hair and the beret wasn't a member of the Resistance but the village idiot, the *Dorfidioten*, who could go where he liked—he knew that Manuel went off up to the hollow beech tree on the Ermerich and stayed there reading his Bible interminably and moving his lips as if he were chewing the words in order to digest them better. Not even the biting cold of January stopped him.

'*Réliyeuss' farick'd!*' (He's a religious maniac!) said some of the sharper tongues in the village.

He was certainly mad, but not in the way they supposed. For Maax, Manuel was mad in the sense in which someone is madly in love. And he was like a lover, displaying his feelings quite openly. In church he could be seen with his head bent forward as if he were asleep, and those who had tried to attract his attention at those times knew that he was somehow absent from the world and from himself. He would stop by the statue of the Mother of God with a radiant expression on his face, and Angela or Fata Ioss would have to give him a shove to get him to move on up the aisle. Yet he was very good at looking after the little one during the fine weather and helping Angela in the garden. And he managed to pay regular visits to Müller, Wilhelm and Dieter. Every time he saw Müller he asked him when this awful war would be over, or so they said. They also said that Müller had become very fond of the *Weisskopf* (White-head), as the Germans sometimes called him, especially the most recent arrivals, and he certainly spent ages alone with him. Wilhelm even told Fata Ioss that the simpleton had become a kind of confidant for the NCO. Maax scratched the back of his neck. How could he go on treating the German as an enemy now that he was Manuel's friend? How would it all end?

It ended gently enough as far as the winter was concerned, with the hedges and woods retaining a white edging even while the clumps of primroses were coming into flower in April. The villagers found it hard to shake off the fatalistic lethargy into which they had sunk once their first excitement at returning had worn off. Some of them just hung about in the street, on the *gasses*, as though numbed by despair. What jolted them out of it, for a while at least, was the first air-raids the following July.

When the *Sturmalarm* first sounded above the rooftops, some people went to the door and stood gazing up at the summer sky with a kind of relief, contrary to all the instructions they had been given. It was the women, prudent as always, who had to take them to task and sometimes even drag them down to the shelter of the cellar. They had the impression that the monster of war had suddenly and violently awoken from a long slumber, and the noisy machines that flew overhead were like the rumblings of its anger, an anger that would have unforeseeable consequences.

Angela had rushed straight down to the cellar clutching Sébastien in her arms. Manuel came down a little later and sat motionless in a corner until the all-clear sounded. By the light of the candle Angela could see big tears welling up in his wide, staring eyes and rolling off his cheeks one by one. In the end she couldn't keep quiet any longer.

'Are you frightened, Manuel?' she asked. He shook his head. Angela had never seen anyone cry like that before, without moving a muscle of the face or making a sound. It was like the rain falling from a clear sky. 'Why are you crying, then?'

'The war, Angela, war is evil.'

That day no bombs fell on the village, but the inhabitants started sorting out and furnishing their cellars in the expectation of having to spend much more time down there in the future.

It was in the second half of August that the next blow hit Lasting-en-Lorraine. Germany had decreed that all the young men should be forcibly drafted into the *Wehrmacht*, and a few days later the news came that Hitler had granted full German nationality to the good people of Lorraine.

'The bastards!' groaned Marx. 'We'll never go, never. We're French, we are, not Germans!'

But what could they do?

On that evening of the twentieth of August 1942, despair came home to roost. The mothers wept, while the men sat drinking themselves slowly under the table, glass by glass, like ships scuttling themselves.

'But they can't let our boys go and shoot at Frenchmen!'

In every heart there rang the echo of Sister Irma's words. They told each other with conviction that they were French, that they had been French first, even if they spoke the Frankish language of Clovis—that's what Sister Irma had said—rather than the French of France. Of course they knew the German songs of Eichendorff which their grandmothers had sung while they were in the cradle, of course they could understand the Germans from Saarbrücken, and Müller and the rest of them, but that wasn't to say . . . Some people claimed that often enough, in the old days, a young man would go off to the Saarland to find himself a wife, but then there would always be those who found a reason for siding with the apparent winners. The others refused to listen, indeed they ostracized them. Fata Ioss rapped out: 'We're French, and we're staying French, and there's an end to it!'

The next day there was a rumour that the new recruits would be sent off to the Russian Front.

'O Iérum Maria!' Bêa-Yasse'Kette crossed herself hastily.

They got together at Ioss' house. He'd been to Russia in the last war, so he could probably tell them something of what awaited the reluctant conscripts, *Malgré-nous* (Despite ourselves), as they were later to be called. When they arrived, they found Maax and Shong deep in discussion, or so it was later claimed. Ioss did his best to reassure the families. He also kept repeating to anyone who would listen that it wasn't anything like as bad as the present horror.

'What on earth was that supposed to mean?' the mothers wondered.

They could have been forgiven for envying Manuel the

simpleton when they passed him in the street with his jacket pocket bulging with his famous book, on the way as always to the hollow beech tree on the Ermerich. 'It's all right for some!' sighed Mother Houbad.

'In a manner of speaking...'

Müller had informed Angela that Manuel was not affected by the decree, being unfit for service in the *Wehrmacht*, and deep down she was glad, although she was careful not to say anything.

The first one to receive his call-up papers was Roger Berdaning, or *Rüdiger* as the Germans insisted on calling him. He went off meekly one fine morning with his cheap suitcase in his hand, accompanied by tears from the rest of his family. If a smile seemed to be hovering on his lips it was because he was thinking of the idyllic night of love, his first, that he had just spent in the arms of his Milou. She couldn't bring herself to be cruel enough to resist his advances yet again. Who could resist a man who was off to the Russian Front, anyway? So off he went, waving as if he was just going down to see his Aunt Mélie in Grandbourg for a few days. Some weeks later the news of his death in *Roussland* plunged the whole village into darkness.

They said that the hospital in Sarreguemines was overwhelmed with cases of acute appendicitis, and the *Amtsarzt* had no hesitation in speaking of a complaint called *Wehrmachtsblinddärme* or 'army appendix'. They soon saw through you, and had you up and off to the Urals in no time.

They said there had been summary executions, on the border with France, of lads who had tried to escape.

The strangest accidents happened. Werner cut his finger off when chopping wood: 'Clumsy fellow!' said his grandfather with a meaningful laugh. Sepp had his big toe crushed by a falling barrel, and a nasty cut on the ankle wouldn't stop suppurating. Conrad, whose parents had bought up Siébert's Mill, got his arm caught in the mill-wheel and it had to be amputated. What a lot of misfortunes!

Every afternoon, the older women, Rak'Onna, Madamilla, Bêa-Yasse'Kette and others went up to the church to pray the rosary aloud, and Müller the NCO could hear them from his office in Sister Irma's house. Sometimes he got up in annoyance and slammed the window, making the sentry outside jump. Manuel often accompanied the women, and they were quite happy for him to kneel down on the stone floor of the choir like a mysterious celebrant. Then he would be seen striding off across the fields towards the Ermerich with his halo of white hair and Maax's beret perching uneasily on top.

Maax had had his marching orders too, and so had Shong. Everybody saw them go off together, with their kitbags on their backs, after leaving Müller's office in the schoolhouse. It was a surprise when the police swooped on their parents' houses a few days later. They had never arrived at the *Kaserne* (barracks). The police carried out a *Hausuntersuchung* (search), but naturally failed to find any trace of them. Their families were threatened with reprisals, but only half-heartedly, since the whole village swore blind that they had seen them go.

'*Ish konn's shvé're,*' said Bêa-Yasse'Kette with her hand on her heart, '*ish konn's shvé're, minne hêrre!*' (I can swear to it, gentlemen!)

'*Schon gut!*' (All right!)

The policemen couldn't wait to get away from the old woman who smelled so strongly of *Knoblauch* (garlic). These Lorrainers...!

They made two or three surprise return visits, but in vain. There was no trace of *Deserteure* in Lasting-en-Lorraine. Müller assured them that he was being vigilant. But how far did they trust him?

Manuel knew that he could trust Müller. He went to say hello almost every day when he got back from the Ermerich, not hesitating to go out of his way through the orchards to have a chat with him, or with Wilhelm and Dieter. It was only after that that he would go off to Fata Ioss' house for his regular visit.

It was there, in the cellar, that Maax and Shong would be waiting for him with patient impatience. Every day. In the mornings, they worked at excavating a hideout underneath Fata Ioss' courtyard, just big enough to squeeze into if there was an alert. They had to make sure they left enough time to empty the three sackloads of potatoes in front of the board which concealed the entrance. In an emergency, they could always dive into the two large barrels where Ioss put his fruit in the autumn, and he would cover them up. He knew he was running a big risk, and La Vieille with him, and he had taken his precautions.

For instance, La Vieille would never go shopping for four. Everyone would know about it in no time. She carried on the same as before, but buying just the tiniest bit more of everything. Angela, who was in on it, did the same, and Manuel took the provisions round in the evening, hidden under his clothes, on his return from the Ermerich, after visiting the NCO. By tightening their belts a little in both households they managed to feed the two outlaws, whose stay in the cellar had not affected their appetite in the slightest.

The only thing was, they were bored silly. September and October seemed interminable that year. They soon got tired of playing cards, and draughts, and chess. And Fata Ioss could hardly spend all his time down in the cellar with them. So the arrival of Manuel every evening was quite an event, an occasion for celebration. He told them about the grey autumn skies, occasionally pierced by the pale rays of a white sun; he told them about the swallows on the telegraph wires, and their departure one fine morning; he spoke of the murmur of the fountain on moonlit nights, for he sometimes went out at night now, when all the world was asleep, to go up to the far end of the choir and speak softly to the One whom his soul loved; he told them of the clouds sweeping over the Ermerich from France, bringing sometimes light and sometimes darkness. And the two young men listened to the simpleton as to an oracle.

'And the war, Manuel, what about the war?'

At that, Manuel's eyes filled with tears, and they watched in astonishment as their friend cried silently for several minutes.

'Why don't you read us something out of your book?'

They had discovered that it was the only way to bring the joy and sunshine back to his eyes.

So Manuel would take the book from his pocket, open it and read a few lines at random. Maax and Shong were always fascinated by the expression of his face with its halo of white.

One evening, while Manuel was reading the words: 'We find nothing wrong in this man. What if a spirit or an angel spoke to him?', Fata Ioss came rushing in. 'The Schupos are at your parents' house, Shong, quick, take shelter!'

The two lads crawled into the narrow tunnel that led to the hideout under the yard, Ioss slipped them some ham, a loaf of bread and a bottle of wine, put the board over the entrance, tipped the sack of potatoes in front with Manuel's help, and set about obliterating all traces of human habitation from the cellar. As soon as they had finished, Manuel quickly got dressed and hurried off to be with Angela.

'Goodnight, Mother.'

'Goodnight, Manuel.'

La Vieille was uneasy.

As Manuel was crossing the square he ran into the Schupos' car.

'*Halt!*'

Manuel stopped and was quickly seized by two *Polizisten*.

'*Jetzt haben wir dich!*' (Got you at last!)

Before he could stammer a word, the simpleton was bundled into the car and driven off to the schoolhouse, where the *Polizist* barked at a dumbfounded Müller: '*Der Kerl ist verdächtig, er trägt eine Perrücke . . .*' (He's a suspicious character, he's wearing a wig.)

'*Aber nein!*' Müller tried to interrupt.

'*Heraus mit ihm!*' (Get him out!)

They hustled him out of the car and into Müller's office, where they pulled his hair and stripped him. He was dumb before them, trying merely to hold his trousers on with both hands.

Müller had taken the *Polizist* over to one corner of the room, and Manuel, under close guard, could only catch a few scraps of what was said: ' . . . *Dorfidioten . . . Weisskopf . . . Krankheit . . . Arzt.*'

'*Und das? Was soll das bedeuten?*' (And that? What is that supposed to mean?)

He was waving the *curé* of Lidrezing's book under Müller's nose.

'*Das Evangelium.*' (The Gospels.)

'*Der Kerl ist zum Schluss noch Träger von Geheimbotschaften!*' (I'll tell you what he is, he's a secret messenger!)

'*Aber nein, ich kenne ihn doch.*' (No, he isn't. I know him.)

And Müller told the *Polizist* about Manuel's religious devotion and his visits to the church, but also about Angela and Sébastien and a young man who was killed in the Ardennes in May 1940.

'*Doch dieses Buch . . .*' (But this book . . .)

'*Der Kerl kann ja kaum lesen!*' (The lad can barely read!)

At that moment the two of them turned round and surprised Manuel with his eyes closed and his lips murmuring over and over again: 'Mother of God, pray for us. Mother of God, pray for us. Mother of God, pray for us . . .'

'*Was hat er denn?*' (What's the matter with him?) said the man, involuntarily lowering his voice.

'*Er betet*' (He's praying), Müller replied in a whisper.

There was a sudden silence in the room, and then the Schupo said: '*Solch ein Haar hab ich noch nie gesehen. Seltsam!*' (I've never seen hair like it before. Most odd!) He turned to his men and ordered: '*Gibt ihm seine Kleider zurück und lasst ihn gehen.*' (Give him his clothes back and let him go.)

They had to touch Manuel's arm to bring him out of his prayers. He got dressed slowly, quite calm all of a sudden. When he was ready, he came towards the *Polizist* and held out his hand like a beggar.

'*Was will er denn? Hast du nich gehört, du kannst gehen!*' (What does he want? Didn't you hear? You can go!)

Manuel didn't move.

'*Das Buch...*' (The book...) said Müller.

The Schupo stiffened. '*Nein. Der welsche Plunder...*' (No. Foreign trash...)

'The Word of God,' Manuel murmured almost inaudibly, and he stood there with his hand still outstretched.

Müller intervened. '*Geh, Manuel. Zurück zu Angela.*' (Go, Manuel, back to Angela.)

Manuel hesitated, turned slowly away, and walked despondently towards the door.

From behind him came a shout of '*Heil Hitler!*' Manuel didn't turn round, didn't even stop.

'*Heil Hitler, du Idiot du!*'

Manuel went down the steps and away. Once again the tears poured down his cheeks as he walked down the main street, and he didn't bother to wipe them away. Some of those watching from behind their curtains said to themselves that he must have been beaten.

Back at the house Angela was frightened to death, for Maax, Shong, La Vieille and Fata Ioss. She was horrified when she found out about her brother's arrest. 'You mustn't go out any more, Manuel, you mustn't...' But she knew as she said it that it was quite impossible. Who would take the provisions to the two men in the cellar?

'The book...' stammered Manuel. 'They've kept the book.' And he withdrew into a kind of absence, while continuing to cry silently but inconsolably.

The Schupos didn't leave the village until late that night. Even later there was a knock on Angela's door.

'*Entschuldigen Sie mich bitte*...' (Please excuse me.)

It was Müller.

Angela took him to Manuel. The German NCO bent down before the simpleton, almost kneeling.

'*Ich bitte dich um Verzeihung, Manuel.*' (Please forgive me, Manuel.)

Manuel looked up at him with eyes still filled with tears.

'*Da ist das Buch*...' (Here's the book.)

Manuel seized it, and kissed the hand which held it out to him.

'*Nein,*' said Müller, '*nein. Es ist nicht*...' (No, no, it's not...) Then he added: '*Kannst du mir verzeihen?*' (Can you forgive me?)

Manuel looked at him, raised him to his feet and gave him a big hug. 'Thank you,' he said. 'Thank you very much.'

When he left shortly afterwards, Müller hadn't revealed the subterfuge he had used to pacify Manuel.

Fata Ioss' household continued in fear and dread for a good part of the night. The Schupos hadn't gone off in the direction they'd come from... It was not until late the next morning that the old man felt able to go down into the cellar and pick up all the potatoes one by one—three sackloads!—before letting the two lads out of their hiding place, pallid and unshaven, as though they had been shut up in a tomb.

'That was dreadful!' said Maax.

Shong was shaking all over. 'We thought we were buried alive.'

They had eaten practically nothing and they stank horribly.

Ioss did his best to comfort them.

It was not until Manuel brought them their provisions that evening that they heard about his experience. Would they understand that his arrest had spared the village plenty of *Hausuntersuchungen*? Fata Ioss looked at him in silence for a good long while, as one gazes at a treasure that has been nearly lost. And to think that not once during the interminable hours of last night had he thought that anything might have happened to Manuel! To think that...

But it was no good dwelling on it.

'You'll have to be more careful in future, Manuel,' he ventured to say in the end.

The simpleton looked at him without replying. Why be careful when life itself is waiting for you?

And life gradually returned to its normal pattern. Each evening Manuel went up to the hollow tree on the Ermerich, before coming back down to call on Fata Ioss and his lodgers. November had come, with its greyness and its mists which took ages to clear and gave audacious ideas to the two young men: without Fata Ioss' knowledge they now came out occasionally at night. That was how it came about that in the morning the Germans found their bicycle tyres slashed, the posters which had been put up the previous day defaced, and the new road signs with their Germanized names—Lastingen, Zinzingen—turned round or simply removed. The NCO was getting more and more perturbed, he told Manuel so, and the villagers wondered and laughed up their sleeves.

One evening someone said that the Allies had launched an attack in North Africa. On another occasion, it was reported that the Germans had crossed the unoccupied zone of France, and that part of the fleet had scuttled itself at Toulon. But who could tell what was true and what was not? It was also said that over in *Roussland* there were major battles around Stalingrad.

'They've had it!' exclaimed Shong. 'I tell you, they've had it!'
Fata Ioss had some difficulty getting him to calm down.

Meanwhile, two more young men from Lasting-en-Lorraine had fallen on the Russian Front.

How could they think of celebrating Christmas in those conditions? They hadn't the heart for it. Manuel himself was often seen in tears as he walked down the street wrapped in his great cape. People had got used to the way he just cried silently, and no one bothered to ask him what the matter was. They simply followed him with their eyes until he disappeared, and then walked on shaking their heads.

'Poor lad!' said Bêa-Yasse'Kette sympathetically.

On Christmas Eve he went round to the parents of Maax and Shong and told them where their boys were, 'as a Christmas present for them'. They wept with a mixture of joy and terror. Shong's mother could only just be restrained from rushing round to Fata Ioss' house. 'No, no, you mustn't.'

That very night, Shong slipped out of his hiding place once more and tapped on the shutter so that he could give his mother a kiss.

Fata Ioss was worried. He hadn't dared to leave his house with the crib, and so Angela was due to bring the child round to his house instead, early, to see the candles round the babe in the manger. It was fortunate that Dieter and Wilhelm weren't in the village for Christmas that year. Ioss would have preferred the secret still to be kept, but the young men couldn't stand it any longer. Of course there was the dreadful anxiety of their families to take into account, being without news for months and months.

... How would it all end?

6

It was the following spring that Seraphim arrived in the village.

From his vantage point in the hollow trunk of the great beech tree on the Ermerich, Manuel watched the pale light of dawn growing steadily brighter over the meadows, watched the shifting splendour of the sky, watched the dance of the seasons.

Sometimes he would set off at first light, ready, like the Psalmist, to awake the dawn and watch the sun rising over Germany, for God makes his sun rise on the evil and on the good, and there were good people on the other side of the Saar, just as there were evil people on this side. He avoided treading on the primroses which were about to come into flower, and he jumped over the slug on the grassy bank. He felt the bud bursting with sap, gazed in wonder at the exquisitely fine serrations of the first tiny leaf, and listened to the birds greeting life from the bushes. He sat quite still for hours on the seat which he had made for himself in his tree, with his eyes shining with the joy of spring and his hands open on his knees, palm up, in an attitude of expectancy.

From time to time his lips would move imperceptibly, but no ear could hear the murmurings of his heart, mysterious as a spring of water. After the midday angelus he would make his way calmly back, and he never returned without bringing some little surprise for Sébastien, whom he would take out in the afternoon to the Pré aux Pucelles. Much later on, after spending time in the church and with Müller in the schoolhouse, he would go back up to the tree and sit again for hours, watching the slow transformation of dusk into night.

Anyone bold enough to follow him on one of those luminous spring evenings might have been surprised to see the simpleton slip from his perch and climb further up the Ermerich to the edge of the wood. Every other day he went up there, entering the trees at the same point and then following a grassy path that ran just inside the wood until he was near the *Winckelstation*. There he would stop, look round cautiously, give a whistle like a blackbird's danger signal, and wait. After a while Maax would appear, or Shong, bearded and shaggy-haired. Manuel would hand over the provisions that he had brought, exchange a few words, pass on messages and advice, and then go back as he had come in the gathering gloom.

Unable to stand being cooped up any longer, Maax and Shong had left Fata Ioss' cellar at the end of the winter and taken up residence in the woods, based at the *Winckelstation*, a kind of hangar with plenty of places to hide: in the old days it had served as a depot for the wagons which brought clay from the *Lettcoul* (claypit). That was their H.Q. now, giving them good views over the village and the whole valley, as far as the hilltops of Nazi Germany in the distance. Apart from Manuel and Fata Ioss, no one knew where they were, not even their parents. With the help of the old man, Manuel kept them supplied with provisions as best he could, and no one appeared to suspect him, they were so accustomed to seeing him go off regularly to the beech tree on the hill. When he came back to the village at nightfall his tall, slim shape flitted down the street under the eyes of the German sentry, who watched him until he disappeared and then abandoned himself to the gentleness of the spring night, silent except perhaps for the song of a nightingale.

It was in the spring that Seraphim arrived.

Manuel saw him as he got back one lunchtime, splitting wood on Le Voisin's *gasse*. He stopped and stared in surprise, and Seraphim also stopped work, leaving the axe stuck in the block of wood to put his hand up to his fur hat, at the same time as Manuel took off his beret and revealed his remarkable mass of white curls.

The man had bristly red hair, and his rugged features, chiselled by the chill winds of the steppe, were regular without being harsh, and illuminated as if from within by his bright blue eyes. He kept rolling his hat up and unrolling it again, intimidated like a child by the sight of Manuel, who stood looking at his old tunic, his coarse trousers and heavy boots, as if they were the costume of a savage.

'*Kriegsgefangener!*' (Prisoner of war!) announced the stranger at last in a hoarse voice.

Manuel understood. Tears started from his eyes, bathing his cheeks with clear water, and the prisoner stared at him in amazement.

'*Nicht weinen*' (Don't cry), he said.

Manuel smiled at him through his tears.

'Russian,' said the man. '*Gefangener, hier Arbeit.*' (Prisoner, work here.) He pointed to Le Voisin's house.

Manuel shook his head as though not wanting to understand: how could Le Voisin...? But luckily Angela appeared in the doorway at that moment. 'He's only just arrived this morning,' she explained. 'He's a Russian prisoner, and the Germans have let Le Voisin have him to help in the fields. He's better off here than in a camp, don't you think?'

'Oh, yes,' said Manuel. Then, turning to the prisoner, he asked: 'What's your name?'

The man's face broke into a smile. 'Seraphim,' he said, '*Ich Seraphim.*'

Manuel was astonished to find someone bearing a name that belonged to the angels. He pointed to himself and said: 'Manuel, *ich* Manuel.'

'Manuel,' repeated the Russian. Then, all of a sudden, leaving Angela and Manuel baffled for a moment, the *Kriegsgefangener* made a large sign of the cross with the thumb and first two fingers of his right hand together, starting at his forehead, then down to his chest, then to his left shoulder and finally to the right.

'Manuel,' he repeated again, fervently.

The simpleton looked at him in amazement and then crossed himself in turn, in his usual manner.

The Russian's face shone with a deep inner joy, and he bowed to Manuel, who bowed back before going to join Angela.

'He's nice, I like him,' said Manuel once the door had closed behind him.

'He seems to like you too,' Angela replied.

Seraphim's arrival in the village of Lasting-en-Lorraine was the major bit of news that Manuel hastened to take to Maax and Shong up in the Ermerich the next night. They took him into their den and questioned him about it.

'So, he's a Russian, you say?'

'Yes, a Russian prisoner of war, and he's called Seraphim.

'And he's working for Le Voisin?'

'That's what Angela said.'

'Does Fata Ioss know?'

'Yes. We were talking about it this morning.'

'A Russian,' Shong broke in. 'So they're sending us Russian prisoners to try to make us think they're still taking Russians prisoner. As if we didn't know they were thrashed at Stalingrad last January! As if we didn't know they've had it!'

Manuel was finding it hard to cope with the hatred in Shong's eyes.

'He's a Christian,' he said.

'Who is?' asked Maax, only listening with half an ear.

'Seraphim, he's a Christian.'

The two young men didn't respond.

'Time I was off,' said Manuel, 'it's getting late. Here are your provisions.'

The next morning he knocked on Fata Ioss' door rather earlier than usual.

'Nothing up, is there?'

'Yes, there is,' said Manuel. 'Shong and Maax are letting their hearts get more and more full of evil. It's serious, Fata Ioss. Hatred is evil.'

'But what they hate is evil, Manuel, the evil of Nazism. Isn't it good to hate evil?'

'Yes, but not to hate people. We mustn't hate people. Never.'

'I know, Manuel, but it is very difficult. We must pray for them...' Ioss didn't really know what to say.

But he knew how difficult it is to hate evil without hating those who do evil. And he knew that hatred of the evil of Nazism was always directed at particular individuals of flesh and blood.

Fata Ioss also knew of the nocturnal exploits of Maax and Shong and of some of the dangerous things they got up to in daylight, even if they didn't tell him much these days, which didn't hurt him. Their natural dislike of authority in general and of the German occupation in particular led them to undertake more and more operations to harass the enemy, although 'operations' is perhaps too grand a word.

One day they were seen walking down the main street in Grandbourg in broad daylight—a friend of Fata Ioss' was sure he recognized them—and when the Germans gave chase they only escaped by diving into the lake. Apparently the Schupos were standing only a matter of a few yards away, and they had to keep their heads under water, holding their breath to the absolute limit. Surely that kind of foolhardiness would one day be their undoing? And what would they then have gained by slashing so many tyres and loosening so many screws?

Fata Ioss was relieved when he heard from Manuel in the early summer that the two lads were planning to leave the Ermerich and their *Winckelstation*. Relieved for them, first of all, because they would be safer in the more structured context of the Resistance group in Sarreguemines which they were intending to join, and then for Manuel, who was exposed to constant danger as long as they were still up on the hill. He was even relieved for Müller, the NCO, who must have a pretty good idea of what Manuel was up to on the Ermerich each day: he didn't go round with his eyes shut, and he would breathe more easily once he knew that the *Weisskopf* went no further than the hollow beech tree at sunset.

Soon the whisper went round that Maax and Shong had been seen at the Resistance demonstration in Sarreguemines on the twenty-fifth of June.

'Anything is possible,' said Fata Ioss, 'anything is possible.'

As for Seraphim, he would never have believed it possible that he could find, in France, a man like the *jurodivy*, the 'fools of God', of his native land. It was not long before he was treating Manuel as a kind of *staretz*. Even on their first brief encounter something had stirred in his soul, and when he felt a mysterious force pushing him to cross himself it was as though he had received a secret intimation.

During his first few weeks with Le Voisin, the Russian prisoner scarcely went out to work in the fields. Each time he met Manuel, he bowed as he would to a priest, and the simpleton's smile opened up immense vistas of inalienable freedom in Seraphim's heart. One evening he was bold enough to ask La Voisine, in his German which was steadily improving while taking on the colouring of the dialect of Lasting-en-Lorraine, who Manuel was. But what could she tell him? We never know those with whom we rub shoulders, busy as we are with our own troubles, and sometimes we meet God without recognizing him. He came to his own and his own received him not. La Voisine spoke of Angela and Benoît and Sébastien, of the pigeons that Manuel had released, and even, after several minutes' hesitation, of the scandal at Lidrezing. 'We nearly had a nasty time because of him!'

Seraphim listened, open-mouthed, as if he were hearing the story of his patron saint, Seraphim of Sarov. But he wasn't satisfied, he wanted to know more, and La Voisine had no more to tell him. It wasn't enough.

'Why don't you go and ask him yourself if you're so keen?' she said in some annoyance.

'There's a kind of light that radiates from him just as Motovilov describes.'

La Voisine didn't understand and merely shrugged her shoulders. 'If it's his white hair you mean,' she said, 'it went like that after he fell down the steeple.'

Now it was Seraphim's turn not to understand, but it was milking time, and the cows were mooing in the shed.

From that evening at the beginning of summer, Seraphim, who, now that he was beginning to be known and trusted, was allowed to go out on his own and wherever he liked, as long as he didn't leave the village, attached himself to Manuel. What he discovered didn't disappoint him: rather, it showed him that his first intuition had been correct.

One night when he was sitting on his chopping-block in a corner of the *gasse*, he saw Manuel slip out of the house wrapped in his cape and stride off in the direction of the church. Without a moment's hesitation, Seraphim set off after him. They walked through the short summer's night unseen even by the soldier on sentry duty, who was dozing on the steps of the schoolhouse. Manuel went down towards the grotto and stood looking at the pale figure of the Mother of God, then along the edge of the cemetery to the rounded east end of the church. From a few yards away Seraphim could hear him murmuring: 'Come, Lord Jesus, come.'

Then everything was swallowed up by the great silence of the night, which was unbroken even by the hooting of an owl. Only the gentle sound of the water trickling from the fountain provided a discreet accompaniment, and Seraphim once or twice thought he could hear the rhythm of Manuel's breathing in the murmur of the water.

The simpleton was motionless against the wall of the choir. All that could be seen of him above the cape that enveloped his body was his mass of white hair, almost luminous in the darkness. Seraphim was fascinated by it, and he felt a new kind of warmth in his heart when he found himself saying the pilgrim's prayer: *Lord Jesus, Son of God, have mercy on me, a miserable sinner*. As the last syllable passed his lips, he was suddenly overwhelmed by remorse, and yet again he had before his eyes the picture that returned to haunt him day and night, the intolerable picture of the isolated house in the birchwood and the ... He could not suppress the sob that rose up in his throat, and there, beneath the starry sky, between the village idiot on one side and the white figure of the Mother of God on the other, the Russian prisoner wept among the gravestones.

When Manuel first became aware of someone sobbing he thought it must be a dream, but when he raised his head and saw the form of a stranger crying his heart out on the ground close by, far from taking fright, he got up, went over to him and laid his hand on his head without a word. There they remained for a long time. When at last Seraphim calmed down, Manuel said in a murmur that mingled with the sound of the water down below the grotto: 'Blessed are those who mourn, for they shall be comforted.'

Seraphim looked at him and then got to his feet. Without

another word, the two men walked back to the street and thence to their houses on the square by the fountain. As they parted, the simpleton looked at the Russian, who hung his head without finding the strength to open his mouth, before disappearing through the open door of the barn.

The summer night was infinitely beautiful. Manuel sat down for a moment on the doorstep, with his eyes raised heavenwards and his gaze lost in the immensity of space where myriads of stars traced the lines of a mysterious message. When he came to close his eyes, he could see the same message written in letters of fire on his heart, and he deciphered them slowly, one by one, until he fell asleep there on Angela's doorstep. He slept so deeply that even the first light of dawn did not waken him, and it was Müller who roused him when it was broad daylight by gently touching his shoulder and saying: 'You mustn't stay out there, Manuel, you must go indoors.'

Manuel looked at him and smiled as though in a dream. Then he got up and went inside without a word.

Müller was intrigued by Manuel's silence. He couldn't understand it, and he certainly hadn't expected it after the unfortunate arrest and the business of the book. It was true that he had returned the book to him that very evening, but he hadn't the courage to tell Manuel straight out that it wasn't the *curé* of Lidrezing's book, which the man from the *Schutzpolizei* had refused to give up, but his own personal New Testament which he had done up to look like the other one. No doubt it was a cowardly thing to have done, but what choice did he have? *Kannst du mir verzeihen*? he had asked Manuel, and Manuel's only reply had been to kiss his hand, raise him to his feet and give him a hug. Müller had felt all churned up when he left the house that night, and the next day he had been most surprised not to see Manuel coming running with the book. What did his silence mean?

Those questions filled the NCO's thoughts as he walked over to the schoolhouse, passing the first of the haymakers on their way to the fields with their scythes over their shoulders. It was going to be a fine day.

Three days later, in the afternoon, as he was bringing home the third wagonload of hay for Le Voisin, Seraphim, perched on the front of the cart, noticed Manuel slipping into the deserted church. He urged his beasts on, nearly knocking La Voisine over at the entrance to the barn, and started unloading at such a rate that she wagged her head and said: 'Easy now, Seraphim! Nobody's on fire: take your time!'

But the Russian had his own reasons for hurrying. He worked faster and faster, perspiring freely, hardly bothered to water the animals, turned them round, and shot off again up the street towards the fields.

'Whatever's got into him?' La Voisine grumbled. 'It's not even as if there was a storm brewing!'

For Seraphim, however, there was more than a storm brewing, and if anyone was on fire he was. He had scarcely reached the church than he leaped off the cart, tied the animals to the gate leading to the grotto, and ran towards the open door of the church. He had never set foot inside a Western church before. He went up the steps and crossed himself. His gaze swept across all the pews on both sides of the nave, and he was surprised to find them deserted. Where on earth could Manuel be? He advanced slowly up the aisle, amazed by the statues of saints and by the absence of icons. He was puzzled by the fact that there was no screen separating the sanctuary from the body of the church. He looked up at the altar and at first failed to see the figure of the simpleton close by him tucked away near the right-hand wall. When he discovered him he stammered: 'Manuel! Manuel!'

Manuel didn't hear. He was once again absent from his immediate surroundings, kneeling back on his heels, with his hands open on his knees and his face lifted up, a face whose brightness was accentuated by the white halo of his hair. As the Russian tiptoed closer he could see Manuel's lips moving imperceptibly, perhaps just trembling, and he fell to his knees beside him.

'Manuel...'

Manuel still didn't hear. Kneeling next to him, Seraphim was conscious of an inner illumination and a gentle warmth filling his whole body, quite different in quality from that of the sunshine. His remorse was almost forgotten, yet he found himself asking: 'Manuel, I'd like...' But he fell silent, realizing that words were of no use. He was simply happy, as happy as he could ever be. He wished he could always stay there, never leave the church, never be separated from Manuel. But the animals mooing by the gate recalled him to the task in hand, and he got up regretfully, bowed deeply several times, crossed himself, and finally pulled himself away, nearly tripping as he came down the steps. He spoke to the beasts as he untied them, and astonished the good folk he passed on the way to the fields by his strange monologue.

'What's the matter with him?' wondered Bêa-Yasse'Kette as she watched him disappear.

Several weeks later, on the evening of the fifteenth of August, the Feast of the Assumption, Bêa-Yasse'Kette came round to see Angela, who was sitting having supper with Manuel and Sébastien in the little courtyard behind the house. As soon as she had sat down she said, 'That Russian is a heathen!'

'What makes you think that?' asked Angela.

'Because he prays to the sun! I've seen him!'

'No, no,' said Angela gently. 'He's a Christian, he told Manuel so. Didn't he, Manuel?'

Manuel looked at old Bêa-Yasse'Kette and said: 'Yes, he is, he's a Christian.'

'But...'

'He made the sign of the cross while I was there.'

'Why doesn't he go to church, then?'

What was the answer to that?

'The sun rises in the morning just as Christ rose from the grave,' said Manuel.

Bêa-Yasse'Kette listened, somewhat bemused, and finally exclaimed: 'He talks like a book!'

Angela laughed, and Sébastien laughed too, and the others soon joined in. It was such a glorious summer evening!

But the summer soon passed. Scarcely was the harvest in than the smell of bonfires started drifting through the streets of Lasting-en-Lorraine, and Seraphim was bringing in cartloads of potatoes for Le Voisin and then, with mist already creeping into the valley of the Sime, more cartloads of beetroot. The evenings turned chilly and people no longer stayed out talking on their *gasses*, even when there was no air-raid warning.

It was on one of those evenings at the very end of summer that the Russian prisoner of war followed Manuel up to the Ermerich. He saw him settle down inside the trunk of the great beech tree, he saw him open the book on his knees, and he heard him speaking as if he was reading, but without ever looking down at the page in front of him. Then Seraphim came nearer, sat down right by the base of the tree and listened.

Come, follow me.

Peace be with you.

Blessed are the poor ...

Blessed are the meek ...

Blessed are those who hunger and thirst after righteousness ...

Blessed are the merciful ...

Blessed are the pure in heart ...

Blessed are the peacemakers ...

Blessed are you when men revile you ...

Rejoice and be glad!

Abide in my love.

Love one another as I have loved you.

Greater love has no man than this, that a man lay down his life for his friends.

The Russian never took his eyes off Manuel. He did not always understand the words, but he tried to repeat them so that they would be engraved on his heart. At last there was a long silence, after which he spoke up imploringly: 'Go on reading, Manuel.'

The simpleton smiled, despite the sadness which veiled his features. 'I can't,' he said.

'Why not?'

'The book isn't in French. The Germans took the *curé* of Lidrezing's book away. Müller gave me this one, his own copy. He did what he could.'

Seraphim could see tears in Manuel's eyes, and he put his hand on the lad's knee.

'It doesn't matter,' said Manuel. 'The Word is written here, and here,' and he pointed to his breast and then his forehead. 'Abide in my love,' he went on, 'abide in my love.'

The Russian heard him and once again saw the house in the birchwood, heard the cries...

'Manuel, Manuel!' he pleaded, and he knelt down in the grass, with his head on Manuel's knee. The simpleton placed one hand on his forehead.

'Abide in my love,' he repeated softly.

The Russian burst into noisy sobs. Manuel stroked his hair over and over again. When he had quietened down a little, Seraphim began to speak in a hoarse, rapid voice, in his own language, and Manuel listened as though he understood every word. His confession was interminable. He lifted his head and looked at Manuel, whose love—there was no other word for it—shone from his eyes. He put his hand on Müller's book, made a promise, said something, and then continued his confession. In the end, when he fell silent and looked up with pleading in his tear-filled eyes, he heard Manuel's voice, scarcely rising above a murmur:

'God forgives,' the voice was saying. 'The Father forgives, the Lord Jesus forgives, the Spirit of love forgives.'

Seraphim crossed himself and bowed himself to the ground.

'God forgives,' Manuel repeated.

'*Seraphim nicht würdig*' (Seraphim not worthy), whispered the Russian.

Manuel leaned forward and raised him up, adding: 'If Christ came along now, he would want to stay with you, Seraphim, with you.'

7

Winter came again, the fourth since their return to the village, and Fata Ioss sometimes had the impression that the darkness was there to stay, for good. Either it was night-time, or there was thick fog, or both. The first fog came with the rain, but later it was associated with snow, when it muffled even the sound of boots in the street. The nights were worrying times for Fata Ioss as he sat by the bedside of La Vieille. She had fallen ill, and Angela looked after her devotedly, helped by Madamilla and Bêa-Yasse'Kette. Manuel stayed at home with Sébastien: a four-year-old is pretty noisy, and La Vieille couldn't cope with that. Ioss paced up and down in the corridor, waiting for the midwife, and then went to the door with her when she left, asking anxiously: 'She's not in any danger, is she?'

'No, Fata Ioss, she'll be all right, but it's going to take a long time.'

How long were they going to have to carry on with this wretched war hanging round their necks? Hitler was bound to fall sooner or later, but when? His henchmen gave the impression of being more and more jumpy when they showed their faces in the village, and Müller wasn't having an easy time of it. It was true that they were suffering constant harassment at the hands of the Resistance. One night when Ioss was watching by his wife's bedside, he heard someone tapping on the shutter. It was Maax, on the run from the *Polizei*, looking unrecognizable. Naturally Fata Ioss brought him in at once. 'Quick, into the cellar!' he said.

The hideout under the courtyard was still serviceable, and the sacks of potatoes were standing ready. Two hours later the Nazis arrived to do a *Hausuntersuchung*, with scant regard for the condition of La Vieille.

'Der Kerl kann doch nicht in der Natur verschwunden sein! Verflixtnochmal!' (The fellow can't have just vanished in the countryside, dammit!)

They failed to find him, and they apologized as they left. La Vieille hadn't been aware of anything. Maax didn't leave until the following night.

'It's going to take time,' Fata Ioss grumbled as he came back into the bedroom, 'plenty of time.'

His wife wouldn't hear of getting the *Amtsarzt*. 'Don't need them,' she murmured weakly.

When Angela came home, Manuel went to sit with La Vieille to let Ioss have a few hours' rest. He settled down by the bed and watched her sleeping. Then the prayer rose from his heart to his lips, which moved imperceptibly: Mother of God, pray for us, Mother of God, pray for us, Mother of God ... And once or twice La Vieille pricked up her ears, a smile transfigured her face, and for a brief moment she opened her eyes and looked at Manuel before sinking back into sleep. Such remissions were rare, but for the old woman and the simpleton they were moments of grace.

When Fata Ioss came to relieve Manuel in the middle of the night, he asked 'Everything O.K.?' And if he heard that she had smiled he would murmur happily: 'She'll be all right.' That's what the village folk said, too, when they heard that Manuel was at her bedside.

They also said that Wag-Nache'Péda's goldfinch had died in its cage the other night. The old man had been heard to sigh: 'What if freedom went the same way?'

But freedom is immortal, like the soul. That's what they should have told Wag-Nache'Péda when they saw him burying the stiff little body of the bird he had brought back from France, but nobody thought of it.

They were all thinking of their cellars, which needed to be properly done up now. The coming year would be decisive, so everybody said, and things might start hotting up as soon as the winter was over... So they cleaned them out and tidied them and furnished them with cupboards and mattresses, and they built up stocks of provisions. Some people even put their rabbits and hens down in the cellar, while others piled straw-bales round the entrance—although manure was said to afford better protection against shrapnel.

After long weeks of waiting the spring finally arrived, and to their astonishment nothing happened. Nobody paid much attention to the news from Fata Ioss' household: La Vieille had got out of bed one morning and was now happily up and about in the house. The truth was that that had been expected, whereas nobody had expected that nothing would happen.

'*Vass soll donn passeere?*' (What's supposed to happen?) asked Bêa-Yasse'Kette naïvely. But they all ignored her, and she stumped off in annoyance.

Easter came and went, then Whitsun, bringing fine weather at last. Fata Ioss and La Vieille now went for a daily walk up to the church and back, arm in arm. Sometimes Manuel accompanied them, sometimes it was little Sébastien and Angela. Whenever Seraphim passed them with his cart he gave them a big wave and a smile. They were fond of Seraphim, who could sometimes be seen with Manuel in the evening, up in the orchards.

One morning the village awoke to a shower of leaflets, falling from the sky like shells. Indeed, from the reaction of the Germans, they might have been real bombs. Everybody in the village pounced on them.

The leaflets announced that deliverance, liberation, was at hand; they spoke of the Allied forces; they called the population to passive resistance; they mentioned...

The German soldiers were immediately under orders to collect up all that 'filth', but there was hardly any to be seen as they went along the street, nor did the people watching them from their doorways appear to have any in their hands. It had all disappeared as if by magic. The leaflets had been hidden away in cellars and elsewhere, buried like seeds in the autumn which survive the long winter to germinate in the spring. But this time winter was already over, and the spring had come.

A few days later a rumour started in the kitchens, where people gathered in secret round wireless sets, and gradually spread to fill the houses, then spilled out into the street, and finally swept through the whole village like a tidal wave.

'They can't have!'

'At last!'

'What's up?' asked Bêa-Yasse'Kette, who hadn't grasped what was going on.

'The Allies...'

'Well, what about them?'

'They've landed in Normandy!'

'Are you sure?'

'It's just been on the news from London!'

'Oh my God! What a thing!' She nearly fainted with the shock.

'They can't have!'

'Oh, yes, they have, it's true!'

'Did you hear the announcement yourself?'

'Yes, I did, with my own ears.'

'But that means we're going to be...'

'Yes, liberated, that's right!'

The men slapped each other on the back, while the women looked at each other more doubtfully.

'It's not over yet,' said Bêa-Yasse'Kette.

The women were afraid. The Germans wouldn't give up and go just like that, they would fight, and there would be more death and destruction in the village.

'That's the price of freedom,' said Fata Ioss.

His wife looked at him reproachfully and pointed to Manuel sitting in a corner. His face was impassive, but his eyes were full of tears. The old man shrugged his shoulders as if to say: 'There's nothing one can do about it.'

Then Manuel spoke, his voice sounding gentle but firm: 'Yes, there will be death,' he said. 'It will come on a day when no one is expecting it, like a thief in the night.'

'What do you mean, Manuel?' La Vieille asked in a low voice.

'Death will come,' he repeated, 'like a great door opening on to the light.'

Fata Ioss and La Vieille sat and waited in silence. After a while Manuel added: 'For you, a big cross, like the one left on the island of fools after the disaster. A big, empty cross.'

'And for you, Manuel?' Fata Ioss asked.

' ... The light,' he replied after a moment's hesitation. Then he added: 'Don't miss the light shining round the cross. There is no cross without light, and no light without a cross.'

'But you're crying,' objected La Vieille.

'You don't only cry when you're sad, Mother,' said Manuel. Then he got up and left without another word.

When he had gone, Fata Ioss repeated as if in a daze: 'Death will come like a great door opening on to the light.'

In the village, joy had given way to waiting, patient for some, anxious for others.

'They've had it now!'

'Yes, but they'll make us pay for it!'

The work of turning cellars into shelters continued. Those whose cellars had vaulted roofs were the object of considerable envy, in view of the greater strength that gave.

'You know, their vaulted cellars will collapse like a house of cards when we blow up the streets,' said Müller to Fata Ioss one evening.

'You're going to blow up the streets?'

"Fraid so: orders from above. To try to delay the American advance as far as possible.' But he added: 'I'll give you plenty of warning. Some houses will have to be evacuated, including Angela's. One of the explosive charges will be right in front of it.'

That gave Fata Ioss the jitters. 'There's nothing I can do about it,' said Müller. 'I'm sorry.'

He looked equally embarrassed the day they came to take down the church bells, in the middle of July.

'What do they need our bells for?' shouted Bêa-Yasse'Kette across the square.

'To make guns with,' said Wag-Nache'Péda.

Manuel, standing only a few feet away, was crying silently. He remained motionless and deaf to everything around him, and when the huge lorry had at last rumbled away noisily down the road he turned and went into the church, shutting the door carefully behind him.

In the days that followed, several people joined the FFI (*Forces Françaises de l'Intérieur*), Forbach region, or so it was whispered in the village. But then so many things were said in the course of that interminable summer and yet deliverance still didn't come, despite the landing of the First French Army at Toulon. How much longer were they going to have to wait?

It was only the children who were really able to enjoy the fine weather to the full. They played round the fountain, splashing each other with water amid much shouting and laughter. Sébastien was among them, and when he saw Dieter and Wilhelm walking up the street, Benoît's boy would run after them and hang on to their coat-tails. They always had a sweet or something for him in their pockets. The other children kept their distance from the German soldiers, no doubt under instructions from their parents. Little Sébastien and Manuel the simpleton were practically the only ones to treat them as friends. The child was readily forgiven, but people were critical of Angela's brother.

They had just about begun picking the potato crop when the first requisition orders for *Schanzarbeiten* (trench-digging) came through. That same day, a letter arrived from Russia for Oche-Dache'Marie, who was next seen rushing off frenziedly to the church and then hanging about the cemetery, searching in vain for a grave which wasn't there and never would be.

'Niclaus and me,' said the letter, 'we were serving in an outpost on the front. On Tuesday morning, they picked men for a lightning raid, and I was one of them. I wanted Niclaus to come too, but he hung back, shaking his head obstinately. He was afraid. I had a sort of feeling that if he stayed with me he'd be all right. But we left right away, before I'd had time to talk to him on his own. It was pretty bad taking part in the raid, but getting back to camp was much worse. There wasn't a soul left alive. The Russians had got wind of our operation and struck while we were away. Our lads were softened up with grenades and then finished off with bayonets. I'll never forget the look of horror on Niclaus' face, his great staring dead eyes, and his mouth, wide open as if calling for help...'

A copy of the letter which appeared as if from nowhere was soon going the rounds of the village, and those who read it were appalled.

'When you think he could have just hidden like so many others!'

But he hadn't wanted to hide. Niclaus knew of the Nazi threats of reprisals against families. If he was found out, it would be his parents, his sister and his little brother who would have to pay. He preferred to go in order to spare them, first of all to the

Arbeitsdienst and then to the *Wehrmacht*. And now he was dead, massacred by the Russians.

'*Herr, gib ihm die ewige Ruh.*' (Lord, grant him eternal rest.)

'*Und das ewige Licht erleuchte ihn.*' (And may everlasting light shine upon him.)

The prayers for the repose of Niclaus' soul went up that night in many houses, without obliterating the new threat of the *Schanzarbeiten* that hung over them.

In order to impede the progress of the American tanks, everybody, men and women, young and old—with the exception only of mothers with young children, the very elderly and those who couldn't be spared from the harvest—was going to be required to go off each morning to dig trenches as deep as houses in the open fields, using pickaxes and shovels.

A few days later, first thing in the morning, the first lorries left, almost empty.

Meanwhile the fields were swarming with indispensable workers picking potatoes at a snail's pace.

The *Amtsarzt*'s waiting-room was overflowing with patients. Never had so many clumsy people gone and stupidly hurt themselves.

In the village the houses were deserted, except for the cats and dogs and the occasional elderly inhabitant, looking even more bent than usual and hardly daring to set foot in the street.

The local SA, responsible for organizing the trench-digging, were furious. They planned a raid on every house in Lasting-en-Lorraine. Müller was in the secret, and he was able to warn Fata Ioss and the others.

Manuel was requisitioned, but not Angela.

Wearing his beret, he stood waiting by the SA lorry.

'*Nimm die Mütze runter!*' (Take that hat off!)

The Nazis didn't like berets.

Manuel obeyed, and his mass of white curls came tumbling

out, making a halo round his face. The man in charge stared at him in amazement.

'*Wie alt bist du?*' (How old are you?)

'Twenty-three.'

'*Und warum bist du nicht an der Front?*' (And why aren't you at the Front?)

Manuel didn't reply. He looked the German straight in the eye but said nothing. In the end the man turned away and barked an order to his soldiers.

They marched into Fata Ioss' house as if they owned the place, two men in uniform, followed by Müller the NCO. La Vieille had taken to her bed.

'*Heil Hitler!*'

She didn't stir. Huddled on a chair by the fireside, Fata Ioss grunted something which they didn't catch.

'*Ist die Oma krank?*' (Is the grandmother ill?)

Ioss nodded. He was hardly recognizable, and Müller smiled inwardly: the old man's knees were shaking uncontrollably, and his hands, gripping a walking stick, were trembling as well. His slippers had holes in the toes, his shirt was done up crooked, and he was holding his head at such a strange angle that anyone would have thought he had terrible rheumatism in his neck.

'*Besorg die Oma gut, Opa*' (Take good care of her, grandad), said one of the Nazis. '*Heil Hitler!*' As they were going out, he added: *Mit diesem Alten ist ja nichts anzufangen.*' (Can't do anything with the old geezer.)

Müller agreed. Down in the cellar, which the soldiers had forgotten to search, two men in hiding listened with relief as the noise of their boots faded.

When Müller reached the lorry he saw Manuel, bare-headed, standing with the others.

'*Warum ist dieser Kerl nicht eingezogen worden?*' (Why hasn't this fellow been called up?) bellowed the *Leiter*.

Müller explained in an undertone.

'*Ach so!*'

But the man hadn't finished yet. Müller tried to reason with him, but to no avail.

'*Graben kann er aber doch!*' (He can dig, though, can't he?)

And Manuel was bundled into the lorry. He was allowed to put his beret back on. He said nothing all the way to Spicheren, but the soldiers who were accompanying them were surprised to see his lips moving the whole time.

They were dropped in the middle of the fields, and the German soldiers issued them with picks and shovels and told them to start digging right where they were. They were surrounded by armed men as if they were convicts.

'*Los! Graben!*' (Get to work! Dig!)

The sun had dried the clay, and the ground was hard. Some of them deliberately hit the white stones that they found, and managed to break the handles of their tools.

'*Scheisse!*' The Germans were furious.

They dug away, but things weren't going very fast.

Manuel was working peacefully alongside the others from Lasting-en-Lorraine. From time to time, if he heard them cursing their slave-drivers, he would murmur: 'Love one another.' Then they would look at him and smile.

One day someone said to him: 'It's not as easy as that, you know.'

Manuel looked at him. 'No, it isn't easy,' he said, 'it's just true.' And he added: 'Love your enemies and pray for those who persecute you. That's what he said.'

Nothing more was heard for a while except the noise of the picks and shovels scraping away at the stony ground.

'That doesn't mean we can't do a spot of sabotage, does it?'

Manuel smiled again. He could see perfectly well that they had just been heaving the earth round without making any real progress for hours.

The Nazis were getting angry. They had notices posted in the village: those who refused to go and *schanzen* were threatened with hanging. The number of *Schanzarbeiter* had been steadily falling. There was an awful lot of 'flu going round, quite an epidemic in fact, and the *Amtsarzt* had his hands full.

And so the weeks dragged on, until at last, in mid-November, the Germans gave up and abandoned the useless digging.

In the last few days before the work on the trenches stopped altogether, Manuel had heard something about mysterious and terrible camps. Once again the tears had rolled down his cheeks under the startled gaze of the soldiers guarding them. With his binoculars, Wag-Nache'Péda had even observed horrible goings-on at the *Goldene Bremm* down in the valley of Stiring. He had nearly been caught at it, and at the mere thought of what a close shave he had had, poor old Wag-Nache'Péda shook in his boots. It was said that he had taken to his cellar for good now, even when there was no *Sturmalarm*.

The siren wailed more and more often these days. Yet, despite everything, the good folk of Lasting-en-Lorraine were preparing to give the children a good time on the sixth of December, the feast of Saint Nicholas. Some had found all the waiting just too much for them, and reacted by burying themselves in the new winter that was beginning, out of terror. It had really seemed that spring had come, and here they were...

On the evening of the fifth, Fata Ioss and La Vieille went to Angela's. For a change, that year, neither Dieter nor Wilhelm was there. Manuel held Sébastien on his lap while Angela and La Vieille got the party food ready next door. 'Saint Nicholas, patron saint of schoolchildren...' Fata Ioss had just gone out and was ringing the bell somewhere to start the ritual, when all of a sudden the siren went. The women came out of the room.

'What shall we do?'

'Quick, down to the cellar!' shouted Fata Ioss, now back in the kitchen.

As they were on their way down, Angela, with Sébastien in her arms, began: 'On Saint Nicholas' Eve...'

That was all she had time to say. There was a deafening noise right above them on the first floor, and they were thrown violently down the stairs on top of each other, landing in the cellar without really knowing how they had got there, but at least more or less unharmed.

Up above all hell seemed to have broken loose. They could hear the menacing drone of the aeroplanes, the hissing noise made by the bombs as they fell through the air, and each time a dreadful explosion followed by the sound of walls and ceilings collapsing and heavy furniture falling.

Dust swirled in the cellar, making it difficult for them even to see each other.

Sébastien was squealing and La Vieille was praying out loud.

It seemed to last an eternity.

Manuel found a flannel, moistened it and passed it to Angela to put over the child's mouth.

When the tumult finally died down and the dust settled, they were at last able to look at each other by the feeble light of the lamp. They saw that their faces were streaked with tears. They hadn't even realized they were crying.

The aeroplanes had gone off into the night, and a strange silence now reigned, as if the whole village were dead. Fata Ioss ignored La Vieille's supplications and ventured as far as the stairs, but they seemed to have collapsed, and it was difficult to do anything in the dark. All they could do was wait.

As soon as it was light, they heard someone in the street calling their names: 'Angela! Manuel!' It sounded very far away. 'Angela! Manuel!'

'That's Wag-Nache'Péda's voice,' said Fata Ioss.

'We're down in the cellar!' Manuel shouted.

There was silence, and then the voice came again, closer to: 'Manuel!'

'Hello, we're in the cellar.'

'Are you all alive?'

'Yes, we're all here, Angela, Sébastien, Mother and Fata Ioss.'

'Ah, so Ioss is with you.' Then, after a moment: 'Hang on! I'll go and find someone to help, and then we can clear the outside steps.'

Soon they heard a hubbub of voices and the noise of stones being shifted. With Manuel's help, Ioss unbolted the heavy outside door. The first to reach them was the NCO, Müller.

'*Niemand verletzt?*' (No one hurt?)

'No, we were lucky,' said Fata Ioss.

Dieter and Wilhelm were there too, with Wag-Nache'Péda. 'We were afraid for you. It's quite a mess up above.' Manuel scrambled out over the piles of rubble. The roof had gone, and only the front of the house was still standing. Through the shattered ground-floor shutters he could see the grey morning of winter.

Seraphim came running up at that moment and threw himself into Manuel's arms. Le Voisin's house had also been damaged, though much less seriously, and their cellar steps were blocked too.

'What about the child, where is he?' asked Seraphim.

'He's still down with Angela. He's all right.'

When she came out and saw her house in ruins, Angela burst into tears.

'Look, you come and live with us,' said La Vieille. 'There's plenty of room.'

Fata Ioss agreed. Dieter and Wilhelm offered to help with the move.

'It won't take long,' Angela murmured.

It didn't.

When the women had gone, the men put everything they could salvage from the ruins into the cellar and made it as secure as they could.

'I'll stand guard,' said Seraphim.

The aeroplanes returned during the day, and again that night. The village was spared, but people now lived permanently in their cellars.

On the morning of the eighth of December the sirens wailed again and everybody rushed for shelter. This time the bombs fell up by the church and the schoolhouse. They thought they heard cries.

As soon as things had quietened down a bit, Manuel slipped out of Fata Ioss' cellar. In the street he met Seraphim, and together they ran up towards the church.

The first thing they saw was the gaping hole where the schoolhouse had once been. There were German soldiers rushing about, among them Dieter and Wilhelm. As soon as they saw Manuel they shouted: 'Müller is under all the rubble! We must do something quickly, *schnell!*'

Seraphim and Manuel helped to shift stones. No one really knew where to dig. The soldiers thought they had heard someone calling not long before.

Manuel didn't hesitate. 'Müller!' he called, 'Müller!'

They listened. Then they heard an answering cry, faint but clear: '*Ja, Manuel, ich bin da.*'

'Are you hurt?'

'*Ja, Manuel.*'

They started digging again furiously. When they eventually uncovered an arm, dislocated and covered in blood, the soldiers looked at each other in horror.

'Manuel, Manuel . . .'

The NCO's face was contorted.

'Hang on,' said Manuel, 'hang on, I'll be right back.' Then to

Seraphim he said: 'Come with me, quickly!'

The Germans couldn't understand why the *Weisskopf* had rushed off dragging the Russian with him. With extreme care they carried on digging round the injured man, who was groaning.

The church had also been hit. When Manuel got there he climbed in through an enormous gash in the right-hand wall, with Seraphim's help. The pews had been smashed by falling masonry, but he saw nothing of that. He ran up to the choir, climbed the altar steps and, watched attentively by Seraphim who had stayed back a bit, he forced open the door of the tabernacle and seized the ciborium. Then he dashed off with it, through the hole in the wall and back to the square, where he arrived, out of breath, to find that more of the villagers had come to help the Germans. When they saw the ciborium that he was carrying in front of him, they stood aside to let him through.

'Manuel!'

Müller had the whole of the bottom half of his body trapped under the wreckage.

'*Manuel, ich sterbe.*' (Manuel, I'm dying.)

Wilhelm was supporting him as best he could.

Manuel spoke to him in a low voice, and Müller's face relaxed despite the intensity of the pain.

'Our Father,' said Manuel.

All round them, the men had bared their heads and were praying with him.

'Mother of God,' said Manuel.

'Pray for us,' responded Seraphim.

'Pray for him,' said Manuel. Then he added: 'I'm going to give you the bread of life now, Müller.'

'I'm a Protestant,' the German whispered.

'You're a Christian,' said Manuel, 'just like me, just like Seraphim, just like all of us. He who eats my flesh will live for ever.'

When he took the lid off the ciborium, some of the men knelt down.

'Your living God,' said Manuel.

He took a wafer and placed it in Müller's mouth.

'He who believes in me, though he die, yet shall he live,' said Manuel.

The injured man had closed his eyes, and his face was strangely calm.

Then Manuel took another wafer and held it out to Seraphim. 'The Body of Christ, Seraphim.'

The Russian opened his mouth, and Manuel placed the consecrated bread on his tongue. Then he gave communion to all those present, who accepted without demur. Finally he returned to Müller and consumed all the remaining wafers himself, one by one, before handing the empty ciborium to Seraphim.

'Take it back to the church now.'

The Russian prisoner of war obeyed. Manuel bent over and kissed Müller on the forehead. The German murmured: 'Thank you, Manuel. Thank you, God.' His head fell back.

Someone behind Manuel said: 'He's dead.'

'No,' said Manuel, without turning round, 'he's alive for ever.'

Then he got up and walked away, leaving the others to see to the body.

Fata Ioss met him as he was leaving. The sight of Manuel's eyes streaming with tears alarmed him. 'What's up?' he asked.

'It's Müller,' said Manuel. 'He's dead.' Then, as if correcting himself, he added: 'He's in the light.'

And he continued on his way without even noticing the people flocking past.

Part Four

Paris had been liberated since August, but in Lasting-en-Lorraine they were still waiting. Hope was in every breast but it could not be given free rein yet. Every evening the men waited eagerly by the wireless for the latest news. People were living more or less on top of each other in their cellars, and because of the tension of waiting, which sometimes became unbearable, quarrels broke out from time to time.

Whole streets had been reduced to ruins. The *Sturmalarm* went every day, for one air raid after another. Saarbrücken was bombed, and from the heights above Lasting the fires could be seen raging until late into the night.

The Germans, Dieter, Wilhelm and the others, had lost their morale. They said that the war was over as far as they were concerned, and that Germany was dead, all through the fault of one man. They reckoned that they themselves would be sacrificed: they had orders to resist to the end. Sheer madness.

'Desert, then!' advised Fata Ioss.

'Where would we go?'

They would simply be shot.

What could they do for them?

'Nothing, you can't do anything for us. If you hide us, you will bring suspicion on yourselves. No, we're like condemned men, just waiting for the sentence to be carried out.'

Manuel said nothing. Whenever he could, he went to find the German soldiers with the book Müller had given him. 'Open it and read,' he would say to Wilhelm, and Wilhelm would open the book at random and read, in German, a few lines from the Gospels. Manuel would listen happily, and, if Seraphim was there, he would listen too. Sometimes the other Germans would all be quiet and listen as well.

When Wilhelm closed the book, there would be a little more light in his eyes, and he would seem more at peace. Occasionally, if Wilhelm wasn't there, Dieter or someone else would read instead.

At several points in the main street they had laid explosive charges, taking care to tell everyone where they were. That led to strange processions night and morning, as certain families emigrated *en bloc* for the night. Some cellars housed fifteen or twenty people.

Angela, Sébastien and Manuel were living with Fata Ioss and La Vieille. Bêa-Yasse'Kette and Madamilla had come to join them, originally just at night, but then for good, at La Vieille's insistence: they were no longer young enough to keep moving in and out all the time.

'*O Iérum Maria!*' groaned Bêa-Yasse'Kette. 'I'll never survive this.'

'That's what people always say,' said Fata Ioss.

The death of Müller the NCO was still very much on people's minds, and they talked about it in the evenings, down in their cellars. Some were scandalized by what Manuel had done, while others approved of it.

'Given that there was no priest to hand...'

'Yes, I know, but to give communion, and without confession too, to that lot of bandits...'

Some were beginning to understand that the simpleton was like a visitor from elsewhere, indicating by his behaviour the pattern of a kingdom that was unfamiliar to them. At the same time, deep in their spirits, they felt the stirrings of a secret complicity which both excited and disturbed them.

On Christmas Eve, Fata Ioss read the Gospel of the Nativity in German, from Müller's book, and Manuel laid the child Jesus in the crib under the enchanted gaze of Sébastien. But none of the women could bring themselves to sing.

They were too worried by the Nazis' latest move. They had once again arrived in force to organize the *Volkssturm* as their last resort. They were requisitioning every able-bodied man capable of bearing arms and training them up to resist the American 'invaders'. Once again the able-bodied men of Lasting-en-Lorraine disappeared as if by magic. The hideouts opening off cellars were still there. Once again the Nazis were furious, and it was the women who had to face their anger. The sound of jackboots was everywhere in the streets, even though it was snowing heavily.

Millache'Pitt's wife had a good idea. She wouldn't hide her man, she'd go and get him a certificate from the local factory. She knew the manager: he must be in need of food!

First of all she killed the rabbit and put it in the saddlebag of her bicycle. Then she sent Pitt off to bed, piled so many eiderdowns on top of him that he was nearly suffocated, made him drink large quantities of boiling hot *tisane*, gave little Sine all sorts of instructions about what to say if the Nazis came while she was away, and off she went with her eldest, Léo.

They got as far as Spicheren without any problems, but then their way was barred by the trenches of the famous *Schanzgraben*. Wheeling the bicycle, she slithered down into the first trench, picked herself up, and squelched about in the snow and the mud trying to get up the other side. A German soldier came to give her a hand. Léo said *merci*, which gave his mother the jitters.

'*Wo gehen Sie hin?*' (Where are you going?) asked the German.

She had to stammmer an explanation: '*Schlackenmühle...Bereitschaftsdienst... Belegschaft...*' (Factory... Duty office... Personnel...)

The German's dog was sniffing at the saddlebag.

'*Ach so!*'

The soldier thought she was very plucky to have come out in the snow, and he wished her a safe journey.

Next it was the aeroplanes. Léo and his mother had to throw themselves flat in the ditch. Bombs screamed all round them, sending tons of earth and snow flying in all directions.

'I really thought my last hour had come,' she told her friends later.

When it was safe to go on, they went down the Brigandal until they reached the factory. The manager stared at her when he saw her, but the rabbit soon did the trick. The certificate was duly made out, and back they went to Lasting-en-Lorraine, eight kilometres through bombs, snow and trenches. Léo was exhausted when they got home.

They found Pitt sweltering under the eiderdowns. The Nazis hadn't been. He leaped out of bed, they rubbed him down and he got dressed and settled himself at the table on which the *Bescheinigung* of the *Bereitschaftsdienst*, dispensing him from the *Volkssturm*, was prominently displayed. Did he realize that that piece of paper had nearly cost his wife and son their lives?

Towards the end of January there were bombing raids every single night.

Word went round that the Americans were approaching.

The Nazis were said to be falling back, but no one dared believe it. In the village, in any case, Wilhelm, Dieter and the others had their orders to stay until the bitter end in order to blow up the street when the enemy arrived. The *Volkssturm* was pretty much a dead duck.

Then, one evening, they heard that the Americans were on the Ermerich, less than one kilometre away. They expected to see them come charging down at any moment, and the German soldiers keeping watch in the trenches at the edge of the village were afraid they would be buried alive.

'If they drive their tanks over the top of us...'

There was no way out for them.

'We've had it,' said Wilhelm when he had a moment to spare and came to see Fata Ioss in his cellar.

Manuel got up and went over to him, with his eyes filled with tears.

'Look, you hide here,' said Fata Ioss at last. 'No one will find you there under the courtyard.'

'Yes, do,' begged La Vieille. 'Hide here.'

Wilhelm thanked them but shook his head.

'I can't,' he said. 'You'd all be compromised then. Ah well, never mind.'

When he left, Manuel went out with him and put his hand on his shoulder. 'You mustn't blow up the street when the Americans come.'

'But...'

'Think of the deaths it would cause, Wilhelm. Love one another.'

In any case, what was the point?

What indeed? 'Yes, you're quite right.'

'Promise?'

'I'm not on my own, Manuel. But I'll do what I can.'

'Thanks, Wilhelm.'

That evening, those whose houses were under threat came out

as usual and went round to the neighbours' cellars where they spent the night. They were unaware that the danger was past. Manuel alone knew.

Someone in the street said: 'It'll be tomorrow morning.' They all looked at each other, not knowing whether to believe it. Why the twentieth of February rather than any other day? There hadn't been any more shooting than on previous days.

Millache'Pitt was uneasy, though. At four in the morning he woke all his family, squashed into Rédache'Momme's cellar. 'Come on! Everybody up! We're going back to the house.'

'What if the Germans blow up the street?' protested his wife.

'I don't think they're going to blow anything up. It's much too late for that. Come along, hurry up!'

The children were quarrelling. 'Be quiet!' shouted their father, and then: 'Léo, you take the slop pail and go in front.'

Léo grabbed the big white pail and heaved it out of the cellar to the gutter, where he emptied it.

'Off we go, then!'

Léo marched in front with the pail.

'Hands up!'

Three giants were blocking their way: two black men and one white.

Millache'Pitt stepped forward and tried to explain. Luckily one of the Americans, the white man, spoke some French.

'That goddam white bucket just saved your life,' he said.

He listened to what Millache'Pitt was saying and then told him to get under cover quickly, with the rest of his tribe. He asked where the Germans were. Millache'Pitt waved his hand vaguely.

They were still not quite safely inside when the first bursts of machine-gun fire were heard.

Down in Fata Ioss' cellar, Manuel leaped out of bed.

'Don't go,' said the old man, 'It's the Americans coming. We're going to be free.' And a few moments later he added: 'At last!'

On their mattresses, La Vieille and Angela were awake now too, but they didn't move so as not to wake the child.

'What's happening?' asked Bêa-Yasse'Kette.

'It's the Americans, they're here.'

'That's all we needed!'

Fata Ioss had got dressed hurriedly, in the dark.

'For goodness' sake put the light on!'

'We can't, Kette. They might shoot...'

From the noise she was making, she was evidently getting dressed too.

Up in the street outside they could only hear a few isolated footsteps, and then, all of a sudden, a stampede. Once again, shots rang out.

'I'm going home.' That was Bêa-Yasse'Kette again.

'You're mad, Kette, they might shoot you.'

But she insisted. She wouldn't leave her house all alone, she didn't want to come back and find it all in a mess like the last time: once was enough.

Try as he might, Fata Ioss couldn't persuade her to stay. In the end Manuel helped him to unbolt the heavy outside door, and he let old Bêa-Yasse'Kette out into the night, grumbling as he did so: 'You're mad, you know.'

When he turned round, Manuel's long white curls shone in the darkness like a halo round his face. His sky-blue eyes were wide open and full of tears, which rolled down on to his cheeks in silence. His lips were half-open and moving. His shirt was open, and when Fata Ioss lowered his gaze before that of the wounded child, he noticed two bare feet sticking out of his rolled-up trousers.

'It's the liberation, Manuel, do you realize? Deliverance at last!'

The simpleton's face displayed no response, but his lips continued to move.

There was a distant roaring noise, like thunder.

'Up you get, Mother,' said Fata Ioss, for the sake of saying something. 'You never know.'

'Is it a storm we can hear?' asked La Vieille.

'No, I think it's the tanks.'

Manuel's whole body started shaking.

'Calm down, old chap, calm down,' said Fata Ioss.

The old man opened his arms, and in the brief moment that Manuel allowed himself to be hugged, he could feel the sobs racking his body.

'Calm down, Manuel.'

But already Manuel had torn himself away.

Outside, the thunder of the tanks was growing louder and louder, until it was deafening. Even the walls of the cellar seemed to be vibrating.

Sébastien had woken up and was huddling anxiously against his mother. Manuel went over to them and kissed Angela, then the child.

'Are you frightened, Manuel?' Angela asked.

'A bit.'

A grey light penetrated into the cellar when Fata Ioss opened the heavy door a crack.

Outside, the din was terrific.

Manuel kissed La Vieille, then Madamilla, who looked at him in astonishment.

'Hurrah!' shouted Fata Ioss. 'Hurrah! We're free!'

Through the partly-open door he had spotted the long barrel of the first tank, and then the white star blazoned on the turret.

'It's the Americans! We're free!'

Fata Ioss' joy had spread to the women.

'At last,' said La Vieille.

Angela held little Sébastien clutched to her breast. Manuel was back by the door, waiting, seemingly unmoved.

'Aren't you glad, Manuel?' said Fata Ioss in surprise.

'Oh, yes, of course,' he replied, but the tears continued to stream down his cheeks. The old man was baffled.

Outside it was now daylight, a grey, wintry light. Every so often there was a burst of gunfire, and each time Manuel flinched. There were cries, too.

Suddenly someone scuttled down the cellar steps screaming. It was Bêa-Yasse'Kette. Fata Ioss caught her in his arms. To begin with no one could understand what she was saying.

'It's horrible, it's just horrible!' she wailed. 'They've shot them all. I was watching from my kitchen window. They all had their hands up in the trenches, but they shot them all like dogs. All of them, the whole lot!' She paused, and went on: 'And now they've rounded up the rest of them by the fountain. Dieter and Wilhelm are there, I saw them. And they're going to...'

Before she could finish, Manuel had leaped up.

'Manuel! Manuel!'

Fata Ioss and Angela both called after him, but it was no good. By the time they got up the steps to the *gasse*, Manuel was already up by the fountain, just as the shots rang out. Ioss saw him throw himself, with arms upraised, between the Americans and the Germans. Almost immediately he fell backwards, and there was the crack of his head hitting the stone. Angela rushed towards him, followed by Ioss.

The three Americans were standing there looking disconcerted. In front of them the only surviving German, Wilhelm, was kneeling down beside Manuel's body and speaking to him gently: 'Manuel! Manuel!'

The simpleton's eyes were wide open, staring.

Angela followed Wilhelm's example and threw herself down by her brother, calling his name and sobbing, sobbing.

The American soldiers had lowered their rifles and were staring in complete bafflement at what was going on.

Fata Ioss murmured under his breath: 'Death will come, like a great door opening on to the light.'

La Vieille had joined him, with Madamilla and Bêa-Yasse'Kette.

Wilhelm was cradling the white head of the simpleton in his hands.

After a moment of fascinated silence when she noticed the three red holes in her brother's chest, Angela had started sobbing even more violently and calling out: 'Manuel! Manuel!'

The first of the three Americans turned to his neighbour and said: 'Emmanuel, huh?'

Neither of the others replied. Only Angela's sobs and the tears of the other women disturbed the silence of the square. The man who had spoken first continued, as if to himself: 'Emmanuel, which being interpreted is, God with us.'

And on his lips there came a strange smile...